The Connection

Jack Simon-Stevens

Copyright © 2019 Jack Simon-Stevens

All rights reserved, including the right to reproduce this book, or portions thereof in any form. No part of this text may be reproduced, transmitted, downloaded, decompiled, reverse engineered, or stored, in any form or introduced into any information storage and retrieval system, in any form or by any means, whether electronic or mechanical without the express written permission of the author.

This is a work of fiction. Names and characters are the product of the author's imagination and any resemblance to actual persons, living or dead, is entirely coincidental.

The views expressed in this work are solely those of the author and do not necessarily reflect the views of the publisher, and the publisher hereby disclaims any responsibility for them.

ISBN: 978-0-244-52168-4

PublishNation
www.publishnation.co.uk

Prologue

Brighton, Sussex
19.00hrs 20th April 1985

MacColl reached the end of Brighton Palace Pier, the light, south-westerly wind picking at his dark hair. Down channel, the sun was sinking below the western horizon. The ebb-tide was creating a small chop in the waves as they touched the pier's rusting support structure but far away, the sea was flat calm.

He looked east towards the marina, as its entrance channel-markers flashed green and red, growing brighter as the day faded. Beyond its breakwater loomed a dark sky.

Deep inside, he knew happiness was an imposter. MacColl turned up the collar of his overcoat as the still light, but now biting wind came in. He looked out to sea and whispered, *"you were like a burning candle, I couldn't hold you for ever."*

The last flicker of sun on the western horizon glinted off the sea, as he thought of her, the incoming darkness overwhelmed him. In his right hand was the *Motorola 8000x* hand-portable phone, and with his left he dialled her number. He felt a question in his mind. *Why am I doing this, when she is no longer here?* He stared absently at the cellular-phone. There was no signal, which he knew would be the case, because the network in this area was still intermittent....

With a combination of frustration and sadness, he threw it into the channel, a seagull crying out, wheeled overhead. The cell-phone, climbed over a wave, like a battling, sinking ship, then it went down, the black rubber aerial rocking relentlessly with a final effort of not giving in, as the sea claimed it.

MacColl gripped on to the pier's rail, swearing at himself in remorseful anger, looking down at the sea's swell, considering taking a leap over the edge, but knowing he would not. He whacked the wooden top of the rail, the pain shooting into his hand, and running alongside the sadness in his mind, like two competitors in the Olympics.

He stared out at the sea, blaming himself but then re-setting control, as the darkness increased. A hooded figure silently walked up behind him, reaching out and touching his shoulder, taking back his life to a different age, in a different world....

Chapter 1

RITON ELECTRONICS MARINE HQ, Croydon
10th September 1984

Linus Simon MacColl sat at his desk in the Croydon office. Back in the U.K, after seven months in Manhattan, he could not stop hearing the words from the Billy Joel song in his head, *'I'm in a New York state of mind.'* He'd travelled the world in his varying roles for RITON Electronics Group, and always felt a sense of loss on his return home.

The group was an electronics giant, employing over forty thousand staff. In some aspects, it was a global leader. From military, security, maritime and opening new concepts, it was no surprise that another Queen's Award for Enterprise had been won.

His Stateside role had been in East 34th Street office, a stone's throw from the Empire State Building. The apartment on mid-town 29th, had been a great place to stay. Most nights he just sat on the balcony and listened to the sirens wail. But on some, he'd been out in bars with the staff, and a few of them were also *sirens,* of a different nature....

Being an analyst was not automated work. No. One had to carefully build relationships through trust, induced humour (he often made minor, deliberately self-inflicted errors) and an on-going charm offensive.

Only then, could the reality of a recently acquired company by the RITON Group, be really understood. It was one thing to purchase an offshore business by statistical analysis, but quite another to gain the personal trust, so as to understand how its people *really* operated, and that was MacColl's role.

Karen Solomon was the area manager in this newly acquired American business. Before being sent to New York, MacColl had asked his boss about her. He said she was *'vivacious'*.

Well, that was certainly the case, and she'd been exciting when out in Manhattan one night, and maybe he'd missed an opportunity. This was always a cynical question which stayed in his mind. *Did a woman want you, or was it merely a ruse for gain?*

As he sat back in the chair considering this, he felt a shiver, like an incoming North Wind, a voice boomed out. "Morning old boy, pleased you are back."

MacColl looked up at his boss, a smart and grey haired but debonair man, formerly a merchant naval captain, but was now, Managing Director of RITON's Ship's Electronics Division.

"Morning Mr Cannon, yes it was certainly an experience." Answered MacColl. "Good, that's the ticket," said Cannon. "I need you to come into my office for a bit of a chat. Something has cropped up that we need to discuss."

He followed Rupert Cannon into his office, catching the eye of Colleen, his boss's attractive, dark haired P.A on route, as they smiled at each other in unison.

"Right take a seat old boy, and I'll give you the SP, what!" Said Cannon. "Now it's a bit of a weird thing, but I've been asked to assign you to a new task with a radio gang, just a short-term thing you know."

MacColl looked quizzically back, somehow feeling a little apprehensive. "What sort of *thing* is that, Mr Cannon?" he asked curiously.

Cannon leant back in his chair and eyed MacColl in a steely, yet what appeared to be a slightly jittery mode. "Well now, do you remember all that hullabaloo a couple of years ago about this new portable radio-telephone thing, when RITON gained that first contract outside of BT and some other lot that was on-offer?"

MacColl nodded. "Yes, that's the thing approved for us by Thatcher, to set up in competition with them."

"That's it, well the radio boys have done something rather bizarre. They have pulled in some help from Ericsson in Norway and created a sort of honeycomb thing called *'Cells'*, to link these VHF style *johnnies* into main telephone lines. The idea is that Fred Blogs out on the road, or wandering about in the sticks, can make a direct call to Mrs Mop and say he's running late for his pie and chips, that sort of thing."

Cannon laughed, looked up at the ceiling, and went on. "I was at a board meeting when a fellow whose name escapes me now, showed us the wall chart. Apparently, it's going to start off in London and Manchester but will cover ninety per cent of the country within five years, not least because Thatcher has insisted on it". He smiled again at MacColl and asked. "Do you know Reggie Potton?"

Linus nodded, he'd heard of Potton, he was the FD of RITON's Military Division, and a rather prickly character. "Well," chuckled Cannon. "He stood up and said that if he was made to have some sort of portable-radio-phone junk, *he'd throw it in a fucking bucket and drown it.*"

MacColl laughed out loud, picturing the situation in the board-room. "Seriously though," said Cannon. "If you are out and about at meetings or travelling, one needs peace and quiet to think, not be harassed by some *nincompoop* in a bloody office calling you, don't you agree?"

He nodded back, and Cannon could see that he absolutely agreed.

"I'm pleased you do Linus, because the bunch at HQ want you to join this new lot for what we both know, is going to be a short one, just for the sake of keeping the numskulls happy."

MacColl was not surprised as such, because his jobs always involved change. RITON called his role 'Field Analyst' and this typified the Chairman's insistence for differing job titles from other large businesses. Linus usually referred to himself as a *'failed analyst'*, which sometimes won a few chortles, both internally and externally.

"Anyway," continued Cannon. "It's going live on Christmas Eve, and the thing, as I'm sure you already know, is called **RADI-CAL.**" He smiled at the name he clearly thought was ridiculous. "You're going to be in of one of the regional teams, at some base in Kent." He scanned through the file again.

"Yes, near Maidstone apparently, and aside from being actively involved in the start-up, the powers that be want a tight watch to be kept on these new *tea-leaves* across the whole operation." MacColl nodded.

"As ever, you'll need to keep this under your hat, and give them the nonsense of *transfer-because-of-your-enthusiasm*," he smiled and winked across. "And you've certainly done that before!"

Despite being a leader technically, RITON was staffing old-school. When a new start-up came on-board or an acquisition was made, the manager's operations needed to fit the style of the group, or they would be out.

This felt like a double-edged sword to MacColl. On the one side, he was going into the '*I-told-you-so*' mould from *some* traditional boys on the board, and on the other, he was to join a completely new concept that was driven by the Chairman, which could succeed, but that surely was an outside chance. Either way, he felt a sudden chill of exposure.

He knew Rupert Cannon well enough to be aware that his reporting back to him needed to be fast, accurate and secretive.

Cannon had a really *joie de vivre* persona, but underneath, like all of those on the board, he was rock-hard.

"Sounds interesting," said MacColl. "So what is the *official* role, and when do I start?" He tried to be positive, but felt his voice probably sounded somewhat tinny.

"Good man," responded Cannon. "Now let me see what it's called." He shifted through the file. "Ah, here it is, seems you are going to be a *G.A.M.*"

MacColl glanced at him trying to work out what it meant. Cannon beat him to the question. "General Activity Manager," he said. "And your *cover-up* role is to sell these new radio telephone johnnies to the irks in the City, apparently they can be fitted into motor cars or be portable."

He looked up at MacColl over his glasses. "They'll need to be tough old bruisers to lug those about," he chuckled. "Make our old VHF's on the bridge wings feel like feathers, what!"

Linus smiled, he was genuinely amused by this. His own experience at sea meant he understood this. Marine portable radios were heavy, mainly because of battery weight, but he'd seen a few of these Motorola cellular-telephones in New York, and they looked like large *bricks* with aerials.

He'd spotted one being used on a street in Manhattan, and thought it was a two-way radio, but then noticed the chap strangely holding it against the side of his head, like a normal office telephone hand-set. He remembered thinking that perhaps he was just a nut-case....

Rupert Cannon scanned through the rest of the file. "There's not an awful lot more in here, except you're going to report in to a chap named Michael Sentinel, who is the... let me see," he looked onto another sheet.

"Ah yes, Regional Manager for the South-East. You'll have to use a new fleet car with all this phone junk built into it apparently, so you can have something *sensible* to drive for once, and make sure you report *everything* you discover to me weekly."

Cannon sat back and removed his glasses and Linus sensed pain in his eyes. "I really do believe this is only going to be a short-term thing. My guess is the start-up is going to get a bit of publicity, then this minor trinket is going to be sold off. Sir Dennis, will see to that. Anyway, you'll have to be there bright and early a week today, so I'll need a full situation report on your last job across the pond by Friday."

MacColl understood. Sir Dennis Ogilvy was the Chairman of RITON Group and was a genius at acquiring a business and increasing profits or rolling out a new-start up, and selling it on to another company. *RADI-CAL* seemed to be fit for the latter. He knew Sir Dennis was the real enthusiast behind this new operation, so would need to be very careful with the reporting. Pointing a finger of blame for a bad idea towards him, was not going to occur.

Whatever the hypothesis, he knew the conversation with Cannon was over, and so needed to get on with it. The analysis work of the NY business had been mainly completed, before he left there, and just needed typing up by Colleen, before a final check and hand-over to the boss.

He took a stroll out of the building, crouched down by the wall on the edge of the car park and lit up a Marlboro. The wind had swung north, and autumn seemed on the cusp. The sun glinted off the bumper of his car, a white, 1973 Triumph Stag.

Often chastised about this, and described by Rupert Cannon as an *'old banger'*, even though the condition was extraordinarily good. In fact, he'd put a lot of time and effort into keeping it on the road over the last three years.

Battling through a challenge, was Linus MacColl's style, he always wanted to do it in a nonchalant way, without argument.

The beauty of the Stag was that it did not answer back, and when it was running on-song, the effort was worth it.

He stubbed out his cigarette and walked back into the office.

By Friday afternoon, everything he'd worked on in East 34th Street was complete. Cannon was happy to put his analysis forward to the board, and wrote MacColl a letter of good recognition.

That was the typical style of RITON. He cleared his desk and headed for the door, on the way Colleen stood up and said. "Just a moment Linus, you're not finished yet, you know!" He looked back surprised, and as he did so, the office team came together by her desk, all smiles.

He recognised them all, except one. A tall and slim, raven haired girl on the front-line stepped towards him, wearing a black, halter-neck outfit. Circling around him, she read from a sheet of paper. "Good luck in you new role, *whatever that is!*"

Someone hit a play button on the Sony ghetto-blaster placed on Colleen's desk. MacColl put a hand over his eyes, he knew he'd been stitched up. He smiled somewhat grudgingly, and said under his breath. *"Bugger, you lot!"*

The music boomed out and was of no surprise in content, *The Stripper,* but everyone still laughed at it. She strode around him and off came the top, then she swirled it round and threw it behind her.

Facing him, she smiled and dropped her skirt, then walked up to him. He felt a weird mix of excitement and excruciating embarrassment, a classic experience of a *Strip-O-Gram* victim.

She was so close. He could feel her breath as she unfastened her bra. As her breasts became exposed, his excruciation hit maximum squirm height. *Double-bugger, you all!* Her hands ran over his torso and then slid down his body, much to the amusement of the gang.

He gritted his teeth as he thought. C*ome- to- a- bloody- end-music,* as if he were a ventriloquist's dummy in *'gottle-of-gear'* mode. And, if that wasn't enough, to cap-it all, she walked backwards, slipped down her panties, swung them around her-head like a cow-girl's lasso in a western movie, and chucked them in his face. The room was filled with laughter, clapping, and cheering.

She strode over, picked up her clothes, smiled, blew him a kiss, and ran out of the door. He recognised *something* about her, it was as if they'd met before....
But that couldn't be, she was in a young style of that fabulous singer, Carly Simon.

Cannon had been standing behind them, and walked towards Linus, beaming and clapping. "Bravo old-boy, well done!" he shook his hand and said. "Right, no argument, you're all out with me tonight and I'm paying."

He looked at Linus. "And you my lad, can leave your bloody old *'Snag'* behind and I'll get you a cab home, what!"
Everyone stood genuinely beaming at him, and despite the embarrassment of this event, Linus felt a great deal of pride in being part of the team. This was indeed, the way it was across the RITON group, everyone exuding genuine compassion, loyalty and fun with each other, which he believed, existed nowhere else.

Saturday was a late start for him. There was no excuse, or maybe there was. After all, last night out on the town had been an exceptional one. As he lay in his bed, MacColl tried to piece together the activities.

Well, they all left the office at 17.00 and then went into the local pub, *The Airport,* pretty conventional. Next step was off to that new Indian in the town centre, then at about 22.30, it was *Scamps* night club time, that was one hell of a Croydon joint.

There was a slight movement on the pillow beside him, and he rolled over then ran his fingers through the lovely raven hair. She turned and smiled at him. "And I thought you didn't like Strippers."

"Well you're wrong on that score," he said. "But bloody wonderful as regards everything else." She laughed and put her arms around him.

"Sorry Sally-Anne, but we've got to get up, I'm having a work car dropped off at mid-day." He passed over a black and white striped dressing gown, and helped her put it on. He pulled on some jeans and a jumper and they went down the stairs and into the kitchen.

"Tea or coffee?" he asked. She pointed to the teapot and sat on a stool. "How old are you?" she asked. Linus looked at her for a moment, as if he was thinking of number to choose. "Twenty-seven." He said. "What, had you forgotten it?" she chortled.

"Forgotten what?" he responded trying to be amusing. "Actually, I am, it's just that everyone thinks I look older." She looked him in the eyes and gently touched his arm. "You look good," said Sally-Anne. "I'm twenty-four, born in August, *Hotter than July.*"

"Where are you from?" he asked.

"Purley," she replied. "You know, top of the game," she glanced snootily out of his kitchen's window, then whispered. "Unlike some."

He smiled at her. "Now don't you knock Upper Norwood, some of Britain's top blokes lived here you know."

"Oh yeah," she said. "Like who?"

"Vice Admiral Fitzroy, founder of the Met' Office, for one." He replied.

She stared back at him and asked. "Didn't he kill himself?"

Linus was about to answer, as there was a knock at the door.

"Saved by the bell." Retorted Sally-Anne.

"That's the delivery of a new car, you know, for the portable 'phone thing they want me check on." She looked at him and shook her head, as that sounded like nonsense. But somehow fascinated, she followed him to the front door.

"Mr MacColl?" asked the delivery driver. Linus nodded. "I have a vehicle to drop-off from the RITON Group.

Linus walked down the path with Sally-Anne, the driver watching them with interest, suspecting why she was wearing a dressing gown at this time of day. He snorted an assumption at them under his breath. *Typical Bloody Norwoodians!*

They walked up to the transporter, both staring at what sat on it. The car was a red Vauxhall Cavalier saloon, and clearly it was new or very nearly, as the registration number started with a 'B'. On the roof and rear offside wing, were two short and thin, black antennas, with a thicker piece in their centres.

Sally-Anne wandered round the car, and stared through the front window, a passing cyclist rang its bell, looked over his shoulder and hollered. "Hello luv, are *yer doin'* anything tonight?" She ignored him, not caring about her bare feet and dressing gown, or that *common, Norwood type*, she was always being propositioned anyway – it went with the job, but was rather fascinated by the strange thing she had spotted.

"Linus, what *is* that?" she asked, pointing at the dashboard. He looked up at her.

"That," he said smiling, "is the future, it's called a cellular-phone, and you'll be able to call anyone indoors or at the office whilst driving, without going through a switchboard, as it's direct-dial."

Sally-Anne and the delivery driver both looked at him, and in unison, laughed.

"Well that's made my day mate," said the driver. "When I put the motor on earlier, I thought it was some sort of two-way thing in there for a black cab!" Their laughter continued, and in the moment MacColl remembered what Cannon had told him, this new role was *definitely* not going to last long. The car was unloaded, he signed the paperwork, and the truck driver headed off.

"Have you got anything on today?" he asked her.

"Only your dressing gown. What did *you* have in mind?"

Sunday arrived, and he pulled back the curtains, the sky above full of tumultuous, dark and ragged clouds. Upper Norwood could feel dull and depressing when the weather was like this. It's old Victorian buildings, from the houses to St John the Evangelist church, looked tired, out of kilter with the modern world.

He'd lived in this end-of-terrace for five years, the location was ideal. Access to the Croydon office, trains into London, and both Heathrow and Gatwick airports, was straightforward. He cast his eye around the bedroom. Yes, it could do with a lick of paint, but otherwise it felt great – he loved this house, it had real empathy, he felt it in his heart.

Sally-Anne was asleep. MacColl looked at her analytically. Not only was she good looking, she had a great personality. Being with her for almost two days, had been an exceptional experience.

They spent Saturday afternoon lazing around listening to his albums and 12 inch singles. In the evening, they strolled over to *The White Hart* pub. He put away a few lager tops, whilst she went for Dry-Martini and lemonade.

 Lighting up a pair of Marlboros and passing hers over, MacColl considered how much he liked the character of Sally-Anne.

She walked over to the Wurlitzer Jukebox in the snug and put on the week's number one, *'I just called to say I love you'* by *Stevie Wonder*. The guys at the bar glanced approvingly at her behind as she swayed back to the table. "And, you'll be able to do *that* from the car, won't you?" She said, pointing up at a speaker as the song wailed out.

"So what made you become a stripper?" he asked.

"Actually, it's called *Strip-O-Gram.*" she replied. "I'm not a cheap whore, you know."

"Oh I realise that," he said nodding over at her glass. "That Martini is over a quid."

"Well as you ask, I can tell you I was fed up with a boring office-job, so started it up myself, you know, put an advert in the *Yellow Pages* and bingo. It's a very popular thing now, in fact, I'm looking to take on some more staff." She held up her hands to him. "And no, don't even think about applying!"

She only had the dress that she'd stripped off in the office yesterday, and a bit of make-up in her handbag, but still looked great. He thought that's all she needed, because she was vivacious and naturally good-looking, not the type insisting on spending hours in front of a mirror before heading out.

But he warned himself to be careful, he knew some women could breed pain. No way was he going to allow that to happen to him again….

Her magical, raven hair flicked on the pillow as she woke again. Linus sat on the bed next to her and ran his fingers through it. "I don't want you to go," he said. "But when do you need to get back?"

She glanced at her watch. "About twelve, we have a family lunch at home today."

"Fine, I'll give you a lift whenever you want."

She looked him in the eyes, he could see she was deep in thought. Perhaps she felt that they had reached the cold light of day, it was fun whilst it lasted but, well…. Who could say, one just had to see how it would transpire.

Heading to Purley was a doddle usually, but today things were in several ways, different. Firstly, he was giving a lift to a woman whose job it was to strip, and driving a new car. And there was one other thing – it was fitted with a mobile telephone. Sally-Anne unclipped the weird hand-set marked PANASONIC from the holder and examined it. On the top was a set of round buttons, ten with numbers on, a star and sort of noughts and crosses box, whilst higher up, were the markings SND, SEL, END, CLR, STO, RCL SIGNAL, MESSAGE.

She waved it under his nose. "What the *fuck* does all this mean?"

Then she put the earpiece to her mouth as if it were a microphone. "Hello, can I have my old job back please?" She said, and clipped it back into the holder.

They both laughed and Sally-Anne put her head in her hands and said, '*Oy vey.*'

Linus glanced at her. "I meant to ask, are you Jewish from both sides then?"

"On my dad's side, my mum's not."

He looked at her and said. "I'm the other way round."

"Figures", she said nodding her head towards his crotch. "Otherwise something could have been, hmm, *adjusted.*"

They both laughed. This was 1984 and not 1934. How the world had moved on, who would have believed then, that a car would have a telephone in it?

She switched on the radio. "Bit tacky, it's only MW and LW."

"That's because this is an L and not a GL, but at least it's got a cassette player."

She nodded and looked upwards like royalty. "Well my car's got FM."

"Oh yeah, and what make is that?" he asked.

"Austin Metro *Vanden-Plas*." She replied.

"Ideal for this place," he said, pointing to the town centre buildings as they drove down into the Wellesley Road underpass. "Nippy and easy to park, and that's useful during the week, given the amount of traffic. My dad used to say how much easier it was here in the old days, you know, buses and trams."

"Yeah, but things have moved on." She said. "The trams finished in Croydon about nineteen fifty and they are never going to come back. It's all about people in cars now, maybe even with phones built into them." She said this in all seriousness for once, looking somehow distant.

Soon, they had passed the old, abandoned Croydon airport and reached Purley Cross.

"Turn right and then left up hill." She said.

It dawned on MacColl where they were heading, it was the *Long Estate*, undoubtedly the most expensive and sought after houses in South London. This was not his expectation, and he felt shock setting in. She was way out of his league.

Sally-Anne sensed this, gripped his hand and kissed it. She smiled and said. "Just over there on the right."

He pulled up outside a mansion- sized building, in the wide-driveway outside sat a gold Rolls-Royce Silver-Shadow and a Mini Metro.

He felt at a loss, drained and then struggled to find words, managing just. "Nice car".

"Told you so," she said. "It's got a *proper* radio in it."

Chapter 2

*Maidstone Kent
17th September 1984*

MacColl drove into the White Lane Industrial Park, on the edge of Maidstone. The Cavalier's dashboard clock was just on 08.00hrs, as he rolled into a parking space. There was nothing at all here, except for a sign over the office door next to a roller-shutter, which said: **RITON *RADI-CAL*.**

The whole place looked deserted, in front of it was a railway line, its fence stacked half-way up with dumped rubbish. Everything was dull, bleak and depressing, and in came the rain.

According to his assignment details from Rupert Cannon, this was one of five regional offices for the start-up. They were in place for both selling and fitting these new-fangled things into vehicles. Each one was to target differing post-codes, issued by the Kingston, central HQ. Cannon was unsure about the number of staff, but had been told there would be sales, tele-sales, installers and a regional manager in each.

This was his second visit, because after dropping off Sally-Anne yesterday, he decided to drive over and check this place out. But it wasn't just for that, he felt a bit lost without her company, not wanting to go home.

She had given him her business card, and said he could call anytime. They finished with a passionate kiss outside her parent's mansion, then she was gone. He kept looking at the card, and when he eventually got back to his house, he put on a fabulous 12inch single he had bought in New York, "M*issing You"* by John Waite.

He smiled thinking about the song's video on MTV, watched in his 29th Street apartment, where Waite smashes up a pay-phone handset because he can't get through to woman who's breaking his heart. *He should have been in a Cavalier,* thought Linus, staring at the bloody cellular phone's red light still saying: '**No Signal**.'

He reclined the seat and watched the site. The first company car came in at 09.00hrs, thirty minutes after the official start-time for all RITON staff. MacColl noted this down for his Rupert Cannon report. A bleak-start to the day for these *numpties* then.

The car was a black, Vauxhall Carlton, with the now familiar looking radio antenna on the roof, it pulled up right outside the front, so it was likely to be his new boss.

A tall, slightly middle-aged man with glasses and a somewhat bizarre flock of blonde hair, stepped out of the car, looked across at MacColl's Cavalier with an extraordinarily supercilious expression, then let himself into the place. "Good start to the day then." MacColl said out-loud and sarcastically.

Linus walked over to the office door, grimacing at the sound of tyres screeching, and the high-pitched pain of an engine being brutally over-revved. Around the corner flew another Cavalier, this one a blue hatch-back. Clocking the antenna on the roof, he knew it must be another one of this mob. *New York, I miss you*, he thought, and this driving style was completely out of kilter with the rules of RITON ELECTRONICS PLC! He made a note of the car's registration number on his pad.

A chap stepped out grinning, and came towards him.

"Hello," he said, nodding at the antenna on the roof of MacColl's car. "You must be the new boy."

Linus stretched out his hand. "Yes, that's right, I'm Linus MacColl."

They shook hands and smiled at each other, and Linus somehow felt an instantly good connection to this man.

"Well, I'm Julian Rayne," he looked at Linus intensely. "I've heard about you, aren't you a died-in-the-wool RITON type?"

"Yep, I've been there for years, worked across quite a few bits of the group, you know, marine division and military coms mainly, but couldn't resist this new thing."

Given his growing belief in the undoubted failure of this new *RADI-CAL* venture, he wondered if Julian would buy into this, indeed, would *anyone?*

"Come on in then," said Rayne forthrightly. "I'll introduce you to the Area Manager, Mike Sentinel."

"What's he like then?"

"Well, how shall I put this?" looking across at the office, giving the impression of trying to find a correct, yet acceptably subtle expression.

"He's one of the weirdest *fuckers* I've ever come across, but he knows his onions."

MacColl thought as they walked to the door, *this just gets better and better; beam me up Scottie.*

They climbed the staircase and turned left into the office. It was a relatively narrow, yet long lay-out, eight desks fitted with tall, red sound-proofing attached on the right, and just one chap sat at the far end. On the left was a sizeable, glass-fronted room, which he rightly assumed was Mike Sentinel's, with an empty Secretary's desk out-front. *Where are they all?* Linus asked himself, glancing at his Seiko watch.

He stared into the manager's space, aghast at what looked like a junk room. The desk and meeting table were piled up with a mass of cardboard boxes, some contained wine bottles, others had wires hanging out of them, magazines were scattered everywhere and on the wall was a photo of a tall, blonde haired man by a roulette wheel in a casino, identical to Sentinel. He looked harder at the picture. Yep, it *was* him alright. *What!*

At the far end of the corridor was a closed door. MacColl and Rayne walked towards this as it flew open, Mike Sentinel coming through it, a thin white plastic cup in his left hand. He was certainly striking. Linus was six feet and he reckoned this man was only an inch or so taller, and if anything, he was slightly slimmer, but there was *something* about him that was extraordinary and very powerful. He couldn't put his finger on it, but there was a strange, almost leviathan presence about him.

He came up close to MacColl, put out his hand, looking down through his thick glasses and said. "Mmm, welcome aboard."

"Mr Sentinel, I presume," said Linus as they shook hands.

He nodded back at Linus

"Well, let's hope *this **isn't** another fine mess you've gotten me into Stanley*, and you can call me Mike."

MacColl and Rayne laughed, but Sentinel did not, he just stared at them and retorted again with that weird *"Mmm"* sounding as if it was a sort of blocked nasal passage.

He pointed back to the doorway he'd just come through. "There's a tea machine in there, follow-me and I'll demonstrate how it operates."

Rayne smiled at MacColl in *'told-you-so'* mode, as they walked behind him into the office. Stood in front of the machine was a man in a boiler suit, wiping the hot water nozzle with a cloth covered in brown filth.

Sentinel looked at the cleaner and said. "Now Henry, how's it all going?"

"All working fine Mr Sentinel, and I've wiped it down inside." He replied, showing him the disgusting cloth. "I've cleaned the bogs too."

Linus stared down at the wooden-handled, rubber plunger on the floor by the machine and decided instantly that he would give it a miss. *No tea or coffee today,* he thought.

"Right," said Sentinel. "I'll explain how this machine operates. It's a GKN Sankey *Super-Compact*, with a built-in *'whipper'* motor, therefore serving coffee in a variety of flavours, and it contains hot water for placing onto tea bags. Let me demonstrate."

He took a thin, plastic cup off the pile by the machine's side, placed it under the outlet and pressed one of the red buttons marked *'café crème'*, looking superciliously at MacColl as he did so.

The machine vibrated and steam poured out of the nozzle, followed by what Linus considered as a microbe of input into the cup, and that was it. Sentinel picked up the cup and stared into what was less than a teaspoonful of thick looking, brown muck.

"Mmm, right, needs a bit of a fine tune, but you get the drift, now into my office."

He strode off, as Julian grinned and said. "Told you, he's a fucking nut-case."

They looked at each other across the round meeting table. Mike Sentinel had dumped some of the weird boxes on the floor, and now had a tray of documents in front of him. He passed the first one over to Linus, a map with circles around the cities of London, Birmingham, Manchester and Glasgow.

A red-line connected the English ones, and inside the circles were those *honeycomb* things that Cannon had mentioned, he seemed to remember these being called *'Cells'*.

"Now these are our target installation areas for the end of December," he said, pointing at them with a pen. "The redlines mean that the main roads in between, are also covered, so that you can drive from the key points here, here and here whilst making a car call to an office or home telephone, or another of our users."

Linus glanced vaguely across, considering the expression of *'car-call'*, he actually quite liked it, especially as this could be from one car to another. Sentinel continued.

"Once this goes live in December, we start the ball rolling, these are the costs." He said, passing over a sheet. MacColl scanned through it, staring at what seemed high numbers. The cellular phone types were broken into three main categories:

R1 Mobile, for in-car use only: £1,600

R2 Transportable, to be fitted in the car but could also be carried around: £1,750

R3 Hand-Held "Brick" thing: £3,999. Available from March 1985.

On top of this were the extras, including; £250 for car install, and £90 for a spare R3 battery. Then there were the call costs of 25p per minute during the day, and 15p at night. On Sunday however, it was down to 10p a minute. Every month, a 'line-rental' charge of £25 was required, and everything was plus VAT at 15%.

Linus was in two minds on this. On the one side, he felt these costs were high, but on the other, was starting to see how an attraction could be there for some businesses. It had dawned on him that organisations for example, running transport deliveries, coaches or managers driving to meetings, could be contacted in the event of a change of circumstances, like a cancellation perhaps.

Saving time, could improve not only efficiency but *maybe* offset costs. It *might* be possible to justify investment in these things. But this could surely only work if the parties involved were within the signal area, which seemed very limited.

Sentinel went on, passing over another sheet. "Now this shows the alternative lease-purchase plan, so costs can be spread over three to five years, but also means an additional opportunity for businesses to sign up."

Linus looked at the sheet. He could see the potential here from a financial perspective, because this thing was going live in the near mid-financial year for most companies, so the lease-purchase option might be a consideration.

"It's being financed by City National," he said looking superciliously through his glasses at MacColl. "Who as you know, have been working with RITON for years."

He nodded at Mike Sentinel. That was true, he did know of them. City National Bank PLC had always financed a mass of the RITON group's customers.

"They've included *peppercorn rental*," continued Sentinel. "So once the full amount has been paid back, the buyers shell out just another pound every twelve months, which means it's even cheaper."

Linus could see some benefits for the businesses, because *'peppercorn'* meant these cellular radios would stay technically owned by *RADI-CAL*, but still be used permanently by the customers, which could be a tax saving attraction. Even so, there were still a lot of doubts in his mind. How could they *guarantee* this network would be working by the end of the year, how reliable would it be, and would people *really* want such a thing, or would it just fizzle out and die?

He heard several cars pulling-up outside and then, the slamming of the building's front door, as more of the team came in. He glanced at his Seiko, it was now after 10.00 hrs and they were only just arriving! Not good at all.

He made a mental note of this, considering inclusion of it in his Rupert Cannon report.

Linus watched them walk past. Three smart looking types went into the area on the right, and a dark-haired woman now sat at the desk outside Sentinel's office, and he guessed this was his PA. Although the office door was closed, he could hear them all talking as clearly as if they were in here, making any privacy completely useless. *What a mess,* he thought. A bunch of questions were spinning, he needed to mentally draft these out fast.

The phone on Sentinel's desk rang and he strode over the take the call.

He put his hand over the mouth-piece and said. "Mmm, I need to have a chat for a while, give me ten minutes." MacColl nodded and walked out, checking that he'd remembered to put the Marlboro's in his pocket as he shut the useless door behind him. Sentinel's PA was also on the phone as he walked towards the stairs, and the other lot who'd just entered, were now engrossed in a conversation up by the coffee machine. *Good luck with that,* he thought.

Out front, four more cars had arrived. There was a white Ford Sierra, and two red Austin Montego saloons, on a mixture of "A" and "B" plates, each with a roof antenna. At the far end sat an older Ford Fiesta, which he assumed was the PA's motor. He glanced at the British Leyland cars. *Monteno-goes,* he thought. Next to the office was the vehicle installation area, so he decided to take a look.

The roller-shutter door was now half raised, and he spied round the edge, hoping to see what was in there. Two men in overalls were removing the front headlining of a Ford Sierra.

He noticed there was some cabling hanging out of the lower dash-board on the left, and that a black box had been fitted in the boot area, as the hatch-back was up. They were fitting an R1 mobile, he surmised.

Must be another *RADI-CAL* company car. The older one of the pair, an angry looking, thin, red-haired bloke, spotted him and strode over, waving a spanner aggressively.

"What do *you* want?" he snarled with a Scottish accent, coming up close.

"Sorry," replied Linus, looking around as if he were lost. "I'm a new boy, just finding my way around, you know."

"That's as maybe," responded the spanner man. "But our work requires health and ***fucking*** safety, or were all doomed, *dae ye ken that boy?*"

Before Linus could reply, the man hit the wall switch, the motor whirred and the door rolled down in front of him. Discussion clearly now over. '*I need a fag,*' he said to himself, this always helped him think, and he needed to do a lot of that.

He walked to the far end of the building, away from the entrance road. The dumped junk-piles, from this miserable estate ending, as a wall came up against the fence. A train shrieked passed, kicking shock into him. Probably heading to Victoria he thought, watching a mass of carriages doing at least 70mph. A narrow path-way went behind the building, leading up to the main road. Linus stopped just beyond the corner, out of sight, crouched down and lit up a Marlboro.

This had been something of a habit for as long as he could remember. There were no restrictions on smoking in RITON offices of course, and quite rightly so. But working on tankers before he joined the main group, there were very few areas where one could light-up, especially up on deck, the ideal place being under the bridge wing. Just choose a side out of the wind, and crouch down out of sight. Luxurious.

He inhaled and considered this situation. It was essential that he understood the process of how *RADI-CAL* was going to pan out. Everything seemed all over the shop, at least in this regional merry-go-round and he needed clarity. So he took focus on the essential RITON way: 1. Strategy, 2. Tactical 3. Operational. The Group's board clearly had knowledge of what this business was *planning* to achieve, but making it happen within Thatcher's Government allotted time-line, was another matter. And a critical one.

These cellular phones *had* to be live at the end of January, or the contract would be cancelled. *RADI-CAL* was going for 24th December, he understood why. It would be newsworthy, and some *rich numpties might* purchase for Christmas Day presents. If the phones failed to work, at least it provided a bit of time for the technicians to solve the problems. Not good for newspaper reports though, he surmised.

Despite his growing misery, there was no excuse to lose the plot. He needed to go back in, ignore all the junk, and get as much out of Mike Sentinel as possible. This was about the plan, clarity of action and target numbers. RITON was a group that prided itself on success of acquisitions and start-ups. MacColl had to assimilate this situation, then report it back accurately, his job depended on it.

RADI-CAL was not about going out to specific corporate markets. For the first time in RITON's history, this affair was to be aimed at significantly smaller businesses than normal, then there were those wealthy individuals, so brand image was vital. He fired up another Marlboro and focussed on what he needed to do.

As he walked back to the front door, a car came into sight, being driven steadily, so he assumed this was not a *RADI-CAL* person. But as at it came closer, he noticed it was another Cavalier, fitted with the now ubiquitous, black antenna. He stopped, and watched it pull up slowly into the last clear space opposite the door.

A tall blonde stepped out, opened the rear door, and bent over, picking up a bag from the rear seat. He glanced at her gratifying rear-end, looking away as she turned towards him. She smiled and walked forwards with a rhythmic gait, sending him out a subliminal message. Coming closer, he realised how strikingly familiar she was to the actress in a Western TV show he'd watched in New York, called *"The Yellow Rose"*.

They came together and shook hands. "I'm Linus MacColl, one of the new G.A.M's."

He said, noticing the gold wedding ring on her other hand.

"Jeannie Sands," she replied. "I'm doing that too and setting up dealer relations."

He smiled back like an idiot, feeling somewhat tongue-tied by her striking looks, and a voice sounding both smoky, and as rich as honey.

"Good stuff." He said, realising the words were coming out like Rupert Cannon's, but in a stupid mode. "Pleasure to meet you."

She grinned back, glancing down as he continued the handshake.

"Sorry," he said, finally letting go and pointing at the door. "Shall we?"

At the top of the stairs, she headed away down the room, as he walked back into Mike Sentinel's office.

Two hours later, MacColl had grasped the full picture of how things needed to work over the next three months, but his expected tasks had not yet been confirmed.

RADI-CAL's operation seemed theoretically viable, but held together by sticky-tape.

He'd been allocated a desk opposite Sentinel's office, in the area for G.A.M's, and he was now a member of this regional team of five. Linus laid out the notes he'd made and stared through them, things were a little clearer now.

Firstly, the radio receivers were now installed in the areas on the map shown to him earlier, and he was told they were already live.

These, high-frequency wireless antennas, picked up the car signal at around 900mhz and connected it somehow, to a BT line, *transitioning the radio-waves into words!* The box of tricks inside a small building under the aerial, doing this automatically, and in the event of a mains power failure, they had back-up batteries. The system being two-way, meant a driver could make *and* receive a call.

But how do you keep connected over anything but a tiny driving distance? thought Linus. These things operated on low voltage, and so would be like VHF sets on ships; once the two antennas were out of sight with each other, the calls would crackle then die, and cars moved faster than ships....

Sentinel had taken pleasure in superciliously explaining this in his usual style.

The clever part, was that when the car moved out of signal-range, the *cells* inside the *honeycomb* thing, automatically connected the caller to another aerial, then the next and so on. Theoretically, one could ultimately drive from Lands' End to John O'Groats, and spend the whole trip chatting to the wife.

Two of the problems being that the network would probably never cover such an expanse, and the call cost would be about £300. Third problem being around sixteen hours talking to *her indoors*. He remembered the Reggie Potton comment about *'chucking the thing in a fucking bucket and drowning it.'*

Was it all just like something out of *Fantasy Island?* *'Here come da plane boss.'*

Well, this had been quite a day. But at least this thing would soon be over for him. The report to Rupert Cannon would need to be subtle though. He began to feel a little happier, and expected to be back in his old role within a few weeks.

MacColl looked at his Seiko, it was just after 17.30hrs, so he decided to make a move, intending to go home and start drafting up his notes on *RADI-CAL*.

As he put the wodge of paperwork in his brief-case, Julian Rayne came over. "Boozer time now Linus, we're all off for a quick one."

Yeah, or two or three or... he thought looking up at him. Although not wanting to go out with this lot, he knew it was important because he had to get under the skin of this operation and chatting to people after a few drinks usually opened up some interesting doors. And another thing, maybe Jeannie Sands would be there?

He nodded in agreement as Mike Sentinel shut his office door and walked over, wearing a Macintosh rain coat, as if he was a detective in an American TV show.

"Now you've got the gist of things, this is your next task, alrighty." Linus looked at him steadfastly. Sentinel continued. "Mmm, well tomorrow I'll assign you to an area, where you'll be expected to sign up a number of companies, prior to us going live."

MacColl stared at Sentinel somewhat aghast and retorted. "Sorry Mike, but as the system is not yet in place, how could that work?"

Sentinel looked down through his glasses as if staring at an idiot. "By getting signed contracts in place to ensure these *yuppies* can get cellular radios fitted before we go live, then they'll be ahead of the game, so won't be affected when we run out of stock. And if they are not happy when it does go live, contracts can be cancelled without any cost to them, and we'll take back the items."

"I didn't realise we had a stock issue," replied Linus. Mike Sentinel stared back at him again, supercilious as ever."

"We don't," he said, looking over his shoulder, as he strode through the door. "It's called a *puppy-dog* close."

Julian and Jeannie came over to him, both smiling.

"See what I meant?" said Julian. "He really is a *fucking* nut case but …." Linus interrupted him. "Yes, yes I get it, but he knows his *onions*."

They all drove their own cars to the *Anchor* pub, which was only about four hundred yards away. He pulled his Cavalier up beside Jeannie's, and they both stepped out.

She laughed, watching Linus stare at the place. It was an absolute dump. Yes, he was used to some rough drinking dens in South London, who wasn't, but this was beyond any of those. It was like Frankenstein's Castle, on a bad day. All the upstairs windows seemed to be broken and repaired with tape, and the ground floor was covered in wall cracks. In the distance, some excavators had just packed up for the day on a new building site, so perhaps the vibration had not helped.

He walked with Jeannie to the entrance, moving cautiously, faking the walk of a nervous actor in a horror movie. She laughed, put her hand on his shoulder and said. "Come on, get a drink inside you, and you'll be fine."

Just that one touch, made the hair stand up on the back of his neck.

Inside the place, it was mayhem already and only fifteen minutes into opening time.

On the far side of the large public bar, he doubted there would be a *snug* in this place, was a *Rockola 445* jukebox, and stood right by it was Mike Sentinel, slotting in a 5p coin.

He walked over to them, a pint of bitter in his hand, looking down at the change in his other. "Mmm," he said shaking his head, those odd, blonde hair strands flicking. "Five new pence for a song, was a fraction of that in the old days, what can I get you?"

Before they could answer, *'Smooth Operator'* by *Sade*, blasted out across the bar. For some reason, it was excessively loud and Linus had to shout in Sentinel's ear.

"Pint- of- lager-top- please." Jeannie gave Mike the thumbs up, so MacColl assumed, this was to confirm her usual drink.

The three of them reached the bar, with Jeannie looking quizzically at MacColl, as the song hit the next chorus: *"Face to face, each classic case. We shadow box and double cross, yet need the chase."*

Beside them, the other *RADI-CAL* team members, stood in a circle nodding with the music and grinning away at each other. Julian Rayne came forward and took Linus around the group, shaking hands with each of them. The problem was, it was so bloody loud, he couldn't clearly hear their names, so it was a waste of time. Still, he got the impression they all meant well, and that was a good sign.

Sentinel turned and handed the drinks to him and Jeannie, pointing out two men at the other end of the bar, then he walked towards them. MacColl recognised one straightaway, it was that workshop bloke that had told him to fuck off this morning. *'Oh well,'* he thought looking at his pint, *'takes all sorts.'*

The music blared out, then Linus and Jeannie looked at each other, as she mouthed the song's words. *"Coast to coast LA to Chicago, western male, across the north and south to Key Largo, love for sale."*

He had no idea what these meant, but she looked bloody amazing. They both walked over to join the team. One of the guys he'd just met, whose name he couldn't remember, stepped to the bar and said loudly. "Does anyone want some food?" they all shook their heads automatically.

There was a heated, glass cabinet, with pies and sausage rolls inside.

MacColl watched him take one of the sausage rolls away on a plate, as he paid the miserable looking, fat barmaid fifty pence. Re-joining the group circle he bit into it, his face cringing. Examining it closely, he said. "It's bloody mouldy!"

The group all laughed, and instantly Linus felt sorry for him, wishing he hadn't joined in with that. The buyer took the plate back to the bar and shouted. "Excuse me, but this is off." The group looked on as the barmaid lumbered over. She picked the sausage roll off the plate and sniffed it. "Seems alright to me," she said, taking a bite from it. "Tastes fine." Chewing it with her mouth open and staring into the guy's eyes savagely, she put the un-eaten lump on the plate and handed it back to him.

There was a change in the music, on came *'Two Tribes'* by *Frankie goes to Hollywood*, blaring from the Rockola. *"When two tribes go to war, one is all that you can score."*

Two, old looking men clambered on to a table, right by the *RADI-CAL* team. One of them had his right hand and forearm in plaster, with the thumb stuck up in the air.

As the song went into overdrive mode, they started shouting out the words:

"Comrade number one, a born again poor man's son...."
The man without a plastered arm, dropped his trousers, danced some more, tripped, and fell off the table, knocking a pint mug out of someone's hand as he went down. Mike Sentinel looked down his nose and sniggered at the bloke, lying in a pool of beer and broken glass. The plastered arm man stepped down off the table and moved aggressively towards him.

"Do you think we're a couple of *old cunts* then?" he shouted at Sentinel.

"Quite frankly," he replied looking down at the man snidely, giving a full nasal effort, "I haven't known you long enough to form an opinion."

The man threw out a punch at Sentinel with his left hand, missed and then Mike grabbed the plastered-up thumb on his right one. The man letting out a screech of pain, as Sentinel grinned with pleasure.

"When two tribes go to war, one is all that you can score."

Linus looked at Jeannie and said. "Come on, we need to get out of here."

She nodded, and they walked, fast-paced out of the door and back into the car park.

Outside, they heard more bawling and glasses smashing, as the music screamed on.

She could tell what he was thinking, and said nonchalantly. "There are always a few scenes in there, never amount to much though. It's got worse since that building site mob started to come in."

Linus suddenly felt a bit overcome. There was so *very much* that he wanted to get off his chest to her about his experiences today, but just could not find the words. He always considered this to be a miserable downside since childhood.

His *real* mother had been a wonderful word communicator, and taught him how to respond to people quickly, and with a little humour. But she went away when he was only seven, and then he'd slipped into a sort of conversational catacomb. He felt the words were stuck in his mouth, like peas in a pod.

Was this the problem that took Anna away from him all those years ago? Did he lack that sort of suave, fast-paced personality that she scrapped him for? One thing was for sure though, he needed to avoid any serious involvement *ever* again, it had been too painful. He could only go so far, that was his self-taught rule.

They stood together by his Cavalier and she nodded at the window. "Have you made any calls yet?"

He mentally stepped back, looking at her with surprise. "I didn't think it was possible." He said.

"Officially, it doesn't go live until the end of the year, but we are supposed to do some 'guinea pig' testing, wherever the network is live - only in a few places."

"Nobody told me," he said, surprised by this. "So is my radio-phone actually activated?"

"Should be," she replied. "Give it a try on your way home, once you get onto the M25 of course, or you'll get nowhere with it."

"By the way," he asked. "What do you know about Mike Sentinel, only he seems well, bonkers." She laughed at him and said. "Actually, he's a really good bloke, I should know. You see, I worked with him for almost ten years at Rate-Syrex. We were both in the corporate copier sales division. He's a bit odd I grant you, but if anyone can make this work – it's him."

She extended her hand, and he gently shook it. "You in tomorrow?" he asked, as they both walked up to her car. The setting sun glinted off her blonde hair as she opened the door. "I'm out in the morning, but we'll catch up later on, I'm sure."

He stood and watched her drive away, and then remembered who the actress was from *"The Yellow Rose"*, that she was the spitting image of. It was Cybill Shepherd.

MacColl headed out onto the M20, the trip home was less than 40 miles, so an hour or so should do it. He glanced over at the Panasonic handset, which of course, was now to be called the *RADI-CAL R1*. Whatever, the SIGNAL light stayed on red, as usual.

He switched on the radio and tuned into Capital 194, and '*99 Red Balloons*' by the German group *Nena* was playing. He laughed out loud, thinking about what happened in the *Anchor* pub earlier. Rayne was right in some ways about Sentinel being a '*fucking nut-case*', but he did deal with that idiot in the pub pretty well.

Hitting the M25, he continued to watch the R1, in case a miracle occurred, but nothing did, it just stayed on red. Thoughts of Sally-Anne came back to him.

He had a real urge to speak to her, maybe he could arrange to see her again soon. The journey back was going to take him close by her place, perhaps he could call in?

But given the *'palace'* she lived in, this was not an option. Then he had an idea, if he left the M25 at the Godstone village turn-off, there was a phone-box in the street. If she was in, then maybe he could arrange something?

He took the Cavalier onto the slip road and headed off for the village. The red light stayed fixed on the R1 as a light shower came on to the windscreen, dropping down the hill into the centre of Godstone, the rain turned heavier. Just up ahead on the left, he saw the red phone-box, and pulled the Cavalier in as close to it as he could.

As per usual, the phone-box stank inside, a mixture of fags and fish and chips, with some greasy wrapping paper on the floor. He glanced out at the car, the side-lights left on, lit-up a Marlboro and placed Sally-Anne's card in front of him as he dialled her number, putting 10p in the slot, ready.

There was no response from the handset, and he tried again. Nothing but silence. Once more, in frustration, he dialled the number. *"Fuck it!"* he shouted. *"Fuck, fucking everything!"*

The bad weather had gathered pace as he stepped back into the Cavalier, his jacket was wet, even though the phone box was close. A thunder storm had come in, right overhead.

Could things really get any worse? Although he anticipated the wipers would operate OK, it might be better to sit this out, for a while at least.

He reached over to switch on *Capital Radio194* again, and noticed something odd. The R1 cellular telephone red light had now turned green.

Unclipping the handset, he considered the electrical storm might *somehow* connect this thing to the *RADI-CAL* system. He looked at Sally-Anne's number, on her now damp card. Maybe, this was worth a try.

He keyed in her nine numbers, the handset lighting up and bleeping for each one. Outside the storm increased, lightening flashing across the village, like a scene from yet another old horror movie, the rain turning to hail-stones that sounded as if they were going to dent the car's body. Not that he cared.

He pressed the SND button and put the handset to his head. The green and white glow from the buttons, cast shadows over the passenger seat. He waited, listening intently for a sound. Nothing.

He was not surprised, and sighed, about to re-clip it onto the dash-board holder. But then something strange happened, through the ear-piece he heard a noise with long '*burrs*', sounding like he was making an overseas call. Then a click came and a voice he recognised said.

"Croydon Strip-O-Grams, can I help you?"

"You're not going to believe this," said Linus "but I'm calling you from the car phone."

"Well, I'm afraid we don't do stripping in motor-cars, you'll need a prostitute for that. I can let you have a number if you wish."

Linus continued. "Listen Sally-Anne, it's me Linus and I'm calling you from that new cellular phone thing. I'm actually in the *fucking* car!"

It went quiet for a moment, she was clearly thinking about this, then replied.

"Is this for real, or a wind-up?"

"No, it's real I promise you. I know I said it wasn't going live till the end of the year, but this is a test-run."

"Where are you?"

"I'm in Godstone, in the middle of a thunder storm."

"Not far away then," she said. "I'll tell you what, you can pop over if you like, all my folks are away tonight, we can have a private chat, so you can tell me all about it."

"Right," he said. "On my way, over and out." As he re-clipped it to the holder, the rain eased and the red, **'No-Signal'** light flashed back on.

Linus pulled up outside Sally-Anne's mansion, although the driveway was empty excepting for her Metro, he knew it was not appropriate to park in there, so he left the Cavalier on the road. Not once had the *RADI-CAL* live signal come back on since they had last spoken.

The rain had completely stopped as he walked somewhat gingerly, up to the front and rang the bell.

The door creaked open slowly. Her raven hair flashed under the hall lights as MacColl stared at her in disbelief. She stood looking coy in her black stiletto shoes, black bra, stockings, suspenders and micro-knickers.

"Any specific music, you'd like me to work with?" she asked, straight-faced. "I'd hate for you to have to put your hands over your eyes again like last week, especially given how much I'm going to charge for this."

He walked in and she closed the door behind them. *Laura Branigan's* new hit, *'Self-Control'* rang out from the lounge.

Maybe these cellular radio things might have some use after all, he thought.

Chapter 3

Heath-field House, West Sussex
24th September 1984

The gravel crunched under the Cavalier's tyres, as MacColl pulled up outside Heath-field House. Despite working at RITON for over six years, this was his first visit to the Group's prestigious training centre.

It actually looked better than in the photographs back at base, and they'd been pretty impressive. A huge, Georgian period mansion, that was more like a palace. He should have brought his *Kodak, Instamatic* camera. Having been told there was so much technical kit in Heath-field House, they probably had a dark-room. Then, he would have posted the photo to Sally-Anne saying, *I'm staying in a bigger palace than yours this week, so there.*

The time was just on 07.30hrs, so he was well ahead of schedule, with the training course not due to start for another two hours. Linus thought about where to park, because he wanted that usual privacy whilst observing the scene. By the far end of the building to the left, he saw a number of oak trees on the edge of the gravel. This looked an ideal place. He reversed the car close to the largest tree, reclined the seat, wound down the window, and lit up a Marlboro, moving into his usual *think-mode*.

A week ago, he'd started out at *RADI-CAL*, his initial feelings reflecting the negative comments from Rupert Cannon, and many of the traditional RITON team.

But now, a different view had started to nag at him, he couldn't stop thinking about the huge benefit that using this R1 car phone had given him during the storm last Monday. He'd been running the extreme, sensual experience of the night with Sally-Anne through his mind ever since. He glanced down at the hand-set. Without *that*, it would not have happened.

Since entering Heath-field, the SIGNAL light had flashed to green, because a *cell* had been installed in the grounds for the training course. Still staring at the R1, he reflected on the mayhem of last week.

From the crazy start in the Maidstone branch, to now understanding how these cellular phone things could be of real value, had been a somewhat fraught journey. The *RADI-CAL* approach, was very different to the standard group behaviour he'd been used to. But, as the week went on, he had built up a strange kind of respect for the staff. This felt weird, given that he had known them for such a short time, in which he had experienced a threat with a spanner and witnessed a pub brawl. So it took some self-explanatory work to perceive why this should be.

Maybe it was because they were fundamentally *'doers'*. He glanced at his watch, and the R1 again. It was almost 08.00hrs, and he thought about calling Sally-Anne. No, this was not right at this time of day, she had probably been working late. He considered what she might have been doing last night, and shuddered.

For some reason, which he could not fathom, his mind flicked to computers. These were now increasing massively in numbers across the business. They were odd looking things called *Apricots*, with huge green screens taking up a lot more desk-space than the IBM and Olympia electric typewriters. The three-and-a-half- inch *'floppy disks'* were also annoying, and Rupert Cannon's PA Colleen, was always complaining about them. "Why not just type and photo-copy, rather than all this *storage* rubbish." She said, quite rightly.

But things were on the change, no doubt about that. Front-wheel drive cars, some with five gears, four television channels, portable *'Boom box'* stereos, these bloody office computers and now, cellular telephones. George Orwell was close to *really* being right about *1984,* then.

But it wasn't just the new machinery and electrical stuff, people were changing too. Linus often thought about his dad's regularly spoken opinion; "The world's gone mad." But he'd aimed this at the seventies, and look at us now.

Maybe it was all these new-fangled contraptions that were affecting people's lives?

Anything automatic and press-button meant you could use it on your own, without needing any input from another person. Changes. He hummed out the David Bowie song: *"Changes are takin' the pace I'm going through."* Too right, and how would the future affect the traditional relationships of the RITON group staff? The irony of this hit home again, because it was now a world-leader in technical development.

He lit up again and inhaled from the Marlboro. *One day*, he thought, *I'm going to give this up*, staring at the red-glow on the fag's end. He set himself another target, the age of 30. The last one was at 25 and that failed, but this time, it would be different....

He muttered out-loud, sarcastically *"Anyway, fags are probably going to be electric too one day."* The stupid comment amusing him, as he thought back to reality.

He considered the events of the past week again. Leaving from Sally-Anne's in the small hours of Tuesday, returning home for a quick change, then dashing back into the Maidstone office.

Everyone arrived there earlier than on Monday, in fact the majority before 08.30hrs. Linus had at least *something* positive then to scribe into his report to Rupert Cannon. Mike Sentinel had a weekly meeting required for 09.00hrs in the large, downstairs room on the edge of the installation workshop. Linus was surprised at just how tidy this place was. As he entered, all of the team excepting Jeannie Sands, were present.

Considering the riot at the *Anchor* pub last night, they all looked fine with one exception, the workshop manager from Scotland whose name he'd found out, was Derek Tweedy. He had a black-eye, but otherwise was alright, in fact he was smiling at everyone. Turned out that he stormed over to join in with Mike Sentinel, and then took on the building-site crowd. He'd obviously put *health and fucking safety* on the back burner. '*And why not,*' thought Linus.

They all sat down and Sentinel opened up. "Mmm, alrighty everyone, I need to give you an update on the situation," he said, looking around at them all. The group stared at him in silence.

"As you are aware, the system goes live on the twenty fourth of December in Hyde Park. The first *official* user of a *RADI-CAL* cellular telephone is going to be the comedian, Frankie Howerd. The whole thing is going to be covered by the gutter press and might also be seen on television sets."

The team stared around the table at each other in shock.

"Och no," said Tweedy. "Why choose a *poofter*?"

"Mmm, well that's because he is a celebrity chap," replied Sentinel. "I would suggest he is a good choice as there are a growing number of queers in the world, and we should be politically correct, alrighty."

Linus, was tempted to pinch himself, wanting to awake from this ever increasing nightmare. The door opened and in walked Jeannie Sands, blonde hair flashing under the room lighting, wearing a tight red dress and carrying a light-brown case.

She sat opposite, sending out that magic smile, removing a sheaf of papers and spreading them out gently in front of her.

"Sorry I'm late," she said looking directly at Mike Sentinel. "Contract is now signed."

He looked back at her with genuine delight, then around the table at each member of the team and said. "Well everyone, I'd like you to applaud Jeannie for gaining our first, decent sized deal."

Linus joined in the clapping, now understanding how this could be achieved before the system went live. It was clearly an advanced contract agreement, based on a method explained to him by Sentinel yesterday. But then he thought, with a touch of jealousy for Jeannie Sands. *Contract is now signed, oh is it really, how wonderful! Blah, blah, blah.*

"There are nine R1's and two R2's going to be installed into lorries and vans on a five-year contract, and the company has asked for this to be carried out by the end of next month. That way, everything will be in place for when we go live." Sentinel looked at each of the G.A.M's around the table and continued. "And I expect you all to follow suit."

Linus sat back in the chair, his mind calculating the value of this deal. The basic cost was £17,900 for the 'phones, £2750 for the installs, and then £275 monthly line rentals. Then there were the call charges at 25p per minute in peak time, and probably some additional costs that he wasn't aware of, and no guarantee it would work. He glanced over at Jeannie and she smiled back, admittedly, she had some real ability.

Mike Sentinel stood up and walked over to the large paper chart on a tripod. In front of him was a clear, white sheet and he pulled the cap off a giant red, felt-tipped pen, whacking it on the paper. It broke in half and the nib flew up to the ceiling, then landed on Derek Tweedy's head, rolling to a stop on the table, red ink everywhere.

"Mmm, sorry," said Sentinel examining the pen. "Clearly a defective device."

Sentinel picked up another one, as everyone around the table put hands over their heads. All except Tweedy, who sat staring at him and whispering under his breath.

Och you Sassenach idiot, look what you've done to my heeed!

Linus stared over at him, and there *were* some significant red streaks on the top of his *heeed*. He should jot this down for Rupert Cannon, but would not now.

Jeannie was laughing out loud, in her unusually deep, yet sensual way. Linus was fascinated by this, as he was by the way she spoke, when occasionally her voice went low and made him shiver. He'd never heard a woman speak or laugh like her before. Given this alongside her looks and work ability, he felt her husband was a lucky man.

Sentinel stood back up by the sheet again. "Now these are the figures *RADI-CAL* needs to reach within the first year." He started to jot down the numbers from a piece of paper he held up in front of him.

$R1 = 7,000$ units
$R2 = 2,300$ units
$R3 = 700$ units
Target Value: £15.5m expected discount 10%
Actual Value: £13.95m

The whole team looked across at Sentinel. Linus noted a level of surprise from most of them, but not from Jeannie Sands and Julian Rayne. He knew they had a close working relationship with Sentinel, and so were probably already aware of the numbers.

But, given the map of where the systems would be in place across the country, showing such a small area of connections, *how could these numbers be possible?*

"But the most important area is the profit from monthly line rental and call costs." Sentinel continued. "Once these target figures are achieved, the R1 volume alone would bring in one hundred and seventy-five grand each month and be on at least a three-year contract. Additionally, most calls would be twenty-five pence per minute."

Linus was noting this down and tried to work out how many minutes' worth of calls would be made on average. Maybe half an hour was reasonable, the R3 hand-portable would not operate for more than this anyway, and then would take around 10 hours to charge up again. The car fitted, R1 and R2 would be connected to the 12v supply, so they would have no time limits. But 25 pence per minute he thought was quite steep, because thirty minutes equalled £7.50, which would be £225 plus VAT every month. And that was assuming the call levels did not go higher.

The *real* value of *RADI-CAL* was now dawning on MacColl. For years, his RITON commercial focus was always on profit in supply of equipment and on-going maintenance and repairs. With this outfit, it was going to be very different.

Linus raised his hand and asked Sentinel "Mike, how much profit is there in the call charges for us per minute?"

"Mmm, that's still under negotiation due to the land-line connection costs with British Telecommunications, and that is going to remain confidential to the board." He replied, as usual, looking down his nose at Linus. "That's not relevant to our work, and we should focus on new business for mobile sales at this stage."

Linus felt a little dejected and mentally shrunk down. Then he thought, *British Telecommunications, why on earth would anyone* say *it like that*?

Sentinel carried on speaking across the group. "We are one fifth of the target number from January to December next year, and I expect us to sell significantly more than two thousand units. With the seven G.A.M's in the team, our target is twenty five per month each. Jeannie is also opening up the dealer trade programme in our region, so she'll be bringing in additional orders from vehicle suppliers, retail shops and others."

The group looked up at him seriously, as Mike Sentinel nodded separately at each one of them. It went without saying, that the pressure was about to begin. Linus thought Sentinel was a mad-man in many respects, but there was no doubt he was results driven, so was beginning to appreciate why he had been brought on-board.

"Jeannie has brought in the first corporate order for the group. I appreciate there has to be a time delay before this can go live, but in my opinion, this is a piece of history."

He continued glancing and nodding at them all one-by-one, that extraordinarily weird blonde hair flicking about as he did so. "In thirty years' time, this *first* will be on national news as a piece of history, because there'll probably be a million people using mobile telephones out there."

Everybody started laughing, but Sentinel kept a serious look about him. He clearly believed this could happen. *Madness.*

Linus jotted everything down, realising the importance of his forthcoming meeting with Rupert Cannon. This was only day two, but he'd already pieced together a lot of important observations for him. Mike Sentinel continued his presentation.

"As from today, everyone is to diarise at least seven and most likely, ten meetings per week. I want you to follow the style of Jeannie in this when it comes to closing the deals.

We need to be the leading regional team, and have every chance because we are well located, our key area being in the City of London EC1 to EC4 post codes. Everyone is going to get their allocated areas from me today. As you are aware, we are recruiting two additional G.A.M's, so I'll reserve certain post codes for them."

He looked across at his PA. "Julia will hand out your target areas this afternoon." He glanced at his watch, as he flicked up the wrist, the strap came undone and it flew off onto the floor. "Mmm, poor engineering, certainly not my fault."

Linus glanced at his own Seiko, it was getting close to midday.

"Right, let's get down to McDonalds Restaurant and I would suggest the *filet-o-fish*," concluded Sentinel as he walked to the door, the whole team with two exceptions, following him out.

Linus and Jeannie sat looking across at each other, then both burst out laughing.

"Like I told you before," said Jeannie, just finding enough laughter control to carry on. "He is no ordinary person, but if anyone can make this work, it's him."

The whole gang walked into *McDonalds* in Maidstone High Street, right by the local prison. *It just gets better,* thought MacColl as he followed them through the door.

There was a large table close by, and everyone sat down except Mike Sentinel and Julia, who went up to the counter to place an order for them all.

Sat within the group, Linus glanced at each member of the G.A.M team. He needed to provide a brief for Cannon about these guys, and committed each of them into his mind, using the usual memory retention tool of putting pictures of people and their detail captions together.

Although he was a lover of McDonalds, the background noise during a busy lunch time would not help, but he compiled it anyway.

1.Julian Rayne – age 24, bright ex-public school, technically astute, well connected across the City of London.

2. Robert "Robbie" Robson – age 40ish, experienced in office equipment sales, ex-army, smart in every way, except when it came to buying a Sausage Roll.
3. Kevin Aaron – age 28, ex BT man, skilled in sales and the phone industry, calm and dependable.
4. Jean (Jeannie) Sands – age 30, Looks like a TV star, beautiful in every way, most successful member of
RADI-CAL, not that I'm obsessed by her at all.
5. Linus MacColl – age 27, new boy on a learning curve, constantly pinching himself to see if this thing is real or a dream. More likely a *nightmare.*

He'd run through these with Cannon, but would also briefly tell him about the rest of the region, avoiding reference to the cleaner, spanner man, and pub fighting, for obvious reasons.

Sentinel and Julia brought two trays of food over, burgers, French fries and *filet-o-fish,* of course.

Back at the office, Linus and the G.A.M team went again into the downstairs meeting room. Julia came in with a file for each of them, except Jeannie. Linus had already thought she wouldn't need one, her role was already established.

Mike Sentinel came in and everyone sat down. He opened his own file and scanned through it, but Linus assumed he already had all this information in his head, because he was the decision maker, and apparently, remembered every detail.

"Now, these are your post-codes," he said, looking around at each of the team in his usual, eccentric way.

"You'll notice that everyone has a London area included, to keep things reasonable."

They opened up the files, looking at the contents. A City post-code had been allocated to each of them from EC1 to EC4.

The other areas were across Kent and Surrey, completing regional coverage, with the exception of some gaps, which would be allocated to the new team members about to be recruited. Everyone appreciated the importance of the City of London, as it was expected to have a significant interest in *RADI-CAL* products.

Linus considered the allocation to him of EC4. He was not particularly knowledgeable about it, but knew of some large shipping HQ's where he had a few contacts. Maybe they could be of use?

But the other areas given to him, across Kent and over the Surrey borders were a very different challenge. He felt it could be the equivalent of trying to sell sand in a desert. Massive areas out in the sticks, probably full of *local-yokels* and most critically, no cellular radio call coverage. He looked up at Julian, Robbie and Kevin, they all seemed quite comfortable with their own allocations. Maybe he was missing something? Sentinel interrupted his thought pattern.

"Linus, you're booked into the Heath-field House training centre with the other *newbies*, starting on Monday. You'll get a full overview of how the network operates and how to target and sell the units." Then Sentinel looked around at the whole group, stood up and said. "I'm off," and walked out. That was it.

Kevin Aaron looked over at Linus and said. "We all knew these would be allocated, so it's good that the guessing-game is over, at least we can all get started now." He continued. "It's probably a good idea if you were to wait until after the course before you get started."

Linus appreciated and understood his advice. All the other team members had done their earlier training course at Heath-field, so were better placed to get on with things now than he was.

"Thanks Kevin, I'll do that," he thought for a moment and added smiling. "I'll find something else to do before Monday, no doubt."

Jeannie looked over at Linus and said. "If you want, I've got a potential new customer meeting tomorrow, in Rochester. We can meet up here tomorrow at nine and go straight over there."

"I'd be delighted," he said, sincerely meaning that.

Linus glanced at the Cavalier's clock, it was just coming up to 08.30hrs. Whilst he'd been mulling over the events of last week, around ten cars had now turned up at Heath-field House, which were clearly part of the *RADI-CAL* fleet, all had the now ubiquitous, black antennas on the roof. They were in the main car park, and given there was another hour before the course was due to start, more were likely to arrive.

His fag packet was empty, and he opened the glove box for another. The R1 handset was mounted very close to it, making it fiddly to open. He ripped off the cellophane, pulled out the silver foil and lit up another, considering how good it was that these had the *safety* of filter-tips. He inhaled deeply and blew the smoke out of the driver's side window again, as his mind returned to last Wednesday's time out with Jeannie Sands in Rochester.

As usual, Linus had rolled-up earlier than the official RITON start time at Maidstone. Then in came Julia followed by Robbie, Julian and Kevin, all early doors. Tweedy and his assistant pulled up outside the workshop in a white Transit van, both looking haggard in their overalls, and each with a roll-up dangling. He guessed they'd put a few away last night.

Given that this operation was just starting out, and was not going officially live for almost three months, he was unsure of what these workshop blokes did all day. Following the team to the entrance, he wondered why Mike Sentinel had not shown up yet, being the Regional Manager, then Jeannie's Cavalier pulled in.

She opened the car door and stepped out, smiling across at Linus. She strode towards him with a truly sensual gait, like a movie actress. He sensed a slightly autumnal feel in the atmosphere and noted Jeannie had dressed accordingly, wearing a cream roll-neck, black skirt and high-heel boots. The early sun caught her blonde hair.

"How are you today?" she asked him, the smile continuing. "Nice suit, I really like the cut."

He felt a little uneasy, because he wanted to say how lovely she looked, but did not want her to get the wrong impression, even though that was the *right* one.

"Thanks, yes I'm fine and you?" He asked.

Her smiling continued. "Good thanks, looking forward to our trip out, shall we nip in for a coffee first?"

They strolled in together and up the stairs. She went ahead of him, and he found that both awkward and exciting. As she strode up, he couldn't help looking at the shape of her body, from the blonde hair down to the beautifully shaped back-side in her pencil skirt, ending with the very high-heels of the black boots. Like the majority of men, he had to be prepared to look away in an instant, should she turn her head round and spot a *letch*.

At the top, she held the door open for him and said. "What coffee, would you like, *Nescafe Gold Blend* maybe?"

He thought about Monday's *GKN Sankey machine* palaver. "No thanks, I'm off coffee just now." She smiled, nodded and walked off.

"Hello," said a voice from behind one of the desk screens. "She's lovely but deadly!"

Linus looked over and saw Robbie Robson smiling up at him. He decided not to respond to this, although was rather puzzled as to why he should have said that. Maybe it was just guesswork, or perhaps he knew something about her past?

Linus decided to avoid the subject and took the opportunity to explore further about Mike Sentinel, who was still missing.

"So is Mike out today?" he asked, glancing across to his office, then noticed yet another bizarre item in there, walking across to the window thinking *that can't be for real*, but it was. Sat on the meeting table was a massive cross-bow, with arrows strewn beside it, next to a huge book, entitled *"An easier way to fish using archery."*

Looking up at him, Robbie realised Linus was shocked. He removed the glasses, closed his notebook and said. "I appreciate people think he's crazy, we all do at times, but there is no one and I mean *no one* that I would trust more than Mike when the chips are down, and I don't just mean in McDonalds. Besides, *they* call them *French Fries*."

He sat back and, brought his hands up to the lips in a steeple fashion and went on. "Let me tell you something." Linus moved closer to Robbie and listened intently, assuming this could be a private matter as he went on.

"Back in Sixty-Seven, we were in the Army Transport Corps together. I had just become a Sergeant and Mike was a Lieutenant. Anyway, the Six-Day War had ended five months before, but we were told we might have to go over there with UN Peace Keeping, so we needed some training on new kit. They packed us off to a place in Scotland, right out in the middle of nowhere."

He shook his head at Linus, the memory clearly flooding back.

"Anyway, we were in a makeshift camp in the Highlands and at night things got boring, if you know what I mean." Linus nodded, but didn't have a clue what he meant.

"Well I was fed up one night, so decided to slip out and go over to a town about twenty miles away. There was a pub there with a nice bar maid, and I'd met up with her on a day's leave the week before, so I thought I'd just go for it. There was a

Norton Commando on the fleet, so I filled up the petrol tank and took it. Well, there was no one to stop me as we had no gate-duty. The weather was so bloody cold."

Robbie shivered as if time had gone all the way back, and he was actually setting off again. "Anyway, I took a few swigs of whisky and put the bottle in my coat pocket for later, to keep me going on the journey."

Linus nodded his understanding as Robbie went on.

"First few miles were fine, but as I went up a steep hill, a blizzard came in with all this snow swirling around. I thought it would ease up as I dropped down the other side, but it didn't, in fact it got worse. The headlight hit the snow storm and my goggles were covered, so I lost sight of the road, came off into a field and hit a tree. Wallop."

Linus stared at him genuinely shocked by this, imaging how awful in every way, this must have been. "Wow." he said. "Were you badly hurt?"

"Not good." Robbie continued. "Broke my leg, cracked my ribs and smacked my head on a tree, so went out cold. We didn't bother with helmets then of course."

"So what happened next?" asked Linus. "Did a local come to rescue you?"

"No, there was absolutely no one in the area, the nearest farm house was about a mile away. I was on my own, freezing and unconscious, with broken bones, so would have been done for had it not been for one thing."

"What was that?" Linus asked again.

"Well." he said, nodding across at Mike Sentinel's office. "He was *that* thing."

Linus continued his confused look as Robbie went on.

"Mike was in the officer's quarters apparently, got fed up with having the piss taken, so thought he'd find me for a quick chat then have an early night as it had been a long, cold, old day. Anyway, he walked over to my hut, but obviously I was gone, so he decided to check if the Norton's were all up together outside the store room, and he noticed one was missing. The weather had really cracked on badly, and he put two and two together and guessed I'd taken off on one of the bikes. I'd already told him about the barmaid and Mike being Mike, he remembered every detail of her name and what the pub was called, you know."

Linus nodded, he'd noticed that Sentinel was exceptional when it came to detail.

"Well, he went into the guard-room and made a call over to the pub. They told him that no army types at all had turned up. Then he tore the road map off the wall, took a Land-Rover from the storage barn and headed off. He later told me he could hardly see out of the screen, which is not a surprise given his eyesight, but slid open the door's window, so he could check if I'd flown into the bushes, which I had."

Robbie sat back in the chair again, staring across at Linus and shaking his head.

"To this day, I still can't believe how he managed to find me, but he did. The Norton's engine had died obviously, but the lights stayed on, bloody lucky. Anyway, Mike just caught sight of the tail-light in the field and pulled over, then came through the bushes with his torch. I was in a right state and out cold. But he checked me over, gave me a face slap to bring me back to life and then carefully wrapped me in a blanket. Lifting me up was painful, but he did a good job at carrying me back to the Land-Rover.

He put the seat cushions from the passenger side and the centre one in the back, so he could lay me in some comfort, then took the whisky bottle out of my coat pocket, how that didn't smash I don't know."

Jeannie walked back in with her coffee in the plastic cup, catching the story. Robbie assured Linus. "It's fine, Jeannie knows about this."

She said. "Oh yes, it was quite amazing." Robbie carried on.

"He took me something like twenty miles to a hospital emergency department, no way was he going to risk me with the camp medic, and it seemed to take bloody hours, but we made it. Then he carried me in and plonked me on a bed, demanding the doctor get on with matters, looking over his glasses and down his nose at him as per usual."

Linus, Jeannie and Robbie all laughed at that typical, Mike Sentinel style.

"Anyway, they found my left leg was broken and so were two ribs and I was suffering from concussion of course, other than that I was fine. The doctor suggested that I had been drinking because my breath still smelt of whisky. I remember that but Mike stepped in, showing him the bottle he'd taken out of my coat pocket and said. *Mmm I gave Robson some of MY whisky as I collected the body, so as to bring him back to life, alrighty.*"

All three of them laughed again, picturing this.

"Anyway, *he saved* my life and stopped me getting court-martialled, but didn't half give me a *bollocking* when I came back to camp, and I missed the trip to Israel, but there you go. Needless to say, I think he's bloody marvellous, even if he can be bonkers."

Jeannie looked at her watch and said. "Come on, we need to go."

They headed down the stairs and out to her Cavalier.

As they drove out to the main road, Linus continued to smile about Robbie's tale.

"I told you Mike was an exceptionally good man," she said. "He helped me so much as well, when I split up with my first husband."

Linus looked across at her and nodded, he said nothing because it *wasn't* a surprise. There was an element of Jeannie which made that the case. He could sense there must always be a mass of men trying to attract her. She had this unusual quality of presence, but could always engage as one of the gang, not that aloof, *look at me, I'm so glamourous* type, who seemed everywhere in the modern world. Each element of her was stunning, but it was somehow natural, and not contrived.

"What did he do then?" asked Linus.

"Like I said, we were working together at Rate-Syrex and Mike was my manager. When the *you- know- what*, hit the fan, things were very difficult. I had to disappear off for a month or so to sort things out, with nowhere to stay. It was complicated and nasty and I won't bore you with it, but Mike gave me the spare room for as long as I needed it at his house, which by the way, is a beauty called *Green Trees."*

She waved in the opposite direction to their journey and continued.

"It's up in that way, near Sevenoaks. Every night he and his wife sat in the lounge with me, and listened to all my concerns and emotions, and this was for over a month. Not only that, but he covered my work for all that time without saying a word to the board or anyone else. Lots of business came in, and it was all down to him, but I got the recognition for it. And do you know what?"

Linus had no idea, so just shook his head aimlessly.

"He has still never told anyone or even reminded me. People sometimes struggle to *get* him, but he is a one-off. One of kindest people on earth, no doubt about it."

They rolled up outside the **Trans-ship Ltd** building on the Rochester trading estate, where Jeannie had arranged a second meeting. She'd already met the transport manager, presenting how the *RADI-CAL* system could make things more efficient for their deliveries. It was a large place, with a mass of articulated lorries parked up beside what Linus thought must be the storage area. Shutter doors opened and fork-lifts headed in and out, full of pallets.

They walked in through the entrance and Jeannie said to the receptionist. "Hi, we're here to see Mr Dave Grant."

"Certainly, I'll ask him to come down, please take a seat."

"Well, this is a first for me." Said Linus quietly to Jeannie.

"It might be a first, but it certainly won't be your last." Replied Jeannie, with her usual smile.

A tall thin guy, slightly balding came down the stairs and over to them. Jeannie and Linus stood up and the man shook her hand. He immediately seemed to Linus a straight up and down type.

"Good to see you again Jeannie," he said then glanced over at Linus.

"This is Linus MacColl," she said. "We're working together today."

He shook hands with Linus and said. "Nice to meet you, let's go upstairs."

They followed him up and into a large area, which had around thirty desks in it, pretty much all with staff on the phone and jotting down information onto clipboards. Walking over were guys in overalls, who picked up the boards, and took them back to the stairs. Linus guessed it was about incoming orders being taken, then organising despatch with the drivers. Dave Grant led them towards his office, at the far end.

Jeannie was in front of Linus, and as they went across the floor, he noticed that some of the deskbound blokes stared at her and one or two whistled out.

She turned and gave them a smile, bouncing along and the blonde hair flicking as usual, then the wolf-whistles started to increase, right across the place and then loud cheering kicked-in.

Linus had never experienced anything like this, and he'd walked across a lot of offices around the World. There was something about this *RADI-CAL* thing which was starting to become infectious. The relatively few members of staff he'd met were extraordinary, from the craziest, yet seemingly, most caring manager, an aggressive workshop lunatic, through to a woman who had totally and effortlessly proven to be the most attention catching he'd ever seen.

How would he explain this to Rupert Cannon? Maybe, he wouldn't bother even trying, because one had to be within *RADI-CAL* to understand it.

Grant sat behind his office desk and ushered them to a couple of chairs. The glass walls were covered in sheets of paper with details of items which Linus thought were for freighting. There were dozens of them, with ticks and crosses on the bottom, which were probably to confirm whether deliveries had been completed or not.

"Tea or coffee?" he asked, smiling at both of them.

"Coffee please," said Jeannie. "Me too," piped in Linus, then went on. "Quite a place you've got here." Instantly regretting stating, the *bleeding obvious*.

"It's always a challenge, and growing all the time as imports and exports are increasing, which of course, is good news." One of the warehouse's doors screeched open and a lorry's diesel engine fired up, then it's **T.I.R** signed trailer reversed onto the floor below.

Grant waved up at the sheets around the office and continued. "Trouble is the more you do, the harder it is to monitor."

A lady in overalls knocked and came in with a tray, placing it on the desk. "Thanks Monica," said Grant. "Very nice of you." He waved at the china-cups and saucers for them both.

Jeannie stirred her coffee and sipped it. "That's lovely she said, just what the doctor ordered," glancing over at Linus and then said to Grant. "We've had a busy day."

"So are you already taking orders?" asked Grant directly to her. "Only I thought nothing was starting until next year."

Jeannie sipped again, and with her cup and saucer in hand, leant forward towards the tray to put it down. As she did so, the sunlight came across through the warehouse's open door, caught her blonde hair and at the same time, enhanced the shape of her breasts under the cream jumper.

Linus noticed that Grant's eyes looked as if they were coming out on stalks.

She sat back again and said. "We are going live on the twenty fourth of December, and committed to getting everything in place before hand." She glanced down at the lorry in the warehouse. "Thing is, by installing now you can have everything ready for when it happens. We've been very busy on this, and our install schedules around the country are very full aren't they, Linus?" He nodded back, dog-style as she continued.

"But we are aware that even though our testing has shown it works very well, we don't expect any company to take a gamble. So our contract with you would make it clear that if you were not satisfied, we'd remove everything and close it down without any charge, except for the calls you might have made. What do you think?"

She sat back and looked at Grant as he glanced around, clearly thinking it over. Then he said. "I'm in favour of your offer, it is far better than BT's and I like the look of your stuff. Only thing is, a board member had a call from another supplier and wants to look at theirs."

He looked down and sifted through the mass of paperwork on his desk, picking up a note. "Yes, that's the one," he said. "They are called *Motafone,* apparently."

Chapter 4

Heath-field House, West Sussex
24th September 1984

Linus stepped out of the Cavalier, it was 09.00hrs as he walked up the steps into the entrance of Heath-field House. The five-day training course for *RADI-CAL* was to commence in thirty minutes. Before going in, he turned and looked down at the car park. He estimated around twenty company cars in there. A mixture of Cavaliers, Sierras, Montegos and Orions, each one naturally, with antennas on the roof. So there would be at least that number of new starters on the course.

Walking inside, he noticed how modern the place's interior looked, a complete opposite to the outside of the building. Apart from the very high ceiling, all the furnishings, fittings and colour schemes were right up to the minute, and there was a smell of fresh paint in the atmosphere.

In front of him was the reception desk, and a number of bag holders were forming a queue to check in. *Damn it,* he thought. *I should have come in earlier.* He left a gap between the last in line and looked them over. It dawned on him that there was no need to check in yet because he wouldn't need to go to his room until tonight, and the suitcase was still in the car anyway.

He took a step to the side and glanced at them all again. There were five men and a woman waiting. They were not communicating with each other, so probably hadn't met before.

His brief experience in the Kent branch was different from the new starters, he'd already made a few connections.

As far as he knew, he was the only RITON staff member to have made the switch. Not a surprise, given his role was to secretly report the activities he'd seen in this new thing back to the main board. *I already know more than you lot,* he said under his breath, looking somewhat superciliously towards them.

They would be in training before going into their regional offices. *Good luck with that,* he thought. Mind you, it wasn't all bad in the Kent office.

As he mulled this over a striking, tall man came walking through the entrance and straight over to him.

"You're Linus MacColl aren't you?" He asked, putting forward his right hand.

"I am," said Linus, as they shook hands together. "You're Mr Rider aren't you?"

"That's right," he responded, smiling back. "Call me Steve."

Linus had already been given a description of this chap by the Maidstone team. He was the Sales Director, and had a reputation for driving new business to high success rates in office equipment markets, before being one of the first to join *RADI-CAL*.

In fact, he now remembered being told by Robbie Robson that he was a former Rate-Syrex man, so might have a connection with Mike and Jeannie too. This was confirmed as Steve continued.

"I know you are over in the Kent regional office. There are some exceptional people there, not least being Mike Sentinel and Jeannie Sands. How are you finding the place?"

"It was a good week in there," responded Linus, trying to think of something positive to add. "They are a dedicated team and certainly know their stuff."

Steve glanced over at the door left of reception and touched Linus on the shoulder, his mind clearly moving to another matter. "Good man, anyway I've got to get things started for the training, see you in there."

Linus watched him walk away and checked his Seiko. Twenty minutes and the course would be starting. Glancing down the lobby to the court-yard, he noticed there were now a considerable number of types stood outside chatting. The weather was good, with the sun coming in as the clouds disappeared. *Now that's always a good sign,* thought Linus positively, as he walked down the steps and back to his Cavalier.

He strolled past the group smiling. Nobody returned it, but he wasn't surprised, they were obviously *RADI-CAL newbies*, and not the traditional RITON people. This was yet another supercilious, internal comment. He felt a shiver of concern that he was becoming Mike Sentinel like. *This needs to stop,* he thought.

Opening up the Cavalier's door, his intention was merely to pick up his brief-case from the back seat and return into the building. But he still had a bit of time left, so another ciggie would not go amiss. As usual, he lit up the Marlboro and reclined the seat, wound down the window and blew out the first cloud of smoke.

His thoughts returned to Trans-Ship in Rochester. After the meeting, Jeannie took him into the high-street, and they went into a cafeteria. It was a traditional, Victorian style place, as befitted a town well-known for its Dickensian history.

"What do you fancy?" She asked.

Linus had an answer in his mind, but stuck to the menu.

"Oh, err scrambled eggs on toast please."

Jeannie smiled and walked up to the counter. As she did so, most of the customers glanced up at her. Linus did the same, he just couldn't help it.

She strolled back and stood, smiling. "I need to whip up to the bank, I won't be long." He watched her walk across the street, sunlight now touching the blonde hair, as usual everyone she passed turned and stared at her.

Linus sat considering the situation of today's meeting. He thought about Grant's mention of a new competitor, *Motafone*.

He'd been made aware of this by Mike Sentinel last week. Apparently, the Thatcher lot saw it as a back-up, in case of any problems with them and BT. Perhaps this might create an issue with the Trans-ship deal? He thought for a moment about Rupert Cannon, smiling to himself, as he would probably have said, *"Trans-ship johnnies."*

He continued to giggle as Jeannie walked back in and sat down. "What made you laugh?" She asked quizzically.

"Nothing much, I was thinking about my old boss." He said.

"I've been meaning to ask you something," she said staring across at him. "Are you gay?"

He looked at her in shock and stammered out.

"Err no, I've never been one of those." He paused trying to think of why she would have asked this and felt suddenly on a depressingly downward path. "Do you think I look like a *poofter*?" He asked, angry with himself for using such a terrible word.

She laughed out loud and smiled in her unique way, causing those at the next tables to stare in wonderment at her, which did not improve things for Linus.

"No," she said, continuing the laughter. "I just keep thinking about you walking strangely into the *Anchor* the other night and your camp sense of humour." She nodded down at his crossed legs. "And I think doing that could be a sign."

He quickly uncrossed his legs and sat upright, thinking, *I am never going to do that again, for the rest of my life.*

"Sorry if I gave the wrong impression." He said.

She held up both hands and smiled back at him, the light catching her wedding ring. "I don't have a problem with it. Anyway, I like to be open minded about everything."

Linus was unsure where this conversation was going, and his initial reaction was to mention his previous relationships with women, including Sally-Anne.

But he decided not to do that. He was convinced that Jeannie had no interest in him physically, so this wasn't just done to sound him out. And even if she did by a very unlikely off chance, she was a woman in her second marriage.

"Anyway," he said. "When do you think Trans-ship are going to make a decision?"

He primarily wanted to change the subject, but also was keen to know the answer. Driving into Rochester town centre, they also discussed the mention of their new competitor.

Jeannie felt confident in winning the order, and had made that clear whilst driving. But considered there would be more work to do before this could happen. She believed that Trans-ship were considering other bids, but at least that meant they were seriously planning a go ahead with cellular radios, so that box was ticked.

She looked at him slightly puzzled, as she felt they had already discussed this.

"I think it's going to be soon and as I said before, primarily down to the costing, but installation time is important and we are well placed to do that. Our contract is a real benefit, because if they are not happy when things go live, we can remove everything at no cost."

"What's the next move?" he asked.

"Well, I'm going to call Grant and arrange another meeting. Then I plan to put a proposal in, which has agreed dates and times, and can be carried out on their own site, that way it would take all the hassle away from them." She drilled down into the detail to help Linus understand. "They won't need to bring their lorries to us, because we'll come to them and do the installations."

Linus nodded, he already understood but Jeannie clearly liked to reinforce clarity.

The waitress arrived with the plates, and both of them were having scrambled eggs on toast. Linus liked that, the small bond made him feel somewhat better.

It was now 09.25hrs, so he stepped out of the car and walked back into Heath-field House. As he went up the steps, the volume of people in the hallway seemed to have increased dramatically. He estimated around twenty were in there now.

A side-table had been set up with tea, coffee and biscuits. Linus decided to give that a miss, it was a bit too close to the start time.

Good job, because there came a hand-clap and a loud voice from the training area door. "Right everyone, let's get started, chop-chop." It was Steve Rider.

The crowd turned and made their way towards the entrance. Linus hung back, so he could be at the back of the chain, the room filling up like a classroom of new kids.

There were four rows of tables across the room, each with eight chairs, so the number of trainees was higher than his estimate. There was a large white-board at the front, and what looked like a film projector in the centre aisle. This was clearly an up-to-the-minute event. Linus slipped down to the back of the room, so he could watch over every element of this new idea extravaganza.

Three senior looking chaps now stood in the front. Steve Rider was in the centre and held up his hands, pumping them up and down to the students. *Pray silence for the King,* whispered MacColl under his breath. A ginger haired chap sat next to him glanced over quizzically, so Linus turned his head to the courtyard window.

The silence kicked in and Rider looked theatrically around the room at each of them in turn. Linus felt a slight grin come his way. He was still not sure if Steve knew of his RITON monitoring role or not. Either way, he would keep *schtum*.

Steve kicked off his opening speech. "Morning everyone, and welcome to your first day at *RADI-CAL,* a life changer for you *and* this country." He looked around at them slowly as they drank in his first sentence. "We are going to lead the way in adding a new light to the world." He then shook his head and swept his arm round the room, his finger pointing at each and every one as if he was Billy Graham on acid.

Everyone stared back in silence and concentrating, waiting for the next words to come out.

"But this is only going to work if you follow every aspect of this course and apply what you have learnt, when out in the field." He turned and nodded at the room's entrance. "If you don't get it right this week, you'll be out of there."

He looked round at them all again. Linus noticed gulping had started with the three next to him, and he reckoned the rest were reacting in the same way, although he could only see the back of their heads.

"We don't have time to waste and I expect everyone here is going to make it." He said, changing his voice to a friendlier note. Linus picked this up and felt a slight sense of stress recovery across the team. *This bloke is good,* he thought. Steve pointed at the other two men by his side. "Shortly, I'd like to introduce the training guys, who are technical and sales experts. You need to listen and remember *everything* they are going to explain about the way the network operates and how to sell it."

Linus noticed the *newbies* seemed to go even calmer. But Rider came back in with another of his test approaches.

"But first, you are all going to introduce yourselves to us." The stress levels went up again. He looked around the group as they sat drowning in silence, and in some cases, perspiration. "Let's start at the back." He looked across at the other side of the room from Linus. The chap in the far left corner wearing a dapper grey suit went pale as he pointed at himself mouthing the words. "Who me?"

Steve Rider nodded. "That's it, carry on."

The man stood up looking somewhat uncomfortable. Linus noticed some beads of sweat on his brow, as he clearly struggled to put some words together.

"Morning everyone, I'm Terry Johnston." He stopped, clearly thinking about what to say next with everyone staring at him. "I'm thrilled to be here. My last job was in sales for Armitage-Shanks." The entire group looked over at him with surprise. *From lavatories to cellular radios in one step then,* thought Linus as he went on.

"I know it's going to be different, but I have good sales results and contacts in large industrial companies, so I am confident. This is going to be a rip-roaring success."

That was it. He sat down and Steve started clapping, as did the rest of the crowd. A few whoops and whistles rang out. The bloke beside him got up, clearly more confident now after this, and then opened up.

"My name is David Ellis and I'm a specialist in commercial vehicle sales. In my last job, I was selling lots of thirty-eight tonners around the country."

He looked over at Johnston. "And like Terry, I've been involved with big companies, so am aiming to get back to them for our *RADI-CAL* cellular radios, as soon as I have finished the course."

More clapping came across the room and the introductions continued with a growing increase in confidence. The way the movement around worked, meant that Linus was the last one to speak. He needed to be careful here, as mentioning his RITON position was not an option. The group in front all twisted around to look at him as he stood up.

"Morning all," he said breezily. "I'm Linus MacColl, from the Kent regional office."

Pausing, he glanced around the room and noticed one of the guys in the front row snigger at his name. He ignored it, thinking, *are you the first to do that? I doubt it.*

"Anyway, I'm very much like you all, because I have come into this with a real feeling of excitement for the future." He looked around again, a few more smiles had set in, but so what. He went on. "I can tell you this, if it wasn't for my R1 last week, I would have missed out on something of *vital and personal* importance. What we have here is a game changer."

With that, he sat down and Steve started a hand-clap, then all of them followed suit...

Having finished the intros, it was now time for the first presentation. Steve pointed at the *RADI-CAL* technical director, Geoffrey Rodgers. He looked older than Steve, was bald and wore horned-rimmed glasses.

Linus considered him to be rather like a science teacher. He opened up his speech in a mono-tone style.

"I'd like to welcome you chaps to our new venture, and am going to explain the background of how the network possibility was perceived, and give you a broad-brush of the technical aims."

Linus sat back sighing. This was understandable, but he'd already gone through this several times at the Maidstone office. Even so, he realised he needed to be seen playing the part, so took a notepad and pen from his bag. As he steeled himself for the next diatribe, Steve Rider came over, placed a hand on his shoulder and said quietly. "I know you are already up to speed on this, so I'd like you to come out with me for a quick chat."

Steve turned and walked to the door, with Linus following and feeling somewhat concerned, wondering what he wanted to discuss. They went past reception and down a long hallway to the right. Another ten yards or so, and the modern updates of the building's lobby area started turning into its dusty, dark past. The spider-webbed walls looked cracked and old, the lighting faded and their footsteps echoed uncomfortably along the worn corridor. Linus considered this place to be rather like a gargantuan mausoleum. The bright image of RITON group, went further away from him as they marched on. He felt a shiver inside, his instinct was delivering a concern.

Rider spun left and turned the handle on a room door with dull, flaking paint, then stepped back, holding it open for Linus.

"Thank you Steve." He said, looking around at this dark hovel, with a tiny window casting a small shadow of light over a grimy single desk and two worn out plywood chairs. On the wall sat a black-board, and a paper filled wire basket on the floor. The room smelt dank and felt ghostly. This was not going to be good.

"Don't thank me Linus, you're the one who has made some excellent efforts for the group in the past. Your reputation is very well respected. In fact, we really need you at *RADI-CAL*, perhaps more than you think, so I just wanted to clarify matters." He looked around and smiled pointing to one of the crappy chairs. "Sorry if it's a bit grim in here, but we need to speak privately and needs must."

Linus considered Steve Rider, as he sat down. He certainly had a *chutzpah* about him, that was for sure. The guys in Maidstone had rated him. He looked good in his modern, blue pin-stripe suit, with the now popular *peak* lapels and a bright red, silk tie. Very nice. He had a sort of RAF style moustache, blonde, just like his hair.

Come to think of it, most ex-Rate-Syrex people seemed blonde and good looking. Steve pulled up the other chair and stared at Linus in a friendly but somewhat curious style.

"The reason for coming in here, is because I need a favour and wanted to ask you in private." He looked around the room disparagingly, appreciating Linus's dislike of it. "Yes, this could do with a new coat of paint, but that's by-the-by. The important thing is how we go forward together."

Linus felt the wind was rising. "Always pleased to be of assistance." He said.

Rider smiled back and carried on. "The thing is Linus, we need everyone out on the road to be a success story. Now, I appreciate that you have been brought in initially to monitor things, but there are a number of issues we have to address. We need everyone, and I mean *everyone* on board to reach their target goals for *RADI-CAL,* there is no leeway in this, we don't have the man-power."

MacColl thought back to Jeannie *well, someone certainly has the woman-power.*

Rider droned on.

"So you will of course keep Mr Cannon in the groove, but your priority is to do what Mike Sentinel wants. Do you understand my point?"

Linus nodded back. He understood alright, this was his fear about the whole exercise. Everything at *RADI-CAL* hinged on one thing, getting 10,000 units sold in the first year.

He glanced around the room again, this was a dump in a gargantuan palace, but what he perceived to be his future, was undoubtedly worse. He whispered under his breath. '*The spy who came in from the cold.*'

"What was that?" Retorted Rider.

"Nothing. But I'd like to understand the expectation you have of me. I was brought in primarily to monitor things and report back, not to be responsible for a sales target."

Steve Rider looked back suspiciously, as Linus picked up upon his changing attitude. The smile now gone, and a dark shadow cast.

"The breakdown of the numbers is actually quite simple. When we go live, we should have a total of forty in the sales team. Given the initial target, that means theoretically each one is supposed to hit a minimum of two hundred and fifty unit sales by the end of next year. But as some areas are going to have more effective coverage than others, there needs to be some flexibility in this."

It dawned on Linus what was coming, as Rider continued.

"You are in a good position, covering an area with a decent number of cells inside it. And, most important of all, you have the City of London on your doorstep. Subsequently, I'd expect you and the Maidstone guys to deliver better numbers than the other regional offices, so you'll have a slightly higher target. I expect you to be at up at three hundred each by the end of year one."

The wind had already hit a gale, and now was heading to storm force ten. So the target numbers given by Sentinel last week were *actually* going to apply to him.

"So, I'll need to sell at least twenty-five of these per month. Surely, given that this is a new venture we can only consider this to be guesswork". Linus took a deep breath and continued, remembering the team's area allocations from last week's meeting.

"I've been through the first year's network coverage with Mike and understand your point about London, but given there are going to be three of us allocated to the City, it means seventy-five need to be sold in the square mile every month, and that's a lot of cellular phone users."

"I hear what you are saying," responded Rider. "But you'll be signing up about a quarter of these *in the sticks*, so it won't be that many and the advertising campaign starts in December, which as Mike probably told you, is aimed at the big money lot. What is it he calls them? Ah yes, *yuppies,* that's it."

Linus remained unconvinced. He had started to actually see the benefits of these cellular phones, but the majority of people would have no interest in them, especially given how much they cost to buy and run. But he felt at least he had now got an overview of *RADI-CAL* and some of the staff. So, maybe he should switch off his involvement immediately, then report his findings back to Rupert Cannon, and get his old role back. Yes, that was what he needed to do.

"Well, I appreciate the information Steve and I picked up some good stuff over the last week and can see how things could go forward. But it's not for me to be actively involved with getting these numbers in, so probably best that I just agree a report with you and head back to my old role."

Steve Rider sat back in the crumbling old, thin plywood chair. He set up the steeple hands to his lips, rather as Robbie had done last week in Maidstone and said.

"I hear where you are coming from Linus. Really I do, but that is not an option. We need every *man-jack* in our lot, because the volume of business is critical, not only for our development, but for the reputation of RITON."

Linus looked uncomfortably back at him as he carried on.

"You are going to help us get to where we need in the next twelve months and there is no argument or going back on this. I made it clear to Rupert Cannon that this would be the case."

"He didn't mention that to me." Responded Linus somewhat shocked and in came Rider's eruption.

"Well, he bloody well should have done! There is no time to waste here, you just need to get on with it. Now I understand you have to report back, and please carry on doing so. But we have only one real objective and that is to reach the given target by the Chairman, you should realise that. I don't want any more *shilly-shally.* You must get on and help make this work." He smiled gently at Linus, then switched his style to a friendlier gait. "The benefit for you, and the guys, is there is a lot of commission payments coming your way if you hit these numbers, *and I mean a lot*."

Linus realised that he was now clearly painted into a corner. His initial reaction was anger towards Rupert Cannon. He remembered there was something a little jittery about him when their conversation on this nightmare started a fortnight ago, although now it felt more like months rather than weeks. A lot had happened since then. There was nothing he could do except carry on. That was abundantly clear.

He felt clammy, heart-rate up, swallowed hard and said. "I understand Steve. I'd better get started then."

Linus slipped into the training room and sat down again at the back. But now it felt very different. This was no longer going to be a walk in the park. *Fuck it.*

The next part of the training course was an insight into how the system design had been achieved and approved by the Thatcher lot. Geoffrey Rodgers droned on in his dull way, occasionally looking over the horn-rims when he picked up some class members on the edge of dozing off.

The sixth slide was now up on the screen, and Linus stared at the honeycomb image of the cells. These things were starting to affect him when he went to bed. He dreamt there were bees all over him last night. The fear of being stung was appropriate, given his last meeting.

He needed to put this on the back-burner and concentrate on the technicalities of the *RADI-CAL* network. Opening up his A4 notebook, he began to write down Geoff Rodgers' instructions, and draw diagrams from the slides. The system was certainly complex, and took a lot of engineering and electronic know how to get it in place. He thought about his first call to Sally-Anne, and how clear it had been, as his mind drifted off again to its outcome....

Linus dragged himself back to the training. Geoff moved onto the next slide. He disliked these old-style things and wondered when the cine-film would start. The next picture was a black and white shot of the first car radio call made in 1959. Apparently an MP made this to some car manufacturer. *Boring* thought Linus, no wonder these *newbies* were dozing off. Anyway, it was all fake. The car had to be stationary, then the wireless went to a local telephone station, then was tuned manually onto the next and so on before it finally reached a land-line connector. No movement, no fast connect and no privacy.

He understood Geoff's plan, present this old rubbish, then re-inforce his point about the dynamic miracle of cellular radio. *Wow*. Linus was fast losing interest and steaming with anger of probably being dropped in it by Rupert Cannon.

Geoff flicked up the next slide, which showed the ground work involved in the installation of one of the cell structures. He carried on with his monotone.

"This shows how much work has to go in from theory to practice, and every cell base-station has to have this done, unless it goes on top of a building like this." He flicked to the next slide, showing a huge aerial complex on top of a tall office. Linus immediately recognised this as the RITON group HQ. *Smashing*. He thought.

Linus glanced at his Seiko, it was just on 12.30hrs.

Geoff saw him do this and checked his own watch.

"Right gents, lunch time. Back in by one thirty please."

The gang stood up, scraping their chair legs and made for the door, starting that classic *newbie* interaction as they walked together. Linus followed them, as usual, hanging back to observe. He didn't want to go in with them, was not hungry and felt depression kicking in. This had to be sorted out, because it always brought in a mix of time wasting, damage to relationships and anger about what he believed was his consistent naivety. *Right; food, coffee, fags and kick arse.* He thought.

The restaurant area was large, there were twenty tables, each with five seats. It was designed to provide for all RITON staff on courses, irrespective of the division. But on this occasion, there was only the *RADI-CAL* lot in here. As they queued up, lifted trays, and approached the counter, Linus was able to do an accurate head count. There were twenty-four, three of them being female.

He'd noticed the course had some empty chairs, so Linus guessed a sensible few had made a last minute decision to keep off this mad adventure. He didn't blame them, and would have done the same, but he was trapped. He strode up to the end of the line.

Terry Johnston, the ex-Armitage-Shanks guy, turned and grinned at Linus, extending his hand. As they came together and shook hands, for some unknown reason they both laughed at each other.

"I like your style Terry," said Linus, unsure of why. "Quite a change from your old role."

"Yep, I've *flushed* that away now." Said Terry.

Linus and the guy in front of Terry both groaned in unison. This Armitage-Shanks joke was undoubtedly *always* occurring.

A few further down the line heard the laughs and looked around, smiling back.

The counter assistant came over and asked Terry what he wanted. As she did so, Linus felt suddenly stifled by this place. The smell of beans, meat, gravy and boiled greens was not good. He put his tray back on to the stack, and walked away. Terry turned and watched him go, wondering if he'd offended him in some way. Linus picked up on that, but didn't care and carried on towards the door. He needed some air.

Walking down the steps, then across to the Cavalier, he glanced up at the sky. Clouds were rolling in and the wind was getting up. He unlocked the driver's door and stepped in. With the seat wound back and the window open, he lit up a Marlboro with his Zippo, he didn't want to wait for the car's lighter to spring out.

Exhaling the first lot of smoke, he checked his Seiko. It was 12.40hrs, so plenty of time before the class re-started. That made him feel a bit better, as he looked across at the R1 phone. He switched on the car ignition and pressed the button marked '**PWR**' on the hand-set.

His first thought was to call Rupert Cannon. But where would that get him? Because he felt so irate, matters could get even worse.

Anyway, he wouldn't get through to him. His PA, Colleen took every incoming call for Cannon, and would insist on knowing exactly what it was about. They had been friends for years, and she'd undoubtedly pick up on Linus's mood.

Maybe this was a good thing he thought, as the Marlboro started to calm him down.

His mind turned back to Steve Rider. He sounded very convincing, but what if his talk about Rupert Cannon was made up? After all, *RADI-CAL* needed everyone. Today's numbers of *newbies* were lower, so Rider convincing him that he was locked in could just be a con.

Linus opened his wallet and took out Jeannie's business card. He considered this for a moment and decided to call her, dialling in her R1 number: *0890 100007*. "*My names Bond*" he said to himself as the call connected with the usual long blur.

She answered, he could hear road noise in the background.

"Hello Linus, how are you?" Clearly she had recognised his number on the handset, which made him feel of some tiny value at least.

"I'm fine thanks, and how are you?" He realised they were in the *small talk* area, and was there *ever* a phone call, where this didn't happen? But admittedly, it was very unusual if you just happened to be driving a car....

"I'm fine too. Now this is a co-incidence, because I was wondering earlier how your training course was going."

He was pleased to hear this, as he could now tell her what happened earlier with Steve Rider. But he was also sure that he should not criticise him. There was a good connection between Steve, Mike and Jeannie, and he needed to choose his words carefully.

"Yes, it's going fine. There's twenty odd *newbies* here and so far, they seem alright. A few of them are pretty entertaining already, and I'm sure they'll get funnier as the week goes on. You know how it is."

She laughed and said. "Oh yes, I shall never forget doing the first one. Most of us were a bit nervous, but Julian and Robbie were like Morecombe and Wise on acid. I had a good trip anyway."

Linus thought about *"good trip,"* and wondered what she meant by that.

"Well that sounds like fun. Anyway, I could do with some advice, if you have a minute."

"I've just got on the M25, so your timing is good. We should have a bit of time before this goes dead."

Linus thought about her words. Perhaps they also applied to her last husband. Anyway, that was stupidly irrelevant, she had just left the M26 and joined the M25, so had no more than ten minutes before the phone coverage would collapse at the next junction. He needed to move on with this now.

Although they had not discussed it directly, he was absolutely sure that Mike Sentinel would have been told about his role of reporting back to RITON by Steve Rider. So it stood to reason, that Mike would have then advised Jeannie and probably Robbie at the same time. Possibly even Julian, come to that.

"Jeannie, I came to this *RADI-CAL* thing primarily to report the operational style to RITON's board. I was expecting a brief time here, and then move on back to my previous role with the marine side of the group. But it appears this is not going to be the case according to Steve Rider. He wants me in for the long-haul."

He left it at that and waited for her response. She said nothing, and all he could hear through the R1's handset was background road rumble and increasing engine noise from her car. She was clearly both thinking and focussing on her driving. Then came her response.

"I understand where you are coming from Linus, but let me make something abundantly clear. This *RADI-CAL* **thing** as you put it, has the potential of being a game changer, not just for RITON GROUP, but for the whole country and maybe, even beyond that."

He noticed her voice was becoming louder, and her words were not what he expected, so he moved the handset away from his ear as she continued.

"To make this happen, we all have to work together as a new business team, that is our priority. So it doesn't matter what time people turn up to the office, if they have an untidy desk or even get into a fight in the local pub.

This is about reaching our target numbers and leading the field as the largest supplier of cellular phones. Now, as Steve probably told you, we need to get out and make this happen and that includes you."

She went quiet, clearly letting this sink-in and waiting for his response. Once again, he took in the background noise as he tried to come up with an acceptable response.

"Well, I told Steve I'd get started on this longer term. I just wanted to let you know because, well, it's a big change for me." He thought about saying he was miffed, but decided against it and went on. "I'm sure I'll get my head around it, but just need to work out how I am going to take on the sales responsibility for this."

She came back quickly, her voice now sounding brighter.

"I tell you what, lets meet up as soon as you are back from the course next week. I can then work with you, to help you plan it out. In fact, let's make a start on Monday. I'll clear it with Mike and we'll get going. What do you think?"

He realised there was no choice, but also appreciated her support and needed to stop being pathetic and kick himself up the arse.

"Yes, that would be very kind of you." He responded, trying to sound positive.

"Great, see you on Monday morning. I need to get going, enjoy the rest of the course."

She hung up and her signal died.

Chapter 5

Croydon Aerodrome
Saturday 29th September 1984

MacColl pulled up outside the *Aerodrome* Hotel on Purley Way. Today, he was in the Triumph Stag and there were a number of reasons for that. He wanted to give it a run, get away from the Cavalier and remind himself of driving to his *former* place of work. The engine idled with a quiet, V8 burble and he switched off, then stepped out.

Over to his left by the hotel's entrance, he noticed a shiny, gold Ford Granada 2.8 GL. It was Rupert Cannon's company car, issued by RITON Group at Director level. Linus assumed he was inside the place already. Looking at his Seiko, it was just on 10.00hrs and he walked into the building.

The bar on the left was a quiet little café up until boozer opening time at 12.00hrs. In the corner sat Cannon, a large coffee pot and two cups in front of him and a big smile on his face. Linus grinned back as he walked over. Irrespective of the outcome of this meeting, Linus still felt a great connection with this charismatic man.

"By Jove!" said Cannon, now stood up and extending his hand. "You've lost weight in the last fortnight, I need to feed you old boy." Instantly, he looked around for a staff person.

"It's fine Mr Cannon, I needed to get rid of a few pounds. Anyway, I had something before I left this morning."

Rupert Cannon eyed him back with an element of suspicion. A Ship's Captain was always concerned if any crew member went off his food. This never went away, even after they had finished working at sea. Linus realised where he was coming from; smart as paint, dyed in the wool and genuinely kind. But also, of course, hard as nails. The classic RITON, director type.

"Well, at least you can have a Nescafe and biscuits, whilst telling me *all* about how this new thing is going, and I'm sorry I had to postpone last week's meeting."

Linus sat down as Cannon handed over the cup and saucer. He put it down on the table, sat back in the chair with his arms folded, looking up at the ceiling, searching for a good starting point from his experiences in the last couple of weeks. Actually, he was quite pleased that their previously agreed meeting had been postponed.

It had become a little bit *political* now, given the sordid discussion with Steve Rider, so he needed to choose his words somewhat carefully.

He decided to go *Liberal* with this, although definitely did not want to be mistaken for Jeremy Thorpe, in *any way, shape or form.*

"I've learnt a lot about this thing's plan for next year and I can actually see some potential. Bearing in mind, that I've only been there for two weeks, of course."

"Oh absolutely old boy," retorted Cannon as he sipped his coffee. "I fully appreciate that, just let me know what you have experienced so far, that's all I expect."

"My initial reaction to the office in Maidstone was that it was a bit of a dump."

Cannon looked quizzically over his glasses at him. "How so?"

"Well it's on a cheap and nasty factory estate, right next to a railway track," he thought back to when the train screeched by after his threat from Tweedy. "But I then realised it didn't matter. It's not somewhere that customers, partners or press are ever going to visit, so nothing like our normal RITON offices."

"But what about the *people*?" Cannon put down his cup. "Did they turn up on time, were they smart *Johnnies*, did they speak decently, that sort of thing?"

Linus considered this for a moment, then did something he'd never done to Rupert Cannon before. He lied.

"As a matter of fact, they were all there before me, so I assume they start around zero eight hundred hours every day. It's still new for me of course, but they all seem well mannered and quite organised."

"What about the manager, Sentinel, Is he a decent type? Sort who could engage in a good way with members of the public? I ask this because, we don't want any complaints written to group HQ when the television adverts go live."

"He seems to be a normal, decent bloke as far as I can see."

Cannon probed him further. "Been out for a pint with him yet? As you know, this can usually get the chaps to open up."

"No, only been in the office with this mob, they seem to be just focussed on the job, not very social."

Linus thought back to the punch-up in the *Anchor* pub. He was getting further into deep water, and needed to change the subject.

"Actually, they all seem pretty good, but it is early doors. Shall I run over the course stuff with you?"

"That's would be good, old boy. *Top hole*." Said Cannon.

He realised the notes he made last week were still in the Stag.

"I just need to go and get the stuff out of my car."

"How are you getting on with that *RADI-CAL* motor? Cavalier isn't it?"

"Yes, it's quite good. The main thing about it is the cellular phone, I'll tell you about that later. Anyway, I left it at home today. Fancied a run out in the Stag."

Cannon glanced up at the ceiling shaking his head and laughed. "Linus, when are you going to learn? Old cars like that '*Snag*' are never going to be anything but scrap metal."

Linus smiled back and walked out to the car park. He stood looking at his Stag, the pale sun glinting off the roof, then quickly lit up a Marlboro, planning a few drags before going back in as Cannon was a virulent anti-smoker. As he blew out the first cloud, he thought, *one day this old car might be worth a few quid. Could even be as much as one of these new portable cellular phone things.* He inhaled a final drag, laughed at his madness, ground out the fag, took the file from the passenger's seat and walked back into the *Aerodrome* Hotel.

Rupert Cannon looked over the sheets of diagrams showing the design of the cells, that *honey-comb* thing indicating the connection between them, and the time-scale statistics of how it would pan out.

He sat back with his cup and saucer, now clearly thinking about *RADI-CAL's* operational possibility. It was a slight change from his attitude of two weeks ago.

"I'm still struggling to understand how they can switch from one place to another without losing the signal," he said, peering over his glasses at Linus.

"Well, that was my biggest concern too. A bit like when we compared this to using VHF sets at sea. But it is very different from that because it can find and switch to the closest cell and then the next, etcetera."

Cannon nodded as Linus continued, and he felt a degree of enthusiasm now, but realised this needed to be managed.

"The cells don't disappear over the horizon like radio aerials on masts. There are eventually going to be so many close to each other, that the car-phone is never going to be out of signal range, because the *honey-comb* automatically works out when radio-wave power is starting to drop and then, electronically hands-over to the cell which is now closest to it. Because they are so close, the car-phones need no more than ten watts of power."

He finished on a more cynical note. "Mind you, it sounds alright in theory but in practice it's probably going to be a different matter."

Cannon nodded back in agreement. "Yes, installing all these two-way signal contraptions around the country looks like a big old task, and bloody expensive I shouldn't wonder. How many areas are to be in place when it goes live then?"

"They have to cover the areas agreed with the Thatcher lot, as we touched on before."

Cannon nodded, remembering this. "Yes, she wanted ninety per cent covered in five years' time. Typical of that old, hot-air from politicians. I'd be surprised if that came directly from her though, she's not a bad old cow is she?"

Linus thought about a response, but steered clear. "Anyway, I have been told that the idea is to cover most places inside the M25, particularly Central London, and then up to Birmingham, Manchester and Edinburgh. They reckon most *yuppie* buyers are there so..." He remembered another point he needed to clarify to Cannon about the Thatcher lot.

"Oh yes, that ninety per cent is not land mass, it's about the *people* volume."

"Ah," said Rupert nodding his understanding. "So if Fred Bloggs *was* out in the sticks and *not* on the road, he probably couldn't call Mrs Mop then?"

"No, so he'd end up *without* pie and chips." Replied Linus.

Cannon laughed, then reached over and patted him on the shoulder.

"I'm already missing you old boy, but I'm sure you'll be back soon."

Linus felt an opportunity here. "Do you have any idea when that might be? I appreciate gathering info' is important before this starts, but it's going live at the end of the year, so I won't be required to carry on by the Board after that then?"

He sat back waiting for the response, as Rupert Cannon looked thoughtfully up at the bar room's ceiling again for a few moments, and then responded.

"Personally, I think you're right and I expect you back by the beginning of next year." He looked into his cup, swilled it around with a thoughtful look and continued.

"You know Linus, there is a wind of change everywhere, I feel it in it in my water. Every day, I see something in the bloody newspapers about these computers. You know, *Commodore, Macintosh, Casio and Lotus,* to name but a few."

He leaned forward and looked around the bar room like a spy in a movie, even though there was not another soul in there, lowering his voice darkly he continued.

"Maybe it's me getting old Linus, but I think a combination of these bloody things and cellular radios is going to *do* for this world. Ever since these computers have come on mass in RITON, a growing number of the team have become obsessed by them." He nodded towards their Croydon office. "Digital bloody junk." he said and continued. "All they seem to do is sit in front of them, starry-eyed and typing away on the keyboards. I understand spelling mistakes are easier to correct than on the typewriters, and letters can be saved onto these *floppy disc* things, but I am *sure* it takes longer than getting the secretaries to do it. Colleen agrees with me on this."

Their eyes met as he spoke her name. Last year, Linus and Colleen had become more *socially connected*. Rupert Cannon had clocked this, aware they were often having lunch together and going out in the evenings. Irrespective of the fact it was genuinely a social and not a physical connection, and neither of them were in any other relationships to his knowledge, this was still unacceptable by RITON standards.

Men and women employed by the Group, did **not** go out together as a couple, **only** as part of the gang. Sir Dennis had made that clear to the management across every division. If it came to light, then woe betide the guilty party. And on that occasion, it was Linus MacColl.

At the time, he was on leave, taking a day off at home. The phone rang in the lounge and Cannon came on directly, which was most unusual.

"You are to come into the office NOW! Do I make myself clear?"

Linus gulped, realising straight away what this was likely to be about.

"Yes, on my way Mr Cannon."

They both hung-up and he made his way there, knowing that he was in for a verbal spit-roasting. As he drove, the guilt set in. Linus was initially angry, he considered this as unnecessary interference.

Sure, Colleen Walker was Cannon's PA and had access to all the letters and faxes communicated within the RITON board. But he knew this was not why he had been pilloried. It was about the rules of *the connection* between staff.

As he stepped out of the Stag and looked up at Cannon's office on the second floor, he mentally kicked himself.

Years ago, when he was a *newbie*, based at the Group's head office, a somewhat middle-aged, but very direct and to-the-point PA to Sir Dennis explained something crucial, which he should have always remembered.

Linus was sitting in the canteen alone, when she came over with a tray of tea and cakes and plonked herself opposite. She made no polite request for taking the seat, but merely lifted off a tea cup and slice of cake, placing them carefully in front of him.

"Hello, I'm Margaret Ellwood. Sir Dennis has always been a stickler for building an exceptionally close team." She commenced with this immediately, as if her time schedule took her straight to the point. "I must say, I admire that about him."

Linus said. "Yes, I have only just started here, but there is a sort of *family* feel about the place."

She sipped her tea and looked back disdainfully. "No, that is not the RITON way. In fact, what you said is a total opposite! Families are very different, as they tolerate each other even if they misbehave or communicate rudely. In fact, the majority get away with it because they revert back to that *close, blood relative* thing, which is a most bitter irony of fate, because if they were not related, they would have nothing to do with each other. And quite rightly."

Linus nodded back, listening determinedly as she took another sip of her tea, and carried on.

"What you must remember is this. RITON Group has grown to where it is now for a number of reasons. The commercial development has been immense, with all the acquisitions and manufacturing across the world, and our technical genius."

She lent closer to him across the table, lowering her voice. "But Sir Dennis is always adamant about his view that the *honourable* quality of RITON's staff is the *critical* factor for success, in every one of our divisions."

She leaned back and looked him in the eyes. The fluorescent ceiling light above her, shining off the curly, dark hair. Linus considered it might have been dyed, but certainly was not a wig.

"May I ask how that *honour* gets accepted?" asked Linus, with genuine sincerity.

Margaret stood up and looked down at him, then gave out a breath-taking smile which lit up with such power and glamour, that the fluorescent strip above her head became redundant.

"You'll find out," she said still smiling stunningly. "And don't worry, you would not have got the job if you were seen as unsuitable."

She walked away, with her crockery now on the tray, and back to the counter.

So when Rupert Cannon tore into him on that dark day last year as Linus stood solemnly in front of his desk, he remembered the subtlety of what Margaret had said so very long ago. He really *got* that now....

Clearing this thought of the past from his mind, Linus nodded at Rupert Cannon. He didn't like the new computer process for producing documents either, but knew it would not go away. *Beware the ides of March.* He whispered to himself, even though it was the end of September. Rupert Cannon went on.

"So in theory, it is technically possible." He said, looking thoughtfully at Linus. "But my concerns are really three fold. Firstly, can the network be ready by the end of the year? Would people really be interested? And could these *RADI-CAL* sales *Johnnies* actually get anywhere near the expected target?"

Linus shrugged back at Cannon. He really could not answer that, although did feel slightly more confident that something could be achieved. Cannon carried on.

"That is precisely why we need you on board Linus. As an experienced, hands-on RITON chap, you need to keep up with the activities of this bunch and report them back to me."

Cannon looked as his watch and carried on. "Let's meet here again at the same time next Saturday. By then, you'll have a bigger picture."

As he stood up, Linus noticed a significant twinge of pain in Cannon's eyes. Despite not making any comment as he knew it would simply be swept away, he suddenly felt concern for the old man. They walked through the door and out under a clear, blue sky, the flickering sun of autumn made them squint across the old, abandoned airfield together. They stood in silence and then, Rupert Cannon quoted a Lord Tennyson poem, 'Crossing the Bar.'

"Sunset and evening star,
And one clear call for me!
And may there be no moaning of the bar,
When I put out to sea."

He smiled like a father figure and Linus felt a distinct touch of sadness coming from his boss and respected friend.

"Right," said Cannon, clearly getting back up and dusting himself off. "Let's inspect your bloody old *Snag*, what!"

They walked to the car and Cannon made no comment, just laughed at it as most people did. They stood on either side leaning on it's hard-top and looking across at the remains of Britain's first international airport runway. There were still a few remnants of history here. Over to the left was the original control tower, apparently the first in the world. In front of the *Aerodrome* hotel stood a four-engine, De Havilland Heron aircraft, welded onto an ugly metal framework, to make it look as if was still in flight.

Cannon said. "I'm fifty-eight Linus, pretty much end of passage."

MacColl cut in quickly with a mix of auto-support and concern. "That's nothing, you'll be with us all for a long time yet."

Cannon held up his hand to stop any further comment and carried on.

"Whichever way it goes; it's made me think. I feel as if I've put my foot on the brake and brought this melee of life up to a halt." Realising this did not sound good he clarified it in his usual, positive style. "Only temporary of course, whilst I think it through."

Linus said nothing, realising Cannon was going to continue as they looked at each other across the Stag's roof.

"I know change must go on, it always has, that's the way it is. But as humans, how can we ever justify the damage we have done to others? When one gets old Linus, this concern kicks in and then grows inside one like cancer."

Continuing to look Linus in the eyes, he swept his left arm across the airfield.

"I know what happened before the war in this place. I was only a youngster, but it filled me with shame. The Nazis flew in their Lufthansa aircraft with swastikas on their bloody tails in the thirties and *we* welcomed them, despite what the bastards had *already* done." He looked down at the Stag's hard-top and shook his head solemnly.

"Yet, when most of the persecuted Jews from Germany and Austria came in here, they were kicked out to Poland, and look what happened there. So off we went and won the war, eventually. Great. And believe me, I have every respect for our boys who risked and gave so much. But what about the things *we covered up*, Linus? Things that are *still* unknown."

MacColl looked across at Cannon, shaking his head. He had no answer. Cannon was deep in sadness, as he looked at Linus in a mixture of devastation and anger.

Then Cannon returned back to his normal, jolly mode. "Pay no attention to me old boy, the important bit now is to keep me updated on this *RADI-CAL* thing."

With that, he turned and strolled back to his car, his final words coming across. "Keep in touch Linus, and don't forget, the board needs your input about what is *really* happening with these *Johnnies.*"

Linus stepped into the Stag, started it up, then powered down the driver's window and lit up a Marlboro. He switched on the radio and on came *"Missing You"* by John Waite. This was now in the UK chart. Typical he thought, everything starts off in America, then comes over to here. Like that bloke he remembered in Manhattan using a *Motorola* portable phone.

Taking another drag on the Marlboro, he looked into the mirror, hoping to see if he could watch Cannon exit the car park in his Granada.

But it was too late, he'd already gone.

Monday came around again, and for the first time in his career at RITON Group, Linus MacColl arrived deliberately late for work. It was 08.50hrs as he rolled up outside the Maidstone office. But despite being twenty minutes behind the official schedule, he was still the first *RADI-CAL* worker to arrive.

He wound down the Cavalier's window, reclined the seat and lit up a Marlboro. The wind had picked up as he exhaled a first drag, the smoke cloud moving fast towards the railway track, just as a morning train screeched past, no doubt on route to Victoria.

He watched the carriages streak past and thought about the passengers. They were undoubtedly, London office workers making their usual daily commute into town.

Never had he been a regular train passenger, and felt for those having to do this day in and day out.

There were challenges in his work at RITON, but changing roles, extensive travel and working alongside a wide variety of staff, tore any boredom away.

But he felt a growing apprehension about his exposure in this new venture. Saturday's meeting with Cannon didn't really touch on this directly, but his comment on the future possibility of computers connecting to cellular phones had been churning over in his mind.

"A combination of these bloody things is going to do for this world...."

Cannon had cleverly sidestepped Linus's concerns about being held captive longer than expected at *RADI-CAL,* as per

Steve Rider's insistence, during their rather terse meeting last week at Heath-field House.

By using his *old man's* style, making negative comments and yet, subtly indicating how big this new venture could potentially be, Cannon might have convinced Linus that staying would be a good thing. If that worked, then Linus could be in a good position, and the Board would be pleased with Cannon's efforts and so, a win-win.

Rupert Cannon was a very smooth operator.

One thing was for sure; whichever way this panned out, MacColl was now in the *RADI-CAL* trap.

He glanced as his Seiko. It was 08.57hrs, and still no one had pulled up. But did it really matter? He considered Cannon's *'wind of change'* comment on Saturday. In fact, he'd been thinking a lot about the old man's rather odd behaviour at the *Aerodrome* meeting.

It wasn't just about him on Saturday, there was something a little strange that happened over by Sally-Anne's place....

Linus pulled up outside Sally-Anne's house on the *Long Estate* at 12.30hrs. In the driveway was her Metro, and the Rolls-Royce. As he walked somewhat nervously to the door, he realised he needed to be on best behaviour. Before he even rang the bell, it slowly opened with that same, memorable creek as it did on his last visit. Only difference being that this time, a glamourous stripper in her underwear was not standing behind it, rather a tall, middle-aged gentleman wearing glasses.

The man smiled warmly at Linus, extended his hand and stepped down onto the path.

"Hi," he said, the smile continuing as they shook. "I'm Sal's dad, Bernie. Pleased to meet you Linus, I've heard a lot about you."

Linus was a little concerned about that, and replied. "Pleased to meet you too," he was a bit lost as to what to say next and nodded over to the *Roller*. "Nice car Mr Cohen."

Her father continued to smile back and patted him on the shoulder. "Please, call me Bernie. Anyway, never mind my *old bus*, I like the look of yours. Come on, let me take a look at it."

They walked down the path together, then Bernie went to the centre of the road, folded his arms and peered over his glasses at the Stag from back to front.

Linus glanced across at him. Bernie had a *Kippur* on his head, as today was *Shabbat*, and continued his concentrated focus on the Stag. A VW Passat came down the hill towards him, but he paid no attention to it. The driver hooted as the car slowed, but Bernie did not move. The road was too narrow for it to go around him.

Pulling up, the clearly annoyed driver, revved the engine. Then something strange happened. Bernie walked up to it, stared closely through the windscreen and gave the driver a V's up, then strolled back to the kerb. The Passat screeched away.

Linus felt shocked at how ridiculous this scene was. Bernie then walked closely round the Stag, nodding his approval and gave Linus a thumbs up.

"I love these old things. You need to hang onto it Linus, one day old cars will be worth a fortune, you mark my words."

A window opened on the top floor of the house. Linus *knew* it was Sally-Anne's bedroom, but was certainly *no*t going to say that to Bernie.

"I saw that dad," said Sally-Anne, looking down on them. "Why are you always upsetting the neighbours?"

He winked at Linus and smiled back up at her. "I have my reasons. Now mind your own business, come down and see Linus."

She blew a kiss to them both, closed the window, made her way down the stairs and came through the front door. Bernie and Linus, now both with their arms folded, giggled like naughty schoolboys, as they stood by the Stag.

The sun left a cloud and its rays glinted off her raven hair, as she sauntered towards them. Linus was pleased to see her, and she looked great in a white jumper and tight jeans. Her brown shoulder bag indicated she was ready for him to whisk her away.

She came over, exuding a lovely aroma and pecked him on the cheek. Linus was a little nervous about this in front of Bernie, but needn't have worried. Bernie just smiled at them both in his infectious style, that Linus was really starting to like, walked over to his Rolls-Royce and opened the boot.

Then he took off his Kippur, chucked it in, closed the lid, and walked back to the house's front door. He turned to them, smiled, waved, then went inside.

Linus looked at Sally-Anne, holding up his palms and shook his head. She laughed back at him and said.

"Don't be fooled by what you see. There is always a method in his madness," she said, looking over the Stag. "Unlike some I could mention."

Her usual mickey-take kicked in, and Linus laughed back. She had exceptional comic-timing. *She'd be a great stage performer,* he thought. Although he remembered she already was a performer, but in a *different* style....

They drove through Shirley Hills, on the edge of Croydon, an area famed for its high position view-point. From there, on a clear day, it was possible to see all of Central London, from the City, to the Post-Office Tower, the West-End, on to Chelsea and beyond. There were public tele-scopes up on the view-point, so for 10p, half an hour could be whiled away. Linus had been there as a child, watching the world move.

Pulling up in the car park of the *Sandrock* pub, Linus switched off the Stag and looked into the eyes of Sally-Anne. On the journey, once her seething comic-cuts on his old car had finished, she asked how that training course on the new mobile phones had gone.

It was a good question. He gave her a reasonably accurate description of how the honey-comb things worked, which she seemed to take on board. But how Steve Rider's strategy for selling the phones would pan out, she did not see as being realistic. Linus made no comment on this, but he was inclined to agree with her.

"I can really see how useful these things could be Linus," she said. "But it's a lot of cost for something that only works in certain places. To get ten thousand people using them in twelve months sounds *really* difficult."

Linus nodded in agreement as she continued. "And like you said, there are two other competitor companies against your *RADI-CAL* lot, and if they have the same target numbers as you do, then that's thirty thousand people in the country expected to be using mobile telephones by the end of 1985!"

She shook her head, flicking the raven hair. "Sorry, but it won't work out. Maybe you should go back to your other job with the Croydon lot?"

He smiled and nodded. She was so right but now of course, this was not an option.

"Oh well," he said, wanting to get away from this concern. "Let's go into the '*Rock,* get a drink and fag ourselves to death, shall we?"

"Ooh, how perfectly charming." She said. "I'm so pleased to be out with a caring person."

Bernie drew the curtains in one of the spare bedrooms. Once Sally-Anne and Linus had driven off, he went back to the Rolls, took his Kippur out of the boot, and placed it back on his head. In the bedroom, he opened the wardrobe, removed his *Tallit* and laid it gently on the bed. Looking down at the white cloth, and slight blue and gold patterns, he quietly read the

Hebrew that would cover him when he placed it over his head and shoulders, and then swept and entwined the *Tzitzit* tassels.

On every Saturday's *Shabbat*, Bernie would read from the *Torah*. Before beginning, he always made sure he was alone in the house, and would then feel emotions for something abhorrently sickening that happened to his family, over forty years ago....

Linus watched Sally-Anne sip her Gin and Tonic, as he lit up the two Marlboro's and passed one across. She had insisted on buying the drinks and then, went over to the fag machine and bought two packs of Marlboros.

"So why did you buy two?" asked Linus. She looked at him as if he were a moron.

"Well, one for you and one for me, as we'd both rather die than share anything with each other!"

They laughed, clinking their glasses together. The autumn sun broke through the clouds as it's rays came in the window opposite them, glinting off her raven hair. Linus felt it was a magical moment in time, hoping that it would never end.

"I like your dad, he is quite a character. But I was a bit concerned when he was stood in the middle of your road as that car came along." He said.

She put down her glass and laughed out loud.

"He's just started to do this, and seems to have got this thing about people driving past in German cars on the *Shabbat*, and today was a classic example of that."

"So he kicked off because it was a *kraut* motor," said Linus nodding back at her. "Only it struck me that it could be because someone, who should have known better, was driving on the *Shabbat*."

"No," she replied still laughing. "Otherwise he would have told you off, wouldn't he? As I said, It's this new thing about German cars on Saturdays. He doesn't care about any other day of the week and dad is not orthodox, so...."

Linus thought about it for a moment, and for some reason joined up the dots with Rupert Cannon's anger about the Airport earlier. "Oh well," he said raising his glass up to her. "Each to his own."

Eddie Cross, the pub's owner smiled at them both from the bar. He'd known Linus for many years and recognised Sally-Anne too, despite her being a rarity in the place. This was the first time he'd seen them together, so he assumed it was a recent connection. "Put that lovely new bird's music on," he shouted over to the barmaid. "What's she called? *Sadie* or something."

The barmaid walked through the adjoining door to the music player, and put on the cassette. *'Smooth Operator'* came on.

"It's *Sade* not *Sadie*," said Sally-Anne quietly in Linus's ear, as she nodded at Eddie walking away from the bar front. "*Schmuck*."

"Oh yes," said Linus, thinking about the scene in the *Anchor* pub almost a fortnight ago. "This song reminds me of my new manager getting involved in a punch-up on my first day with the *RADI-CAL* lot."

She stared at him, looking understandably puzzled. "What?" she said.

"I forgot to tell you before. For some reason, you took my thoughts somewhere else later that night. Anyway, we all turned up at a pub that can only be described as a dump near their Maidstone office, bang on opening time. Do you remember I told you about this weird bloke in charge of the office?"

"Oh yes," she said. "Mr *Sensible* isn't it?"

"His name's *Sentinel* actually, but never mind." Replied Linus. "He is a nut-case. Anyway," he said nodding at the music's speaker in the ceiling. "He put this on the juke-box and then, later on, got into a fight with some old git who accused Sentinel of calling him a *See you next Tuesday*."

"What?" she said again, staring at him, still confused.

"I know," it was bizarre. "But the rest of their team."

"So are they all blokes then, or is there a form of female decency in this lot?"

Linus thought back to Jeannie Sands.

"There is one, an older married type called Jeannie, but she seems ok." he said, taking a sip of the lager-top.

Sally-Anne drew in her last drag from the Marlboro before reaching the filter, stubbing it out in the ash-tray and looking him in the eyes with intuitive interest.

"I'm surprised they have an old bird there, given how much running around there is going to be."

"Well," he said. "They seem a barmy lot. Anyway, like you said, it's never going to work out."

She nodded back and said. "Perhaps she used to be in that show with Larry Hagman, you know, *I dream of Jeannie*."

Linus considered there was a depth of intellect in her, mixed with that sarcastic and infectious humour, similar to her dad's.

"How about another drink?" he asked, nodding at her empty glass. "And some lunch if you like."

"Another G and T would be nice," she said looking around the *Sandrock's* old style, slightly worn bar area. "But I insist on buying you lunch. It's the least I can do, with you having brought me to such a *lovely* place in a *luxurious* car."

Switching off the Stag, he noticed that Bernie's Rolls was missing from the driveway, and only her Mini Metro Vanden-Plas was there.

She guessed his incoming question and said, "Dad's gone to pick mum up from East Croydon Station. She's been up in the smoke doing some window shopping," she looked at him and went on. "As I said, he's not orthodox, same as you. It's fine by me."

Linus nodded back. He got that, and said, "You know I told you I met my boss Rupert Cannon this morning at the *Aerodrome,"* he said. She nodded back as he continued. "Well, he had a strange conversation with me, in more ways than one as it happens. But something he said has been eating away at me."

She looked at him quizzically. A crow flew past, close to the windscreen, and her mind flashed back, as if she'd seen it in another life, in a different world….

"It was to do with him being at the airport in the thirties, watching Nazi 'planes come in. Then he said how the persecuted Jews from Austria and Germany were rejected by Britain and sent to Poland, and how this country had *covered* things up."

"You know what," said Sally-Anne. "The past is what it is. We can't change it and we *have* to just keep on going forwards. My dad is still massively sad about what happened to his family, they were holocaust victims." It's stayed inside him, that's why he hates German cars on the *Shabbat*."

She ran her fingers through his hair and looked him in the eyes. "Changing the subject slightly," she continued. "You are growing on me."

Linus felt incoming happiness, and grinned back at her.

"I know," she said, holding up her hands and nodding over to the house. "You think, I'm going to take you in there, add my charges on to your account from last time, which by the way, has still *not* been paid. Well, I've got news for you, it's for free."

She leant over and kissed him, then opened the Stag's door.

"Come on, there's no time to waste, dad and mum are going to be home soon."

The *RADI-CAL* team were finally arriving. It was almost 09.30hrs, and the only staff member in there was Julia, Mike Sentinel's PA, but Linus didn't care anymore. He'd already lied to Rupert Cannon on this, so would just continue to do so. For some reason which he couldn't fathom, Julian, Robbie and Kevin turned up within a couple of minutes of each other. It was probably a co-incidence. They had all spotted Linus and walked over towards his car, then he stepped out. They shook hands with him in turn and Julian asked.

"So how did the course go?"

"Very interesting," said Linus. "I learnt a lot."

As they went over to the entrance, Jeannie Sands arrived.

All four of them turned and stood in silence as they watched her car pull up. Linus guessed how each one somehow had a connection with her aura of style and good looks.

She stepped out of the Cavalier and came over to them smiling, her lovely blonde hair flickering slightly against the pale, incoming sun of autumn. Today, she wore a long, black leather coat and very high heeled, red patent leather shoes. As ever, there was a swagger in her walk, rather like a fashion model on a cat-walk.

Linus wondered if she could sense desire exuding from all of them. Then he realised she must, considering any alternative would be simply naive.

"Hello you lovely lot," she said. "Have you been waiting here for me long?"

"Only all night." Replied Robbie, the rest instantly laughing.

They entered the main, first floor room, the only occupant being Julia, sat at her desk.

"Morning all," she said. "Mike is over in head-office today, so feel free to use his room if you want."

They all looked through the window at even more piles of junk than Linus had seen when he was last here.

Together, they shook their heads at Julia. "We'll be fine at our desks." Said Kevin, smiling at her.

Julia laughed back at them all. She fully understood. But although untidy and eccentric, Mike was a very generous man. She considered him to be a real *giver* and when you got to understand him, you realised how lucky you were to know him.

Jeannie took off her long leather coat and placed it on the hanger by the office door. Her dress was red, not too long but not too short either. It matched her shoes perfectly. He noticed everyone, including Julia, had watched her as she took off the coat.

He felt a sense of approval in the atmosphere as Julia returned to the IBM typewriter.

But something occurred to him, being so attractive must be ironically difficult, because one always had to plan ahead for what to wear at work. *Well, that certainly is not something that applies to me,* he thought.

Jeannie looked at Linus and said. "Shall we go downstairs to the meeting room, then we can have a chat about you going forwards with the new business?"

Linus thought back to the slightly awkward cell-phone conversation they had last week when she was out on the road, but appreciated her generosity.

"Yes please," he said waving at the door. "You lead the way."

Then he realised this might have been the wrong thing to say, in case she thought he was going to watch her behind. A torrent of anguish piled into him. Every time he spoke to her, he messed it up.

Jeannie gave out her infectious laugh and said. "Right, let's get on shall we?"

She led him into the downstairs meeting room and switched on the lights. They sat and looked at each other across the table, then Jeannie asked.

"So, how did it all go on the course?"

A simply put question for a complex issue. Thought Linus. Something he'd discovered she was really good at. He needed to manage this carefully, having already dropped himself in it to her by admitting why he'd *really* joined *RADI-CAL* during his frustrated call last week. He had exposed himself to the RITON Group rules, and if this got back to Rupert Cannon....

"It went pretty well. Not least because of your advice," he said as she smiled and held up both hands in a generous style. "But I'm keen to get going now as I believe it is going to work out, and I genuinely like everyone here."

Jeannie sat back and looked at him with deep consideration. Linus felt on the precipice. Steve Rider knew why he'd joined, but had he advised others? Linus had already felt a suspicion from Mike Sentinel, maybe because of this. Had Jeannie told them anything about his admission to her? Everything felt out of control.

"I need to get in the first part of that Trans-ship deal today," she said looking at her watch. "I said I'd be there at eleven, so why don't we run through a few elements of the sales tactics as we go back there together?"

Linus immediately felt her suggestion was a positive, and the pressure came off.

"That would be great," he replied, now genuinely relieved.

Jeannie drove towards Rochester in her steady and careful way. Everything she did seemed well planned and carried out thoughtfully. Linus suggested that he drive today but she insisted on doing it. He was starting to learn that this was the *Jeannie way.*

Back in the office, she had listened to his view of the training course. Putting the technical aspects to one side, she quizzed him on the sales side of it.

Linus gave her an over view of this, and the way the group were given a number of scenarios across differing potential markets, which were recorded using a portable film camera. Everyone in the class then gave their personal feedback on how the individuals performed.

Linus had found this quite stressful, not just because it was being filmed, but as others could give their opinion.

Jeannie had told him she had felt exactly the same when on the first *RADI-CAL* course. In fact, the trainer for the sales side had previously been an ex Rate-Syrex guy. As a former staff member there, she had been used to it, but still had sympathy for the stress that Linus had felt.

She continued to drive steadily towards Rochester, and felt a sense of concern about Linus as he sat in silence, staring through the windscreen.

There was something about him she was starting to like. It wasn't a physical attraction but rather, a really good mental connection. It was as if there was magical link from her mind to his. She strangely felt as if she'd known him forever.

Determined to break the continuing silence she said. "I think the most important thing we do for new business is use the *Spin* angle."

Linus had no idea what this term meant and shrugged his shoulders. She laughed in the deep husky way that everybody was fascinated by and smiled at him.

"Well I'll tell you, it's *easy-peasy lemon squeesy*, but needs some practice to make perfect."

"Please, carry on." he said, genuinely fascinated.

"It's about asking the right questions. *Spin* stands for situation, problem, implication and need-payoff. So you should always start off by understanding the prospect company and its needs.

The questions you ask should be thought through before you visit the site really, and aimed at someone who can actually sign the order off. Now, that tells you about the overall *situation*."

Jeannie looked into the mirror and indicated right, then carried on as she changed gear. "Then it's about *problem* solving, or *pain- points* as Mike calls it. Like we used to ask at Rate-Syrex, *how do you currently carry out business information copying?"*

She looked over at him to check his understanding as she changed into top. He glanced at her wedding ring on the gear knob as she did so, trying to imagine what her husband was like. *Probably like a film star on a good day.*

"Next," she continued, "is the *implication.* It's about the outcome of *not* doing something. Actually, a prime example is with Trans-ship, because if they do not sign up with us for fitting the Panasonics into their lorries now, there could be a big delay until this can be carried out. Personally, I think this is our key point for the meeting."

Linus nodded back, very impressed with Jeannie's outlook on this and he was now beginning to *really* understand why she was so revered as a successful sales expert. It wasn't just about looks and style, but her *technical* commercial ability.

Up ahead was the industrial estate that encompassed the Trans-ship *Johnnies.* Linus reminded himself to never cross his legs or come across as gay.

"Finally," said Jeannie Sands, "it all hangs on *need-payoff."*

She pulled up in the visitors parking area of Trans-ship, switched off the Cavalier's ignition and glanced over at her Panasonic R1 cellular phone handset. The red light stayed on, indicating no service. Looking him in the eye with what he considered to be a heart-felt passion for the next thing, she asked.

"Given how this new mobile system is going to greatly improve transport efficiency around the country, how would that impact on your business?"

Linus imagined for a moment that he was that bloke Dave Grant who they were due to see here again within minutes. He thought over Jeannie's question as she stayed completely silent, yet continued to look him in the eyes. Finally, he came up with a response.

"We *need* it. Where do I sign?"

She laughed and smiled in her beautifully infectious way and shook his hand. "If only it was that simple," she said. "Come on, let's go."

They stepped out and walked to the door together, both feeling the real connection of a seriously growing friendship.

Chapter 6

RADI-CAL, Maidstone
2nd October 1984

Mike Sentinel looked over his glasses and smiled with a clearly genuine delight for Jeannie and Linus. In the centre of his meeting room table, a brown cardboard box sat with a giant Meccano toy crane's yellow jib sticking out. Linus MacColl, didn't care, he thought nothing of the eccentric junk in this man's room now. It was irrelevant, in the same way as the team turning up after the *official* RITON Group time. Everything now depended on the success of *RADI-CAL's* performance.

"Mmm, this is a good start to the week," said Sentinel as he studied the agreement from Trans-ship. "So Linus, I see you managed to get the northern warehouse signed up. So how did you go about this?"

Linus felt rightly uncomfortable, as Mike continued staring across at him in what he concluded to be a suspicious manner. He passed a concerned glance to Jeannie and responded.

"Well, it's like this, you see—"

Jeannie cut across Linus and said, "Actually Mike, it was very fortunate that Linus was with me yesterday. You see, Dave Grant, who signed our area contract, had arranged for the guy responsible over in Manchester to be there, so we could explain things for use on their northern based lorries." She looked across at Linus with her captivating smile.

"Linus had to do this," she continued, "because I needed to fill all the Kent based paperwork out with Dave, so I couldn't explain our systems to the Manchester guy. As you can see, Linus did a great job in getting the other contract signed."

Mike sat back and nodded, smiling again as he was clearly happy with Jeannie's explanation, even though he didn't fully believe it. For a brief moment, his mind went back to a situation, where he'd helped her out when they were at Rate-Syrex together, after she had broken up with her first husband.

He'd felt for her so much then. Nobody should have to go through that, but if they did then you had to support them in every possible way. This was his code of conduct. *For the rest of his life,* he thought, *he had to make up for the terrible error he made seventeen years ago in Aden.*

"Mmm, well good on you both, I suggest we go into the back room and get a cup of tea to celebrate, *alrighty.*"

They stood up and walked to Mike's office door. He put his hand on Linus's shoulder and gave it a gentle squeeze of thanks. Jeannie walked on ahead of them in her dynamically beautiful saunter, the seams on the back of her stockings, straight as dyes as the sun came in through the windows and glinted off her blonde hair.

Something in Linus was creating an infectious connection with this thing he was starting to feel part of. Was it because of him now understanding the team, and so formulating a genuine personal liking and respect for them? Or perhaps it was his growing, albeit crazy belief, that cellular phones *could* be a real game changer?

But there was also a special emotion to consider. In all his years at the RITON Group, despite the decency and pride of the staff, he had not experienced generosity like that given to him by Mrs Jeannie Sands.

When they had gone into Trans-ship yesterday, Dave Grant had taken them straight to the boardroom. Sat in there was John

Edwards, a Company Director who was also the senior transport manager at their Manchester base. Linus realised this opportunity had now grown much larger. Dave introduced everyone and set the scene.

Apparently, since their last meeting, Dave had taken matters further. It was now clear that other transport companies were starting to consider using these cell phones for the future, although none to his knowledge had committed as yet. He had advised the board to go with this, and be ahead of the game, as he saw it as not only a method of improving efficiency, but a very clever move for their advertising.

He'd suggested they go with *RADI-CAL*. He liked their products and they were part of a long established, technical electronics group. He also understood how trucks could be kitted out on their own sites for convenience, and should these things not work, they could cancel, have them removed and get a full refund, except for any call charges.

On a personal level, Dave Grant had been *most* impressed by Jeannie Sands, and considered it possible there *might* be a chance for them to meet up quite regularly, if the board decided to go ahead with *RADI-CAL*...

The meeting opened with the Director, asking confirmation of the contract position, which Linus thought, was a positive start. Jeannie went through the process in a straightforward way. Then this most senior looking, grey haired and rather rotund man said.

"So Mrs Sands, despite you being based in this area, can you arrange for our Manchester fleet to have your equipment fitted at the same time?"

It was a good question, and hugely positive.

Even Linus knew that if this was correctly responded to, it would mean a go ahead with Trans-ship, and this was now all down to how Jeannie handled it.

She looked over at this senior man, who was clearly the decision maker, then smiled at him and said.

"The way we can ensure this is going to work Mr Edwards, is if I look after all the installs here in Kent," nodding at Linus she continued, "and my colleague manages bringing in our technicians from one of our other sites to your Manchester depot, then we can all work together to reach the agreed time-line. This is very much the RITON Group style, isn't it Linus?"

Linus nodded back and said. "Oh absolutely, we always work as a team to ensure we always get installations done on time."

Jeannie responded to this instantly. "And that is why we need to move quickly on this, as things are getting very busy for us now, so if you sign this off today it would ensure we can do all the installs before the system goes live. That way as Dave said, you'd be ahead of the game in the transport market."

Silence then kicked in for what seemed to Linus an age as the Director looked down onto the meeting room's table and tapped his pen on it several times. Then looking over at Jeannie, he said.

"Very well then Mrs Sands, where do I sign for our *seventy* vehicles?"

Jeannie took the contract sheets from her brief case and laid them carefully in front of her, running her fingers gently and somehow, sensuously over them as if they were beautifully designed, silk underwear on her dressing table.

Once again, Dave Grant's eyes came out as if they were on stalks.

She is a total one-off, thought Linus.

They finished their meeting with Mike at the *RADI-CAL* office, and decided to have lunch in McDonald's. It was just on 12.00hrs, and they sat at a table in the corner.

She brought two quarter pounders over, and handed one to Linus, which had no cheese in it. She watched him bite into it with some interest.

"You know," she said. "I quite like to go in gently and lick the juice off, *then* start the nibbling."

Linus, put his down, covered his mouth with his hand and laughed at her as she continued to smile at him. He now understood her sense of humour.

Going back what happened in Mike Sentinel's office, he said. "I felt he was a bit suspicious about my involvement with the Trans-ship situation."

"Even if he was," she replied, smiling, "he wouldn't care. We are a team."

"That is kind, Jeannie. I feel humbled with your generosity."

She took a sip of her tea and said. "Look Linus, it is vital *RADI-CAL* has you on-board. Steve Rider knows this and so does Mike." She looked into his eyes with a depth of concern. "I know I came across as a bit angry and frustrated last week when we spoke, and I wanted to make up for that, as we *have* to make this work together."

She sat back, glanced up and took a deep breath.

"I know you have to report back what you see to the board via your old boss, Mr Cannon. I get that. But Linus, there is *something* huge about this. What we are starting up I believe, is going to change the world." She tapped her hands on the table, laughing as she threw her head back and smiled at him again.

The mid-day sun's rays touched her hair. Linus MacColl held his breath. He wanted this moment never to end. But as ever, the world turns and this split-second of magic breezed away.

She had not only made it clear how he needed to support them, but generously let him have a large sale he'd not really been involved with, and opened her heart with how *RADI-CAL* could be involved in *changing the world.*

Apart from that last bit, he was now completely on-board. A lot can happen in McDonalds it seemed. Being in there *could* change your life....

"Anyway," she continued, "Mike has requested Steve pays you the commission on the thirty trucks based in their Manchester depot."

She took out a piece of paper from her handbag and slid it across the table to him.

Linus read over the figures several times and then looked over at Jeannie in total disbelief.

"But that's almost *four grand!*" he said.

Rupert Cannon stood looking down into the car park from his second floor office in Croydon. He smiled somewhat sadly at the empty parking space of Linus MacColl's Triumph Stag. It was the same when he was out in New York, but now things were different. The storm came in from the south, across what used to be, the old airport's runway. The sky darkened and the rain took out his view from the office window.

Although he always laughed about the Stag, or *bloody old 'Snag'* as he preferred to call it, deep inside he understood why Linus kept it. After all, he could have a company car, and the only reason he used one of these now was because of this bloody *RADI-CAL* thing and if and when it ended, he'd back to the *old banger*.

He knew it was because something in Linus's mind was always battling away, as if two armies inside of him were constantly fighting, pushing him to the edge.

The Stag could let him down, yet raise him up, but could not speak. *That was why he kept it*.

Rupert had seen this in the lad for the last nine years. There were times when they were at sea together on tankers, that he'd wanted to hug his young friend's pain away. But a ship's captain could never do that to crew members, and quite rightly so.

Then RITON Group bought out his old employer's fleet and a lot of the gang came into their marine division. Cannon, with his seniority as a captain, knowledge of operations and contacts in shipbuilding, had risen right to the top. In some ways he missed working at sea, but absolutely loved being in this role. Even Sir Dennis Ogilvy was an admirer of him, although he would never say that of course.

For Cannon, getting some of his old team into their new jobs had not been easy. But Linus had fitted in with the RITON style, apart from the odd hiccup….

Colleen Walker, his PA knocked on the door and opened it without waiting for his response, as per usual. "Private call for you on line two," she said, then closed the door. There were two phones on his desk, a black one for international and a grey for local calls. He walked over and picked up the grey handset.

Later, one of the managers from the far end of the office came over to Colleen's desk and asked if Mr Cannon was free. His door had been closed for over half an hour, which was very unusual, so she asked the manager to wait while she checked if he was available.

Looking through the door's glass panel, she realised something was wrong. Rupert was up on his feet, but lent over the desk, resting on his hands. Staring out of the office window into the rain on the airfield, she saw a tear fall from his cheek.

She turned to the manager by her desk, making sure her back was up against the door, so he could not see through its glass panel. "He's still tied up I'm afraid," she said. "I'll let you know when he's free."

Back in the Maidstone office, Jeannie and Linus entered the downstairs meeting room to plan the Trans-ship fit outs. The Rochester site was close, so would be ideal for their workshop guys to make the lorry installs. The problem was how to manage Trans-ship in their Manchester base. Linus was determined to arrange this, because after all, it seemed the least he could do following Jeannie's generosity.

Anyway, he was used to managing operational work within the RITON Group, so could pull all this together and supervise it as necessary. At least, that's what he thought.

Derek Tweedy opened the door and came over menacingly. As usual, he was wearing overalls and had a roll-up hanging from the corner of his mouth. He stared at them, seemingly friendlier than usual. Linus noticed the brown tobacco stain on his fore-finger as he took the roll-up out. *I'm definitely going to give up smoking,* he thought.

"Right," said Tweedy to Jeannie. "We can do this *wee* thing for *yer.* When is it needed?"

"Thank you Derek," she said smiling at him. "This could never have been possible without your help. Next week would be great."

Linus watched with interest, the attitude changes in Tweedy increasing still further. "*Och,* it's *nay* bother Jeannie," said Tweedy, now smiling. "I'm here to help *ye.*"

She has this effect on everyone. Linus said to himself.

As Tweedy turned to walk out of the room, Linus stood up and said, "Oh, Derek, just wanted to let you know, I am responsible for getting their lorries in Manchester fitted out. I'd be very grateful if you could help advise me on this."

Derek Tweedy stopped in his tracks, slowly turning around, his roll-up now back between his lips, light perspiration on his brow and the ceiling lights glinted off his red hair.

"Och ye are, *are ye?"* he said staring aggressively at Linus. "Well, good luck with that. *Ye'll* need to sort it with the regional office boys up there."

He turned and walked out of the door. Discussion closed.

"Thanks for that," said Linus to the closed door.

Jeannie laughed and responded. "You seem to have really made a friend for life there. Anyway, Manchester has a new regional office in place as you know, so the way to sort this, is by getting Mike to approve it with Steve Rider."

Linus nodded back, he understood how the regional sites worked.

"I'll go and ask Mike now," he said. "Then I'd like to travel up there and make sure everything goes according to plan when the installs start."

"Really?" she asked somewhat surprised. "It's a long way for you to go and I'm sure the fitters would be ok, there has been a good workshop training course on this."

"Even so, I feel I owe you on this and want it to be *glitch* free."

She smiled back, understanding his genuine commitment to her for making it work efficiently. Her suggestion for him *not* to bother going, had been merely a ruse to test him. She wondered if he realised that. On the other hand, so what? She was starting to quite like his decency.

"So let me get this straight," said Sally-Anne Cohen. "You are suggesting picking me up Sunday, we drive to Manchester and stay three nights in the Hilton? Explain the catch please."

Linus glanced across into Mike Sentinel's office. He was also on the 'phone, and looked superciliously over his glasses towards the General Activity Manager area.

"There is no catch," he'd lowered his voice into a whisper, turning away from Sentinel's office. "They want me to make sure an install is done properly, but much of the time we can spend together."

"Ok," she replied. As it's you I'll do it. Don't forget though, that you already owe me a *wodge* of cash, so I shall be adding my time for this onto your account."

He was about to respond, but she had already hung up. As he looked at the handset, with a fifty-fifty split of humour and annoyance, Mike Sentinel approached him.

"Mmm, come on in to my office Linus, I want to fill you in on the game plan for the promotional events of next year."

Now this was interesting, he thought. Something he would discuss at next Saturday's meeting with Rupert Cannon.

They sat down at his round table, which amazingly, had been cleared of junk. On it were two A4 sheets. Mike handed him over one and said. "Right, let's go through this. Most of the others were given these when you were away on the Heathfield course, so I need to update you."

Linus looked down at the page list. He was already aware of the bizarre start-up event featuring the comedian Frankie Howerd on 24th December, but had no idea about rest of it.

Mike sat back and looked over his glasses at Linus in a friendly and relaxed fashion. He was clearly waiting for him to absorb the file's content list before speaking. It certainly was quite something to take on board.

"Ring in a change" 24th December 1984,
Starring Frankie Howerd in Hyde Park.

List of events agreed for 1985 so far:

Parliament House event - April

Goodwood Gold Cup - August

European GP Brands Hatch - September

London Motor Show - October

City of London show – November

Exact dates TBC.

"So when do we get the exact dates?" asked Linus.

"Should be next week," responded Mike. "Not all of these have been confirmed yet by the organisers, so a new sheet is to be printed when this is done."

"Would I be required to be at all of these?" asked Linus.

"Mmm, assuming you are still with us, I would suggest so." Mike replied, then went on. "So have you got organised for Trans-ship in Manchester yet?"

"Yes, I'm planning to be at the Northern regional office first thing on Monday. Then I can oversee the procedure when they start on Tuesday."

Sentinel stood up, walked over to the door and closed it. The whole group in the main room lifted their heads, realising a private conversation was about to be made in Mike's office. And of course, the paper-thin walls meant that they would be able to hear everything. Linus looked down, shook his head and whispered '*oy vey,*' as Mike sat back down at the table.

"Now, I have spoken with Steve Rider about this, and he is happy for you to go up there. But you need to be aware of the political aspect of this, *alrighty*."

Linus looked across at him, guessing that the Manchester regional office was expecting this area part of the deal to be allocated to them. Mike carried on.

"Trans-ship's head office is in our region as you know, so we are completely in the right, but given we are the first area to have signed up any *RADI-CAL* business so far, the Manchester lot are likely be a bit *pissy* over this. Their manager is Jason Lord. He is alright, but can be somewhat terse. We used to be at Rate-Syrex together, so I know."

Linus thought, *yet another Syrex one on board, is anyone still working there?*

"Thanks for letting me know Mike," said Linus. "I'll handle this very carefully and keep you posted."

"Well make sure you do, *alrighty*," he replied looking over his glasses. "Don't let us down, c*heers*."

Mike stood up, walked to the door, opened it and headed off, Linus suspected, to the coffee machine.

As the day ended, Kevin Aaron asked Linus if he would come over to the *Anchor* pub for a quick one, to celebrate the Trans-ship deal.

A quick what? he thought. *Room full of lunatics, rotten sausage rolls and a punch-up.*

"I'd be delighted." He replied, rather hoping Jeannie would be there, but she wasn't.

"Do you know what?" asked Robbie. Linus shook his head as he had no idea what was coming next. "I think you made a good decision in joining us."

They were standing by the bar and clinked their pint mugs together as Linus smiled at him and said. "Cheers Robbie."

Linus offered him a Marlboro, but he held up his palm and carried on. "Thing is that I reckon we are all in the right place at the right time. Because when it goes live, our lot would already have some experience. Your trip up north being a good example of that."

"I've been meaning to ask you about that Robbie. I was surprised when Jeannie passed this over to me. After all, she had done all the hard work. Not that I'm complaining, on the contrary, I'm delighted."

"And so you should be," said Robbie. "Jeannie is a very generous woman."

"I know," said Linus taking another sip of his lager-top and a drag of the Marlboro. "I feel really indebted to her."

Robbie put his pint on the bar and looked Linus in the eye in a serious manner.

"She is a *very* clever woman Linus. I worked with her at Syrex too, don't forget."

Am I the only one on the planet who didn't work there? he thought, nodding back at Robbie, and said. "Oh yes, I remember you telling me."

Robbie looked over his shoulder to make sure none of the team were close by and said. "Few things to be aware of. Firstly, she is very close to Mike and Steve Rider, and could well be reporting stuff back to them. Secondly, there is *no way* she was going up to Manchester and that's why she brought you in." He took a sip of his bitter. "And thirdly, she kicked her first husband into touch for the current one. You see, I know the first one, and the bloke still cries over her *every single day*."

Linus looked at Robbie with a multitude of surprise and said. "But she told me the fitters would sort it up there and that I didn't need to go, only I wasn't comfortable with that, so I volunteered."

Robbie took another sip of his bitter and shook his head. "As I said, she knew someone had to go up there, so handed the Manchester deal over to you. If I was a sarcastic git, I might think she was covering her own arse instead of being generous to you. After all, it's all going to be fine down here with *bonkers* Tweedy running it, but up in the *frozen* north, who knows?"

Linus glanced across at the Wurlitzer. Mike Sentinel had now entered the bar and stood by it with Julia, Kevin and Julian, and then he put a coin in the box. The song was by Wham! – *"Wake Me Up Before You Go-Go."* As it blared out, Mike began to dance like a robot; start, stop and twisting, his blonde hair flicking about over his glasses. Linus shook his head in disbelief as Robbie continued.

"Linus, generosity means there is *a price* to pay. It can be a *big one*, so be careful."

Robbie lifted his now empty pint glass across the room, saluting towards Mike Sentinel. "There is only *one* person I have ever known who is *totally* genuine, and expects *nothing* in return."

Linus put up his hand towards the bar maid, for the next round....

Chapter 7

Long Estate, Purley
7th October 1984

Linus arrived at 14.00. He'd agreed to pick up Sally-Anne at 14.30, so stopped on the back-road, about quarter of a mile from her place. He was really looking forward to spending three nights away with her. This was for many reasons, and not least because of her genuine listening ability. He needed to talk. Sally-Anne was aware of the awful thing that had happened, because Linus called her about it yesterday.

Sally-Anne had only met Rupert Cannon once, when Linus was moving to his new role, and she had been called in to provide *entertainment*. He'd seemed like a really nice guy. In fact, had it not been for him, the relationship with Linus would never have happened. His PA, Colleen had organised her show, but when it was over, Cannon had caught up with Sally-Anne as she was leaving the building, and asked if she fancied coming out with the gang.

She had no other work planned for that night or the next, so thought *why not?* Anyway the bloke that she had been *presenting* to seemed interesting. Although she'd never tell him of course, his shyness she felt, had been genuinely special. There was *something* that made her want to be with him. It was as if she'd known him before.

Reclining the Cavalier's seat, Linus wound down the window and lit up a Marlboro. He blew out the first cloud of smoke, watching as it rose into the sky. The feeling of guilt kicked in again. *If only he'd realised this last week. Damn it!*

Yesterday morning at 10.00, Colleen's Renault 5TL was already in the *Aerodrome* Hotel's car park, covered with rain droplets from the dark sky. Linus had driven there in the Cavalier, because his Stag had developed a fault, which was not unusual.

On his way back from Sally-Anne's last Saturday, it had started to miss-fire. He was actually lucky to get home, as the further he drove, the worse it got. Later in his garage when the engine had cooled, he found the distributor cap was cracked. There was a spares place called *'All-Parts'*, close to West Croydon train station, but they closed at 12.00 on a Saturday and would stay shut until Monday. He'd been too busy last week to go there, so the '*bloody old Snag was off the road – again,*' to coin Mr Cannon's phrase.

Walking into the café-bar area, Colleen was at the same table where he and Rupert Cannon had met-up a week ago. Linus could not believe that he would never see his boss, long-term friend, and genuine confidant again. Now, the emotions kicked in and the tears began to well up. But he *had* to keep it under control. Rupert Cannon would never tolerate crying.

Colleen was looking down at the table, it was completely empty. She seemed to be just staring into *nothingness*. She was wearing large glasses. Linus knew she didn't need them, Colleen had perfect eyesight, they were fake-lenses, worn out of respect for Rupert, because she also knew he'd never abide tears. *Never.*

As Linus approached the table, she stood and came towards him, still wearing her khaki, lightweight Macintosh with some droplets of rain on the shoulders. Linus guessed that she'd only just arrived.

They hugged each other silently and then sat down at the table, trying to find the words to start a conversation. The search continued for a moment, and Linus asked.

"What happened?"

Colleen looked down, shook her head and raised her hands up towards him. "He had spinal cancer Linus, and didn't tell anyone. It seems he suffered from back pain for months and did nothing. Then two weeks ago, went into hospital for a radiography test. Then he was told last Tuesday that it had spread massively."

She took off the fake glasses and wiped the tears on her sleeve. "Here," said Linus, passing over a clean handkerchief, "use this."

"Thanks," she said, wiping her eyes and continued. "I passed the call through to him from the hospital, but had no idea what it was about." She looked up at the ceiling and said angrily. "Damn it Linus, I could tell *something* wasn't right, but I did nothing about it!"

Linus sat back fighting against his own tears, he wanted to console her somehow, but knew it was impossible.

"Let me get you a coffee, or something." He said.

Colleen shook her head and blew her nose. "No thanks," she replied. "I don't want anything."

He felt full of sadness, responsibility, self-anger and confusion. But really, knowing Cannon as well as he did, he could guess how his death had manifested. He had to play this straight but sympathetically with Colleen.

"He was always a very active man, so whilst his loss is tragic, the *frustration* he'd have been facing would have been impossible for him."

She nodded back and said. "I know, but taking his own life is so difficult to bear."

This confirmed his thought, and it wasn't a shock, but a very sad, macabre thing.

Colleen went on. "He did this at home on Tuesday night or in the small hours of Wednesday morning, apparently."

"How?" asked Linus.

"I spoke to the head of medical at Group HQ yesterday, you know Brian Callaghan."

Linus nodded back. This man was responsible for the all the private medical care services for RITON on a global basis. Every staff member had this available to them. Callaghan always ensured that families and appropriate staff were advised and kept up to date, whatever the situation.

Colleen looked confused, as if there was an element here that she just could not fathom.

"Linus," she said looking him in the eye. "He took a *cyanide* pill. How on earth did he manage to get that?"

That was not what he expected to hear. In fact, he had no perception of what he might have used for this tragedy. But *cyanide!*

"I have no idea," he said as they continued looking shocked at each other.

A tall, grey-haired man wearing a long black overcoat, also damp across the shoulders, walked with a slight limp up to the bar counter. He glanced at them both in a distant fashion as he passed their table, then lent over the bar to catch the eye of a staff member.

Colleen carried on, lowering her voice as this man was now close by.

"Anyway, I've been given the details by Brian. It's so *bloody* sad." She reached down to her bag by the table leg, and removed a notepad, flicking through to the appropriate page. "He died sat on the sofa in his lounge. On his lap was a framed picture of his wife, who as you know passed away over ten years ago, also from cancer."

Linus knew of this, although it was something Rupert Cannon rarely talked about. He remembered her being referred to as his *'tower of strength,'* once. They had no children and their relatives had apparently all sadly departed. In his final years, Cannon had been a personal loner, but at work he was a vibrant man, gregarious and generous.

"So who found him?" asked Linus.

"I was coming to that," she replied back in her frosty, PA tone, continuing her focus on the notepad. "It was his cleaner. She usually only came in on a Monday, but for some reason had returned to his place on Wednesday."

"That must have been an awful shock for her." Said Linus.

"I'm sure it was," continued Colleen. "And once she had called the police, I'd imagine they had to question her and then bring in the medical people for the post-mortem. Which, by the way, was carried out on Thursday."

"That is unusually fast isn't it?" he asked. Colleen nodded back.

"It is, and then the report on this went straight over to Brian by fax, following a call to him from the doctor. Then he rang me first thing yesterday."

This is a whirlwind of bloody sadness, thought Linus.

"Where on earth could he have got cyanide from?" he asked, knowing she would have no idea.

Colleen shook her head at him. They continued to sit silently, in a quiet storm of sadness.

"What about the funeral?" he asked.

"That's going to have to be sorted out by Brian, and he also has access to the will documents, so I can only keep you posted. I believe he's being kept in the *Lansdale* Hospital cold-room until this is arranged."

Linus nodded back in understanding. Lansdale was a private hospital available to all RITON staff in Isleworth. They continued to sit in silence, then Linus said.

"Are you sure I can't get you anything."

She seemed calmer now, as she glanced at her watch.

"No thanks, I need to get back home." Linus understood Colleen. He knew that the wave of emotion was continuing to kick in, and she didn't want to show it. They stood up together and walked towards the main door.

"Oh," she said, coming to a stop right by the table where the grey haired, limping man was now sat drinking a coffee. Then she reached into her bag again, taking out a white, A4 sealed envelope. "I nearly forgot. This had been put in my desk draw."

On the front was his name, **Linus MacColl**, written in black ink. He knew straight away it was from Rupert Cannon.

Linus's fingers gently ran over it, and as they did so, in came another wave of sadness.

"I wonder what's in this?" he asked, continuing to look at the envelope.

"I've no idea. Maybe it's to do with the *RADI-CAL* thing. But whatever it is, it was surely hand-written by Mr Cannon, otherwise I'd know." Linus understood her point. If something was entirely *personal* it would not be given to a PA for typing.

The grey haired man glanced up at them both, his gaze particularly focussed upon the envelope. They both automatically felt annoyance, after all this was a personal matter. But as Linus reached the door, he realised they were probably just stressed by the sadness.

Outside, the rain had stopped, although the sky was still overcast and the wind continued gusting across the old airfield.

"It's been like this all week," she said looking up at the clouds, "I remember on Tuesday, when Mr Cannon was looking across at the car park and…"

The emotions were now really coming out from her. The tears, the shaking, the wind tousling her dark hair. Linus hugged her, wishing he could fix this. But no loss of life could ever be recovered, no matter how clever this new world of communications and computing would become. This was a *humanity catastrophe.* It was reality, it was pain and it was guilt.

She stepped back from Linus and walked over to her car without saying another word. He could see that she was absolutely choked with sadness.

As she drove away, he thought about the additional pain she'd now experience in the workplace. He knew the RITON group would look after her, as if they were parents of a heart-broken child. She could stay away from the office on full-pay for a long period and then choose her new PA role from a list of options.

But the pain was going to stay within her. Colleen and Rupert were so close and supportive of each other, that many of the team believed they had a magical connection. Linus MacColl wholeheartedly agreed with this.

He walked across the car park to the Cavalier, opened the door and looked at the envelope from Rupert Cannon. It was certainly going to be about the *RADI-CAL* situation, and as he got into the driver's seat, he opened up the glove box., gently folding it in half and placed it in. He didn't feel up to reading it now, it would have to wait.

He reclined the seat, wound down the window and lit up a Marlboro. He blew out the first cloud, the strong wind grabbing it, as it flew towards the old runway.

Glancing into the mirror, he noticed a black Volkswagen Passat parked near the fence. *Good job Bernie's not here today, he thought,* given it was *Shabbat* again.

Then he noticed there was someone sat behind it's steering wheel, looking over the bonnet towards him. It was that grey haired man who had been in the café-bar earlier, now wearing a trilby-hat. *Why would he be doing that?* he thought.

He started up the Cavalier and drove towards the car park gate. Turning left onto Purley Way, he took another look in the mirror at the Passat. It remained parked up, with the man now looking at the gate as Linus drove away thinking, s*trange sad old git, you need to get out more*.

Linus pulled up into the driveway of the Cohen's house. Sally-Anne had told him to *stop* calling it a *mansion,* as it was now becoming boring. "Besides," she had said, "as you are correct about that, in return I should call *your place* something accurate too, and you wouldn't like that would you?"

Bernie's Rolls and her Metro were both parked there, as the gravel finished crunching under the Cavalier's tyres. Linus switched off and stepped out. The *house's* front door creaked open slightly in it's now familiar style, with Sally-Anne staring through a narrow gap.

"No cleaners on Sunday," she shouted. "Oh Linus, it's you. I am sorry, please come in."

She stood back and swept her hand along the hallway. He walked in and stood shaking his head at her somewhat inane sense of humour. She clocked it and said tersely. "It's called *comedy*. Anyway, come and meet my mother."

He followed her along the hallway towards the lounge entrance. She looked good; wearing her tight jeans, red high-heels and that fabulous, raven hair shining on the back of a cream jumper.

As he walked into this massive room, he felt on edge. A first meeting with a woman's mother was usually somewhat nerve racking. But he needn't have worried. On the far side of the lounge, Sally-Anne's mum stood up from the stool behind the Steinway baby-grand piano, and walked towards him.

She was an exact, older replica of Sally-Anne. Sure, the hair was greying, but her face, height and image were *so* similar. With her black dress, high-heels and subtle gold jewellery, she was a seriously classy lady.

They shook hands and she gave him a gentle kiss on each cheek. "Nice to meet you Linus, can I get you anything to drink?"

"No thank you Mrs Cohen, we must get on the journey, unless Sally-Anne needs something?"

Sally-Anne replied. "No, I'll just get my bag, then we can go."

She walked out and Mrs Cohen put her hand towards one of the leather arm chairs and said. "Take a seat Linus, and please, call me Jane."

He looked at the chairs, trying to give out the impression that he had never been in this room before, wondering if she would buy that.... They sat down and Linus asked.

"So is Bernie around today?" trying to find the start of an engaging conversation.

"He's in town today Linus," she replied. "I dropped him off at the station about an hour ago. He's got a work thing on at the South-Bank studio."

Linus nodded back. "Yes, Sally-Anne told me about her dad's business, and that he made it a real success."

She smiled back at him and said. "I was an actress, never film or TV, just a stage person and not a great success. But that's how I met Bernie. He started out as a talent scout." She looked up at the ceiling and laughed, as clearly her memories were flooding back and went on.

"He never got me very far, but I married him anyway!" Waving her hand across the fabulous room she went on. "Then he did pretty well with quite a few others."

I like her, thought Linus, *she has a classy, understated style.* He smiled back at her, his legs, as ever, now, uncrossed.

"I really like Bernie, we met here last week." He said.

Jane looked back and shook her head. "I know, Sally-Anne told me. Apparently, he went for a VW car driver. Sorry about that, I'd like to say it was a first, but it wasn't."

Linus said. "I understand why he does that."

The room's window panes had diamond shaped, lead panels across them. Outside, the garden was huge, with oak trees standing proudly and a beautifully trimmed lawn, with perfect mower lines running down it. Then the sun came out from behind a cloud, and its rays flickered through the panes with a stunning intensity, like that film production company *Columbia's* lady figure on the big screen.

"The thing is Linus," continued Jane, "Bernie had a sad childhood and a lot of that is still trapped in his head. I know he tries to hide it, or if not, make a joke out of it, but it can't ever go away." She looked up at the picture of her daughters on the wall by the door. "Sally-Anne knows about the *basics* of course, as does Esther, my eldest, but Bernie and I have never gone into too much detail."

Linus looked at her concentrating deeply, his mind flashing back to Rupert Cannon's emotions about what had occurred at Croydon Aerodrome in the nineteen thirties. What had Britain's Government *really* done?

"Anyway," she went on, "I'm not Jewish, but have so much sadness for what happened to Bernie's parents and so many others in those awful times. Sally-Anne told me about your mum's background." She said, and then laughed warmly at him.

"So you two are a good fit!"

She had made her point, then turned the tide from sadness to humour. Good one.

Sally-Anne came in with a brown leather hold-all over her shoulder, clearly ready to go. Jane and Linus stood up.

"Very nice to meet you. Bernie and I would be delighted if you came over for dinner soon."

"Thank you Jane, I'd love to." He replied.

Sally-Anne gave her mum a hug and said. "See you in a few days."

They walked through the door and Jane called out. "Enjoy yourselves both. Don't let the bed-bugs bite!"

They walked out, got into the Cavalier and Sally-Anne put her hold-all in the back and then jumped in the passenger's seat. Linus started the car and U turned towards the entrance.

"Whoopee!" she said. "Come on chauffer, let's go! Oh, just to let you know, if you *do* come to dinner, the cost is going to be added onto *your* account. And given my charges over the next three days, you'll need a lot of dosh."

Then she took some cassettes out of her handbag and scanned through them. She pushed one into the cassette player and said. "I am not going to sit listening to medium wave whilst we drive to the other side of the *fucking* world."

It was the band *ABC's* '*Poison Arrow*' from their album '*The Lexicon of Love.*'

Sally-Anne started singing the words as the music played out, albeit a little *tinny* sounding, from the Cavalier's rear parcel shelf speakers.

"*Shoot that poison arrow. No rhythm in cymbals no tempo in drums, love on arrival, she comes when she comes. Right on the target but wide of the mark, what I thought was fire was only the spark.*"

Her singing was pretty good; he glanced across as she pulled back the imaginary bow's string and fired off the arrow, looking through the window.

He smiled at the back of her raven haired head. *Although her sense of humour could sometimes be slightly annoying, she was a real character.*

Linus glanced at the car's clock. Only another four hours and they would be there….

Chapter 8

Midland Hotel, Manchester
7th October 1984

"Err, excuse me mister *shmuck* man, but this is *not* the Hilton." She said as they pulled up outside the *Midland Hotel* in Manchester's city centre.

"Oh, didn't I tell you we were now going to be in one of the finest hotels in the country instead of a boring, standard one?"

Sally-Anne looked up at the building. It was very special, no doubt about that, and she was rather taken aback.

"No, you *forgot* to tell me," she replied, still looking up at it, "looks old but has a nice shape." The raven black hair flickered as she turned towards him smiling. "Bit like you, I suppose."

"Well," he said, ignoring this, and looking up snootily. "Mr Sentinel *insisted* upon it."

The journey from Croydon had exceeded the expected time of four hours, and it was now almost 20.00hrs. The darkness had set in up here earlier than down south, so the last thirty minutes of the drive were tricky. Crossing London to the M1 was not bad, probably as it was Sunday, but as for that Spaghetti Junction….

On the outskirts of Birmingham, the Panasonic R1 flicked into green. Linus knew there were now some *RADI-CAL* base stations here, but was not sure where exactly.

In fact, he was somewhat surprised that a signal had not kicked in when going through London to Staples Corner. But of course, the system was not officially live and he imagined the technicians were still connecting the cells up and testing them.

He told Sally-Anne to give her dad a ring, as he'd told Linus last week that he was interested in taking his first call from a cellular radio. She un-clipped the handset and pressed the nine digits for her home phone number.

"You need to press that *send thing*," said Linus, looking across as she put it up to her ear.

"Whoops," she said, bringing it back down and pressing the button. Linus could hear the long ring-tone start up as she lifted it back up to her ear. Then it was answered.

"Hi dad, it's me. We are going past Birmingham on the motorway." She smiled at Linus, now looking genuinely excited. Obviously, he couldn't hear what Bernie was saying, but imagined it was something funny, as she kept giggling.

"Actually, you sound fine," she said and then. "Oh it just clicked then for some reason, no it's alright, you're still there."

Linus realised that the cell the Panasonic R1 had first connected to, had automatically switched over to the next one via the *honey-comb thing*.

Their conversation continued as Sally-Anne looked over at the speedo. "Just on seventy," she said, smiling again at Linus as she carried on with Bernie. "Yes, we should be up there about seven thirty." She listened as Bernie carried on and then said. "I'll ask Linus about that dad, hold on a second."

She put her right hand over the mouthpiece and asked Linus pointing at it with her left. "How much?"

"Sixteen hundred, plus twenty-five pence a minute and another twenty-five quid monthly line-rental." He said. Sally-Anne repeated this to Bernie. She listened to his response and said. "I'll ask him to get it sorted dad, see you soon. Bye."

She clicked the hand-set back on the holder and smiled at Linus. "That's even more dosh you *owe* me now," she said, pointing at the R1. "He wants one of these *bonkers* things fitted into *his* car."

Sally-Anne had been a good navigator, following the map and his notes very accurately. *Rupert Cannon would have appreciated that,* thought Linus.

There were free parking spaces on the main road here, unlike central London. They pulled in close to the main entrance, and walked in with their bags to reception.

They stared around the place together in awe. It was extraordinary, because it somehow retained a real Edwardian style, perhaps reflecting the originality of when it was built, even though that was over eighty years ago.

As Linus went up to the counter, Sally-Anne stood behind him, dropping her bag then doing a 360 degree turn in slow motion and said. *"Wow!"*

A black suited, fair haired and very tall young man came over to him and said. "Good evening sir, can I help you?"

"Yes," said Linus, "I have a room for two booked for three nights. It should be under the name of MacColl."

The receptionist opened a smart, leather file and scanned through some typed sheets, taking one out and raising it up. "Ah yes," he said, "a double room for three nights, breakfast and evening meals for two included."

Linus turned to Sally-Anne and nodded pretentiously, which she returned in exactly the same *'get you'* style.

"I assume payment should be made on check out?" asked Linus.

The receptionist ran his eyes down the sheet and said. "No sir, it seems your stay has already been paid for." He nodded over to the large bar. "It's only the drinks and any other extras that you'll need to pay for." He scanned down to the bottom of the sheet.

"Yes, this was all done last week by a Mr Sentinel, from something called *Radical*."

Sally-Anne heard this and came sauntering up to Linus, then looked at the receptionist dead-pan and said. "No problem, Mr MacColl is used to paying for *extras*," then looking across at Linus. "Isn't that right, my *darling* man?"

Linus ignored her as she continued to glance with the raven hair flicking, from one to the other, like a grinning lunatic.

"Thank you," he said, as the receptionist handed over a key.

"My pleasure sir, your room is on the third floor," the man continued, then waved his hand down the hall-way. "The lift is just there."

They picked up their bags and set off towards it.

She pressed the button by one of the lifts and it opened straight away. Stepping in, they both put down their bags and she touched the button for the third floor. Then as the door closed, she put her arms around Linus and kissed him on the lips.

"Thank you," she said in tenderness and sincerity. "This place is amazing."

The lift was slow but gentle and so, possibly original. As they rode up in it, the connection between them came in. There was a pang of desire, but also a link of *something* that neither had experienced in any other relationship. To both of them, it felt on a higher plane, extraordinary and out of their own control….

The room was truly lovely. It was spacious, beautifully maintained and like the rest of the Midland Hotel exuded original Edwardian style. The double bed was huge, a leather sofa sat by the window and the bathroom was beautifully tiled, with brass taps that could have been there since 1903.

They put their bags on the bed and sat on the sofa, taking it all in. Linus looked at his watch. "It's 20.30," he said, "shall we unpack and go for something eat?"

Sally-Anne nodded back, taking a letter from her handbag, then passing it to Linus.

"Typical," he sighed, as he looked at the envelope. "Just as I was starting to enjoy myself, I get an invoice."

"You had a decent innings, now it's payback time *sucker*." She said, smiling.

Tearing open the back, he took out the white card. He read it, stared at her and then read it again in disbelief and silence. It said:

Mr Linus MacColl and Miss Sally-Anne Cohen.
Request pleasure of your company
Concert commencing at 8pm on Monday 8th October
Location at BBC studio, Oxford Road, Manchester
Performance by Sade
We look forward to your attendance
BBC Invitations Department

"How did you get this?" he asked.

Sally-Anne punched the air with excitement, laughing, then said, "Dad gave it to me yesterday. He's got a load of contacts in the BBC, and told someone we were coming up here. It seems we timed it right because Sade- or perhaps I should say *Sado* like that land-lord in the *Sandrock*- is in their studio for a private concert that's being filmed tomorrow." She nodded at the card as Linus continued staring at it. "So, they gave this to dad for us."

"That's great," said Linus, genuinely amazed, continuing to stare at it. "It's so nice of your dad."

She held up her hands at him and said. "It's a pleasure, I always like to give *extras* to my customers, so I'll add this onto your account. Come on," she said, looking with approval around the room, "let's go to the bar and raise a glass to *Mr Sensible.*"

The old man drove slowly into Queen Anne's Gate, the sidelights of the black Passat now on as dusk set in. He pulled up into a public space, knowing that there would be no parking charges on Sunday from the City Council. The street lamps now glowed with an amber hue, and he parked in the darkest space between them, switched off, then waited, sitting absolutely still and checking for any signs of life. There was nothing. He gave it another thirty seconds, as old habits die hard. A spasm of pain kicked in from his leg. *Bugger* he thought, it always did this when autumn came in, so was nothing new. But it still *bloody hurt*.

He stepped out of the car wearing his raincoat and a brown trilby hat, another element of his standard procedure. The upturned collar and hat's large brim helping to cover up his identity. *It didn't prevent that sixteen years ago in fucking East Berlin,* he thought, approaching the entrance to the most refurbished looking building in the road. Staring up from the first step to the first floor, he could see the lights were on. It was time to face the music....

There was no lift, so he made his way up the stairs, walking slowly with continuing pain. When he reached the office door, he stood up straight, and mentally told himself not to limp in. His image to the man in there *had* to be one of normality. Anyone walking with a crippled gait, slight or otherwise would not be tolerated by his *Lordship*.

Everyone in this game had to be normal in every respect, because if not, they might be remembered by a passer-by after their *task* had been completed, and could be tracked down more easily.

He took off his trilby and knocked on the door, wiping his now perspiring brow with the back of his hand. It was a mixture of climbing those bloody stairs and stress of the situation with that bloke Rupert Cannon.

"Come in!" Boomed out a voice with an upper-crust style.

The old man turned down the door's handle and focused on walking in straight and level, standing still and upright in front of the desk where Lord Atkins sat. He was bald and rotund, and his glasses were thick. His focus was still on the desk, and he had not lifted his head to look at the man as he came in. *Round one,* thought the visitor as he continued to stand rock still.

Atkins leaned back and removed his glasses, waving down towards the chair in front of his desk. "Thank you for coming in at short notice, Kelson."

He sat down in the chair, still wearing his raincoat, knowing that it could not be removed, unless Lord Atkins requested it.

"I'm pleased to be of assistance Sir." Said Kelson, hiding the pain of sitting down, following his walk up the stairs.

"Right," said Atkins, "let's get down to it. I think you know this Rupert Cannon debacle is a potentially *serious* issue for us Kelson." He nodded back his understanding as Lord Atkins continued.

"Knowing part of the issue is one thing, and like a number of other events in global history, lighting only a small fuse can be a *huge* danger for this sacred land Kelson, rather like World War One."

Dick Kelson swallowed hard, the perspiration growing on his brow. He really wanted to take his raincoat off, but knew that was impossible.

If necessary, Lord Atkins would look at *every* inch of him and examine *any* bodily function, no matter how small, in order to diagnose his honesty. Weird but effective, Kelson knew that.

Lord Atkins took a deep breath and sat back in his green leather desk chair. Kelson considered this to be rather like something in a gentleman's club, befitting the man's upper-class style. Atkins now looked at him in a slightly warmer fashion. *Typical of the type,* thought Kelson, *give you stress, then turn all friendly with you. Fucker!*

"So, explaining the reason for concern is why I needed you to come in today," continued Atkins. "And if it makes you feel better, I wouldn't have been here on a Sunday either, had this not been such an issue."

Kelson continued to look at Lord Atkins nonchalantly, although felt his tide was going out fast.

"The thing is, Dick," said Atkins, his tone becoming even friendlier, "the problem is not down to your *medical help* for Mr Cannon. In fact, you completed the task well and so took away any current, direct communication risk for us. No, it's not about that, but more connected with the *aftermath*."

Dick Kelson felt relieved but still confused, as his *Lordship* continued.

"I'll get straight to the point. You did a good job in taking out Cannon. True, the cancer gave us an advantage and so we made it look like suicide. When his father was removed back in nineteen thirty-eight, it was because of a contrived accident. In those days, the Police did not have the forensics and other *claptrap* that's in place today."

Atkins stopped talking, allowing this to sink into Kelson, then glanced down at the photo-copied sheet of paper on his desk, tapping it with his right hand.

"My concern is the fake letter you produced from Cannon.

I appreciate that you managed to have it placed in his PA's desk drawer. I also realise you're an experienced man in this activity, so no finger prints are going to be found."

Dick Kelson was feeling more confident now and said. "So what's the problem?"

"Well, let me tell you what the *fucking* problem is, *Kelson!*" Atkins shouted, waving the copied document in front of his face. "Your *forgery* of his writing is *atrocious!*"

Atkins put the document back on the table, clenched his fist and whacked it down, his face turning red with a mixture of anger and pain.

"I thought this matched his hand-writing very accurately," responded Kelson, and *his* mixture was of indignation and fear. "I even used that old fax he'd written on that we got from *SICS,* to check this."

Lord Atkins shook his head, the beetroot colour in his face now subsiding. S*ICS* was a *Special Input Collection Section*. It was designed to access information by getting undercover people into companies that communicated using fax machines.

Rupert Cannon would often write a quick note to the board or others, then pass it to Colleen for faxing. When it reached RITON HQ, an undercover *SICS* member (usually acting as a cleaner), would gather up any faxes and make copies of them. Later, the copies would be dropped in a post box, addressed to an empty office in North London, registered to a *'hair stylist'*. Then they were collected and used as required….

But, this situation was much simpler, and so massively frustrating for Lord Atkins. Because when Kelson had finished the job on Cannon, he just needed to remove the dangerous information inside the envelope addressed to Linus MacColl that Cannon had *previously* written and put into his PA's desk drawer.

One of the *SICS* cleaners was to remove this, and replace it with a forgery made up by Kelson, with just a few words of friendly*, cheerio old bean* to MacColl on it. The cleaner would simply insert the fake letter in the *same* envelope, because Colleen would be keeping it in the draw unopened until her meeting with MacColl took place.

Then she would just pass it over to him at that *Aerodrome* Hotel. The *original* letter would be given to Kelson, by the undercover cleaner. Kelson would in turn, hand it over to Lord Atkins.

"What you have to do now is monitor the situation," said Atkins, reducing his anger slightly. "As you are aware, this *whippersnapper,* Linus MacColl, was given this by Cannon's

PA. As I see it, you have two choices. You can either arrange it to be stolen from him *before* he has looked at it and realises it's fake, which is frankly a long-shot, given that she handed it to him *over* two days ago."

Atkins tapped his pen on the desk, turning his head away from Kelson towards the window. It was pitch black out there now, with just a dim shadow coming up from the street lights. The sweat on Kelson's brow and his heart rate increased as he waited for the next choice. One that he'd already guessed of course.

"Otherwise, you shall monitor him. If you find he is digging into this, then you shall take *defensive* action. Is that clear?"

Kelson realised there was no alternative, he had to follow the second instruction.

"I shall monitor the situation and report back to you Sir." He noticed that Atkins had turned his attention to another file, so this discussion was now over. There would be no '*goodbye*' or '*good luck.*' This meeting was over.

Dick Kelson stood up, and despite the pain made a straight-line for the door, opening and closing it quietly.

He hobbled down to the main entrance, turned up the coat collar and put on his trilby. The street lights on Queen Anne's Gate were always quite dim, and there were relatively few of them. Kelson thought this was because it was more residential than a work place. As he came closer to his car, he stopped and looked at the building on his right. It was further back than the others, and was of special interest to him.

In 1970, the TV Show called *The Persuaders!* had quite a few scenes here. Roger Moore and Tony Curtis were the stars. Kelson and his wife had been fans of it.

Fourteen years ago, he thought, continuing to look at this, shaking his head in sadness, then staring at the pavement. *If only things had been different.*

He limped over to the Passat and climbed in. Before starting the engine, he opened the glove box and smiled into it. There was a photocopy of Cannon's *actual* letter in there. Sat in the darkness, he glanced up at Lord Atkins's window. "Fuck you," he said out loud, "that's my safety net." Then he drove away.

Lord Atkins stood looking down as Kelson's car as it disappeared. He walked to the office door, switched the lights back on and sat down again at his desk. The hands were now set steeple-style, touching his lips, his right one still throbbing from whacking the table in frustration over Kelson. *Still* he thought, *at least that fuckwit is expendable.*

He looked at the fax machine over by the door. Those things were the most secure way of sending information. Letters could be removed from postal delivery depots and 'phones could be easily tapped. But having to smuggle faxes out of offices was not easy, that's why they recruited those bloody fake cleaners to do it.

Speaking to a *'computer wizard'* in the Whitehouse, when paying a visit to the American Secret Service Department, Atkins was told something interesting.

He said that before long, people could communicate to each other with computers, interconnected with phone lines. That way, files could be sent across and viewed on monitors. But he also mentioned his concern about something called *'hacking.'* This was the same method as telephone call recording, using additional computer units. Perhaps it was yet another future nightmare.

The world is getting more dangerous, he thought. But, whatever the future might hold, he needed to resolve this potential Cannon issue before it spun out of control. The buff coloured file now sat open, as he leant over it and switched on the large, gold hued, desk lamp. Page one stated:

**Secretary of State, Home Office
Visa Regulations
Subject to the Official Secrets Act
March 29th 1938**

This information is to be kept permanently under lock and key.

Lord Atkins then turned to the next page; something he'd read many times over the years. It confirmed the importance of immediate actions.

Section one:
Following the annexation (Anschluss) of Austria by Germany on twelfth of March 1938, Britain is no longer to sanction any currently existing Visas of Austrian citizens when immigration is being attempted into this country, effective from third of April 1938.

Any attempted arrivals into Britain considered as non-sanctioned, shall be deported under the auspices of local Police stations with written confirmation by officers at the rank of Inspector or above. All confirmations are to be returned to this department using instructed procedures.

None of these written confirmations are to be shown to any other officers or relayed to members of the public or any other government departments. Any such activity is to be treated as a violation of the official secrets act.

All deportations are to be made to Germany or its occupied zones.

Section two:
In the event of a declaration of war, there shall be no accepted emigration from any country that is allied to, or is an occupied zone by Germany or associated nations.

The Aliens act of 1905 is to be repealed in the event war being declared with Germany to ensure that further Jewish migrations shall not be sanctioned in Britain.

Lord Atkins then turned over the last page and glanced at the footnote.

'Visa regulatory administration completed for the Permanent Assistant Home Office Secretary, March 29th 1938. by **Walter John Cannon Esq.**'

Sitting back in his chair, he looked up at the ceiling, considering the dark history again. The danger lay in that small detail that had been kept locked up since 1938. Atkins was pushing the boundaries of his contrived role for government secrecy dangerously far. Aside from that, his sympathy for the potential greatness that *Nazism* could have brought to this country, overpowered him again.

He slid open his desk drawer and placed the buff coloured file in it, continuing to think about history. Yes, a lot was known about what happened during Hitler's reign by the people of Britain. But some things had been hidden from virtually everyone, even those who ran the country, thank goodness.

Walter Cannon had been dealt with after he had completed this in 1938. But what if he knew the truth and passed it over to someone before his removal? The catastrophe of this was too much to even think about, it could bring the image of this sacred land to its knees, at a key time when global economies were about to grow staggeringly, with Britain as one of its leaders.

That letter written by Walter Cannon's son, Rupert was frightening. It might not have been completely accurate, but was very close. If it hit the press, especially globally, it could be like that *Watergate* thing. Somehow, Walter Cannon might have given this secrecy to his son and perhaps, others.

Lighting up a slim-panatela, his multi-facetted mind spun, as he blew out a cloud of smoke. *I need to go rouge.* He said to himself. *This cannot go any further. One day a glorious leader shall come back and make this place a new fatherland.*

Then he took Rupert Cannon's *real* letter to Linus MacColl that Kelson had previously collected, out of his top drawer, ripped it to shreds, screwed it up and set fire to it in his large ash tray. He smiled as it burned and crackled. "You all fucking deserve that," he said.

He stood up, took the panatela from his mouth with his left hand, extended his right arm from the neck, and it went up into the air with a straightened hand.

'Sieg Heil,' he shouted.

Chapter 9

Trans-ship, Trafford Park Estate, Manchester
8th October 1984

The distance from Midland Hotel to Trafford Park industrial estate was just four and a half miles, and took less than fifteen minutes along the A56. He pulled up outside the office of Trans-ship's warehouse at 08.40, so had twenty minutes left before the meeting. This place was much larger than expected. In fact, Linus thought it was bigger than the Rochester site.

Considering this winding back the seat, opening the window and lighting a Marlboro, it made sense. The vehicles operating out of here covered a larger area for deliveries than those in their southern base.

A number of warehouse doors were already open, as fork-lift drivers put pallets on board the articulated lorries, all of which had five axles. There were four being loaded up and another three waiting in line. They were clearly the recently type approved, thirty-eight tonners.

Staring across at the Panasonic R1, the signal was still on red. Heading into the City yesterday, it had gone green for a few minutes, but that was all. This was not a problem because the network wasn't going officially live until the 24th December, and up until then, was merely being spliced-up and tested.

He thought of Mike Sentinel's speech about there being *'a million users in thirty years.'* This made him laugh so much, he choked on the next Marlboro drag. *I need to stop this*, he thought, looking wistfully at the fag.

On the subject of Mike Sentinel, something had unfolded on his journey this morning, that underlined the man's bizarre personality, but also his thoughtfulness. On the A56, about halfway to the Trans-ship site, Linus had seen the Hilton Hotel. *As it was closer and probably cheaper, why did Mike change the booking to The Midland?* Then his naivety disappeared, and he realised why. *He did it out of kindness*. Robbie was right about him.

It was time to go in, so he lifted his brief case off the front passenger seat. Glancing at the glove-box, he thought about opening Mr Cannon's letter, which was still sealed up in there. No, he could not bring himself to do that, and decided to wait until he was with Sally-Anne later, that way he could get her moral support.

The reception area was old-style and very basic. The paint was peeling and the entrance space was empty, the walls had a number of old lorry photos on them, some in black and white, looking like pre-war images.

The drivers stood by them, wearing caps and what looked like leather overalls, with smiles on their faces, as pleased as punch. *I hope those guys made it through the war,* he thought. The lorries were marked **Edwards & Co Ltd.** He understood this. There had clearly been a brand change at some point, but the man he was meeting today *must* be linked to the founder. He could see a number of staff behind a glass-fronted area at the far end of the room.

A middle-aged woman with dark hair, wearing a telephone headset, slid open the window. "Can I help you?" she asked.

"I'm here to see Mr Edwards said Linus."

She passed him a large book full of previous visitors names, their company titles and the Trans-ship staff members they had come to see. Linus filled out the information and handed it back to her.

"Take a seat," she said. "I'll let him know."

Within a minute, the lady had contacted Mr Edwards, then she came into reception, via an access door at the end of the glass-fronted area.

"Follow me," she said, still wearing the headset but holding its disconnected cable in her left hand, whilst opening the far door with her right. "He's up on the first floor."

As they walked up, Linus considered the building to be around fifty years old. The stairs, walls and bannister giving out a slight image of *Art Deco* style.

The head-phoned lady knocked on the first door they came to on the second floor, and opened it, not bothering to wait for an approval to enter. Linus went in as John Edwards stood up. They shook hands and the man walked round his desk, waving at the comfortable looking pair of seats at the far end of the room, with a small table between them. On it sat a tea pot and two cups and saucers.

"Tea for two," said Edwards smiling as he poured it into the cups. "Thanks for taking the long journey up."

"I'm pleased to be here," said Linus. "You have got a really impressive facility."

Edwards nodded back as he sipped his tea, then placing the cup back on its saucer said. "We started up here in the early thirties, and although Rochester is now the head office because we have a higher volume of smaller traders in the south, the *largest* deliveries are still done out of here."

"I can only imagine how busy you must be Mr Edwards, which is why we want to do all the installs to suit you," said Linus, putting down his cup. "If you were to let me have the availability times of the lorries, then I can co-ordinate this with our local office, so the installers can come over to fit in with what works for you."

John nodded over, looking quite pleased to hear that and said.

"That would work well for us. We have read your contract of course, and are aware that the system doesn't go live for a while yet, so there is no panic. But we are always very busy in the last month of the year, so would like everything in place both here and in Rochester, by the end of November."

"I know that Jeannie Sands is planning to arrange that with Dave Grant, and our local installers are ready to start work." Responded Linus.

Edwards smiled at him, as he sipped his tea again and said. "You know Mr MacColl, Dave Grant was really keen on us going with *RADI-CAL* instead of the other lot." He put his cup down as Linus wondered what was coming next and Edwards continued. "Don't get me wrong, I think you are streets ahead because of your site installs and you have a very reasonable contract. You were the right decision, but for Dave, I think your Mrs Sands was the *tipping point*."

Linus understood that, but could find nothing to say in response. Fortunately, John carried on talking.

"Anyway, we have a plan. All our vehicle movements for the next fortnight after Wednesday have been listed, and we have set aside a bay-area in the depot, where your installers can have access for all the fitting work. So we can probably arrange for two lorries a day to be there."

"That sounds good," said Linus and then went on. "It should take around four hours for each to be fitted, which would enable twenty out of the thirty to be done."

Then he realised they probably operated seven days a week in shifts and added. "But if you are open over the weekends, we can cover that, so should manage all thirty."

"That would suit us," said Edwards as he stood up, "we operate seven days a week. Now, I'll show you around and introduce you to the foreman."

In the Midland's bar, Sally-Anne sat with her coffee, smoking a Marlboro and reading *Cosmopolitan*. It was now 13.30hrs and she wondered when Linus would be back. After they had an early breakfast and he'd set off for his meeting, she decided to take a stroll around part of the City. She had never been here before and wanted to see what it was like, but also needed to find the BBC studio for tonight's outing.

The weather was dry but overcast. She walked down past the massive Central Library, then turned right into Oxford Street, as she wanted to see the *Palace Theatre*. It was huge and she noticed it was Victorian style in some areas, but in others there seemed to have been more recent changes to the building, perhaps this was because it had taken a direct-hit in the war. There was no indication of the next show over the entrance, but a bill-board was up by the front doors, it said: *Coming in December. Pantomime Aladdin, starring Tommy Trinder and Annika Rice.*

She strolled on, and many of the buildings looked drab to her. There was a mixture of boarded up old ones and dull and grey newer places that didn't co-ordinate. And then there were the gaps. She considered that these were still a left-over from those huge bombing raids this City had taken.

There was less traffic than she thought there would be. In fact, more people seemed to be moving around in single-decker buses and street walking than driving. But *something* felt decent about the place.

Looking around, she worked out why. The majority were together, not isolated like more and more were in every part of London. *I like this place.* She thought. *Maybe Mr MacColl and*

I could end up living here one day? She laughed and shook her head, the raven hair flicking.

Heading south, she noticed that Oxford Street then became Oxford *Road*. Strange. Up ahead, she saw the BBC studios. It was a big, grey building and a pretty short walk from the Midland, so they could have a couple in the bar, then stroll down before tonight's event. She guessed that was going to be something very special, there was every chance they would *actually* meet *Sade*.

Sally-Anne turned back, then crossed the road into Portland Street. On the left, there was something rather strange. A Chinese market, full of stalls with pots, cups, saucers, plates and lots of *objet d'art*, and at the far end, a mass of food, with rice, meat and fish, being cooked in metal pans over burners on *Calor* gas bottles. The stench was overpowering. *Yuk*.

It was manic and crowded in here. Walking along past a long stall, she noticed a rather eye catching China doll, with bright red cheeks and a sort of high-browed, black hair. She picked the doll up from the stall and examined it carefully. It was the kind of thing her mum would like.

A short Chinese man in full, far-eastern regalia, clearly the stall-holder, came towards her and said. "This doll very rare, was made *specially* by my *friend* in *Hong-Kong* for me."

Sally-Anne looked at him deadpan and said. "How much?"

"Normally it would be at least ten pound, but I do *special* deal today *missy,* you pay eight pound."

She put the doll back down very gently, looked him in the eye and said. "No thanks."

Then turned her back on him, ready to walk away.

"No *missy,* as you are nice person, I do you a special deal, you give me seven pound."

She smiled, her back still turned on him, her heels clicking on the concrete floor as she took a very slow step to the exit.

"Sorry *missy,* I take six pound."

Sally-Anne stopped for a second, then took another, slower step forward.

"OK, five pound is last offer."

She spun round, holding up four fingers. "And that's mine," she said.

The man took her four pound notes and handed over a plastic carrier bag, then she walked out, checking her watch so that she'd know roughly how long the journey would take them tonight, as the BBC studio was only a short distance from here.

Kelson had been across the floor at another stall, pretending to look at this '*chink crap*', but was actually watching that dark haired cow. Today, he had his black overcoat on. It was bloody chilly up here, so he'd left the rain mac in the car. His trilby was pulled down and he didn't want anyone to see his face. He limped to the exit and watched her strut across the road, fast and confident like a stage actress, wearing very high-heels. *Fucking Yid bitch.* He said under his breath. *Be careful about crossing this road again luv, especially when darkness falls…*

Linus shook hands with Mr Edwards by Trans-ship's front door and walked back to the Cavalier feeling pleased with the outcome. Edwards and the foreman, had shown Linus around one of their many *Seddon Atkinson* trucks, so he could see available space for the Panasonic R1 installs.

There was plenty of room for the handset on the dashboard, and the *black box* power and aerial signal unit, could be fitted under the seats.

The truck's voltage was 24, but access to both its batteries meant the fitters could install onto just one of these, because the R1 only operated at 12volts. Linus measured up for cable lengths, then wrote all aspects onto his notepad. He used his Kodak Instamatic to take a few shots of the fitting areas, including the cab roof, for options on the aerial position. And all thirty of the lorries were the same. *Seddon Atkinsons.*

He felt sure there was enough information in his notes for presenting to the *RADI-CAL* technical team tomorrow. And if he needed anything more, the foreman said he could give him a call anytime via the switchboard.

As Linus walked into the Midland's café-bar, she placed her *Cosmopolitan* on the table.

"So, how did it go?" she asked.

"It was better than I thought," he said. "They have got a timetable and a place on-site ready for all the installs into these lorries. And the Director I met with has requested an HPU for his own use."

Sally-Anne looked at him and asked. "What's an HPU then?"

"Well," he said as he sat down across the table from her. "It's a *Hand Portable Unit.* They are made by *Motorola* in the States, imported by us and we put our *RADI-CAL* brand on them." He reached into his bag and took a brochure out.

"Take a look," he said, passing it over to her, remembering back to his time in Manhattan. "I saw a guy using one in New York, when I was working there."

"Oh yeah, that's called the '*brick*' isn't it?" she flicked the brochure over and looked at the back page, where a man stood out in the *sticks* with it against his head. "So how long does the battery last then?"

"Thirty minutes," he replied. "Then about ten hours to re-charge it."

She shook her head at the thought of that, still looking at the brochure. "That's a long time. What is the cost?"

"Just under four grand to you," he said, spitting on his hand and extending it over to her.

She laughed back and said. "Good one! I'll take that off what you owe, which includes what happened on *your* return from New York. Thanks for reminding me of that. *Shmuck.*"

Sally-Anne put down the brochure and looked Linus in the eye with a real depth of soul.

"Seriously though, why would anyone ever do this? I mean, supposing you're in London, this place, or *anywhere* else in the country," she shook her head, glancing at the room's window, the sun flickered across and touched gently onto her raven hair. "Why not just walk up to someone's door and say. *Hello, can I come in for a chat?"*

Sometimes, a magical gift came from her; he could never describe it, even to himself. It was like a connection in their souls*, like they had been together in a former life, in a different century and in another place in the world....*

"Well," he said, swallowing back the power of emotion that he felt. "They are not available until the end of March, but he's made an advance order."

"Why?" she asked. "Is it because he thinks they are going to be sold out if he doesn't do it now?"

"Could be," said Linus.

"He travels regularly from their site up here to the one in Rochester, by train apparently, but unless you are in central London, it won't work on the railway and I told him that.

The power is only about one watt, whereas the Panasonic fitted in the car I've got is *ten* watts. The *brick* won't ever pick up a signal or switch across the cells on a train."

"So why bother then?" she lit up two Marlboros and passed one over to him.

"Thanks," he said, taking in the first drag. "Well, apart from using trains he's got a Jag and doesn't want any holes drilled in it, so he can just keep it in the glove box I suppose."

She blew out a puff of smoke from her nose and said. "At least it's not a Rolls then, as it would be even worse, wouldn't it?"

˙He ignored this and said. "More importantly, I've finished for the day. Everything is set up for Trans-ship, so now all I've got to do, is go over to *RADI-CAL* on the edge of Manchester tomorrow morning, and that shouldn't take long."

She took the cigarette out of her mouth with her left hand, and gave a thumbs up with the right.

"What have you been up to?" he asked.

She reached into her bag and placed the doll on the table in front of him, then sat back, folded her arms and nodded at it and said. "So what do you think of that?"

"Well," he said staring at it, then shaking his head, "I think we should go up to our room…."

It was just coming up to 16.00hrs and Linus was up and about, wearing his blue polo neck jumper and jeans. Sally-Anne lay on the bed in a white fluffy dressing gown, with the Midland Hotel badge sewn onto it, as she read *The Times* newspaper. And that had been delivered free to their room, yet another good thing about this place.

"I'm just off to get something out of my car," he said. "Won't be a minute."

She lowered the paper and waved at him as he went through the door.

He walked into the lift, pressed the ground floor button, and it slowly took him down.

The door opened and he noticed the reception and café-bar were virtually empty. There was a group at a table, and over on the far side, a man sat with a newspaper hiding up his face, only the very top of his trilby hat was visible.

Linus opened one of the front doors and walked out into Peter Street. The Cavalier was just a few yards away and he only wanted to do a couple of things. One was to see if there was any live signal on the Panasonic, so he could call Mike Sentinel, although he doubted that, so would call him from the hotel later, and to collect the envelope from Rupert Cannon. He felt he just had to open it now, and would do this back up in the room, with Sally-Anne by his side.

As he went out into the street, Dick Kelson put down his paper and stood up. He limped slowly towards the door, and the gang at the bar table glanced up at him. He was used to that, but it was always bloody annoying. But there was something else that worried him. If Lord Atkins found out how bad his limp *really* was, well that didn't bear thinking about…

Linus opened up the Cavalier's door and jumped in. He switched on the ignition and pressed the PWR button on the Panasonic R1 and waited to see if it went on to green. There was a lot of test work going on by *RADI-CAL's* site engineers, and if the local cell was powered up, it *could* be live.

He waited a few minutes, but it stayed on red. Deciding to be patient a bit longer, his mind went back to that Motorola 8000 *brick's* running time.

The battery type had been a big point of discussion during the training course. It was called a *Ni-Cad or Nickel-cadmium.*

These new things had specific rules. The battery had to be initially run flat and then steadily charged over ten hours, or the thirty minutes of call time would not happen. He needed to make this clear to Mr Edwards.

The instruction manual would include this when he finally got the *brick* delivered, but Linus felt it could bring *RADI-CAL* into disrepute with Trans-ship, if he didn't warn Edwards beforehand, and they were now a *big* customer. Besides, the RITON Group way was always to be forthright and honest in all aspects of business.

That's it, I'm going, he decided as the Panasonic was still on red. He switched off the ignition, pulling out the Cavalier's annoyingly modern, double sided key, with a plastic square top on it. Then he opened the glove-box and took out the envelope.

Kelson had gone into a green-grocers shop on the other side of the road, and slightly behind the Cavalier. He'd chosen this spot because it meant he could look across the road through the shop's window, and see if MacColl took what he was hoping for out of the car.

In front of him were two large trays of potatoes, one being *Whites* and the other *King Edwards*. He made it seem as if he was making a choice between them, but kept glancing across the road. The shop keeper looked over at him as he twirled the top edges of a brown paper bag around and handed it to an old lady, who stuffed it into her grey, *wheelie bag ankle scraper.*

The shop keeper was about to ask the trilby-hatted bloke what he wanted, but then saw him hobble out of the door, not buying a single spud. *Time wasting old git.* He thought.

Linus had already passed the shop on the opposite pavement carrying a white envelope. Kelson knew exactly what was in it, and hoped this had been left in that car since the meeting at Croydon Aerodrome with Cannon's PA.

This was all about luck now. If this *git* hadn't opened it yet, which was possible, otherwise he wouldn't be carrying it into the hotel, then it all depended on *when* he was going to.

He guessed MacColl was going out on the town with that *bitch* tonight, so it would be straightforward for him to get into their room and check.

He had the replacement to put in the envelope ready. If this worked, then MacColl would be none the wiser and Lord Atkins's concern would be over. But, if this envelope *had* been opened, then he would need to *remove* both of these annoying *fuckers*.

Sally-Anne was still lying on the bed reading *The Times* as Linus came back in. "Hello," she said. "And how can I help you today?" she tossed the paper on the floor, rolled onto her side, pulled open the dressing gown, flashed her body's front and closed it back up. "I can do you a discount as there is no music."

"Thanks but no thanks," he replied. "I already owe you more than I can afford."

"Oh well," she sighed, "you're the looser. Anyway, the least you can do is organise an early dinner. We need to be out of here at seven."

Linus called Mike Sentinel from the pay-phone in the Midland Hotel's reception area. Julia put him through, as he pushed a 50p into the slot. Manchester was a long way from the Kent office and he knew this would not last very long and so did Sentinel.

He knew that, because Mike opened up very quickly on the subject of Trans-ship. "Mmm, is everything fixed up for the installs?"

"Yes," replied Linus, "availability of the thirty trucks has been diarised and a reserved install place has been set-up. "I'm off to our Manchester office to get everything arranged in the morning."

"Alrighty," said Mike. "And make sure that Jason takes responsibility for that and keep a copy of his full commitment. If something goes wrong, it'll be down to his lot."

"Understood," said Linus, minimising the call time, it would not have long left.

"Good, and how is the frozen north?"

"The Midland Hotel is a great place Mike. I appreciate you organising this. Tonight I'm out on the town and…"

The pay-phone started bleeping and he rummaged in his pocket for another 10p or 50p but there wasn't any. The call died and that usual, long *burr* was coming out. He looked at the handset and put it back on the hook. *Oh well,* he thought, *job done.*

He stepped back from the booth and looked over to the café-bar, considering the potential of opening time. Then he saw that man again, the trilby hat over the top of the newspaper reminded him of that old comedian, Tommy Trinder.

Linus glanced at his Seiko, this bloke was still sat reading the same paper when he went out to his car an hour ago. *Bit sad*, he thought. Anyway, he needed to get on. The restaurant opened soon at 17.30hrs, and the plan was to eat and then get in the bar for a quick one, before heading out to the BBC studio.

It was 19.00hrs when they arrived in the bar. Sally-Anne wore a plain black-dress and a touch of red lip gloss. Her shoes were the same red stilettos she'd worn most of the day, and the raven hair was extraordinary.

But it always was as if she was a star in a movie. The other thing which made her so very different, was her speed of being ready to go in a few minutes. There was no *try on this, try on that* and then spending ages stood in front of a mirror. No, she was a natural in every way. His love for her was now for real. He trusted her completely. But *why* did she want to be with him?

Linus ordered a Dry-Martini and lemonade and a lager-top. They touched glasses and he lit up two Marlboros and passed one over to her.

"So, how do think tonight is going to pan-out?" he asked.

"Well," she said taking a sip from her chilled glass. "If you think about it, *Sade's* album *Diamond Life* came out in July, and dad said it's sold about a million copies already. He also reckons there is another coming out next year, so maybe some of the new songs are going to be played tonight in the studio."

"Is there a chance we could get her autograph?" he asked.

She took a drag on her Marlboro and said. "Well, if you were generous enough to buy her and the band a drink in the BBC's bar after the first session, she might."

"I didn't know they had a bar in there," he said somewhat surprised.

"They have but it's not for all the *plebs,* and dad would have arranged for us to go in."

"That is truly amazing," said Linus taking another sip of his lager-top.

"It is, but of course guests are only allowed in if they have paid what they owe someone." She replied, pointing at herself.

They walked out onto Peter Street and crossed over, now heading towards Oxford Street. Daylight was fading, they both turned and looked back to the Midland Hotel, as Linus quietly sang:

"Hitler has only got one ball
The other is in the Albert Hall
His mother, the dirty bugger
Cut it off when he was small"

She laughed. It seemed Hitler was a lover of the Midland Hotel and after he had invaded Britain, would steal it and stay there, so he insisted that the *Luftwaffe* made sure their bombers didn't dare drop anything on it. And they didn't. Unlike what they did to the rest of Manchester.

They walked on arm in arm, and Linus had a flashback to what Mr Cannon had said to him at Croydon Aerodrome. But he was not going to allow past sadness to spoil tonight.

Under cover of darkness, in an empty building's doorway on the side of the road, out stepped Kelson. He watched them turn the corner, now heading towards Oxford Street.

Fuckers, he said under his breath. *This country would have done away with scum like you if Adolf had won.* He was in his raincoat now, as he felt the storm was coming. In his inside pocket sat the replacement for his faked up Rupert Cannon letter. He turned up his collar, pulled down the edge of the trilby and limped across the road to the Midland Hotel.

Chapter 10

*Sevenoaks, Kent
8th October 1984*

Mike Sentinel sat back in one of the lounge chairs. His large detached house *Green Trees,* sat on the edge of a wooded area near Sevenoaks. It had been impossible to be accurate about the age of this place, as it had been altered so many times over the years. But he considered it early seventeenth century. He didn't care. Low beams, open fires, curved walls, large garden, no passing traffic and an atmosphere of delight, made him content.

It had been a busy day at the *RADI-CAL* office, but an exceptionally good one. Linus was doing better than he thought *up north*. There was *something* decent about him. Jeannie had signed up another transport company, albeit smaller than Trans-ship and her previous one. But it proved that delivery businesses were starting to realise how important cell phones *could* be. He thought about her for a moment, remembering their days at Rate-Syrex. She was a *bloody good sales woman.* She never missed a trick.

Then, his mind edged back to when she split up with her first husband. He glanced around the room as the open fire crackled and passed out its warm glows. Yes, she'd stayed here with him and his wife Matilda for quite a while then. But he often wondered what had *really* caused the split.

Jeannie had used an expression to them, one that he'd never forgotten. *"We've run out of road."* She said, shaking her head.

He put down the paperwork and removed his glasses. He *needed* to help people. Sometimes they were not what they seemed, but it didn't matter. Always be there for them, guide them down the right path, pick them up when they fell. He could never make up for the terrible thing he did so long ago. It was a mistake, if only he could turn back the clock. But ever since, he'd always tried to give help wherever he could.

Then he picked up his glasses and held them at arm's length towards the fire place. He shook his head, the weird mop of hair flicking about as usual. He could see nothing without these thick lenses. As a child, his father had constantly scolded him for taking his glasses off. "You are a boy with poor eyesight. Don't be an idiot, you must wear them and keep them *clean*. If you don't then I shall punish you, or one day, you'll make the *devil of a mistake*."

Despite his father being harsh, he was always right. Mike thought about this constantly and would for the rest of his life. If only he had *understood* his father. He should have really *listened*, just because he was a child, was not an excuse.

The tiredness of today kicked in and as he dozed off, the nightmare came back ….

Aden, 10th November 1967. The Westland Wessex MK V helicopter took off from *HMS Albion*. Below it dangled a large bag of stores for the men of 42 Commando, but also included necessities for the *Ferret and Saladin* armoured cars, that were out of action and needed fixing before they could make it to the beach, and then onto a landing craft. This was thought by the Head of Operations to be safer than bringing. *HMS Albion* into the docks. Otherwise, she could be subject to attack by the enemy, the National Liberation Front or *NLF*.

It was not so much the loss of these *scout* armoured cars that mattered, they were all old and clapped-out in some cases. It was more the embarrassment caused if they were captured by the *NLF*. Bad press for Britain.

Mike Sentinel sat in between his six mechanics. The de Havilland *Gnome* engine was loud and that heavy bag dangling and swinging below the Wessex, caused a vibration throughout the helicopter, but they were coming in close from the Arabian Sea, so landing would not take long.

They came in near the perimeter fence, around it circled a squad of RAF patrol troops, watching attentively through the wire, their FN rifles held at the ready. The temperature was up to eighty-eight degrees Fahrenheit, even though it was still only 07.35hrs. It was stifling in the helicopter, despite its fuselage door having been open all the way from *HMS Albion*.

Before the wheels touched down, a group of soldiers came in and put the hanging bag onto a large trolley, disconnecting the cable and then moving it away. The Wessex touched down and Lieutenant Mike Sentinel and his team jumped out, crouching low, as they moved away under the spinning rotor.

A number of RAF men ran over to the Wessex and climbed aboard. The British military were now reducing in numbers quickly, as their presence in Aden was nearly over. Sentinel and his team marched towards a building around one hundred yards away by the entrance gate. An RAF Sergeant stood by it, started moving towards them. He noticed Mike's shoulder pips, came to attention and saluted.

"Morning Sir," he said. "Can I be of assistance?"

"*Mmm*," said Sentinel. "We are responsible for armoured car work before shipping out, *alrighty*." He pointed over at the trolley containing the bag from the Wessex. "Some of our kit is in there, the rest is for Forty Second Commando."

"Right Sir, I'll get that put into the office here, then I'll arrange transport to the broken down armoured cars."

"Carry on Sergeant," he said as they both saluted.

Corporal Wallace drove the Land-Rover 109 towards the perimeter about one kilometre away, where all the broken down, six-wheeled scout vehicles were laid up. The screen was down, and so the wind coming towards them as they hit thirty miles an hour brought in a tirade of dust. The desert air was humid, and the temperature felt as if it was up in the nineties now. Mike's glasses were covered in dust and he had the taste of sand in his dry mouth.

This was not what he had been expecting. The plan for assisting the UN peace keeping force with vehicle maintenance in Israel had been changed at the last minute. They had been switched to Aden. It was about the politics of not leaving some old armoured vehicles behind, as Britain pulled out of here for good.

Mike would have felt happier about this job, if Sergeant Robbie Robson had been here. Robbie was good mechanic, a brave soldier and had good *people skills*.

But, he was still in convalescence after that cock up in Scotland.

Wallace pulled up the Land-Rover by the row of *scouts*, all backed up against the fence. Mike stepped out of the passenger's seat, took a handkerchief from the pocket of his khaki shorts and wiped his glasses, they were caked in dust and sweat. There were a total of ten scout vehicles, the majority *Ferrets,* fitted with Rolls-Royce engines. They all been hand painted in a desert fawn colour and in some areas, the original olive green was still visible. These things were not really designed to work in these conditions. No wonder they had often over-heated, causing engine damage.

The rest of his troops jumped down from the tailgate and lifted out the parts bag, placing it up onto the front of a scout. On some of them, a few of the tyres were flat, but luckily these were only on the *Saladin's* and being six-wheelers, they could still make it down to the beach.

Wallace told each of the five Privates to check out a vehicle and report back the *sit rep* to him quickly. This was the first part of the plan that Mike had told him to carry out. The next was to assess the others. The ones that could be saved would be worked on, and taken to the beach. Those not repairable would have the engines drained of oil and started where possible to seize them up, wiring ripped out, weapons removed and tyres punctured. They would not be useful captures for the NLF.

The men got started efficiently as Mike walked around the vehicles, glancing at his wrist watch. But his glasses had misted up again in that mixture of soaring heat and sweat from his brow, so he had to wipe them before he could see the time. It was 08.10hrs.

The boys had stepped in through the turret hatches and were checking as much as they could by using their torches. If there had been fuel leaks, they needed to find these before switching on any of the electrics. The process of then working through the problems that had caused them to be out of action, would then be followed. It was a step-by-step procedure that Lt Mike Sentinel was excellent at managing.

Another RAF patrol guard walked past behind the scouts and didn't even look at Mike, the guy was clearly very focused on any movements he could see in the desert behind the road around the aerodrome. He held his FN rifle tightly, the barrel down but he was clearly ready if the NLF started up an attack.

Mike watched the man continue to walk slowly along, by the perimeter fence. He saw him cover about one hundred yards, then looked round at the scout armoured cars.

The mechanics were still inside checking carefully. *Good men*, Mike said to himself, *I'm very proud of you*.

The sun was dazzling now and more sweat trickled down his brow. He pulled out his handkerchief again, then took off his thick glasses and wiped them. He put the hanky back into his left pocket, behind the holster of his *Browning Hi-Power automatic*.

In the distance to the left, he saw a faint dust cloud starting to rise. The cloud increased and as it did so, the sun glinted off a vehicle creating it, on the road behind the perimeter. As it got closer, it began to slow down. It was now only a few hundred yards away.

Mike looked over towards the RAF patrol guard, but he was now a good three hundred yards away. He stared at the car's front as it came closer, and could see it was a *Morris Oxford* saloon. Mike was quite an expert on these. He knew they were also made in India, and were called the *Hindustan Ambassador* for the last ten years.

It was dark in colour and covered in dust, and he couldn't tell where it had been built, because the bonnet's name badge was filthy, but also his glasses were becoming soaked in sweat again.

The car ground to a halt by the perimeter fence, opposite the second scout from the end. It was a *Ferret*; Corporal Wallace was inside it.

The dust cloud started to ease off now the car had stopped, Sentinel walked slowly towards the perimeter fence.

Both front doors opened and two men jumped out. It was left hand drive, and the man on the far side was taller and larger. *Must have been the one behind the wheel then,* thought Mike. But although he'd wiped them again, his glasses were now picking up the dust created by the car as it pulled up.

He unfastened the flap on his holster, in case he needed to take action. They could be NLF attackers.

Both men stood looking at Mike as the dust settled. They had black *thobes* and *khurtas* on their heads. Although they were surrounded by dust and his glasses were picking that up, he noticed they were smiling and his gut instinct told him they were decent men, probably just stopped to take a look at the armoured scout cars. The pressure was off and Mike walked on.

Suddenly, the hatch on the *Ferret* flew open, as Corporal Wallace climbed out of the turret. In that instant, Mike saw the smaller man on the nearside of the car reach back inside it and take something out. The mist on his glasses had increased, this situation having caused more perspiration. Everything was a blur. The man held something black and he moved it up to his face. *He's aiming a pistol at Wallace!,* thought Mike.

Sentinel felt as if he were in a slow motion film scene. His right hand took the Browning from his holster and as he brought it up, he flicked off the safety catch and held the pistol as far away and as close to the man who was clearly aiming at Wallace, as possible. He squeezed the trigger and fired through the fence. He saw the man fall, the *pistol* he'd been aiming at Wallace leaving his grip and hitting the ground.

He turned the Browning across to the other man, but could see, even though the blur was even worse, that he had now run over to the one who was down.

Mike moved towards the fence, still aiming at the man, who was kneeling down by the one he had shot. A huge cry of emotion came from him, and Wallace now up alongside Mike, stood looking through the fence and then turned very slowly to his officer.

Mike Sentinel took off his glasses, wiped them and put them back on. He stared in horror as he saw what he had done.

The man kneeling down and crying, was desperately trying to revive a teenage boy. Mike looked across to what he'd believed was a gun that the boy had held up to shoot Wallace. Even though he was only a youngster, he *could* still have shot him. Only he hadn't done that.

The *pistol* was a black *camera*.

The man on reception duty had already spotted Dick Kelson in the Midland Hotel's café bar earlier today, so gave him a smile, nodded over to it, and said. "Good to see you again sir, how did you find the service?"

Kelson clocked it as being useful, and if he did this right, it would be easy to find MacColl and that *bitch's* room. "Very good," he said, lying as he didn't order anything this afternoon, "I was hoping to give something to my nephew, who's staying here. He's Mr Linus Simon MacColl."

The receptionist looked down into his room file, scrolling his finger across, clearly looking for MacColl's name. Kelson jumped in with a classic method of finding a potential victim's room number.

"Linus mentioned the number to me earlier, twenty-four. I think he said."

"Actually," said the receptionist now finding it in the file, "it's thirty-five."

"Yes," said Kelson. "That's it. Silly me."

The receptionist looked down to the room key hooks under the counter. "Looks as if Mr MacColl has gone out. Oh yes, I remember now, it was only a few minutes ago."

"Blast," said Kelson, "I've just missed him. Never mind I'll go and get myself a drink and I can see him later."

The receptionist smiled and nodded at Kelson as he walked over towards the bar area. But when the receptionist turned his back to him, he hobbled as fast as he could to the lifts. One of them had just arrived on the ground floor and the door opened. *Lucky one,* thought Kelson as two guests came out and he went in, quickly pressing button number three.

The lift bell sounded as at it arrived on the third floor. Kelson hobbled out and walked down the corridor, trilby hat still on, collar turned up and looking for room thirty-five. As he came up to the door, he looked up and down the corridor and listened for any movement. From his coat pocket, he took out a bunch of brass *skeleton* keys.

Kelson had done this thing before. He looked carefully at the door handle's key slot and measured this up in his mind against one of the skeleton's that might work. He needed to move quickly, one of the lifts was on the move and he heard laughter from the next room, he reckoned the occupants were getting ready to go out.

The first key was too thick and the second too long. But the third slipped in and he turned and wiggled it very gently. The door opened and he went straight in, just as the next room's occupants came out. He shut the door behind him and lent against it. *Phew,* he thought, *just made it.*

He left the room lights turned off and took his small torch out of the coat pocket.

The curtains were open and he was not going to touch them or anything else for that matter, except an envelope. He'd already put on his gloves in the lift and now started to look around the room. It was actually tidy in here. This was a surprise, as he thought the *bitch* would have left clothes and bags all over the place. But no, apart from a dressing gown on the bed and a newspaper on the sideboard, it was clear.

He moved the torch around the room again and it picked up on the wardrobe. He carefully opened one of its two doors and shone it onto the clothes. Apart from a suit, an overcoat and a dress, it was virtually empty. Then he pointed the torch down and saw a brief case. He put his gloved hand on the handle and lifted it out.

Opening it up carefully, he saw this was full of paperwork and brochures. Gently lifting one out, he put it up to his face and shone the torch over it.

He laughed as he looked at the *unbelievable shit* on the front cover.

RADI-CAL CELLULAR RADIO TELEPHONES.
*GO **OUT** AND PHONE **IN** AT ANYTIME!*
For business and pleasure!

There were three photos alongside each other underneath this. One had a bloke sat in a car with a sort of narrow plastic strip covered in round buttons against his head, then a man on a building site wearing a safety helmet and holding a big metal box with a different shaped strip connected by a curly cable. The last one was a *geezer* on a street corner holding a grey coloured *brick* by his head, with a long *rubber duck* aerial.

Fucking mad, he thought as he slid the brochure back in and continued to look into the bag, holding the small torch between his teeth, and there it was. The envelope from Cannon's PA. *Yes!*

He took it out and looked at it carefully. The crux was if this had been opened or not.

Kelson examined the envelope's flap. It looked untouched. Now was the difficult bit, to open it without tearing. He took a small plastic sleeve out of his pocket and slipped out the razor blade. He looked down, and eased the blade under the edge of the flap, keeping his torch steady between his teeth.

He eased it in and very steadily moved it across as the flap came up, undamaged.

Taking the fake letter from Cannon out, he examined it for anything that would indicate it had been looked at. There were no marks or tears on it. This was good news for him and maybe he'd get a thank you from Lord Atkins, although that was *fucking* unlikely.

He would not have to *deal* with MacColl and that *bitch* either. Whilst it saved him a difficult job, he'd wouldn't have minded that – especially with *her*.

He took a folded sheet from the inside pocket of his suit jacket. The torch picked up the details. *Triumph Stag, Road Impressions, September 1973, Motorsport Magazine.*

Kelson smiled as he slid it very carefully into the envelope and smoothed down the flap. He placed it back in MacColl's bag and closed the wardrobe door. He folded the original letter and slid it into his inside pocket. Job done.

They walked into the BBC studio's reception in Oxford Road. It was bright in here, with modern, flush ceiling lights. The front desk was silver coloured, with the **BBC** logo in large black letters. A red haired young woman stood behind it smiled at them, as Sally-Anne showed her their event pass.

"Hello," she said, "welcome to the show. The film crew and the band are doing a sound check, so please feel free to use the bar as you have a *special* invite."

She waved towards a door on the left. Linus and Sally-Anne both smiled and thanked her, then made their way across the floor. He held open the door and followed her in, thinking about the *special invite*. There were only a few people in here, mostly stood together at the bar. Sally-Anne opened her purse, taking out a fiver.

"What would you like?" she asked and then carried on. "No don't tell me, let me guess, it's coming to me, yes that's it. A lager-top."

Linus looked at her with no reaction or humour and said flatly. "Thanks."

"My pleasure," she said lighting up two Marlboros and passing one over to him. "I'll just add it on to your bill."

In the studio behind the bar, the band started to play. A crescendo of sound came in; everything from drums, guitars, piano and the incredible, soulful voice of a singing goddess. It was Helen Folasade Adu. *Sade.*

They stared at each other, as if *imagining* being somewhere is one thing, but the *reality* is something *very* different.

The band continued, keys and harmonies going from one level to another, clearly checking the BBC's sound recording equipment before the filming event started.

Linus looked at Sally-Anne and said in all seriousness. "This is going to be one heck of a night."

He imagined that one of her sarcastic humour responses was on the way, but it wasn't. Instead, she reached gently out with her left hand and touched his face. One of the bar's ceiling lights glinted off her silver bracelet's Star of David for a split second.

A feeling of mystic connection came into both of them. *I want to tell you where my mind is, in a different country, in a different century, both of us together in a different life. But I can't, because you'll think I'm crazy.*

She moved slowly to the bar, both looking at each other, strangely overwhelmed.

The cameras were manned, the lighting was in position, the audience were all there and then *Sade Adu* came up onto the stage. She was wearing a black top, slightly off the shoulders, black trousers, hair swept back with a long pony-tail, large black round earrings, bright red lipstick and black leather gloves. The band followed, with their instruments ready and everyone in the studio cheered and clapped with passion.

The group was up on the centre stage, and they were almost completely encircled by the audience. There were seats slightly behind the band on the right, but most were stood waiting for the music to start.

Sally-Anne and Linus were to the left of the stage and near the back of the studio. The lighting was extraordinary, with so many electrically lit colours behind panels around the room and in the ceiling. The band had tube lights in pairs vertically around them, that flashed around continuously from one to the next and created a sort of maroon glow effect. The whole ambience was stylish, yet very laid back. The BBC had done a good job, because it really matched Sade's style.

Sade stood behind the microphone and all the band were with their instruments and clearly ready to start. The studio producer raised his hand and did a *three, two, one* countdown for the band, as the camera men began operating.

The musicians started, the saxophone player leading brilliantly, and then Sade stepped up to her microphone, lifted her gloved hands and started the vocal of *Your love is king*. It sounded *just* like the album track, but Linus was convinced this was being played live, because every action from the band was *exact* with the music.

The atmosphere was electric.

Sally-Anne Cohen was giving out a *lip-sync* of the words from the second line, as she looked into the eyes of Linus MacColl.

Your love is king... never need to part
Your love is king... round and round and round my head
Touching the very part of me
It's making my soul sing
Tearing the very heart of me
I'm crying out for more.

Everyone was rocking slowly and gently, right across the room. The camera men continued to move around, and as the song finished, the audience all cheered and clapped towards the band. The musicians began to get ready for the next one and as they did, the studio producer lifted a finger against his lips, and looked around the room, so that all the audience members would realise they needed to keep quiet.

The band started and everyone knew from the first notes that it was *Smooth Operator*.

Despite the studio producer's insistence, there were whistles of excitement, but the band carried on. In fact, it added to the content of the filming.

The guitar, conga drums and saxophone came in, and then the voice of Sade.

The entire audience began to dance slowly, swaying to the music. Sally-Anne did the *lip-sync* again and moved around Linus. For a split second, he imagined she was going to strip, not sure that the BBC would approve of that.

Thinking back to meeting at the RITON office in Croydon a month ago, he never believed they would have been together in Manchester at a live concert, performed by someone who would surely soon be a global superstar.

The song also reminded him of his first experience when out with the *RADI-CAL* lot in the *Anchor* pub, and then, being played in the *Sandrock* with Sally-Anne, a little over a week ago.

All the tracks were played from the *Diamond Life* album. The band then received a huge round of applause and shouts of delight from the audience. It seemed the show was over, the camera men came away, the band left the studio and moved towards the bar door, being patted on the back by the audience as they went.

Linus guessed the band were going in for a well-earned drink. He fancied one or two pints himself, but assumed the bar would now be private. The audience were guided to the exit door by the BBC staff, and Linus and Sally-Anne were the last in line. As they moved slowly towards it, a few of them lifted their passes and the staff waved them towards the bar door. Sally-Anne smiled at Linus and he remembered they also had the *special* invite.

They walked in, and it was full of atmosphere. There was laughter, the bar staff were busy, and clouds of cigarette smoke were in the air. Over to the left stood the band, but Sade was not with them. Linus and Sally-Anne stood waiting for the barmaid to come over. Then Sade came through the entrance. Both of them gasped together. She looked exactly as she did earlier in the studio and when on television. There was a real sense of style and class about her that exuded beautifully. She was a natural.

The barmaid came over and asked them what they would like.

"Gin and tonic and a pint of lager-top please." Said Linus, guessing what Sally-Anne wanted. He could see her mind was still focussed on Sade.

Linus lit up two Marlboros and passed one to her. "Do you think we could meet her?" he whispered into Sally-Anne's ear, as if overcome by the fear of Sade hearing his question.

She looked at Linus, took a drag of her Marlboro and said. "Once we've got the drinks, we should wander over."

As they approached the band, the BBC studio producer had joined them and he offered ciggies around, and most including Sade, lit up.

Linus and Sally-Anne were close now, and stood looking as if they were in a discussion, but were actually trying to get a glance, and then a link to an introduction. A long-shot, but worth a try.

Sade looked over and smiled at them, no doubt aware of what they were trying to do, thought Linus. But then she seemed to recognise something about Sally-Anne.

"Excuse me." She said to the guys standing next to her, and then came over.

"Hi," she said to Sally-Anne, who looked back in surprise. "I saw you across the floor tonight, and liked your moves."

Sally-Anne recovered and said. "Thank you so much. We thought you were fabulous." Linus nodded in agreement, trying to find something appropriate to say. But he couldn't.

Sade took a drag on her cigarette and then went over to the bar's ash tray, stubbed it and came back to them. *She has got real class*, thought Linus. *Not an over-privileged celebrity who might have dropped that and then, ground it in to the carpet.*

"I hope you guys are staying the for the next session." She said to them.

Linus looked at her smiling, not realising there was a *next session.* Sally-Anne said.

"Absolutely, we're looking forward to it. That'll be for the new album, won't it?"

"It is. Not all of the tracks have been made, but some have and we'll play a few."

Sally-Anne said. "That's great. Have you got the new album title yet?"

"No, not yet," replied Sade, looking back over at the band. "There's a lot of ideas, but it won't be out until next year. So what do you guys do?"

Linus and Sally-Anne looked at each other, neither sure who should speak first on this subject. *A stripper or someone trying to sell mobile radio telephones.* Tricky. Linus went first.

"I work for a company that is networking cellular mobile phones next year." He said.

"Wow," replied Sade. "I've heard about these coming in. I've seen people with them in America. That's *really* interesting. I think that's going to be *massive*."

Linus smiled at her, and one of the band members looked over tapping his watch. It was clearly time for them to get back on the stage.

She smiled, shook hands with them both, then walked back to the band and the BBC studio manager. All the group headed off to the door.

Sally-Anne looked at him, shaking her head, the raven hair flicking and then sarcastically said. *"Oh, that's going to be massive!"*

"Jealousy," said Linus, looking at her pretentiously, "gets you nowhere."

Kelson was in a phone-box on the outskirts of Manchester, with his collar turned up and trilby-hat pulled down. Over the mouthpiece, he'd placed a handkerchief and, as Lord Atkins answered, he pushed in the 10p.

"Hello," said Lord Atkins. "Who's calling?"

"It's Kelson sir, I just wanted to let you know the mission is completed and the item had not been read."

"Right, before you say anything Kelson, take that *fucking* hanky off the mouthpiece."

Kelson removed the handkerchief, cursing under his breath, *fuck you, your Lordship, it's supposed to be for our safety.*

"All previous information removed and replaced Sir." He said.

"Are you *sure* this had not been read?" asked Atkins.

"Yes, I am sure." Replied Kelson.

"Well you'd better be right old man. Because if it turns out you are not, then being shot in the leg when you were in Berlin will be *nothing* to what I'll do to you. Get in here on Thursday at 6.30pm."

Lord Atkins hung up. Kelson stared at the handset, shook his head and placed it back in the hook. He opened the door of the phone-box and hobbled out.

Lord Atkins slammed down his phone, annoyed with Kelson as usual, but at least he seemed to have removed this problem. He'd been in thought about the potential danger of the Cannon issue again. It was all down to the complexity of history, economics and national pride that most people would be unable to understand, become bored and then put their focus on nonsensical activities. Britain was a good national example of this. Full of television shows, then the advertising of *crap* such as electrical goods, furniture, cars and *fucking* holidays.

Were today's public bored with history, being too thick to understand it, or just scared to face up to what certain *scumbag* humans had *really* done to the world?

He remembered the words of a German philosopher, Hegel;

"We learn from history that we do not learn from history."

Well, the finest leader in world history knew what the *Jews had done*. Ruination of Germany after World War One for a start. *Every* nation should have joined Hitler in their total destruction.

Atkins whacked his fist down on the table again in anger and the pain hit him hard. Then his smirk came in. *If Adolf had been with me now, he would have agreed,* he thought, placating himself.

He stood up and began pacing around the office. The desk light was on, casting its shadows around, but the rest was in darkness. On the wall behind the fax machine, there was a photograph of his father. Atkins walked up close to it and stared him in the eyes. *What a man. Someone who knew how dangerous the Jews were to the world, who secretly helped with their annihilation, who worked with one of the finest members of the Nazi party. And out of this, made a fortune.*

The secrecy of this had been held, until now. And it was due to that bloody clerk, Walter Cannon having given out *something* before he was removed back in 1938.

It seemed the only person to have received this was his son, Rupert Cannon, now out of the game. But what if someone else knew about this? It would ruin Atkins, and be a massive global story. It could make this country loose its honour, and maybe a lot more….

Walter Cannon ordered another pint and a large whisky chaser from the bar-tender. He'd been in the *Sun and 13 Cantons* public house for almost two hours and had put a few away already. The pub was right on the corner of Beak Street and Great Pulteney Street in London, W1. Sitting down at the table near the door, he took another swig of *Charrington's mild bitter* and looked down at the front page of the *Daily Sketch* newspaper, probably left behind by a lunch time drinker, because it had today's date on it. **Friday, 1ˢᵗ April 1938**.

He turned over the pages, but his mind was so focused on another matter, that he could not concentrate on the articles. On the back page he saw the words **Joe Louis is favourite to win world title.**

Looking up at the bar ceiling he thought about Joe Louis probably knocking out Harry Thomas in the Chicago Stadium. *The same as stopping refugees from entering Britain.* He shook his head in disdain of himself, there was no comparison.

He was sure that he'd been caught up in a melee of a potential humanitarian disaster, and a method of gaining money for his senior officials. The *connection* he had found between Mr Atkins and Adolf Eichmann had stunned him, and he was sure that Britain's parliament would be too, if they found out. But Cannon knew he must say nothing because his life and more importantly, probably his family's would be in grave danger.

He took another swig of the mild, and thought about what he now knew.

The secret document sent out from the German Embassy Ambassador, von Ribbentrop, had been left on *his* desk two days ago instead of in Atkins' office. *Why on earth did this happen?* He asked himself, as he'd now done so many times. *And why the hell did I open it and read it anyway?* But it was too late, the damage was already done, he knew too much….

When he read this thing that came in on Wednesday, the office was empty as it was after 5.30pm. In fact, if anyone had still been there, he would have taken it straight into Atkins' office and handed it over or left it on his desk, unopened.

Instead, he'd read it, and then placed the letter onto Atkins' secretary's desk.

He recalled the words with a shiver, as he took another swig of the *Charringtons*.

German Embassy
8-9 Carlton House
London, SW1

Mr Gregory Atkins
Permanent Assistant Secretary
British Home Office

Dear Mr Atkins

In reference to our discussion regarding German liberation of our now native Austria from Jewish residents. The Central Office for Jewish Emigration is to manage action as follows:
  A) All Jewish exiles shall be required to obtain initial applications and required papers
  B) Exit visas, transit visas, tax and other required payments are to be made at suitable Embassies or Consulates
  C) In the case of Jewish Exiles being deported to Britain, all required payments for visa entry shall be made to official departments aligned by agreement with the SD sanctioned officials of the Finance Ministry
  D) Passports issued for exile shall be valid for a maximum of 14 days
Administration of Emigration for Jewish Exiles is to be carried out under the auspices of the Permanent Assistant Secretary to

the British Home Office via the German Embassy and Consulate in Britain.

*Yours sincerely
Joachim von Ribbentrop
Ambassador*

Walter Cannon had worked out the underlying possibilities for Atkins. This agreement had been sanctioned by von Ribbentrop, but was certain it was part of the Adolf Eichmann plan for the removal of Austrian Jews and in doing so, taking all of their possessions away. Money, property and anything they owned would be taken by the Nazi government.

This thing was like a *conveyor belt* used in modern factories. The Jews would start at one end. trying to get their exit visas produced, then payments would be demanded by Embassies of the countries they would try and be deported to.

They would then have to pay these embassies, and he suspected some of this would be returned to the Nazis. A visa could then be potentially issued, but it would only last for fourteen days. So if the emigrants could not get to the border of the new country they were hoping to be in within this time, they would be deported back. And *what* would happen to them if they had to return to Austria or any other German held country? Would it be prison camps, or perhaps worse? He had no idea.

He was sure there was potential for both the Nazis and the countries the refugees would attempt to go to, for taking all of their money. Cannon did not know how this would operate, but was sure Atkins was somehow doing something behind the back of the British Government, and could be in cahoots with the Nazi's. What Cannon had been forced to produce, and the letter from von Ribbentrop, seemed to underline this.

The thing that worried him the most was the term *non-sanctioned,* in the document *he* had written. Atkins had insisted upon this.

What if desperate refugees were forced to pay money or gave out any other possessions to this country on arrival here, undercover? What if that money and those possessions were somehow filtered behind the British Government's back to sophisticated criminals.

And what if the Nazi's were collaborating with this? Was that why he had been told to use the term *non-sanctioned?* Because if it was, then he could be responsible for conspiracy and should the refugees be sent back, possibly murder of a massive number of people. This was potentially genocide, and he was involved with it. He looked down at the table and shook his head in sadness and anger.

But it was no good. He just has to get on, because despite his suspicions about Mr Atkins lying and cheating behind the government's back, the man was his senior and so he had to do what he was told. Looking at his pint mug, he thought about his young son, Rupert. It made him smile and he finished the rest of his beer, followed with the whisky, and then stood up. Time to go home.

Outside, the fog was coming in thicker now. He turned up his coat collar and glanced at his wrist watch. It was 8pm. It wouldn't take long to get to Piccadilly underground, then a short trip to Victoria Station and a late train to Croydon.

He could go home, see his wife and boy and try to put the worry behind him. Yes, that's what he would do.

As he walked along the pavement, it was becoming more difficult to see anything. The street lamps were on but were dull and very distant, due to a combination of darkness and the swirling fog. A Morris Eight saloon went slowly past in the opposite direction, it's headlights on, but probably making it more difficult for the driver he thought, as the fog must be reflecting the light's brilliance back through the windscreen.

He walked on, swaying on the pavement, feeling a bit worse for wear after a lot of pints, and looking out to make sure he didn't hit a lamp-post. There was no one else on this side of the road, he knew that at this time on a Friday, they'd either be home or still in a public-house. Then he heard another motor-car coming towards him. The engine and gearbox whine sounded familiar, it was an Austin Heavy Twelve he thought. These were usually taxis, so typical of it being out at this time of night.

Looking ahead he could not see any lights from the motor-car, so thought it was a long way from here. But the engine noise was increasing, so it *must* be getting closer.

Then a black shadow came through the fog, around twenty yards away. It definitely looked like a taxi. His initial reaction was that he could hail it, and get a lift to Piccadilly underground or even Victoria Station, it could save him time and the danger of walking into a lamp post.

As he was about to raise his arm to do this, the engine noise increased, the driver opening the throttle. The taxi suddenly turned towards him, the headlamps came on and dazzled him, as it mounted the edge of the pavement. Cannon stood dumfounded as the Austin Heavy Twelve hit him. The driver continued up onto the pavement and drove on until Cannon was crushed under the front nearside wheel and then the rear.

The flat-capped driver sneered a smile from one side of his mouth, as the *Players* fag hung out of the other. Then he selected reverse, switched off the lights and backed over the body. Cannon was already dead, but the driver always liked to be sure. *Another earner from Mr Atkins then,* he said to himself smiling, *four quid and five bob. I can take the Mrs out, leave me son indoors, fuck a whore and still have enough left for a booze up.*

He turned back onto Great Pulteney Street, drove off into the fog and disappeared.

Chapter 11

Midland Hotel, Manchester
9th October 1984

It was only a short walk back to the *Midland* Hotel, and all they did, was talk about Sade. Talented, professional and kind. Sally-Anne knew that her dad had not been angling with them to create a business connection. And besides, the band had their contract in place with *Portrait Records*. Bernie just wanted them both to have a good time, and they did.

Earlier, when they left the bar and went back into the studio, most of the audience had left, except for those with *special* invitations. The BBC were not filming, so this was a dedicated performance to them by the band, with tracks from an album that was being released next year.

There were two songs that were going to stay in their minds. One was, *It's a crime,* and the other, *The Sweetest Taboo*.

Sade and the band smiled and waved at the audience as they danced around. It was an experience tonight that would stay in everyone's memory. Unique and without pretence. A super band, with a small group of enthusiastic fans engaging with each other. A quiet storm of real connection.

It's a crime, brought Sally-Anne and Linus into the slow dance. As they touched and looked into each other's eyes, Sade sang out, looking at them, as if she had an inner feeling of their relationship and future lives….

As they crossed the Midland's entrance to the lift, Linus glanced at his watch. It was ten past midnight. Stepping in, he pressed the third floor button and it started to move very slowly. He put his arms around her and asked. "I'd like to open that letter from Mr Cannon. Do you think I should do that now?"

She knew this has been on his mind since he'd been given the letter by Colleen on Saturday. Colleen was the one who had booked her for the *event* she had performed for Linus in their office, and she seemed alright.

"I think we should go in, get ready for bed and then sit together whilst you open it." She said, gently stroking his head with her left hand, the silver Star of David from her bracelet touching his dark hair.

Linus opened the hotel room's door and switched on the lights. He walked over to the window and closed the curtains. Sally-Anne stood by the bed looking at him. "Strange whiff in here," she said. "Smells like after shave."

"Well it's not me, "said Linus, "because I don't have any."

"Ha-ha," she said sarcastically. "But something does smell odd in here. Maybe the cleaner has been in, anyway I'll ask reception in the morning."

They got undressed, and then put on their dressing gowns.

He took his bag out of the cupboard, rummaged through it, removed the envelope, and sat on the bed. Looking down with her arms folded, she watched him, sensing a mixture of sadness and fascination as he opened it up.

Linus took out the content and then looked up at her rather dumfounded. An old, *Motor Sport* magazine page about the Triumph Stag, then he held it up towards her. he said nothing.

She knew how close Linus was to Mr Cannon and no matter what she felt, it was *never* appropriate to say anything in such a sad and personal situation. In fact, she felt a wave of emotion for Linus, but would never share that.

"Well," he said, feeling somewhat disappointed, but then realising it reflected that joke between them, "He always used to laugh about my *old banger, as* he called it."

She came over and sat next to him, then looked at the article and noticed the date.

"Same age as yours," she said. "That's a nice touch. I think he must have been a very brave and clever man. He wanted to give you a message, not words of emotion, but a *connection* between you two. Something like that, I reckon."

"You're right," he said, nodding at her, then looking down again at the article. "I'll miss him."

"*Genuine* relationships," she said, looking into his eyes. "They are the key to our lives. The real ones come at us from good fortune and maybe, guidance from our god. It's not about being a *family* member, that can just be an excuse. When these come at us, we must grasp them, you did that with Mr Cannon and the sun will always shine on you for that."

She gave him a hug. "Come on," she said. "Let's get some sleep, tomorrow's another day."

The trip over to *RADI-CAL's* regional office on the outskirts of Manchester was faster than he thought. It was easier to get around this city than London. *Could be a good place to live*, he thought. *Maybe with Ms Cohen, one day.* Something touched him inside, and he wanted that now.

As he pulled up outside the office, it was only 08.10hrs, and there were plenty of *RADI-CAL* cars there already. But there was no longer a requirement to make any notes of this for Mr Cannon....

He stepped out of the Cavalier and took his case off the rear seat. This place was on the edge of an industrial estate, which was much tidier than the Maidstone site.

On the side of the entrance door was a buzzer. He pressed it and the door clicked open. *Very efficient*, he thought.

This was a one-story building. The small reception area was empty, so he knocked on the first door he came to. It opened immediately and a tall man in a blue pin-striped suit stood smiling at him, extending out his hand. "Hello," he said, "you must be Linus, I'm Jason, pleased to meet you."

Linus shook his hand and said. "Pleased to meet you too Jason, thanks for taking the time to see me."

"My pleasure. Thanks for coming all this way." Jason said.

He followed Jason Lord towards his office. There were a number of staff in already, not a surprise due to all the cars outside. He passed a man sat at a desk on the right that he instantly recognised. It was the bloke from the training course, who used to work for that *bog* making company. Terry Johnston.

Terry smiled over at Linus and said. "Good to see you again, what brings you over here?"

"Hello Terry," he replied. "I'm just here to pass some install information over for the Trans-ship company. We signed them up in their head office, close to us in the Kent region."

He wanted to make the head office point clear, so there would be no question as to where the sale would be attributed to.

"Well," replied Terry. "You have *flushed* us away then."

Linus smiled back remembering his humour at the Heathfield House training course.

"I hope we can catch up later before I head back." He didn't intend to.

Linus followed Jason into his office. It was much tidier than Mike Sentinel's, which was not a surprise. But in comparison it was very bland, it was clearly under the domineering control of its manager. He weirdly felt a pang of wanting to be back in the Kent office.

They both sat down at his round meeting table, and Jason said. "Can I get you a cup of something?"

"No thanks," replied Linus, his thoughts going back to the Maidstone office coffee machine. "I'm fine."

"We've got the installation guys out-back, so I can introduce to them later," said Jason. "Have you got all the vehicle and contact details at Trans-ship for us?"

Linus opened his bag and laid all the information he'd got from John Edwards yesterday.

She sat back in her chair in the Midland Hotel's café-bar, and thought about that strange whiff of after-shave she had noticed in their room last night. There was no reason for a cleaner to have come in so late in the day. Sally-Anne took another sip of her coffee and looked over at the reception desk. She decided to ask if they had sent someone in, but then realised that was unnecessary, and a waste of time. *Who cares*. She said to herself.

She lit up a Marlboro, and her mind went back to the thing Linus received from Mr Cannon. Given their relationship, she could see why he would do that, but it didn't make sense if there was something he'd needed to communicate. She took another drag on the Marlboro, then exhaled it down her nose and thought back to what Linus had said about their Croydon Aerodrome meeting. She had thought there might be *something* linked to that in the envelope. Not an old magazine article on a Triumph Stag.

Looking across at the reception desk again, she noticed the guy who was there last night was back on duty again. She stubbed out her Marlboro, stood up and walked to the desk.

The meeting at *RADI-CAL* had been alright. Jason had taken Linus out to the workshop so that he could meet the installers. They were clearly efficient, and had already worked out what they needed to do with the Trans-ship's lorries. What really impressed Linus, was the large number of Panasonics already delivered into this workshop area.

He went through the notes he'd made at Trans-ship with them, and found they were already ahead of the game on every technical aspect, and were even planning to discuss the options for the positioning of the handsets when on site. The installers could match the timing that Trans-ship had requested. This was a factor that he'd been concerned about, it would not look good if they could not have agreed this. Then he thought back to what Robbie had said to him about Jeannie not wanting the responsibility of this.

It was a balancing act. She had got the cachet of having achieved something excellent of course, but had removed the risk of it going wrong by engaging Linus with the Manchester division of *RADI-CAL*. Clever.

The upside for Linus had been several fold. He'd potentially earned a significant payment, the job so far had been much better than expected, and he'd been out at great event. Being in the Midland Hotel with Sally-Anne, was the icing on the cake.

Jason asked him to return into his office, to finalise matters. Linus shook hands with the installers and gave them his R1 number, so they could try him on the off chance it might be in coverage, if they could not reach him in the Maidstone office.

"It seems everything is in order now, and we'll keep you informed." Said Jason.

"I very much appreciate that. This is a big ask for you guys, especially as their head office put the order into Maidstone." Replied Linus.

Jason looked across and shrugged. "It's fine, these things always go in circles. We'll probably get something from your neck of the woods one day, you know how it goes."

Linus nodded back, he understood that. Jason seemed like a decent bloke. He remembered Mike Sentinel telling him to get a document from Jason showing the details of the installs.

"Mike has requested a confirmation on the work you are going to carry out at their Trafford Park industrial estate. It's something we have to keep for the contract department at their Rochester office apparently."

Jason held up a typed sheet and passed it over smiling. "I know Mike's attention to detail," he said. "He's always been that way. He was at Rate-Syrex when we worked together, and I heard he was the same in the Army."

Linus remembered Robbie telling him the story about when he rescued him. He was an ex Rate-Syrex man too of course.

"Robbie Robson told me how he rescued him years ago after his bike accident. He said Mike had saved his life."

Jason nodded at him. "He did that alright," he said, then sat back in his chair staring at Linus in a serious manner. "He took a boy's life too when he was out in Aden. But, he managed to get away with it."

This was a shock, and Linus felt a distinct mixture of Jason stirring things up, and the need for him to find out more.

"What happened?" he asked.

"I don't know all the details, but heard it through the grapevine years ago." He said, looking over to the window, giving an indication of casting his mind back.

"It seems Mike had gone out there in '67 to fix up a few broken down tank things. A bloke and his son got out of a car and came up towards him at some airfield, and then Mike shot the youngster."

Linus looked back in shock and horror as Jason carried on.

"Anyway, it seems the boot of the car was full of Russian *Kalashnikov* assault rifles, so they were probably terrorists. Called the National Liberation Front I think. Mike was deemed to be a *hero*, despite shooting a youngster."

Linus glanced at his watch, it was just on 10.30hrs. He stood up, took the sheet of paper that Jason had passed over and said. "Thank you for all your help Jason. I must get going as I've got a long way to go today. I'll keep in touch."

Jason Lord got up, clearly not expecting the meeting to reach a close so fast.

"That's fine," he said as Linus walked out the door, then raising his voice "Pleased to be of help, just let me know if you need anything." He sat back in the chair, a smug expression on his face and thought. *Got one over on you for a change Mr Sentinel, you fucker.*

Linus walked out the front door and over to his Cavalier, got straight in, started the engine and drove out fast through the site gates. Then he pulled over, reclined the seat and lit up a Marlboro. He was *very* angry.

Jeannie Sands sat considering the situation. It was a sunny morning here in Rochester and the café was quiet. The last time she came in here was with Linus, and coincidentally, they had sat at the same table. She wondered about his Trans-ship visit in Manchester yesterday. The information Mike gave her about this was positive. She took another sip of her tea. It was good that Linus had done alright.

But if she had gone up there instead, then she might have avoided the problem with Dave Grant.

Being approached by men was something she was used to. It was not because she set out to be *deliberately* attractive. At least she didn't think so. No, it was more of a connection she had with men that was different from *normal* women.

Even considering this made her feel uncomfortable. So how did these *normal* women feel about her then? They probably disliked her. What was she to do? Change her personality and dress down perhaps?

She looked at her watch. It was getting on for 11.00hrs. Going back into the Maidstone office and having a chat with Mike would be good. At least she could open up to him, albeit in a controlled fashion.

As she stood up, she felt depression kicking in and knew she had to fight it. Walking to the door, two men at another table both looked up at her with desire. This was the irony of her life. She had been fortunate to have been created with the looks, style and voice of attraction. But the situation with Dave Grant underlined how difficult this was for three reasons.

Firstly, it meant she had to handle things courteously, but make it clear to him that she was *out of bounds*. Secondly, if that annoyed and belittled him, then the *RADI-CAL* deal could be in trouble. And thirdly, despite all her hard work commercially, the order might have been placed because of his attraction to her, and not for what she had achieved.

She walked slowly along the high-street towards the bridge and crossed over the road to her car. Looking over at the River Medway, she switched on the Cavalier's ignition and then waited to see if the Panasonic R1 would come up with a green light. She felt the need to speak to her husband, Paul. It was strange because there was nothing specific she intended to say. She just wanted to hear the sound of his voice. *Pathetic, but I really need to.* She thought.

She stared down at the R1, but it stayed on red. Not a surprise as the network pre-testing was only minimal in this region. She waited a while longer, but still there was no signal. For some reason Paul became distant, and in her mind, disappeared over the horizon.

It wasn't his fault the network didn't connect her to him. Something else inside her brought this on, almost as if he was her first husband.

Then she started up the Cavalier and headed back to the Maidstone office.

The bar was virtually empty as he expected. There was not even an old bloke wearing a trilby and reading a paper in there. Linus walked over to Sally-Anne.

"I've never seen *you* in here before," he said. "Can I get you anything?"

"Nothing *you* can afford," she said snootily. "You're back early. Don't get me wrong, I'm really pleased, but how come?"

He sat down at the table and said. "I shan't bore you with it, but the manager pissed me right off. Anyway, everything on the job front is sorted. How about you?"

"I've been doing nothing except thinking about work when we get back tomorrow," she replied, then looked over at the reception desk. "Oh, there was a strange thing. The bloke over there told me an old man had asked for you last night. Your *uncle* it seems."

He looked at her in surprise. "What? I don't even have an *uncle*."

"Well that's what he told me," she said raising both hands. "A nice old man it seems, who *thought* you were in different room from the one we are in."

Linus sat back and thought about it. "The receptionist must have got this wrong. Probably because so many people are staying here, he got the guests names mixed up."

She lit up two Marlboros and passed one over to him. She took the first drag then exhaled and said. "You could be right, but why then did we pick up that stink of after-shave in the room?"

"That's a point," he replied. "Maybe it was a cleaner then."

"I asked him if there was a cleaner in last night and he told me there wasn't." She took another drag and said. "Anyway, nothing seems to have been touched in there, so it'll remain a mystery."

"Oh well," he said. "What would *you* like to do now?"

Jeannie walked into the Maidstone office with a spring in her step and a smile on her face. When it came to being in the workplace, image was everything. But inside, she was going downhill fast. She was a fighter though, and would map out her list of problems and manage them. Workwise that would be sorted, not least because Mike Sentinel would help, as ever. But what about her husband Paul? He'd done nothing wrong, but she felt they were moving apart. For her, the excitement of their relationship was on the wane, just like her first husband. She wanted a drink and a fag, despite having given up smoking.

Julia looked up at her as she came towards Mike's office. "Hi Jeannie, can I get you a coffee?"

"Yes please, a white one without sugar would be lovely."

Julia smiled and headed down the office towards the *GKN Sankey* machine. Mike waved Jeannie in as he came off the phone.

"So, how did it go at Trans-ship this morning?" He asked.

"It was alright," replied Jeannie somewhat tentatively. I just needed to sort something out." She said it that way, because she knew it would open up the door.

"Mmm, what was that?" asked Mike Sentinel, *exactly as she had expected.*

She leant over his desk, putting her hands gently on it and looked him in the eyes with total sincerity. It was the *Jeannie way.* Despite Mike Sentinel's intellect, she was in control.

"The guy who runs the Rochester site, Dave Grant has been a little bit tricky for me, but I've sorted it out now."

She moved her plan onwards by saying this, passing the next step over to Mike.

"What do mean by *tricky?*" he said, looking superciliously at her through his thick glasses.

She looked down with an intonation of huge embarrassment, shook her head, then stared back up at him.

"Mike," she said. "He tried to *touch me up*. I was in his office and he sat beside me and made a move."

He looked across at her in genuine shock as she continued.

"I didn't over react, but told him to back off. You know, said he was a great guy but I was a married woman, usual sort of thing."

Mike nodded. He understood that was the right way. The boat should not be rocked with this deal coming in. "What happened next then?"

"He backed off," she said. "Then he apologised. All a bit awkward as I'm sure you'd agree." *Job done*, she thought. And she was right.

"Mmm, that's a bloody nuisance. Tell you what, I'll take over this for you. You can tell Dave Grant you have to go somewhere urgently. Make it sound like a really important support thing for another customer, that way It'll tick the box positively with Trans-ship in case something ever goes wrong for them. You know how it works."

"Are you sure?" She asked with a mixture of concern and relief.

"Yes, that'll be fine. And besides you've got loads of other things to do." He smiled at her in genuine friendship. "You didn't deserve that."

"Thank you so much," she said. "You are the greatest."

They both stood up and Mike felt a little embarrassed. He always did when someone said something kind to him.

As usual, he came back with a bad joke, to cover up his emotion. "I'm not *Cassius Clay* you know."

She gave out her infectious laugh, even though she did not find this funny and left his office. Passing Julia's desk, she picked up her coffee brought back from the machine, thanked her and walked to the end of the room. Robbie, Kevin and Julian were already at their desks, watching her come towards them.

"Hi guys," she said. "Any of the new boys started yet?"

Chapter 12

Midland Hotel, Manchester
10th October 1984

It was just after midnight. They had been drinking too much in the *Midland Hotel's* bar.

He looked down at the now empty glasses on the table and said. "Shall I get us another one?"

She shook her head, the raven hair flicking. "Thanks but no thanks. I've had enough now."

"Me too," he said. "Actually, a bit of fresh air would do us good. Shall we have a walk around the block?"

She raised her hands and said. "That's fine by me."

Their coats were up in the room but both had jumpers on as they walked out into the cold, autumn night. There was virtually no traffic, and apart from a couple walking towards them, no one was out. It was very different from London. This was the City centre after all. Both of them felt a sort of affinity for this place. It was really civilised up here.

They continued to stroll, although with a slight stagger and kept the *Midland* on their right side, otherwise they would get lost. The fresh air of the night was kicking-in to both of them now, and causing the typical, acceleration effect of alcohol into the bloodstream.

Linus came to a standstill, and then took a pair of Marlboros out, trying to find his lighter without success. Sally-Anne reached into her bag and took out hers.

He put the fags between his lips and she lit them up as he inhaled both, and passed one over to her.

"You know what," he said, pointing up at the Midland. "We are a team, that's what we are, a team."

She looked at him and took a drag, as he carried on, now waving up at the hotel.

"This is where *Rolls* met *Royce* and they were a team too. Right where we are staying, how about that?"

"Were they both men?" she asked, now starting to slur.

"Yes," he said, and then thinking about her question again. "Why?"

The combination of night air and fags was now increasing the alcohol effect in them.

"Well," she answered, "if they were gay in those days, do you think they would have been able to share a room?"

He ground out his Marlboro on the pavement, slipped his arm behind hers and said.

"Come on, I think we need to go back in and sleep this off."

"What utter rubbish is in the post today?" The man asked himself out loud, walking up to the front door, wearing an old, woollen dressing gown, slippers, carrying a mug of steaming tea. There were three letters on the floor, and he picked them up examining the hand writing on two and on one, the typing of his name. He walked into the kitchen, ripped the hand written pair in half and threw them in the waste bin.

"You utter *cretins*," he said, looking down at the bin. "Don't you know how to spell my name correctly after all the years I've been around?" But the third was typed and the spelling *was* correct on it. He sighed, knowing who it was from.

Hardly surprising though, considering how much I pay you. He thought.

Sitting at the kitchen table, he opened the envelope and took out the letter. Looking down at it, his toupee very slowly slid forwards, and so he took it off and put it on the table.

Reading the first words, he tutted and then shook his head in annoyance. '*Why did this bloke always start off with Dear F instead of Dear Frank?*' But he actually knew why. In fact, because although Frank was his *real* name, his *stage* one was Frankie. Even this agent got confused. Anyway, at least he got the *Howerd* surname right as opposed to *Howard,* despite that the fact that Howard was his *real* surname.

"*Ah Gaud*" he said out loud, putting his head in his hands. "The world is *so* complicated these days."

He read the letter out loud:

"Dear F
Just to let you know that the timing on 24th December for the RADI-CAL cellular radio telephone event has changed slightly.

They have brought the time forward to 2pm to make sure there is sufficient light for the filming, and so everything should be finished by 5pm at the latest.

Could I therefore request that you meet up with the film crew at 1pm please? They should be near Lancaster Gate, but I'll keep you posted on this.

*Toodle Pip,
Alex Judd*

Frankie Howerd sighed, folded up the letter and put it back into the envelope. He'd read about some of this new technical junk in the papers, but this nonsense was going nowhere. He laughed for the first time today, and said out loud. "Cellular radio telephones, whatever next? *titter ye not RADI-CAL."*

Then he put the toupee back on and stared at the agent's envelope.

"No, it's wrong to mock the afflicted," he said, as if he were on stage in a theatre surrounded by a large audience. *"Please yourselves."*

The journey back from Manchester had been faster than going up there. Rather than just drop Sally-Anne off at home, they had gone to the *Sandrock* for lunch and a quick drink. There was no reason for him to go into the Maidstone office until tomorrow, but she had a work event tonight in Croydon's *Blue Orchid* club.

They sat at the bar and she could sense that Linus was deep in thought about something, and had been since she told him about her job tonight. She picked up her glass and touched it against his. "Thanks for a lovely few days," she said sincerely. "Actually, I loved it so much, that I have decided not to add anything onto your account."

He lit up two Marlboros and passed one over to her. "Can I ask you something?" he said.

"Be my guest." She replied, taking her first drag. She knew what was coming.

"Are you doing the stripping tonight, or is it going to be one of your new assistants?"

"It'll be me," she said, looking him in the eye and then reached out and squeezed his hand. "I know it must seem odd, and I appreciate that. But you need to understand something." She took another sip of her Dry Martini. "My dad started with nothing, and so have I. Yes, I could be a lazy cow and live off what he has achieved, but that is not right. Maybe in part, it's about *competing* with him and my sister, but the main thing for me is to grow this, and be proud of it."

He smiled and squeezed her hand, in total understanding, his mind now at rest.

"I love you." He said from his heart. She swallowed hard and fought back her emotion from his words, held up her hands to him and said.

"Nice try mister *Shmuck* man. But you still owe me the dosh from *before* we went away."

The *RADI-CAL* site in Maidstone felt a whole lot better for him this morning. The sun was out, most of the staff were there already, the rubbish dump by the fence had been cleared up and he was in a really good mood. The most important thing of all, was the phone call he received from *Ms* Cohen at mid-night. After he dropped her off yesterday, he'd felt uneasy, despite his real trust in her. Being cheated on in the past had always made him steer clear of involvement in a relationship. That was his self-taught rule, but things had moved on.

He felt a bit of a spring in his step, as he walked towards the office door. The late call she made when she got home from her job last night was special, it was to let him know that *she* was safe and so was *he*. It was a connection of trust and the bond that was growing between them. *What if she had a Motorola 8000x?* he thought. *She could have called him from the club when she finished.* Going up the stairs he considered this but then returned to reality. The system was not live yet anyway.

And who would spend almost four grand, and then have the twenty-five pence per minute call charges and twenty-five pounds a month line rental, just to do that?

As he went further up the stairs, the thought of this brought in a wave of concern as he remembered the words of Rupert

Cannon: '*When out and about, one needs peace and quiet to think, not be harassed by some nincompoop in a bloody office calling you.*'

He stopped on the landing in front of the office door, and looked out of the window at the railway line, as a London bound train flew past. Julia looked up at him through the door window and waved. He could see Mike Sentinel's head move up, checking who Julia was waving at. It was time to go in.

Mike walked towards Linus as he came through the office door, looking pleased.

"Mmm, its seems you did alright up there *alrighty*."

Yes, it was alright, alrighty. He thought, no longer surprised by the way Mr Sentinel spoke.

"I think we have everything sorted with the Manchester lot for *Trans-ship's* installations." Said Linus, as he sat down at the meeting room table.

On the table today, stood a plastic bucket, which was three quarters-filled with water. Linus looked inside it with interest. There were two tiny *Koi Carp* in there swimming about, one red and one yellow.

Mike was ahead of his question and said. "Picked these up from the pet shop this morning," looking down at them through is thick glasses. "They are going into my pond this afternoon."

"Nice," said Linus, now completely unfazed by anything on this table.

"I'm pleased it's all sorted up there," Mike continued. "We got the order in yesterday by fax for an HPU, so well done with that."

"Yes, that's for John Edwards," said Linus. "He's planning to use it when travelling to Rochester by train next year."

Mike nodded somewhat superciliously at this and turned to another subject. "So what did you think of Jason Lord then?"

Linus thought back to what Jason said about when Mike was in Aden in a different life, and at a different age. Part of him wanted to express his anger about Jason and part of him did not want to open this up with Mike. He decided to steer clear and said.

"He seemed pretty accommodating, but the workshop guy and I spent most of the time together, because it was important to get the practical work and timing right for Trans-ship's availability."

Mike nodded back, his thought process initially being to delve into this a little more, but decided to leave it. He was starting to form a degree of trust for Linus. It seemed clear that if Jason had said anything about his past, then Linus would keep this private. He was after all, very much the RITON group type.

"Sounds good," said Mike. "Jeannie's in today, so I suggest you have a chat with her about the situation up there, and she can tell you where she is with her side of things, *alrighty*."

Linus knew the conversation was over, so he nodded at Mike and left his office.

Walking down the room and past Mike's glass side panel, he noticed him staring into the fish bucket, watching them with interest. How things had changed. A little more than a month ago, he would have been taken aback with the madness of this. But now he didn't care. Unbeknown to him, the cycle of life was turning.

On the back of Jeannie's chair, he saw the red strap of her handbag, and guessed she had probably gone to the coffee machine. He walked through the door and into the end office, and there she was, leaning back against the *GKN Sankey*, stirring her coffee and smiling at him as he walked towards her.

As ever, she was exuding that charm and sensuality that he could never really describe, even to himself. It was in the atmosphere, as if the sun was coming out on a depressingly dark day. Then there was that feeling of trust. He considered what Robbie had said in the pub, but still felt an inkling of generosity from her.

Today she was wearing a blue *coat dress*.

"Hello there," she said. "I hear it went alright up there."

"Yes, it seems ready to go," and then added. "But I'm going to keep in touch with them and our lot, to make sure it's managed properly. How did you get on?"

She glanced down at the floor and then said. "It went fine."

Linus sensed something was not quite right. "Do you fancy going out for lunch?" he asked.

Jeannie looked at her watch and said. "That would be great, we could do 12.30 and then you could tag along to something with me later if that's alright with you?"

As usual, Jeannie insisted on driving. She had worked out a plan for this afternoon, which included lunch in the *Albany Arms* pub, then driving out to a farm for a potential sale, and to have a discussion regarding Trans-ship with Linus.

Mike Sentinel always called this *the Jeannie way*. It was planning, carrying things out and then, achieving results.

The *Albany Arms* was on the edge of town, and pulling up in the car park, they could see that it was going to be quiet in there, only a few cars were outside. The sun had come out and as they walked to the pub, its rays touched her blonde hair, and she gave out that sense of *something* that he felt was mystical.

It was atmospheric and surreal. She was good looking, but it felt as if she had come from another world. Linus considered this as an observation, and not an attraction. He felt truly smitten by his relationship with Sally-Anne and he would be loyal to her. But even if they weren't together, he knew deep down that Jeannie Sands would be like a burning candle. He could never hold her. Strangely, this made him feel relaxed in her company. There could be never be any connection, other than friendship. And of course, she was a married woman.

Inside, the pub was virtually empty. They walked up to the bar and Linus asked her. "What would you like?"

She thought about it for a moment and said. "I'll have a pint of lager please."

Linus looked at her surprised, said nothing, and just nodded.

Jeannie realised he thought this was a slightly odd choice for a woman, laughed in her deeply sensual style and said.

"I do enjoy the odd pint, how about you?"

"A pint and a Marlboro are my favourites," he said and then went on. "In fact, half a dozen and twenty fags, is my usual on a night out."

Jeannie looked at him still laughing and said. "Is that *all?*"

The barmaid put their pints on the bar, and they both lifted them up and touched the glasses gently together. Then they took their first sip and Linus asked. "Shall we get the menu?"

Sitting at a table, they opened up a conversation. There was now, a feeling of trust between them. It was not like a man trying to attract a woman, or her considering the possibility of accepting him.

It was because in their souls, they were counterparts in starting up something that might change the world, but also felt a very personal closeness. Friendship and trust.

She told him about the situation with Dave Grant at Transship and how difficult it had been for her. But it was not the first time she had experienced this in her career.

Then she explained how Mike Sentinel would manage this situation. Changing the subject, she asked him. "So, tell me about your *lady friend*. What did you get up to in Manchester?"

"You are right about that," he replied smiling. "She is a *lady friend* and no, I'm not gay."

Jeannie put her hand across her face, remembering what she'd asked him that day in Rochester and said. "I'm so sorry about that, there is no excuse."

Linus smiled and said. "There was one good thing about that day though."

Jeannie gave a puzzled look and asked. "What was that?"

"Well, you taught me never to cross my legs, at least not in front of a woman." He said.

"Pleased to be of assistance," she replied. "Anyway, don't try and change the subject, tell me about your *lady* friend."

Linus sat back in the chair as he tried to manage his thoughts into words. A song came on through the speakers. It was *Missing You*, by John Waite. This was on its way up now in the UK chart, but it always seemed to come out at a key moment for him such as, thinking about his ex, Anna, when sat alone in the 29th Street apartment in New York. On the Stag's radio as Rupert Cannon left the Aerodrome Hotel and now, out with Jeannie Sands.

"She is a lovely but quite unusual woman," he said, trying to give a simple description of Sally-Anne. "We have good times together. Actually, I think she is way too good for me."

"What do you mean by *unusual*?" She asked. Linus carried on.

"She has a great sense of humour and is very generous, in fact she often mixes the two together." Jeannie looked at him curiously.

"I know that sounds odd," he continued. "But let me give you an example. She runs a sort of *entertainment business,* and that is how we met, by the way. Anyway, the on-going joke is that I still owe her money from when I left RITON's marine department for the move over to *RADI-CAL*."

Jeannie continued to look somewhat confused and said. "So how does that become funny then?"

He knew it was something someone had to be part of to understand. "You see when she pays for something, she always tells me she'll add it to what I owe, and calls me *Mr Shmuck man.* Actually, I suppose it's not that funny, anyway, each to his own."

She laughed and said. "However it works between you, on-going humour is *so* important in a relationship. It takes out the stress and keeps you close. When you lose that, you have to think about moving on. Life is too short."

"I think that's where I went wrong before," he said nodding at Jeannie. "You see, I was overcome with work, and then lost my way with somebody. She got bored, walked away and that was it."

"Nothing's easy in relationships, I have got things wrong too." She said, looking up at the ceiling. He felt a pang of sadness and guilt coming from her as she continued.

"We all need to learn from our mistakes. The thing is, we feel the excitement of starting out together and if we believe that person is *really* right for us, then we go for it and take the gamble. But if it turns out we got that wrong, then we have to get out of it. Too many people carry on, and then throw their lives away."

Linus nodded at her. "And that is what I'm worried about, because Sally-Anne is entertaining and has a real depth of understanding. I am scared about being a bore." He wanted to tell her something. It was about his feeling of being together with Sally-Anne in another life, somewhere else in the world, back in time. When there was no other way of communicating other than being together. But that would just sound crazy....

She thought for a moment and said. "The world is becoming more of a machine every day it seems. Watching TV is bad enough, but what if these computers become even more addictive? We are on this earth to be close, physically and mentally. Life is about *feeling* compassion and even *passion,* face to face."

She looked at Linus as he listened intently to her, then she smiled and said.

"Pay no attention to me. I'm the one being a bore."

"No, you're not," said Linus, feeling a real connection with Jeannie's words. "I think exactly that myself, and that makes it crazy that we are working at *RADI-CAL* doesn't it!"

Jeannie laughed as she raised her glass. Linus touched his against it, then the sun cast its rays on them. They finished the drinks, and headed off to their meeting at the farm.

Driving back down the lane, Jeannie said to Linus. "That proves how much cellular radio is going to help people out in the sticks." The meeting there had gone well.

Linus remembered Rupert Cannon's expression about *Fred Blogs* and *Mrs Mop* and said. "Well he can phone in and say he's running late for his pie and chips."

Jeannie looked over at him unsure of what he meant by this.

"Sorry, said Linus. It was just something my old boss Mr Cannon said. Anyway, you did a good job today." He looked at Jeannie as she concentrated with care on the narrow lane. She always had a focus on what she did. Planning, talking, selling, driving. Everything.

Jeannie had given him generosity from the Trans-ship deal, but also Mike had in booking the *Midland Hotel* for him.

It was as if the RITON group had recruited a very different type of people into *RADI-CAL*, but they somehow matched the integrated kindness of the group's staff. It was a bit humbling. He didn't think it would be that way when he came on board. Mr Cannon would have said it was *"a jolly good show."* He started to consider there was a change coming in the company. A new style of operation and communication, but still with decent humanity perhaps? He really hoped so.

"Well the least I can do is buy you a drink." He said.

The road from the outskirts of Canterbury took them back to the *Albany Arms*, soon after it opened at 17.30 hrs. The sun was on its way down as they strolled into the bar. Although it was early doors, it was much busier than it had been at lunch time. Jeannie went to the bar and ordered their drinks.

"I said I'd get these in." Said Linus, standing next to her.

"You can get the next round," she said looking at her watch. "Then, I'll need to get going. Paul and I are out tonight."

"So what is it that Paul does then?" He asked, taking a sip of the lager top and lighting up a Marlboro.

"He's the Director of a housing trust charity." She replied.

"That sounds pretty impressive." Linus said, taking his first drag. "Where are you off too?"

"I don't know, he's taking me out for a few and dinner in town. I'm Looking forward to it. Have you got anything on tonight?"

"No." He said. "Staying in and I might try and repair my old car."

"What's that?" She asked.

"Triumph Stag." He said, taking a swig of the lager top and another drag of the Marlboro. "My old boss called it a *snag.*"

"Not surprised about that," she said laughing. "Why are you keeping that thing?"

He thought about this for a moment, because despite often being asked, he could never really define an answer. Then he said. "It's hard to explain, but it's like the need to fight a battle to keep you alive. The Stag can let me down with problems, but sort of raises me up again when I fix it." He sat back, then looked up at the ceiling taking another drag of his Marlboro and laughed, then said. "You see, it can't talk, so I don't have to try and answer something difficult to respond to. I just do the job."

Jeannie could sense the emotion of frustration coming from him, she reached across, touching his hand. She had understood this totally.

"It's kind of like walking in the desert alongside someone whose language I can't understand, but we end up as close friends," he said.

"Perhaps we can go out in it one day." She said. "As long as we don't have a breakdown."

She pulled up next to his Cavalier outside the *RADI-CAL* office. "Thanks for today," said Jeannie. "I enjoyed it."

"Well, I wish you and Paul a good night out on the town." He said smiling at her.

"Thanks, I'll let you know how it goes." She said, and then reached over and touched his arm gently, and carried on. "I think I understand why you have the Stag or *snag*. It probably looks and sounds great, but underneath, has a raft of problems. It's not the fault of the car itself, but the way it was built." She looked deeply into his eyes as he stared back, knowing she had worked it out. The only other person who had got this was Rupert Cannon. "It's like you Linus." She said.

He stepped out and they waved at each other as she drove away. Standing and watching her disappear into the growing twilight, he wanted to tell her something he'd been keeping within himself since he was a teenage boy. She was the *only* person he'd ever known except Rupert Cannon, that he felt he could trust. But he never told Mr Cannon. He just could not bear to, even when the time was right. Now it was too late. There was *something about* Jeannie Sands that made him feel as if he could. He trusted her implicitly.

Sally-Anne could never know about this. It wasn't because he didn't trust her. No, on the contrary he loved her *so* much, and that was why he must never tell her….

As he walked over to his Cavalier, another commuter train from Victoria screamed past. It brought him back to reality. He needed to get moving, *but one day* he thought, *I shall tell Jeannie what happened to me.*

Chapter 13

Queen Anne's Gate, Westminster, London
11th October 1984

As he pulled up, the dusk of autumn came in. Dick Kelson reached over and opened the Passat's glove box. He looked at the *Walther PPK* pistol, contemplating. Then he gently shut the box. The time was 6.30pm.

There was no need to put anything in the parking meter, as it was free now until 8am. *Fuck you, council gits,* he thought as he walked towards the entrance. If anything, the pain in his leg was getting worse, and it didn't help that he'd been following those idiots around in Manchester, especially *that bloody yid bitch.*

Lord Atkins had seen Kelson pull up outside, and watched from the office window, as he walked hobbling to the entrance, wearing his overcoat and trilby. Atkins smiled and thought *there is no way Adolf would have tolerated any spy walking with a fucking limp.* It was only a short time before he would be removed for good. He looked at his watch and noted Kelson was now three minutes late, laughed and rubbed his hands together with glee.

There was a knock on the office door as Atkins sat down at his desk. "Come in." He shouted.

Kelson entered holding the trilby in front of him, squeezing his hands on the rim to try and cover his pained expression of walking with a limp. Atkins stared at him with an evil smile and said. "Stop right there, Kelson."

Atkins stood and walked slowly around him, staring at every part of his body. The sweat trickled down from Dick Kelson's brow, as he looked straight ahead at the window behind Atkins' desk. He stood in silence motionless, breathless and in pain from the long climb up stairs. The ceiling lights reflected off his brow.

Atkins was much shorter, and stood looking up at the beads of sweat, smirking. Then he put his face up close to Kelson's neck and sniffed at the after shave smell.

"Give me your hat." He said to Kelson. As he handed it to him, Atkins examined the brim and then threw it to the end of the room. "Now", he said waving to the chair, "go to my desk and sit down."

Kelson moved forwards, trying not to limp. The pain increased, but he knew he had to make it look better than it was. Atkins knew that too, of course, and this was the highlight of the day for him. It had been miserable in the House of Lords this morning, so the more painful it was for this fuck wit, the better.

"Sit down." Said Atkins as he reached his chair, the sweat and red on Dick's cheeks had increased even further. "Thank you for coming in Kelson, despite being late."

"Sorry," said Kelson. "It's just that there was a lot of traffic and…."

"Shut up," interrupted Atkins. "I know what you and your kind are like. *My* father used to employ *your* father."

How could I fucking forget that man? Thought Kelson. *He was the one who promised my dad the earth, gave him nothing and probably did him over.*

"Anyway, at least you're here safe and sound." Said Lord Atkins, as his attitude now became somewhat gracious.

Here we go again, thought Kelson, *the shit storm is coming*.

"Well done in Manchester by the way, it seems the Cannon *debacle* is sorted out now." Atkins continued, now grinning at Kelson. "Those two or anyone else, won't ever see the original letter." He looked over his glasses in a *chummy* manor at Dick and went on, lowering his voice as if he were telling his friend a sick joke in a club. "I set fire to it in here and then gave out a *traditional* salute."

Kelson smiled at him, in a mixture of understanding, but also hiding annoyance of this twit, as Atkins carried on. "It was as if I'd chucked Cannon, that MacColl bloke and the *yid* bitch in an *Auschwitz furnace!*"

Kelson smiled at him again thinking. *what you don't know is that I've got a fucking photocopy of it.*

"Anyway Dick," said Atkins, becoming friendlier by the minute. "It's opened up an idea of how we can improve this country, rather like my dear old father did."

Kelson looked at Lord Atkins trying to show some interest, but knew he'd probably been developing another crazy idea within his right-wing mind. But whatever it was, the truth was that Atkins *was* a member of the House of Lords but had no other role in the government. All his actions in '*Secret Service*' activities were total bullshit. This place, the office information thieves, and even Dick Kelson's role as a *British* agent, were not run by government. It was Atkins that paid for this work, not the public sector.

Lord Atkins was a dominant millionaire, trying to compete with a father, who had been a Nazi supporter. That of course, had made him rich. Although they lost the war, he was able to buy and sell land in Britain and make investments across the world.

The Sterling that came in from the *Reichsbank* was fake. Goring and Ribbentrop had seen to that. After their British invasion took place, then Atkins would have been wiped out along with his henchmen, after they had built the concentration camps for the Nazis to use.

In fact, Hitler wanted to see Atkins and his staff in person, entering the gas chamber naked, so he could stand in front of them tearing up the fake pounds that the head of the *Reichsbank*, Walther Funk, had made for Atkins, and then gas all these *swines*. *WUNDERBAR!*

But it never happened of course. Kelson was unsure how the fake money had been used, but assumed Atkins used his huge gang of *street walkers* to make purchases every day with cash over the counter, and pass back the high percentage of change to his henchmen, who in turn, handed it to Atkins. Simple but effective.

"That's interesting sir," said Kelson, putting his thoughts away. "What is your plan if I might ask?"

Lord Atkins sneered at him and stood up slowly from his desk, moving menacingly again towards Kelson, then he walked around him as his brow sweat increased. Atkins sniffed into the atmosphere around Kelson's head, and stared into his eyes with anger.

"Would you mind if I take my coat off?" asked Kelson.

"Yes, I do mind," said Atkins. "Because the more you sweat, the more you stink of after shave. You better not have fucking well had that on when you swapped over that fake letter in Manchester."

He went back to his chair and looked across his desk at the now hugely perspiring old fool. "Because if you did, you probably would have stenched out their hotel room, and there is every chance that at least one of them would have smelt it when they came back in."

Kelson looked at Lord Atkins and lied. "I certainly would not have done that as today is the first time I've ever used it." He could see that Atkins was considering this, as he stared back, looking to detect any signs of the lie in his sweat covered, red face.

Then Lord Atkins smiled and began to laugh. He pointed at Kelson, as this growing hysteria started to bring in tears to his eyes, and then ran down his cheeks. Atkins took a handkerchief from his trouser pocket, then wiped them away and said.

"That serves you right for being almost five minutes late." He continued to laugh and said. "I know you would not have made that mistake Dick, you might not be the brightest tool in the box, but you certainly wouldn't have fucked up that badly."

Kelson grinned back at Lord Atkins. *This man is getting more bonkers by the minute,* he thought, and asked the question again. "So can you tell me what the plan is for the future then Sir?"

Lord Atkins continued his laughter and said. "No, but you'll find out soon enough, when everything is put in place."

Kelson was clear that he would find out nothing more tonight about any new plans, and so made no response to this. Unless there was another task he was required to carry out, it would be time for him to go, and he guessed rightly what was coming, as Lord Atkins sat back and smiled evilly at him.

"Well *Dicky boy*," he said. "We are finished now, and you better keep that stink-bomb, cheap aftershave off you in future, because if you don't, I shall force you to drink a full bottle of it. Now get up, and walk slowly to the door."

Kelson got up and turned around, doing all he could to move straight and without a hobble to the door. He knew Lord Atkins was staring and smiling, despite his back being turned on him. Then he reached the door and heard a slow hand-clap being made. He said nothing, turned the door's handle and walked out.

Atkins laughed and then looked across the room to where Kelson's trilby lay by the window. *Things are getting funnier tonight,* he thought walking over to it, then opened the window and threw it out into the street.

Kelson was on the pavement in Queen Anne's Gate, and watched his trilby spin to the ground. He stared at the hat as it went into the gutter, waited for a moment then hobbled over and picked it up. Then he dusted it off and slowly looked up at Lord Atkins, standing behind his office window, looking down and laughing.

Next time, Kelson said to himself, *I'll be the one who has the last fucking laugh.*

Linus examined the Stag's distributor cap on the workbench of his garage. He could not see the crack as he removed it, but holding it up to the ceiling light, it became clear. He looked over at the car and said. "Solved your problem, I'll get a new one for you on Saturday." Then he patted the Stag on it's hard top and gently closed the bonnet. "You'll be fine," he said. "I'll never let you down."

There was a knock on the garage door, which startled him at first but as he reached the frosted glass pane, he could see exactly who it was. He opened the door, and Colleen stood smiling at him. She looked across at the car and said. "It's not like you to be fixing the *old snag* is it?" She said, in a combination of humour and the personality of Rupert Cannon.

"Do you want a drink or a coffee?" he asked, taking off his gloves, "and if you prefer a drink, we can go over to the pub."

"I'd love a drink," she said. "But I'm buying."

The White Hart was quiet, with just a few locals in. Colleen went up to the bar, and as she got the drinks in, he walked over to the Juke Box and put *Freedom* by *Wham!* on.

She brought his lager-top and her glass of *Lambrini* over, and then they sat at a table. They touched their glasses and together said. "Cheers."

Colleen looked at Linus and asked. "So how are things going at *RADI-CAL* now?"

He took a swig of his pint and said. "It's alright, but still early doors. The team is actually pretty good."

"So do you think this could really work for the long term, or is Sir Dennis going to sell it off once it's gone live and gets publicity?" She asked.

That was a good question, given the way Sir Dennis took the RITON Group forwards. His style was to build up successful business ventures, and sell off those that weren't so good, but for a buyer, had the benefit of the group's reputation behind it.

Linus shook his head and said. "It's difficult to say for sure, but I've changed my opinion about these cellular phone things. It seems to me that they could be very useful."

He took another swig of the lager-top and continued. "You see, it's a way of keeping in touch when you're out, but there are also some *subtleties* that I have experienced."

Colleen put down her glass looking at him somewhat confused. "What do you mean by *subtleties*?" she asked.

"Well," he replied. "On the trip to Manchester, Sally-Anne called her dad as we drove along the motorway. We covered some distance, and you could hear the phone *click* from one cell base station to another. It might sound weird, but it *sort* of gave out a feeling of confidence, that it would just carry on working, never mind how far you went."

Linus looked down at his glass then continued. "Then next thing was that Bernie, Sally-Anne's dad, said he wanted to buy one. I think he realised the usefulness of these things, and not just because he had *thought* about it, but because he'd *actually experienced* it."

Colleen nodded and smiled at him. "So when this thing goes live, the *right* people are going to buy them quickly." She said.

"I really think so." He replied. "Obviously, they are only going to be of use for businesses that are moving around, but there are plenty of those out there."

"I get that." She said. "They are never going to be bought by the public of course, not at these costs anyway."

Linus took another swing of the lager-top and then laughed, thinking about what Mike Sentinel had said last month.

"What's the joke?" she asked him, smiling.

"The area manager, Mike Sentinel, told us that he reckoned there would be a million users in this country after thirty years." He said, still laughing at this.

"Are you sure the team is actually *pretty good?*" She said smiling back at him.

They carried on laughing, enjoying each other's company, as they had done for many years now. Raising their glasses up together, they both realised inside, that this was not for them, but for Rupert Cannon. *If only he could have been in here with them tonight.*

Colleen went into her serious, senior PA style and said. "I came to see you for a few reasons. Firstly, I need to give you the details about Mr Cannon's funeral, which is at St Leonard's Church in Streatham, at 11.00 hrs, a week tomorrow."

Linus nodded back and said. "I'll be there of course. Is there anything you want me to do?"

"No, it's all sorted out. The ceremony has been arranged by Brian, and there is going to be a number attending, including Sir Dennis. I'll pick you up on the way, as you are on route for me."

"Thanks," said Linus, then shaking his head in sadness. "I still can't believe he's gone." Then he realised if this was sad for him, it must be even more difficult for Colleen, given her work position.

"Anyway," she said, clearly trying to manage her emotions. "I need to tell you about something else that's happened."

Linus took another swig of his lager-top, wishing he could light up a fag, but he would never do that in front of Colleen Walker, as she carried on.

"Margaret Ellwood called me and asked if I would consider taking on the PA role for this *RADI-CAL* bloke called Steve Rider at, so I wondered if you'd met him yet?"

He knocked back the rest of his pint, now *desperately* wanting a fag.

"I have met him, on the training course at Heath-field." He said, thinking back to this bloke's smooth but demanding style. Then he remembered the call he considered making to Colleen, trying to reach Rupert Cannon after his meeting with Steve, but didn't because he knew she would not have put him through...

"So what is he like?" she asked.

"He comes over as a very strong manager, with complete focus on success. There is a charm about him, but he won't stand for any nonsense." Said Linus.

She nodded back and said. "That's what Margaret told me." She took a sip of her *Lambrini* and carried on. "The thing is, Sir Dennis would get reports back from me because of the information I gain. Margaret has been told to arrange this, and she feels that the situation you and I are in, is an opportunity, despite the sad loss of Mr Cannon."

Linus nodded with interest. "So, we would be feeding back information to Sir Dennis via Margaret in *secret service* style then?"

"That's right," she said, "and there are two key requirements for RITON Group. One is that we can pass information back about how *RADI-CAL* is operating and secondly, we can advise on anything that needs to be fixed urgently, that the Group is not aware of. "Now if I accept this, I can be based out in Kingston initially, but they are planning to move over Mr Rider's office to the Croydon site within weeks."

He realised how important this was. As a closely linked, and trusted pair, they could be valuable for the RITON Group board, especially Sir Dennis Ogilvy.

"I think you should go for it," he said. "You could have something good in this. If it goes forward, then it should become quite successful. I can't imagine it's ever going to be massive, but cell-phones might be used in a growing number of larger businesses." He took another sip of the lager-top and carried on. "If it doesn't work, then Sir Dennis is going to be pleased with our reporting back discretely, as it were. So, we could be on a win-win and another assignment in the future."

Colleen looked at him and nodded in agreement, raised her glass and said. "Right, I'll call Margaret and get started."

As they walked across the road from *The White Hart* and up to Colleen's Renault, the darkness had come in, and there was a definite feel of autumn in the air.

"So what did you think of that car article that Mr Cannon gave you?" she asked, turning the key in the lock of her car's door. They had spoken about this on the phone, when arranging tonight's meeting. She had made no comment then, but was surprised, and actually somewhat disappointed for Linus.

She knew Mr Cannon always took the mickey out of Linus about his *old snag,* but surely, given the circumstances, he would have at least written him a letter to say goodbye, not send some old article from *Motor Sport* magazine.

"I was surprised." He said. "In fact, it made me pretty sad. You see, given all the time we had spent working together on tankers, and then at RITON after they acquired them, he felt like a father to me. I could *almost* tell him everything about things that happened in my life that I…." He lost the ability to carry on and swallowed hard to hold back the emotions.

Colleen squeezed his hand, looking into his eyes. She didn't know what he meant, but felt his sadness. They had been *close* friends for years.

Then she went back into efficiency mode and said. "I can't understand it. I'll do some checking around the office, just to be sure there wasn't a mistake by the post staff, or something. Anyway, let's keep in touch and it looks like we'll be back working together soon, which I'm really pleased about."

They hugged and kissed each other on the cheek. Linus watched as she drove off in her Renault 5, its tail-lights disappearing into the night. She was gone, but he stood looking into the darkness as she exited, then he lit up a Marlboro, now deep in thought....

Jeannie walked back from the bar with two large glasses of claret. She didn't have time to change when she arrived home tonight because their table at the restaurant was booked for 20.00hrs, and Jeannie never turned up late for anything.

"Don't get me wrong," said Paul. "You look great, but I thought you might have wanted to get changed when you came back from work."

"Well, I would have done normally," she said taking a sip of her claret. "But Linus and I were running late, and so I didn't have time." She decided not to mention them going back into the *Albany Arms* for a second time today.

He raised his glass up and said. "You are an exceptionally hard worker Mrs Sands, and whatever you wear or *don't wear,* you look fabulous. *Cheers.*"

They touched glasses, *both mishaps resolved,* she thought.

The *Clover-Leaf* restaurant's bar had a nice ambience. The low-beams, soft lights, red carpet and open fire all added to the occasion of a good dine-out.

In fact, Jeannie and Paul had been regular customers for some time now. She looked across at him as they sipped their drinks, and then both glanced down at the menu.

A feeling of unhappiness washed over her. It was as if the boredom that made her leave her first husband, was flooding in again.

"So what do you *fancy* tonight?" he said, clearly trying to be a little humorous.

"I don't want much," she replied, ignoring this, moving the menu aside, then looking over at him. "What do you want?"

"I'll just go for the main course," he said. "I think I'll have chicken chasseur."

"Me too." She said, trying to show interest but not having any.

Paul extended his right hand across the table and touched her left one, his finger glancing over the wedding ring.

"I need to tell you something Jeannie," he said looking into her eyes passionately, and clearly trying to get out the words she guessed he'd probably been practicing for days. "I'd like us to have a child."

She smiled back at him; she had been expecting this.

"You know what Paul," she said, looking at him with a real depth of understanding. "I get that, and feel very appreciative. But, as I'm sure you know, this *RADI-CAL* thing is stressing me just now, so could we discuss this when things have calmed down a bit?"

He looked across nodding and with genuine understanding. "I'm sorry," he said. "That was selfish of me, it's just that…."

She touched his hand and then interrupted. "I really do understand, please don't think you are being selfish, these things happen, we'll sort something out."

Paul smiled at her, clearly pleased at not causing an upset.

Jeannie took another sip from her glass and thought. *Like I said to Mike Sentinel about my first husband. 'We have run out of road.'*

Chapter 14

Compiegne Forest, France
22nd June 1940

The warm sun beat down on the great elm and pine trees, and cast pleasant shadows on the wooded avenues. The time was now 3.15pm and a line of German troops, forming the guard of honour, stood on the right side of the long avenue leading to the railway dining car number 2419D. This was the same dining car that had been placed here for the armistice on the eleventh of November 1918.

German engineers had knocked down the wall of the armistice museum building, where the carriage had been proudly kept since then by the French government, and removed it two days ago. Then they made sure this wooden dining car was in the *exact* position it had been just under twenty-two years ago, even though there were no operating railway lines here. Precision of the position was essential for Adolf Hitler, because he was going to humiliate the French to a level that their nation had never experienced before.

Germany had invaded France on the 10th May 1940, and now within a matter of weeks, they had occupied the country. Many other nations across Europe had been taken, but even faster. It seemed there was no stopping them now. The Nazi's were heading to be the world's dominant super-power.

At the end of the avenue and on the edge of the forest, the statue of Field Marshall Ferdinand Foch, Supreme Allied Commander of the first world war and the chief of armistice negotiations in 1918 in this very spot, was now covered with Germany's national flag. Further along and on a tall, white pole, the personal flag of Adolf Hitler was slowly raised, as the Fuhrer and his senior staff officers, marched towards it.

They reached the dining car and then looked around at the site, standing together by a large granite monument block, in the centre of the clearing. Adolf Hitler stood and read the words carved into it, his arms folded.

"Here on the eleventh of November 1918 succumbed the criminal pride of the German empire...vanquished by the free people which it tried to enslave"

A mixture of scorn, anger, hate, revenge, triumph and complete control raged within Hitler, as he put his hands behind his back. He stepped away from the monument, making this gesture a masterpiece of contempt. Glancing back at it, strong and angry. Suddenly, as though his face was not giving out enough expression to his feelings, he threw his entire body into harmony with his mood. He swiftly thumped his hands on his hips, planted his feet wide and then raised his right leg in a marching style.

Hermann Goring looked over at Adolf Hitler, his god of the new Fatherland, and thought.

Once these French scum had signed the demands of our glorious Third Reich, then this whole place would be destroyed, but the dining car shall be taken to Berlin as a reminder to the Aryan race of what had been achieved by Mien Fuhrer and his loyal army. This world is to be ours!

At the end of the dining car on the left, were the steps up into a space that these eight, senior Nazi officers, would enter to assist their Fuhrer.

They took their seats, with Hitler in the same one that Foch had sat in during the humiliating armistice for Germany in 1918. Around the car stood a number of SS soldiers, all proud to be protecting their leaders in this moment of long awaited triumph for the fatherland.

Three senior French men, one of them in civilian clothes, and two in uniform, approached the dining car in the clearing under sunlight, flanked by three German officers. The men had flown up from Bordeaux to a nearby landing field, and then been driven to Compiegne.

Arriving at the dining car, French General Huntzinger, Air General Bergeret and Vice Admiral Le Luc went up the steps, together with Monsieur Noel, the French Ambassador to Poland. They had been chosen due to their acceptability for this event by the new French President, Monsieur Petain, often to be considered as the *puppet* head of France.

The men all sat in silence, with the exception of Germany's General von Keitel. He ordered that all agreement signatures were to made by 6.50pm and once done, Herr Hitler would sign in acceptance. There was no negotiation allowed. With that statement made, Hitler and his other officers stood and left the French behind with von Keitel and the SS guards.

They walked back along the avenue, the guard of honour now on their right, some held various instruments and played out the German national anthem, *Deutschland Uber Alles*.

Hitler saluted and led his general staff, as they walked towards the Alsace Lorraine monument. Something he would order the destruction of, along with the rest of this place, once the armistice had been signed. Only the train carriage would survive, and then be taken to Berlin on a lorry transporter.

At the far end of the site, Hitler's Mercedes-Benz 770 convertible was parked, it's swastika flying from the bonnet's mast, as the sun glinted off of the chrome work. The driver stood bolt-upright, waiting for the Fuhrer.

Hitler turned, then looked at the site. His guards stood to attention and his feeling of satisfaction grew. France now belonged to the Reich. He approached his senior officer and respected comrade, Herman Goring. Soon to be Germany's first *Reichmarschall.*

Goring smiled at Hitler. Today was the making of History.

"It has been a great day for the Fatherland," said Goring. "And it is all down to you Mein Fuhrer."

Hitler looked at Goring and said modestly. "It is not just I. You have always been loyal and deserve much acclaim. This is only the start for us. We now have much of Europe returned to where it should be. Britain is our next conquest. For this, we are relying on you."

Goring nodded, but felt a little pressurized. Hitler said this to Goring, as he was head of the *Luftwaffe.* Then Goring decided to bring up a relatively minor point, something that he felt was associated with the conquest of Britain. Something he wanted the Fuhrer to agree on.

"As you know," he said, "our *conveyor belt* work for sending Jews to Britain by Eichmann and von Ribbentrop had been of some success before war was declared on us. The *undercover* workers we have in their government department, have proven there is no knowledge of how this was being processed with any of their parliament ministers. We sent the *scum* away from countries we now control, and gained for our financial benefit. And those returned to us, of course, we dealt with, mainly in our new Polish *factories.*"

Hitler nodded back, a little frustrated, as this was not what he considered to be relevant to today's, historic event. But he knew Goring well enough to realize there was a specific thought that he wanted to share. Goring continued.

"When we take Britain, then I believe we should use this *connection* to build and manage the Jew *removal* sites we need to put in there. More can be sent there via the *conveyor belt*, from other countries we dominate, and so something has to be done when Britain becomes part of our glorious *Fatherland*." We have to build many *factories* there.

Hitler looked back at Goring, clear in his understanding of this. The sun was still beating down and he felt a wonderful warmth of atmosphere, believing there was a divine inspiration of glory from the heavens for him and his Aryan counterparts.

Back in the railway dining car, the three French leaders stood looking out of its windows. They would not be allowed to sit or leave the car, until Hitler had been chauffeured away from Compiegne. They were here to sign for the surrender of their nation, and there would be no choice.

"Then we must keep our secret assistants in Britain." Hitler said, looking back at the clearing where the monument block and the railway car stood. "We are to be paid four hundred million Francs per day by these French swine. We shall pay these loyal *friends* in Britain one tenth of one percent each day. Tell the *Reichsbank* to arrange this."

He smiled at Goring, patted him on the shoulder and said very quietly. "When their country is ours, this shall be stopped and we'll remove our helpers of course, but until then we should give something to the leader of this *connection*."

Hitler marched towards the Mercedes-Benz, the driver opening the rear door, his SS guards on the other side overseeing everything. Hitler turned and asked Goring.

"Tell me, what is the name of the man who is controlling this?"

Goring replied. "Permanent Assistant Secretary of State for the British Home Office. His name is Gregory Atkins, Mein Fuhrer."

"*Ja*, this man arranged things with von Ribbentrop didn't he?" Goring nodded as Hitler continued. "He is quite efficient but only at a low level. Make sure the *Reichsbank* print fake *Englander* money and have this sent via a neutral country.

Once we have taken Britain, then we shall insist Atkins works on arranging concentration camps. After they are built, we shall dispose of him and his men. I'll leave this in your capable hands, Herman."

Hitler turned and then stepped into the back of his car, the chauffeur carefully closing the door, then got behind the wheel and started the engine, as the SS guard stepped into the front beside him. Goring made the Nazi salute as it drove away towards the shadow of the trees, the sun still glinting off the chrome work.

Watching it head away at speed, Goring considered the daily fee for Atkins. His mathematics were good, that helped him as a pilot in the first war, and he quickly came up with the payment converted to British currency. It was *two thousand three hundred pounds* per day. That sounded acceptable, even though it would be fake.

Goring smiled and thought. *One thing is for certain, the gold bullion I am sending to Atkins in secret, shall be real. Even Mein Fuhrer does not know about this. After we invade Britain, it shall all belong to me.*

Chapter 15

RADI-CAL, Maidstone office
12th October 1984

Linus walked past the workshop and Derek Tweedy spotted him.

"*Och*," he called out, now walking under the roller-shutter and looming towards him, carrying a large spanner. "I want a *wee* word with *ye* boy."

Here we go again, thought Linus, *trouble from him, it's not even 09.00hrs yet, and given last night's Brighton bombing, there is enough to worry about.*

Tweedy came over menacingly, a roll-up in the corner of his mouth and stared at Linus as he tapped the spanner gently against his other hand. His overalls seemed clean, but there was a whiff of beer coming from his breath, now uncomfortably close.

"Is everything alright Derek?" asked Linus, expecting that it wasn't.

"*Aye,*" he said. "Just wanted to let *ye* know that the Rochester jobs are going well, and I've checked in with the Manchester *bairns* and they have started." He grinned at Linus and walked back to the workshop, the roll-up still attached to the corner of his mouth, as if it was glued on. In fact, he'd never seen Tweedy without it

"Thanks," said Linus. "Appreciate you letting me know."

Derek gave him the thumbs up and went back to his work. *Not a bad start to the day then.* Linus thought.

Up in the office, most of the team, were sat at the far end. But Mike Sentinel was not in today, and neither was Jeannie.

Kevin Aaron waved at him and said. "Good to see you Linus, how are things going?"

"Alright thanks, I am starting to get my head around things now. How about you Kevin?"

"We've got a few advance orders in from the City, and one of our boys is going to be a *super-star* now." Kevin replied somewhat sarcastically, looking over at Julian Rayne as if he'd been nominated for an *Oscar*.

Linus sat down and then asked Julian. "So tell me, when are you off to *Hollywood*?"

Julian smiled and said. "Take no notice of him. It's all to do with the publicity when we go live. You see when I was on the first *Heath-field* training course in April, a good friend of mine who works in the Stock Exchange and often trades a lot of overseas shares, saw how he might be ahead of the game because of us."

"So how does *RADI-CAL* help with that?" Asked Linus.

"Well," replied Julian. "It's all about timing. When this guy gets up and heads into the City office, he can call other brokers based overseas when he is driving." Julian looked at the team who clearly already understood this, as he'd explained it to them before. He carried on.

"When the network goes live, he'll be able to call countries anywhere that have finished or not yet commenced trading while he's driving to the Stock Exchange. That way, he can organise to buy or sell shares as soon as London opens."

Linus instantly realised what the potential of this was.

This guy could be ahead of the game from other traders, because they would *all* be out of overseas communication as they travelled to work, but Julian's connection would be *in the know*.

"I'd never considered that." said Linus, realising the great potential of this for *RADI-CAL*.

"That's an amazing opportunity." Now feeling somewhat dumfounded.

"Anyway," continued Julian. "The *R1* was fitted into his *Beemer* months ago. He is the first person to sign a contract for a cellular telephone in this country, so I guess our marketing lot are going to put this out in the press as soon as we go live, and he can make his first trading call."

"So did you come up with this idea?" asked Linus.

Julian looked back somewhat modestly at him, then glanced at the other G.A.M's and said. "Yes, but any of our team would have done the same. I was just lucky because this guy is an old friend of mine."

Linus extended his hand to Julian, delighted for his clever achievement, and also realising what a great publicity coup this was. The *first ever* person in Britain to have sold a cellular telephone was in the RITON group!

"Anyway," said Julian shaking hands with Linus. "I'm not going to *Hollywood*. In fact, the only star I'm going to meet is Frankie *Fucking* Howerd."

The whole team laughed.

The *Anchor* pub was starting to liven up. All the *RADI-CAL* team including Derek Tweedy, were there, so it would be good if that building site mob didn't show up….

The juke box came on with '*All cried out*' by *Alison Moyet*. The music blared out around the bar, there was an aroma of smoke in the atmosphere and everyone was in a good mood, not least because it was a Friday. But he felt that last night's appalling bomb attack on Mrs Thatcher and her party at *The

Grand Hotel in Brighton had brought people closer and even more loyal to Britain, irrespective of their political views. Linus took a swig of the lager-top and inhaled a drag of his Marlboro.

There was a positive atmosphere coming into the country. It was about time. Four years ago, inflation was at a ridiculous high of something like sixteen per cent, now it was down to three, and people were spending more. Confidence in Britain was on the increase. The doom and gloom was leaving, and as long as the nation's trading performance and its reputation of decency and democracy both *now*, and in the *past* to everyone remained, things could only improve. The awful hotel bombing had brought people even closer.

Robbie said. "So how was Jason then?" Linus changed his thought pattern back to the *RADI-CAL* office in Manchester, when Jason Lord had been derisory about Mike Sentinel.

"He seemed alright initially, but to be honest Robbie, then he pissed me off." Linus replied.

Robbie smiled back in understanding. He knew Jason well enough, so his annoying style was never a surprise to him. He took a swig of his bitter and asked. "So what did that *fucker* say then?"

"He seemed determined to slag Mike off, telling me about when he shot a youngster in Aden back in sixty- seven."

The colour drained from Robbie's cheeks and he leant on the bar, banging down his pint mug in anger. It didn't shatter, but the noise brought in the attention of the others who were close by. Silence came in for a second, then things returned to normal.

"Did he tell you how many lives he probably saved?" growled Robbie, his anger growing. Linus shook his head at him as he carried on. "Well he fucking should have done, because those *Kalashnikov* rifles weren't in that car for a joy ride were they?"

"I don't know the details or background to this at all," said Linus. "But I guessed from his attitude that he was somehow trying to wind me up and discredit Mike."

Robbie had started to calm down, took a swig of his pint and said. "Sorry to have lost my temper, but that is typical of not just him, but loads of others that don't *get* Mike."

"I'm beginning to understand that." Said Linus, thinking about what Robbie and Jeannie had told him about how supportive Mike was when they needed help.

"Like I always tell people," said Robbie. "They should remember how much he helped me out and probably loads of others, and that was *before* the Aden thing. If it wasn't for him, I'd be dead, so wouldn't be out with you in a lovely pub talking about cellular phones that are going to have a million users in thirty years' time."

With that, they both laughed and clinked their pint mugs together.

"On another subject," said Robbie, now clearly wanting to move right away from his annoyance. "What are you up to this weekend?"

"Well," said Linus. "I'm going into town tomorrow night for a few beers and then off to a club. How about you?"

"I'm taking my bike out for a run, before the winter sets in." He replied, smiling then said. "And before you ask, no it's not a *fucking* Norton."

Jeannie had pulled over into a tree-lined, side road on the outskirts of Maidstone. She reclined the driver's seat and looked through the windscreen as the sun began to set. Today had been quite a good one, having spent the morning off site with Mike Sentinel. In fact, they decided to meet up at the closest *Hilton* to the office, so they could discuss the way forward with her dealer relationship work.

Being the first in the *RADI-CAL* business to be involved with this was something of a challenge, especially given the need to carry on with her General Activity Manager role. But she had a great reputation for building relationships with dealers to promote Rate-Syrex products, when she worked there with Mike and Steve Rider, not forgetting Robbie and all the others of course....

But her main issue now, was time. She must keep her new business numbers on target, but also needed to put the hours in for laying out opportunities with partners. There was no decent advertising yet, and some of the press had not been favourable, making it even more difficult. She was passionate about work but insisted on personal happiness. She felt time was running short for her life.

In one newspaper, it was argued that *'pagers were good enough, so why bother with these new, unnecessary and expensive cellular phones?'* The reporter said that pagers were much cheaper, and once they *bleeped*, all you had to do was find a phone box on the street, of which there were loads, then call the number that had been sent. If someone answered, you could put your coins in, and speak to them until you ran out of change.

If no one answered, you might be able to leave a message, or find another phone box to use later. Easy. *'Why on earth would you ever need a cellular radio?'*

The sun died away and she watched the car pull up on the other side of the road, about a hundred yards away. It was a blue, Ford Cortina mkV. The driver was wearing a black, baseball style cap and she saw him wind down the window and blow a cloud of smoke out into the air. Then he flashed the headlights once. Jeannie flashed hers twice, and both knew the game was on. She took a deep breath, opened the Cavalier's door, stepped out and closed it very quietly. Then she took a final look around the street to see if anyone was watching her.

The coast was clear, and she slowly walked towards the Cortina, as the darkness came in.

As they pulled out onto the back road of the *Long Estate*, Linus looked down the bonnet of the Rolls-Royce Silver Shadow to the Silver Lady mascot, and asked. "So tell me, *why* are you driving your Dad's car tonight?"

"Well," said Sally-Anne, glaring over at his Stag as she drove past it. "Firstly, there is no way I am going out in that thing and secondly, you'll be paying for the petrol."

He looked over at the fuel gauge and saw that the needle was on full. "But the tank is full already." He said.

They had reached the main road and as she opened the throttle and headed up the hill towards Purley Way, she responded.

"By the time we get back from *Samantha's club,* the tank is likely to be empty. So you can either fill it up or put it onto your account, and I'd prefer the former, Mr *Shmuck* man."

He laughed, and she switched on the radio.

This car's engine was nearly 6.8 litres, but the distance was only a thirty mile round trip, so it wouldn't need more than three gallons. That would be around six pounds.

Accelerating past the *Aerodrome* Hotel, she turned up the volume and the song *Drive*, by a band, *The Cars*, appropriately resonated through the Rolls-Royce's four speakers.

The V8 engine's revs quietly increased, as if they were cocooned in a sound-proofed room. The car felt like a flying carpet, ignoring any bumps in the road. It seemed as if it was in a different world from every other vehicle on this planet. Powerful, smooth, slightly pretentious perhaps, but comforting and dependable. *Just like the driver* he thought, glancing over at her.

As they passed the RITON marine building, Linus looked at it in a mixture of sadness, guilt and happiness. It brought in the loss of Mr Cannon, but reminded him of where he'd met this woman taking him out in a Rolls-Royce tonight, despite him having to pay for its petrol.

Sally-Anne's parents were at a golf-club dinner-dance at Broxbourne in Hertfordshire, and would be staying up there overnight.

"So why aren't we in *your* car?" he asked.

"Because I don't smoke when I'm driving, so I reckoned you would steal *my* fags if we were out in mine. Dad does not allow *any* smoking in this car, so I'm safe. Anyway, I wanted to make the most of it before *your lot* fit that cellular radio thing in here."

Linus smiled at her again. She was a genuine one-off.

"Which route are we taking?" He asked.

"Westminster Bridge, Birdcage, Mall, Trafalgar Square and Piccadilly." She replied.

He touched the electric seat control knob and moved it back slightly. "Thank you chauffeur, wake me when we arrive."

She giggled. Sometimes, he could be funny. *Sometimes*.

Lord Atkins stepped into his red Bentley Mulsanne Turbo in Queen Anne's Gate. Being in his office on a Saturday had become a habit, not least because staying overnight in the *Cariton Club* on Fridays meant he could meet up with his right-wing pals for dinner and drinks until the small hours, then do some work and sober up before heading home. Unbeknown to Atkins, the issue for his *pals* however, was that they universally hated him….

Atkins started up the Bentley's V8 engine and lit his cigar, then he floored the throttle until the revolutions counter went close to the red zone, smiling. He didn't care how much he damaged his cold engine. Why should he? The car was brand new last month, bought from *Jack Barclay,* with a sum of money he felt was peanuts, *thanks to good old Adolf and Hermann.*

Anyway, if there was a problem with the car, he could take it back for repair to the suppliers, and treat them like *shit.* The very thought of this made him rev up again. He pushed in a cassette, which played *Richard Wagner's 'Ride of The Valkyries,'* and turned the volume right up. *What a composer that man was.* He Thought. *Good at music, and anti-Semitic right through to the core.*

He selected *'drive'* on the column gear lever, floored the accelerator pedal and screeched away from the kerb, not bothering to look out for any traffic.

Tearing past the parked cars on the road, he neared the junction with Dartmouth Street and then went straight into it, without looking right. He came onto Storey's Gate and headed towards Birdcage Walk, just up from Westminster Bridge.

Sally-Anne drove the Silver-Shadow carefully across Westminster Bridge, observing the 30 mph speed limit. The dusk was coming in, so she switched on the side-lights. Linus was singing out the words terribly from an old hit on the radio, *McFadden & Whitehead's, 'Ain't No Stoppin' Us Now.'*

She drove across the top of Parliament Square and onto Birdcage Walk. "*Ain't no stopping us now we're on the move."*

She stared in disbelief as a red Bentley came straight out of the side-road junction in front of them. As her foot instinctively touched the brake-pedal, she saw an old man with a cigar between his lips looking at her in what appeared to be delight, as he streaked across in front of them. It was as if it were a slow motion type of movie scene. But then he was gone, tearing up Birdcage Walk like a rocket. He missed them by what seemed like an inch.

"*Fucking idiot.*" She shouted, angry but also relived that they had not hit this lunatic.

Linus touched her arm and they glanced at each other in silence. Her left hand was on top of the wheel and as the setting sun's final rays came through the windscreen, they glinted off the silver Star of David on her bracelet. Miraculous.

There was no need to put money in parking meters after 18.30hrs and New Burlington Street was already full. Sally-Anne drove across Regent Street, into Beak Street and pulled into a parking space on the corner of Great Pultney Street.

They planned to have an early dinner, go into *Samantha's,* and head back about mid-night. Sally-Anne would only have a couple of drinks. That was what she'd planned to do tonight, even if she hadn't been driving, because she had something to tell him, and wanted to be sober when doing so. Anyway, she would certainly have a few when they got back home.

Stepping out of the Rolls, Linus looked over at a pub he'd never seen before. There was a black-board outside the front door, with a menu list chalked on it.

"That looks pretty good," he said, nodding at it. "What do you think?"

Sally-Anne, clunked the driver's door shut, walked around the front of the car and onto the pavement, then stared over at it. "Yep, let's go for it." She replied.

They walked arm in arm into the *Sun and 13 Cantons* pub. She was wearing a black dress, low cut and medium length, with matching high-heels. As she strutted across to the bar, the ceiling lights touched her raven hair and the silver necklace. She exuded class and sensuality.

As they reached the bar, Linus looked around. He noticed she was picking up a lot of attention. But as ever, she ignored this, giving out a slight smile, connected to an image of superiority. *No wonder she is so successful in her business,* he thought.

"What would you like?" he asked.

"I'll just have a coke please." She replied, and then added. "I'll have a couple of Vodkas in *Samantha's,* and that'll be it till we get home."

Linus understood, and lit two Marlboros then passed one over to her as they sat on the bar stools. The bar maid came over and he ordered their drinks.

"All pretty old hat in here isn't it?" he said looking around the place. "Feels like we are in the nineteen thirties."

"Well," she responded. "I know you are getting on a bit, but never thought you went back that far."

He ignored her as he paid the bar maid, then raised his glass against hers and said. "Cheers."

"I need to ask you about something." She said, looking into his eyes with a depth of concern."

"Fire away," he said, taking a sip of the lager top as he held up his other hand. "Don't worry, your cheque is in the post."

She ignored him and said. "My sister, Esther, is working for dad in California as you know." Linus nodded back as she carried on. "Well, things have started to take off there, and she has signed up a large production company that dad is going to link up with for TV shows and perhaps even movie distribution over here and in Europe."

"Wow," said Linus. "That sounds amazing."

"Well, it's not been easy, but she has done a good job out there." She took a drag of her Marlboro and carried on. "The problem is that she needs some help, because there are now doors opening with other producers, but she has to focus on the one she has signed already. Also, another prime opportunity is based over in New York."

Linus realised the distance issue for Esther, and nodded back in understanding. Sally-Anne carried on.

"That is something of a conundrum, which is why Esther suggested to dad that I head out there for a while to help out. What do you think?"

Typically, she had gone straight to the point. Linus felt an overwhelming weight of concern coming at him. New York was not the safest place to be, and what if he lost her to someone else? Then his mind went back to losing Anna, and his head started to spin. It was as if, suddenly, everything good was turning to bad. He needed to control this and said, "I get that, even though I know nothing about the industry, something with that sort of opportunity needs to be managed properly."

She put down her glass, touched his hand, looked in his eyes and said. "If you tell me that you don't want me to do this, I'll say no, and don't worry because both of them will be totally understanding. I assure you, there will be no issue."

He knew she really meant that, but still felt choked and would never ask her to let Bernie down. "When would you have to go, and for how long?" He asked.

Sally-Anne carried on, trying to continue her analysis of his feelings and wanting her genuine commitment to him beyond anything, to come across.

"Well," she said as cheerfully and as matter of fact as she could manage. "Because of the New York people being on hold until a bit later, they want me to go at the end of next month. I don't know how long this is going to take, but it could be a couple of months or so."

Linus nodded, took a sip of his lager top and asked. "So could Esther not find someone over there to do this?"

"If she could, she would," she replied. "But the problem is that dad's aim is all about bringing these American shows here and like I said, maybe into Europe, so it is much better to have us there in conversation with the production companies. There is no simple way to communicate this. All the information details need to be written up and faxed over to dad at the very least. Anyway, he views this as a family business in a critical moment of opportunity."

She sat back and took a drag of her Marlboro, looking up at the ceiling. "Also, I'm not as clever as Esther, but I understand how dad operates."

Linus was now struggling to find words. The bar was filling up and getting noisier. He took another swig of his lager top and said. "I'm really going to miss you."

"I'm going to miss you too," she said and then stubbed out her Marlboro and looked over the table at him. "Why don't you chuck everything in and come with me? I *fucking* love you and it won't cost you a penny, or even a cent."

Linus swallowed hard, covering up his emotions, laughed and said. "But it could be a *pound* or a *shekel.*"

"Ha-ha Mr *Shmuck* man. I'm being serious." She looked around the bar, then leaned across the table and said. "My business is growing faster than you might think. I've got six girls now, and they are all working for me but not as *employees*. They are my *agents*. The calls come in from the adverts in the local paper and then I organise, take the cheques or cash in the post and pay the agents in advance."

"That local paper is not called the *Croydon Advertiser* for nothing then?" He said.

"No, and I can get it managed by one of dad's staff when I am in America. Which means I can give the money to you if you come with me. Then when we come back, I'm sure RITON would take you on again, or something else would be out there for you." She lit up two Marlboros and passed one over to him and carried on. "I totally get it if you feel that's not right, I just wanted you to know."

Linus looked at her realising she meant it. He felt sad, moved and madly in love with her, all at the same time.

Atkins pulled up in front of the black iron gates of the mansion's drive entrance. The Bentley's headlights were on full-beam and glinted off the spikes on top of the gates. He switched off the ignition, removed the key ring and stepped out.

On the gate pillar, was a large, grey metal box. He turned the key in its lock and opened the door. Inside was an alloy button pad with numbers on it, rather like in a new-fangled 'phone box. Lord Atkins pressed *1,9,3,3* then shut the door, and locked it. As he returned to the Bentley, the gate's two motors whirled and they began to open inwards.

Starting the engine, he drove through and pulled up, then he switched off the car again, took out the key, and walked over to a similar box on the inside. He turned the key in the lock and pressed in another number *1,9,4,0*. He locked the second box and the gates slowly began to close. Atkins got back in the Bentley and started it up, looking back at the gates in the driving mirror as they both clanked shut.

"Ah, modern technology." He said out loud. "So much *simpler* than the old days."

He floored the throttle and covered the quarter mile to the huge, Victorian mansion, the headlights on full beam, catching the trees, fields and fences.

A deer stood watching him fly past, and an owl at the top of a tree, looked down as the Bentley crunched over the gravel and pulled up outside the front door, the engine idling and the lights still on, as Atkins got out and walked up the steps.

A tall, elderly servant bowed his head and held open the door as Atkins walked in, saying nothing to the man, just waving down the steps making it obvious that his Bentley should be moved.

Atkins walked along the hall-way, past the wide, red-carpeted staircase, the huge lounge, music room, dining room and men's smoking and billiard rooms. On the walls were a mass of oil paintings, the closest to the lounge being an original *Van Gogh*, a gift from Hermann Goring.

Coming towards him and looking down graciously as he approached, was his butler.

"Are you running late for some *fucking* reason *Smithy*?" Said Lord Atkins, angrily.

"I'm sorry your Lordship," replied Smith. "I wasn't expecting you back yet."

Atkins smiled at him and said. "That's not an issue *Smithy*. Plenty of servants get things wrong. Luckily for you, I'm not my father, because he would have *fucking scalped* you."

Smith's face went pale and said. "I'm sorry Sir, it won't happen again, I'll be waiting in the entrance the next time you return."

"You can bet your *bottom* dollar it won't happen again *Smithy,* and talking of which, don't expect to get paid this month." Snarled Atkins. "Now take my coat off and bring me a whisky and soda."

The secure room was at the far end of the building, and Atkins turned and made his way towards it, as Smith stood in sadness and anger staring at the overcoat he gripped in his hands, the label was from *Gieves & Hawkes*. He looked down the hall as Atkins walked on and shook his head, thinking.

If only I'd been born with a father like his Lordship's, and not to a pauper.

Atkins opened the room's door with a brass key, then closed it behind him and switched on the lights.

They crossed Regent Street just before midnight, and began the stroll back along Beak Street. The music had been loud in *Samantha's* night club, and as usual when leaving, there was still ringing in their ears. The DJ had been using turntables fitted behind the bonnet of an old, scrapped, E-Type Jaguar, on the edge of the dance-floor.

The club lighting was low and the spinning, over-head mirror ball gave out colour flashes, making it look as if the DJ was actually driving this old car.

Sally-Anne was singing *Caribbean Queen*, as they strolled along the pavement. Linus stopped by a lamp post and lit up two Marlboro's, passing one over to her.

"Actually," he said, somewhat smugly. "The version played in there was *European Queen.*"

"I know that," she said, taking her first drag. "And I am aware *that* was the *b side*, but so what?"

He was about to respond, and then a black cab streaked past, the diesel engine loud, and with only the side-lights on.

"For *fucks* sake," he said, watching it speed up towards the *Sun and 13 Cantons* pub. "Why hasn't the driver got the headlights on. Bloody dangerous."

"The thing is," she replied as they walked on back to her dad's Rolls-Royce, "cab drivers might drive looking a bit crazy, but they always concentrate hard on what they are doing." She looked snootily over at him and said. "Unlike some."

They reached the Rolls as Linus stood thinking about that cab flying past the pub, feeling a shiver run through his body for some unfathomable reason, as Sally-Anne opened the driver's door and stepped in. Then she pressed a switch inside, near the armrest, which somehow magically unlocked his door. He looked at it in disbelief as he stepped in and she stared over at him, flicking the raven-hair back, and superciliously said. "It's called *class*."

She turned the key in the round panel on the dashboard near her door, clicked on the light switch, selected *drive* from the gear lever on the right of the steering column, flicked up the indicator stalk on its left, and carefully pulled away.

Sally-Anne decided to take a different route to the south of the Thames. She headed back to Regent's Street, around

Piccadilly Circus, down the Mall towards Buckingham Gate, then left towards Victoria and over Vauxhall Bridge. There was no way she would go back to Westminster Bridge following what happened earlier tonight….

Crossing the bridge to Vauxhall Cross, she pressed a button on her door and Linus felt his lock gently from the arm-rest. This could be a rough area. As they pulled up at the lights in centre of the three lanes on the south-side of the bridge, she pushed a tape into the *Blaupunkt*. *'A night to remember* by *Shalamar'*.

Alongside them, a red Ford Escort XR3 pulled up, the driver revving the engine, clearly looking to race them when the lights went green. She ignored it, and the Ford streaked away when the traffic lights were still on red, both of them laughing at the stupidity of this. *You can drive as fast as you want, but can't ever beat being out in something like this.* Thought Linus, looking along the bonnet at the Silver-Lady.

They went through Brixton and reached Dulwich Village. As Sally-Anne drove past *Dulwich College*, Linus, began to think about Rupert Cannon's funeral next week. Then his mind went back to the last time they'd met at the *Aerodrome* Hotel.

Sally-Anne glanced over at him. She knew something was nagging at him inside. Linus had brought the sun back out from the clouds of her life. She had been cheated on in the past, although never told anyone. There was *something* about him. It was as if they had been together before in another era. A bit like a dream, where you wake up, desperately trying to keep the details as they fade away. Every time they went out now, this kicked in again.

"What's on your mind Mr *Schmuck* man?" she said. "No, no don't tell me, I'll guess, it's about how *you* are going to pay for the petrol isn't it?"

He looked across at the gauge next to the speedometer on the walnut veneered dashboard, shrouded in a soft green illumination.

"Quarter of a tank used up," he said. "Might have been less with a slower driver."

"So what's bothering you apart from fuel costs?" she asked glancing over.

"Oh, quite a few things," he said looking over at her. "You going *stateside* for one."

She concentrated on the road ahead as they went through the toll-gate, which was free this late at night. The headlights caught the tall trees on both sides of the steep hill's bends.

"Yes, I get that." She said. "And I really want you to come with me, even though I realise how impractical that is for you, it doesn't stop me wishing you could."

"I've been thinking about that since you told me." He replied. "The problem is that the Chairman of the RITON group wants to discuss something with me about this *RADICAL* thing, according to Colleen. That could happen at Mr Cannon's funeral on Friday, so maybe the outcome would be a reason for me to stay or chuck it all in."

They reached the top the hill, and she turned right towards the *Crystal Palace* tower.

"I understand that." She said. "It was unfair of me to ask you to leave. I think I'll be finished over there by the end of February at the latest, then you can pick me up from Heathrow and pay me back what you owe, which by then, is likely to be loads due to interest."

They went past the Crystal Palace tower and headed down towards Croydon.

The tall structure Linus felt was the same as the Eifel tower in Paris, even though it was only here to bring in radio and television signals to the south of London. It had red lights on it up to the very top, no doubt to warn aircraft of its presence. On the hillside below it stood a block of flats. He'd been told that his mother had stayed here after she left his father. Sally-Anne looked over at him as he pondered what had *really* gone wrong between his parents, so very long ago.

"I love America," he said. "There is a special feeling of acceptance there for everyone, no matter what race or religion. It starts off at the airport passport control, and then you feel it on every street in the city. It's always straight and to the point but *kind*."

She continued to concentrate on the driving, coming up to the red traffic lights near Norwood Junction rail bridge as he continued.

"It's like when Thomas Jefferson said in the American Declaration of Independence.

"We hold truths to be self-evident, that all men are created equal." He looked at her as the lights changed to green and she drove off. "Course, he meant that applied to *women* also."

"Ooh, *Mr History*." Said Sally-Anne.

Chapter 16

Hertfordshire
14th October 1984

Lord Atkins sat back and lit up his cigar, looking across at the long cased, flame mahogany, moon clock made in 1795. On the clock's top plinth, stood its original brass eagle statue, between the curved, gold painted swan necks, on top of the moon-phase dial. The lights in the room were dim but touched the eagle's wings, reflecting its position as leader of every element of the clock's design, materials and function.

Midnight had chimed a few minutes ago. Atkins took a swig of the whisky from his crystal glass. He swirled the remainder around smiling, the lights glinting off his glass. '*Kristallnacht*', was what he called it….

He was feeling tired. Things were moving too fast in life, and he sighed as he felt age was withering him. On the wall staring over, was an oil painting of his father looking stern and confident, in the late nineteen thirties.

Despite his enormous wealth, Lord Atkins was internally self-hating. Everything he owned was made possible by his father's money. He felt a huge pride in this, but it wasn't just about the money. It was how his father had achieved this in his relationships with that wonderful *Fuhrer* Hitler and *Reichsmarschall* Hermann Goring. Atkins loved his father, but was riled by constant jealousy.

Although the Nazi's lost the war, his father had used *their* money to his advantage, investing in land and businesses across Britain and the Commonwealth. Up until his father's death, he had done nothing. But then he began to become more like his father. He was able to grab onto the coat tails of his old man, who had received a knighthood when the war was over, due to his diligent hard work as Permanent Assistant Home Office Secretary. Following his father's death, being made a Lord was a natural assent for such a loyal and respected man's only son....

This opened the door to start a new activity. He created the fake secret agency, and that enabled him to enjoy the satisfaction of arranging bribery and corruption, by using his people to steal information from businesses.

Then, their owners would be threatened, and unless they paid, their businesses could be destroyed if his agents forged the stolen information and then sent it to the press. Atkins often liked to compare this with *The Protocols of the Elders of Zion*.

Many of his staff believed they were *actually* carrying out work for the government, and that always made him smile. However, those who didn't were expendable. Dick Kelson could be quite useful in seeing to that, like *his* father did, many years ago. Atkins looked around the room and over to the huge safe door in the far wall. Yes, the money they made from the immigration *conveyor belt* was good. But that was only the start, thanks to how it opened things up so much more.

He stubbed out the cigar and stood up, moving towards his safe. Now was the chance of some payback to the activists in Germany, who were supporters of a *new* Third Reich. But they would have to earn it.

The safe's door was set into a steel frame, and had a bronze securing rod wheel, a number lock, opening lever and massively strong hinges. It was an old bank vault door, over seven feet in height and bought by his father when he acquired this place in 1938. It was bomb-proof, and only one man knew the code and owned the key....

Atkins entered in his numbers by moving the chrome knob, then turned the large key in the lock and pushed down the brass handle. The bronze wheel released the steel door securing arm, and Atkins turned it to the right, then pulled it back. He needed all his strength to get the door open.

The safe-room was in total darkness and silence as Atkins walked in. He stood for a moment, basking in the knowledge of what was surrounding him, then took a deep breath before reaching out to the light switch. It was always like that for him, the overwhelming feeling of respect for his father, and the Nazis who supplied it all....

The fluorescents flickered off the four gold bars on the central table, and then settled in brilliance around the room. The walls were covered in classical artwork, much of it from *Carinhall*, the summer house of Goering. Metal cabinets surrounded the room below the paintings, each with closed, locked doors.

Atkins walked to the table and looked down at the gold. He picked up one of the bars and smiled at its markings. It was quite heavy, about twenty-six pounds and stamped with an eagle, its wings spread as it stood on top of the encircled swastika. Underneath, the year 1938 was engraved, as was the number 799884. He never understood why these numbers had been conceived by the *Reichsbank,* but so what? He owned over *five hundred* bars, and each had a different one on it. One thing he did know; their total value was around ten million pounds. Although, he'd need to smelt them before they could be sold, and never wanted to damage their history.

He put the bar back down on the table with the other three. Atkins always liked to have these on show, even though he was the only one who would ever go in this strong-room, and all the other bars were securely locked away.

But despite his enormous pride in the gold, the artwork and so many other glorious gifts from the Nazi's, there was one thing that he felt was the crown of it all.

Atkins slid open a draw beneath the table and looked at a buff coloured file, it's cover with the eagle and swastika in black, on the top. He gently ran his fingers over it and then opened the file. Inside was the letter from Heinrich Himmler to his father. Atkins read it in silence, swelling with pride. He'd done this so many times, but it always moved him intensely.

Herr Atkins

It is with respect and honour that the award of an Iron Cross has been made for your loyal support of our Third Reich, and your future Einsatzgruppen dedication across Britain.

Heinrich Himmler Reichsfuhrer – SS
10th August 1939

Atkins continued to savour this brief yet magical sentence from one of the most intelligent men in military history A man who took the SS from a mere 290 men to being a million strong. A man who created more extermination camps than any other human in the history of this world. Lord Atkins shook his head in sadness. *If only they had won.*

Under the envelope was a small, black velvet bag. He took it out and opened it. The Iron Cross shone as the room's lights touched it, but what he liked most, was the Swastika in its centre. *That should always have been in the heart of this world.* He thought.

Manfred von Sterne left Berlin's *Paris Bar*, walked across the *Kanstrasse* and got into the Volkswagen Jetta. In the driver's seat, a dark haired man in a black leather jacket looked at him with interest.

The street lamp caught the side of the driver's face as he continued to stare at von Sterne, a scar ran from near his right eye, down the cheek, ending close to his lip. *Another centimetre during that slash and you'd be dead.* Thought von Sterne.

"So, what was the outcome?" the man asked, his English both clear and precise.

"I believe we have an agreement in place to go ahead," replied Manfred then continued. "If we play the game correctly with Atkins, there is the money to come from him or he can melt down the gold bars, removing the swastikas, and then re-cast them."

"That's both good and bad," said the driver, resting his hands on the steering wheel and looking along the bonnet. "We can use that to our advantage, but it's not good for our pride Manfred."

"I realise that Gerhard, but at least we know the gold is genuine, and we can store it in the *Neuruppin* site." Von Sterne replied.

Gerhard nodded over at the office door near the *Paris Bar* and asked him. "So how did he sound on the telephone in there."

"He seemed alright, in fact clearer about what he wants from us than normal." Replied von Sterne.

"What *exactly* did he say he wants from us?" asked Gerhard, now sounding frustrated.

"He wants us to organise an on-going rally across his country, and we take on a number of historic supporters of the Third Reich and re-establish it under our *Fourth Reich*. He wants something similar to the *Kristallnacht,* as he believes this would increase the support of many in Britain, maybe even the majority."

"The man is crazy," said Gerhard. "Our country had already taken control of Austria in 1938 before we started that, and *Kristallnacht* was to show the power of the Third Reich to the world, as well as our hatred for the Jews of Austria."

"I appreciate that," said von Sterne. "Which is why I have been thinking about how we can actually use, and then sideline Lord Atkins to our advantage." Von Sterne, watched the cars continue to drive past. A little over one kilometre away, on the other side of the wall, there would be no traffic. *Checkpoint Charlie* would see to that.

"I see," said Gerhard, as the rain fell onto the windscreen. "Perhaps you could fill me in on this?"

"The trick is to do this with subtlety. Before the second war started, there were supporters of Germany in Britain. These *intelligencers* knew how the French had destroyed our old country when we surrendered in Compiegne in 1918. That is why our *Fuhrer* took us forwards, to recover what was *ours* again in Europe. Hitler *knew* the Jews were *not* influential on causing our losses during and after the first war. But he wanted revenge against France and its allies, quite rightly, and so would use them as an excuse to gain from it."

Gerhard nodded, listening intently despite already knowing this, and passed over one of the two cigarettes he'd lit to von Sterne, who took a drag and continued.

"Britain is now heading forwards and to the *right* as its economy grows. We can use this to connect with the *contrived* evil loss of our old country caused by the Jews. By growing the numbers of sympathisers in Britain, we can restore anti-Semitism." He nodded towards the Berlin wall. "There's a good example. How *fucking* unfair was that?"

"I understand your anger Manfred, and I feel the same. But I don't see how this could work," said Gerhard.

"I'll tell you how I believe it *can* work." Replied Manfred. "We create a subtle version of *Kristallnacht* again, but this time, in Britain."

Gerhard took another drag of his cigarette, the rain was now hammering down, then he shrugged his shoulders as Manfred continued.

"We bring in an attack on the Jews in Britain. It gets negative stories in the press of course, but I believe the level of support in this from their nation will grow, because we can offset the bad press by giving out the *truth* of how the Jews destroyed us after the first war. We can knit back old Nazi ways with the British people, convincing the majority of how much better their lives would have been if we had joined together before the war started. Not least, because no debt of billions would have been owed to the Americans by the British. In short, we *claim* that if the Jews had not ruined us in 1918, then no second war would have come, and maybe not even our *Fuhrer*."

"That's an interesting hypothesis Manfred." Said Gerhard, smiling at him. "And I suppose, even if this fails, we shall still put a match to a powder keg that might go off in the future."

"Exactly," said von Sterne. "And the advantage is that Atkins is going to ship us forty percent of the bullion agreed in advance. My estimate is that should be over a million *deutsche marks* as the down-payment, so even if it doesn't work, we have a nice contribution for our *Fourth Reich*."

"Yes," replied Gerhard. "Once we have the first payment from *Herr* Atkins, we can get our other *associate* in London to take over anyway, so whatever happens, we shall get more. After all the gold was always *ours* anyway. So let's get on with it."

"*Ja*," said von Sterne. "*Das ist gut mein Freund.*"

"*Nein*," responded Gerhard. "I told you, we *must* play this game in English."

Manfred nodded back and said. "I shall prepare matters including the down payment."

"Good," said Gerhard, turning the key and starting up the Volkswagen's engine, then lent over to Manfred as he stepped out and said. *"Auf Wiedersehen."*

The car then accelerated up the *Kantstrasse*, the tail lights disappearing into the darkness and rain. Von Sterne dashed across the street and back towards the *Paris Bar*. As he reached the door, a couple walked out onto the pavement. The man was speaking, not to his woman, but into a grey *brick* looking thing with a black aerial on top.

Manfred reached the long bar and thought about that *brick* cellular phone. These had just gone live in West Berlin.

He ordered a *Berliner Pilsner* and lit up a *Karo* cigarette. Leaning against the bar, he felt it vibrate, as the music was loud. The song on now was by *New Order*, called *'Blue Monday.'* It had already been a hit in West Germany. The bar was packed, despite it being past mid-night, everyone looked merry and plastered. A short distance to the east, across the wall, it would be silent and in darkness, and the poor people there would be in their beds. He shook his head in anger at how things had panned out almost forty years ago.

The beer foamed over the edge of his glass onto the bar and he took a sip, thinking about his friend, Gerhard. They'd been together in the undercover *Fourth Reich* now for ten years. But the man had never told him anything about his past. And now, Gerhard Baum was the most senior man in their new order.

Manfred took a swig of his beer followed by a drag of the cigarette. Two things had always puzzled him about Gerhard. How did he get that scar, and it seemed an extraordinary co-incidence that the name *Gerhard*, was the same as Himmler's adopted boy? Sure, his surname was faked, and that was the case for of all of the *Fourth Reich* members. But what if his Christian name was real, and he was Himmler's adopted boy?

The blonde bar maid winked at him, and he smiled back, noticing that her pale, large breasts that were almost out of her tight, red dress.

But so what about names and the past. What mattered was the future, and now there was a chance. They needed to get moving, and managing the situation with *Herr* Atkins was his job now. Assuming they could open up their Fourth Reich in Britain, one of the main difficulties was how their comrades there could privately communicate with each other, as they ransacked its cities.

He took another swig of the *Berliner Pilsner,* as the blonde leaned over the bar, licking her lips and staring him in the eyes. The song, *Blue Monday* played the words. *'But if it wasn't for your misfortune, I'd be a heavenly person today.'*

Then a thought struck him. *Of course! That man walking out with the Motorola cellular radio phone. When this goes live in England, our 'new order' could use these to communicate and plan with each other. Herr Atkins can pay for this too.*

He smiled at the bar maid, and touched her face enjoying her, and his *schadenfreude* plan for Atkins. It was time to get on now....

"They are a German band, aren't they?" Asked Linus as she put the album on in the lounge.

"Yes, it's *Alphaville,*" said Sally-Anne. She danced towards him, then spun around three hundred and sixty degrees. "But they are *Big in Japan.*"

He stood up and put his arms around her, as they rocked slowly to the music. She ran her fingers through his dark hair, the Star of David on her wrist glinting, as the lounge's wall lights touched it.

As the song finished, the next track came on from the *32 Hits Album* on the turntable, *'Self Control'* by Laura Branigan.

"Now this reminds me of a *very* special occasion." Said Linus as they sat on the sofa together, both smiling at the memory of something that happened barely a month ago.

"Talking of *reminds,* then" she said. "You still owe me for that, and more besides."

"Well, at least you didn't include Mr *Shmuck* man in that." He replied.

"I don't have to. Because you *obviously* already know that, don't you?"

He ignored this, picked up his glass of Moet from the coffee table and raised it against hers. As they clinked together, he said. "Seriously, though I'll put the fuel in your dad's car in the morning, if you can drive me to the petrol station."

She looked at her glass, realising that was not going to happen. "Let's put that on hold." She said.

Linus lit up two Marlboros and passed one over to Sally-Anne. Her dad and mum were fine with anyone smoking in the house, as long as they opened the windows.

"So when did your dad come into this country?" He asked.

Sally-Anne took a drag of her cigarette, clearly giving this a little thought before responding. "It was early 1939," she replied. "He was eight years old and came in from Prague by plane." She pointed towards the right window in the lounge. "It landed at Croydon Aerodrome. His parents weren't on the flight, and he never saw or heard from them again, or any other family member come to that. He was the only one who was given an exit visa and survived."

Linus felt a mass of sadness hit in and said. "I'm so sorry."

Sally-Anne held up her hands and said. "Don't be. If he hadn't made it, then I wouldn't be here and neither would mum or Esther.

He was lucky as he was put on a train to Prague from just outside Vienna by his father, who stood on the platform and waved him goodbye. He was desperate to save my dad after *Kristallnacht* happened."

She stared at her glass. Linus could see emotions were building within her and kicked himself mentally, for asking the question. But irrespective of whatever she faced, Sally-Anne had the courage of a wounded lion inside her head, and staggered back.

"It was called *Kindertransport*, but I expect you know that don't you?" she said, taking a sip of champagne. "Apparently, the British government waived some of the immigration requirements to let them in. Although, dad said a lot of older people were not allowed in, and just disappeared. Anyway, dad was put into a hostel and the rest as they say, is history."

Linus knew that she had finished now. He imagined what it must have been like for an eight-year-old coming here with no family, probably no friends and certainly into a strange land with a language he'd never spoken, or even heard before. And what about the possibility of bullying? Then he looked around the lovely room and at the Steinway piano, then finally over to his beautiful daughter. Linus shivered down his spine. *What an amazing man Bernie Cohen was.*

Sally-Anne finished her champagne and re-filled the glass, then reached across and did the same for Linus. They touched their glasses together, with the effects of the Moet now coming into both of them. The next track playing out in the room was *Ghostbusters.*

She looked at him with a depth of real seriousness, it was as if there was something she really needed to get out. And then she did.

"Linus, we have all got to fight this. The aftermath of what happened then has affected us all in some way. But we *don't* communicate it. We don't, so we still can't fully understand it." She took a final drag of the Marlboro, stubbed it out and lit up two more, passing one over to Linus and carried on.

"We can't help who we are, so we bury it inside, and then it eats away at us. I've seen it in my dad."

She leaned forwards and looked him in the eyes and said. "The *fucking* Nazis were not *just* killing our relatives Linus. Irrespective of whether they won the war or not, they wanted to hurt the *left overs like us*, for generations!"

Linus took a sip of the Moet, but as he did so, guilt hit in hard for those that had been destroyed so disgustingly back then. Sally-Anne realised what he was thinking and said.

"And how you feel in this *moment* and if you are not careful, throughout your *whole* life is *exactly* what the fucking Nazis intended. Inbuilt misery, and then if things go well for you, guilt for the ones who *they* murdered."

He wanted to respond, but could think of nothing to say. She was right. Sally-Anne continued.

"They knew in 1944 they'd lose the war, but then increased the genocides. Why? To create hundreds of years of on-going pain for us. And Hitler's plan was to ironically turn attitudes against the Jews, because he knew we would all be committed to make sure this didn't happen again, and so became defensive and angry if anything seemed like a threat."

She took another swig of the Moet, emptying the glass and placing it gently on the table. Linus could see the calm was returning. She laughed with an ironic head shake, put her hands together and touched her lips with her fingers.

"We have to beat this. For both of us, and maybe even if we have a child one day. I don't know."

Linus put his glass down and ran his fingers gently through her raven hair. There were no tears on her cheeks, she was too strong for that. It was one of the many things he loved about her. Their lips touched with a genuine passion, and a magical sensation that they both felt from a past life. Although they had never spoken about this, it was becoming intoxicating.

The train left Broxbourne station for Liverpool Street, it was just after 11am on Sunday morning. Bernie looked across the fields, as the autumn sun caught the bare ground and hedge rows, all the crops had now been harvested.

"What's on your mind?" asked Jane.

"Oh, nothing really," replied Bernie, bringing his thoughts back to today from the past. "I have a *thing* about trains."

"Talking about *things*, do you think Sal and Linus are going to stay together?"

Bernie considered this for a moment, then said. "Yes, I do. They haven't known each other for long, but there is a real connection between them, as if they *had* known each other for many years."

"That's weird," said Jane. "I feel the same. Do you think they'll cope with being apart when she is out in the States with Esther?"

The train speeded up and the fields began to rush past it, like a silent movie from the early nineteen twenties. Bernie stared out of the train's window, his mind heading back to his own experience of the past, that was in 1939. The 11th of January, to be precise...

He waved at his father, the smoke from the steam engine passing the open carriage window as the train moved away. There were many fathers and mothers waving at their children, as it left the station platform in Vienna, heading for Ruzyn airport, Prague.

If his father had not sent him, then where would he have ended up? It could have been in Germany, Poland or even still in Austria. But wherever it was, it would *certainly* have been in a concentration camp, and he would not have survived. The gas chambers would have seen to that. But thanks to his father somehow arranging this, *Kindertransport* had taken him to

England, and *KLM's DC-3* aeroplane landed at somewhere called Croydon Aerodrome.

He was an eight-year-old boy, knew none of the others on the flight and spoke no English. His uphill struggle, was about to begin, but he was *alive*....

For years, he had overcome his memories of leaving the Vienna station, seeing his father disappear as the train steamed around the bend in the track. But now things were changing inside him, perhaps due to age or something. Whatever was causing this, his sadness was increasing and so was his anger. Maybe that was why he lost his temper with that Volkswagen driver on the *Shabbat*. Now, he felt guilty about that, wanting to find the man and apologise. If he saw that car again, he would.

Becoming closer to religious beliefs, was not just about getting older. Maybe it was to help the younger generation to understand that you must stand up to the past. Show pride, not embarrassment and embrace the world for the future. Sure, things will always go wrong again, but we must fight on. If for no other reason, he had to do this for his daughters.

Even now, after so many years, what he'd seen on the streets when *Kristallnacht* came in would never go away. His father's little café was smashed into pieces.

First the windows, then the plates, furniture and food were thrown out onto the street.

Their flat over the shop was broken into by the Nazi's, and his parents were forced to sweep up the street, as the angry people watching them swore, baying for their blood. Many of them had been friendly customers of the café for so many years. It seemed like madness to his confused parents, as they swept the street and were spat upon...

When Bernie's new life started in England, something inside him constantly battled for independence. First he needed to learn the language, then connect with the people and build a way of making something a success out of nothing. He never considered himself a genius, but rather someone who tried and failed but kept going. It was in his blood. The history of his race provided that. But there was more to it than that, fighting back for his parents and giving to their descendants who were his girls, was one thing. Something else was now coming into his thoughts.

"Bernie," said Jane. "You seem miles away. What's on your mind?"

He reached over to her smiling, then squeezed her hand with a heartfelt passion as the train sped on.

"Nothing my darling. Just thinking about Sal and Linus. I reckon they are a real *connection*."

Jeannie sat in the Cavalier and looked at her handbag. It was fast approaching 12.00hrs. She had lied to Paul, telling him that there was something she needed to pick up from the office, and it couldn't wait until tomorrow as she was heading somewhere else early in the morning. He told her that was fine, as he sat up in bed reading the *Sunday Times.* And that was another thing about him which was annoying her. Instead of focussing on *her*, he was obsessed with a *newspaper*. Great.

She drove away and then switched on to BBC Radio 1. The DJ was Steve Wright, who Jeannie liked, not least because of his humour, and she really needed cheering up this morning. He put on a song called '*Shout to the top'* by the *Style Council.*

Pulling up outside the *RADI-CAL* office, part of her felt strangely annoyed given it was Sunday, but the practical and constantly planning elements inside her mind understood why she had come here. The industrial estate would be deserted today.

If Paul suspected her of something, and had followed here out here, then she would have the excuse of picking something up from the office.

But that was the undercurrent of the problem she had with him. The passion, excitement and jealousy that she always yearned for in a man had gone. When it started out, he was obsessed with her every move, just like her first husband, and she threw in the towel with *him* because of the way Paul was when they met, but now *that* was over.

She was now yearning for excitement and happiness in every moment of the day, as if time was running thin for her....

Gently, she placed the bag on her lap and took the folded tissue paper out of it. She opened it very carefully and looked at the pink powder. She was starting to transfer her thoughts on this from a feeling of guilt, to a really useful activity.

After all, it was not only making her feel better, but was keeping her work activity at the top level. The supplier was a reasonable guy and she was only going to need one, or at the most, two *drags* a day. The powder was purer than most *methamphetamine* out on the streets, and so would be safer. Anyway, she could stop when she wanted to.

It was never going to save her relationship with Paul, that was surely finished. After all, she had to move faster and he was getting slower. But it would give her the strength to go on. There had to be *something* better before it was too late.

Then, reaching back into the bag, she took out a paper straw. She looked carefully around the site. There was no one here, but suddenly a train screeched past, heading towards Victoria Station.

Although not unexpected, it rattled her. The expletive of the '*F*' word was close, but she never said that unless it was linked to a *personal* activity. Then she calmed herself, touching the left of her nose with her wedding ring finger, taking the first inhale into her right through the straw. The *Speed* entered her, she took a deep breath and then did the same on the other side.

It slowly kicked in, spinning her mind. She stared over at the *RADI-CAL* office, and within two minutes she began to hallucinate with energy and excitement....

Chapter 17

London, Heathrow
20th November 1984

Autumn was fast turning to winter. Looking out of the café window to the runway, Linus watched the Pan-Am Boeing 747 take off into the gloom, heading for its Atlantic crossing, and then into JFK in New York.

Despite everything in his past, he could not remember such a massive wave of sadness coming at him.

He'd wanted to tell her about the love, passion and trust he felt, and his addiction to her extraordinary personality. But he'd struggled to control his emotions, and so could not get the words out, and now she was gone.

Bernie and Jane had planned to drop her at the airport, but she insisted that Linus did that.

They both wanted to underline their *future* together, and not be at Heathrow today just for old times' sake. Linus took a sip of his coffee, as he watched her aircraft disappear up into the clouds.

Then, a positivity came at him, almost as if Sally-Anne was inside his head, looking after him. *Yes, when she came home, they would be back together.*

Walking out of the terminal and into the multi-storey car park, he tried to imagine she was by his side.

The Cavalier was up on the fourth floor, and as he reached it, the noise of another huge jet came in. He stepped into the car and looked at the bag she had left on the seat. It was made from a sort of fake, *flax* material, ancient in design. He ran his fingers gently over it, thinking of her, then opened it.

Inside, was a cellophane covered pack of 200 Marlboros and a bottle of Moet. As he took them out, Linus saw the envelope at the bottom of the bag. He opened it, expecting a bill, adding these items to what he already owed.... But he was wrong of course. Taking the card out, he looked at the picture on its front. It was a couple, holding hands on a beach, looking at the sun setting on the horizon. The *co-incidence* was amazing. He opened it up and read out the words:

"Don't ever give up. I know we are connected by magic. xx"

The rain came in heavily, as Linus drove back to the newly opened, *RADI-CAL* head office in Croydon. It was on the other side of the car park from RITON's marine department, and he knew this would bring memories of the past. A combination of thoughts on dropping off Sally-Anne Cohen at Heathrow, and back to the Rupert Cannon funeral, were not helping matters.

The rain had turned to hail stones, just like when he'd first used his cellular telephone to call Sally-Anne that night in Godstone village. He switched the wipers onto fast speed, but still the motorway lanes were hard to see clearly. Easing back to 50mph, he thought back to Rupert Cannon's funeral at Streatham on the 19th of last month.

Walking down the graveyard path from St Leonard's church and towards the car park, Linus and Colleen were behind Sir Dennis Ogilvy and his PA, Margaret Ellwood. The mid-day sun had come out from behind the clouds, and they all felt the warmth touch their heads.

It was as if Rupert Cannon was smiling down at them, in thanks for years of friendship and coming along here today. They all felt it.

Sir Dennis stopped by the gate and asked Linus to wait, as he shook hands with the long line of RITON staff and some of Rupert's neighbours. But there were no relatives. Linus looked over at Sir Dennis as he shared his sympathy with the team.

Linus had met the Group's Chairman several times over the years, predominately at events. There was a certain style that set him apart. Sir Dennis was tall and slim, blue eyed and grey haired. He was an older guy, and his suits were always of a perfect style and cut, so were clearly bespoke. The shoes were polished to perfection and his skin always had a light tan, indicative of his global travel with RITON Group.

But it was his personality that Linus really felt set him apart from anyone in the company. He was friendly, amusing and intellectual, but had a very cool way of asking questions. Also, he never made any staff feel as if they were underlings. Linus felt that was a huge reason for RITON's global success, and he was not the only one to think that. It was right across the group, that feeling of respect and comradery.

The last person to shake hands with Sir Dennis was Brian Callaghan. Brian was the manager of all the staff's medical and personal support around the world, and had arranged the very sad event of today. Sir Dennis shook Brian's hand, touching his shoulder with the other, showing his deep thanks for helping in efficiency and care. As Brian walked away, Sir Dennis came across the path to Linus, stood by the gate.

They had already spoken about Linus's background with Mr Cannon earlier today. Sir Dennis nodded towards Brian as he walked towards the road and said. "He did a good job today. I'm sure Rupert would have approved."

"He would have done Sir Dennis." Replied Linus, imagining Mr Cannon saying to Brian Callaghan, *'good show old boy.'*

"Rupert was old school, and very clever," said Sir Dennis, and continued. "He was a *people* person of the highest order, but totally committed to *our firm* Linus, don't you agree?"

"One hundred percent." Replied Linus from the heart. "He told me off a few times, but he was not only always right to do so, but got me onto a learning curve. I'll never forget him Sir Dennis. Never."

Sir Dennis Ogilvy laughed back at Linus, picturing Rupert Cannon in an angry mood and carried on. "He is going to be sadly missed by us all Linus. I liked his old style, but believe we are facing a huge change in the world with people, and some say we have possibly added to the powder keg for this with *RADI-CAL*."

He began to walk slowly towards the car park, as Linus looked at him, wondering what was coming next. As they went through the gate, Sir Dennis then stopped and looked Linus in the eyes with a depth of interest and asked.

"So, what do *you* think of the show so far?"

Linus realised the Chairman was asking a good question with an element of humour. So came back with a reconstructed *Morecombe and Wise*, response. "I'd say from what I have seen so far, it's better than I thought it would be, and it's certainly not *rubbish*."

Sir Dennis laughed back and said. "I'm glad you think so. When we started out on this almost three years ago, there were problems. A lot of time and investment would be required and my biggest battle with board, and shareholders, was convincing them that the world was changing, and methods of mobile communications could provide efficiency and eventually, social change."

Linus walked alongside Sir Dennis towards his Rolls-Royce Silver Spirit, as the chauffeur stepped out and opened the rear door. Stopping before he reached the car, he turned to Linus, now looking seriously deep in thought, then carried on.

"Change is coming Linus, whether we like it or not. I am convinced there is going to come a time when cell phones are going to extend further than our current prediction of business use. People will one day use them to call socially. It's as if *RADI-CAL* is starting out like a British version of the *Wright Brothers*."

Linus chuckled at the connection with the first men to build a flying machine, as Sir Dennis laughed, clearly enjoying his own mirth. Linus realised that he'd probably used this term before. It was his way of touching commercial propositions with humour across the group. But Linus got the impression that he really did consider this to be a potential leviathan for Britain. After all, cellular radios were operational in America, and now even in Germany.

Sir Dennis glanced at his watch and said. "Goodness, I need to get on." He shook hands with Linus and went towards the car, then stopped, turned back and said. "Oh, keep Colleen updated so she can report back to Margaret. But keep it *hush hush*." He said tapping the side of his nose. "Cheerio."

As the Pan-Am 747 reached its trans-Atlantic flying height of 38,000 feet, she took her bag off the empty seat next to her in business class. She remembered Esther telling her this used to be called *clipper class*, and had been moved to the upper deck. The seat was in dark blue fabric and comfortable. The hostess came up and asked her if she'd like a drink, as she handed over the lunch menu. Sally-Anne asked for a Gin and Tonic, then opened her bag.

She took out the envelope that Linus had given to her after they held on to each other, both not wanting to let go, stood by the check-in desk. "Nearly forgot this," he said. "Don't open it until you are on the flight though, I need time to run away."

The sun's rays came in through the cabin port and glinted off the white envelope as she ran her fingers gently over it. Opening it very carefully, so as not to damage it even with a slight tear, she took out the card. Then she stared at the cover in amazement. There was a couple, standing on the beach, holding hands and looking out at the horizon. It was exactly the same as the one she had given him.

If he'd been next to her now, she would have accused him of using *Tipp-Ex* on *his*. Now she was *really* missing him. Opening the card, a cheque for £10 dropped out onto her lap. Then she read the words in it and laughed out loud, an old man across the aisle staring at her over his paper as she did so.

"I realise that I owe you more than this amount, but given how much I'm going to have to spend on you in our future lives together, I think this is fair." xx

The rain had stopped as Linus pulled up in the office car park. Looking down at the Panasonic R1, the red light was still on. That was somewhat annoying, as he intended to give Bernie a call to let him know that the flight had been on time. The building looked drab in the downpour, as he looked up at the top floor. On the edge of the car park, Mike Sentinel's Carlton was parked across two spaces. *That's not like you Mike*. He thought, walking towards the reception. But then he regretted that. *Not everyone was lucky enough to have good eyesight, were they?*

Up on the third floor, Colleen sat behind her desk in front of Steve Rider's office. The place had been recently modernised to a high standard, and had a distinct aroma of change about it. On Colleen's desk sat a new *Apricot Sirius 1* computer. It was huge and Linus looked around it in awe as she held up her hands and said. "Don't even go there." Clearly knowing what he was thinking. "It's called the *modern* world now."

"Do you know what." He said. "I heard some people called them *Apri-clots*."

"Ha-ha," she replied. "And just to make you aware, it runs on *MS-DOS* and is the first one to use only a three-and-a-half-inch floppy disk."

"Thrilling," said Linus, still staring at its green screen. "Whatever *that* is. Can I go in and see Steve now please?"

As he walked in, Steve and Mike stood up from the meeting table and shook his hand.

"Thanks for coming in mate," said Mike. "I know it was officially your day off."

"That's fine," he replied and then continued. "I'd rather be here than go home anyway."

Mike realised what he meant by that.

"Well," said Steve Rider. "You couldn't have timed it better Linus. Because today, another large order has been taken, and we are way ahead of schedule."

"Great, where did that come in from?" Linus asked.

"It was from another transport company, called *Fore Front*" replied Mike. "But this one has placed an order for almost three hundred."

"Wow." Said Linus, looking over at them both in shock. "Who took that?"

"Robbie signed it up this morning." Said Mike. "And there are some branches up north, so it is only *fair* we split it up with the Manchester lot, isn't that correct Steve?"

Linus saw Mike grinning at Steve, as his slight sarcasm was clearly taken on board.

"Anyway, the key point Linus, is that we have now taken orders for a total of almost one thousand units." Said Steve, and then continued. "Considering we don't go live until the end of next month and we now have a target of nine thousand for next year, that is pretty good."

"That is great news." Said Linus, genuinely pleased to hear this, and thinking he should go and have a few pints with Robbie to celebrate.

"It is," said Steve, looking over at Mike then carrying on. "And I'd like to thank you for all your work on *Trans-ship* too. Mike tells me that had it not been for all your efforts, this would probably not have reached the level we are at, because all industries communicate good service support, even if *they* are in competition with each other. I have no doubt that *Fore Front* knew about *Trans-ship's* orders."

Linus understood that, in fact that was very much the RITON approach. He also knew how smart Steve Rider was, so guessed what was coming up next, and he was right.

"Linus, I'm sure you realise how essential it is for good reports to get back to the board and the group investors about *RADI-CAL*." Steve carried on, looking both serious and friendly. "I know you were allocated into us by Mr Cannon, and I was very sorry to hear about his death, but I appreciate he probably felt some negativity about us, in fact a number of group's *older* board members did."

Mike could see that Linus was now teetering on a touch of anger about Steve's words, so he said in an understanding and sensitive style to counteract this.

"The thing is Linus, we really appreciate how cellular phones could be seen as a *fad*, but we have seen the potential with the likes of *Fore Front* and *Trans-ship,* proving that *RADI-CAL* has an even better chance of hitting the target than British Telecommunications and the other lot, *Motafone*."

Steve then took over as Linus looked across at Mike thinking, *here we go again. British Telecommunications.*

"Yes," said Steve. "That is a good point Mike, and it is therefore essential that any reports back to the group are created in a positive style." He sat back in his chair, smiling in the friendliest manner, and carried on.

"Linus, we know Sir Dennis needs information from you about us, but he is, as you probably know, not only the instigator of *RADI-CAL*, but a prime supporter and he knows the future growth of RITON could depend on this." Steve nodded and winked at Linus, as if they were long standing friends in some sort of club house and went on.

"But also, he needs to demonstrate to the board and investors, that he's used a staff member with proven *independent analyst,* experience to monitor and give feedback on the *RADI-CAL* activities, and that person of course, is *you* Linus."

Linus smiled back. He knew the tables had now turned, and somewhat in his favour. In fact, he was in a much stronger position now than he'd ever imagined with this role. His feedback was now not going through Mr Cannon of course, but via Colleen over to Sir Dennis's PA, Margaret Ellwood. His research on the activities of what could be a significant new business for the RITON Group, was an important aspect of this, but it wasn't just about that.

His growing liking for the *RADI-CAL* staff also helped, of course. But more than anything, was the call he'd made to Sally-Anne on that night of the storm, from his *Panasonic R1*.

If it hadn't been for that, would he have ever got to where he was now with her? Connecting with people via these cellular things could one day, be a game changer for everyone….

He looked over at Mike and Steve, then said. "I am one hundred per cent on board. Whatever I report into Colleen, I'll make sure you have it first."

They both smiled back at Linus in genuine delight for his commitment. Steve had considered him to be a *nerd* after their initial meeting at Heath-field, but now was starting to like him.

Brian Callaghan sat in the driving seat of the Sierra, his RITON company car, flicking through the money in the brown envelope. The sky was growing darker now. The mourners had been fortunate that Cannon's funeral had taken place when the sun was out. He watched the old man in the trilby hat walk with a limp towards the corner of the side road and then disappear. Callaghan had known Kelson for years, but had never seen his limp reach this level before.

He opened the glove compartment and tossed the envelope in, then locked it. After all, there was three grand in it.

This was not the first time he'd received payment for a fast tracked disposal. Lord Atkins had used his *expertise* before. In fact, Callaghan's father had been an assistant to *his* father forty-six years ago. He looked along the back street, as the first shower of the day came in. The houses along here looked run-down, the pavements were worn out, and the street was full of clapped out cars. He watched an Asian couple push a pram along the cracked pavement, pulling it's hood up.

If only the Germans had won the war, these streets and everything else in this country would have been clean and managed to high standards. Thought Callaghan, shaking his head, then starting the car and driving away into the rain.

When Linus answered his phone in the lounge at 22.00hrs, he knew immediately who it would be. There was that usual slight delay in words coming across the Atlantic as he picked up the phone. Linus listened intently, not speaking and taking in the sound of Sally-Anne's voice. "I'm here and it's only five in the afternoon, not like where *you* are."

He waited for a second and said. "How was your flight over there?"

"Good thanks, and right on time to the airport, and once I'd waited for ages in passport control, then Esther took me back in a cab via the tunnel on East River, to the rented apartment on 25th Street."

"I know that route," said Linus. "It goes via Long Island and then around the Empire State."

"Is there *nothing* you don't know about?" She asked.

Pausing again for a moment he replied. "Only one thing, and that's how I'm going to manage without you."

Sally-Anne looked down at the street from the tenth floor window, watching the traffic stream past. A siren wailed as a *cop-car* went around the mass of traffic, pulling over to let it go past.

"Considering how much you still owe me. I'd make the most of it if I were you."

"He laughed and said. "Good one. Keep in touch whenever you can, and let me have your number there."

She read it out to him and then said. "I love you, I'll call you tomorrow."

They both hung up and then looked at the phones, each thinking and wishing they'd said something more inspiring. Esther walked across the room and put her hands on Sally-Anne's shoulders. Esther was a little older and slightly taller, but otherwise strikingly similar, and she knew what her sister was thinking.

"It's never easy when you travel a long way from someone." Said Esther. "The first thing that happens is you get tongue tied because it feels odd, you are tired after the flight and then you think, *I wish I had said something better,* after you have put the phone down. But don't worry, you two are going to be fine."

Sally-Anne smiled, turned and gave her a hug, then looked back down at the street and said. "You're right. Can we nip out for a quick one in that bar?"

Chapter 18

Ramsgate, Kent
29th November 1984

Looking across the marina to the harbour entrance, Jeannie Sands asked Linus. "So, when is she now coming back then?"

"At some time in March or April." Said Linus, also looking across the harbour from the front passenger seat of her Cavalier. "The delay has been caused by that production company in New York putting back the shows that her dad has secured a European agency contract for. I don't know all the details, just that Sally-Anne and her sister need to be there for a while longer, until it's all sorted out."

"That's a shame," said Jeannie, continuing to look across the harbour. "You are going to miss her."

"I am." He replied. "Anyway, how are things with you?"

Jeannie considered this for a moment. The dusk was coming in and the harbour lights were now growing brighter. The wind was light and it was dry, but autumn had reached it's close, and winter was coming in.

She looked at the Cavalier's clock, it was just coming up to four PM, and she said, pointing to the right. "I'll tell you what, there is a bar in that hotel and we can go in for a quick one if you like."

"Sounds good to me." He said.

They sat at the table in the corner of a very smart lounge area in the Victorian hotel. It was on *Royal Parade*, just across from where her car was parked. The waitress came over from the bar and placed a lager top and gin and tonic on the table.

They touched their glasses together and said "Cheers." Then Jeannie put her glass gently down and said. "To answer your question about how things are, I'd say they could be better, but maybe a lot worse. So, we shall just get on with things."

Linus realised she was referring to her husband Paul and then decided to change tack. "So we are going live in less than a month now." He said, referring to *RADI-CAL*.

"Yes," she said. "We are, and the timing is really good."

"That is a good point," said Linus. "The government *official* date for going live was the first of January of course, but good old Sir Dennis somehow managed to bring us forward to the head of the game, and *we* go live on December 24th."

Jeannie smiled back at him. "That is a massive result for *RADI-CAL*."

Their meeting today had been near to Manston airport, just outside the town, and opened up some good points to consider. This was a former RAF base, but now had a few transport and warehouses close to it. One of these had originally helped provide supplies for aid flights into Africa a couple of years ago, but now was transporting goods by road into Europe.

The operations guy had shown interest in installing cellular radios into his lorries, but wanted to know if they would ever connect with the networks in France and Germany, when they were on TIR work. His other question was about if and when an answer-phone system could be fitted to them.

Jeannie had explained that at this point anyway, there was no link to any overseas networks. But come the middle of January, an answer-phone could be electronically triggered by *RADI-CAL*, and it was going to be called *Message Link*.

Driving into town after the meeting, they had a discussion about this. Both Linus and Jeannie could not imagine how a European connection of countries could ever be created with cellular radio. Sure, some of the new land-line phone systems were moving to digital systems, rather like computers, but most countries only had analogue networks in place.

"Imagine this," said Linus. "A bar in Rhodes is full of English holiday makers. They *all* have our hand-portable *Motorola 8000x* cell-phones. Instead of just sitting back and looking out at the *Med* with a drink and a cigar alongside their other half, they start to dial in numbers and call people back home."

Jeannie laughed in her unique, deep and sensual way then raised her glass and said. "Rest assured, that'll never be in our lifetime."

Then she looked across the table at him and said. "I've been meaning to ask how the funeral went for Mr Cannon."

Linus began to feel the flood gates open. It wasn't Jeannie's fault for asking about this. Far from it. No, it was more like his mind began to throw darkness and a storm at him. And it wasn't just because of this subject. It was, he now realised a battle within his spirit against mental anxiety. Did it go back to something bad that happened long ago, or had it always been inside of him? He didn't know and probably never would.

He looked across the room to the window. The darkness had come in now, and at the harbour entrance, he could see the lights flash red and green. His mind touched on the poem by Tennyson. He remembered it being quoted by Rupert Cannon several times.

Sunset and evening star
And one clear call for me!
And may there be no moaning of the bar,
When I put out to sea.

"Are you OK?" Jeannie asked.

"Yes," he said. "Sorry, just had something in my head. Sometimes takes me a bit down in the dumps, that's all."

She looked at him, somehow reaching out in a way which he'd never experienced before. He'd needed to get something off his chest that had been haunting him for years, and now this was his first feeling of being able to. He *almost* told Rupert Cannon about it once, but didn't quite make it. But tonight, in Ramsgate of all places, and with someone he'd known for only a short time, he was going to.

She reached over and squeezed his right hand with her left, the bar's lights catching her wedding ring. "Tell me." She said very quietly.

Linus looked straight at her, he'd never told *anyone* about this before.

"I was in a boys' school in South London. I was just on fourteen and given the job of tidying up after a hockey match, in the field, just behind the school. It was getting dark, and the players and fans had gone, so there were just two of us picking up some junk and a few empty bottles, you know how it is after those things. Anyway, he was in the year above me, and I hardly knew him."

She nodded back in full concentration, sensing something bad was on the way.

"We moved to the outside of the bicycle shed, picking up the last junk of the day." Linus shook his head, still angry at himself for not realising what was coming at him, all those years ago, and continued.

"Unfortunately, the bike shed took out any vision from the school building and across the empty pitch were the woods, it was getting dark and there wasn't a soul out there. I bent over to pick up the last empty coke bottle and then…"

Jeannie guessed what was coming, and squeezed his hand tighter. For the first time, his words on this subject were ready to be spoken. Words of self- hatred and embarrassment, and the memory of pain.

Linus held back his anger, looking up at the ceiling, the world reaching a standstill. The barmaid had left and they were the only people in the room, there was no music or passing traffic. Nothing but total silence. She saw him take a deep breath on the last leg of this return journey.

"He whacked my head with a hockey stick that had been left by the pitch. I fell forwards onto the ground. I wasn't fully out cold, but my eyes blurred and I can still remember the grass going bright green. Then, he tore down my shorts and…..."

Linus stood up, placing his hands on his head, remembering the pain, feeling guilt, now wishing he had not told her, and in wild desperation following acute embarrassment, thinking of running out of the door. But he didn't. He just stood still.

She rocked back and forth, half expecting this, but still shocked. The sadness now somehow connecting her with the need for a *speed* drug inhale, right now. Then she stood in silence, walked around the table and held him close, wanting never to let go.

The Stag was running well now. In fact, everything was good today. As he went along Purley Way, he looked over at the *Aerodrome* Hotel on the right. The car park looked full, and he wondered if that sad old bloke wearing a trilby hat, was still sat in his Passat, staring out of the windscreen. It was only about six weeks ago after all.

It had been a good weekend so far and now, he'd been invited to have lunch and spend the rest of the day at Bernie and Jane's.

The postman on Saturday had brought his RITON payslip. Included in it was the *Trans-ship* deal commission payment.

Without Jeannie's generosity, that would not have happened and he couldn't wait to see her again tomorrow, so he could thank her for this.

But there was something else he needed to thank her for. The gift of some huge element of trust, gave him the chance to confess what he'd always felt ashamed of, to her on Friday. Perhaps, getting this off his chest was going to tear the anguish out of him for good. Then, he'd be a better person and would stop annoying people with his *constant, miserable depression.* That's what Anna used to call it. Anyway, he was so glad he was with Sally-Anne now, and not *Anna*.

The Stag's V8 burbled as he slid the switch on top of the gear knob into overdrive. He'd fitted a new *Blaupunkt Toronto SQR45*, as recommended by Julian Rayne. By co-incidence, Julian was a car stereo buff too. The DJ, Steve Wright's show was on BBC Radio 1, and a record called *The Power of Love* came on, instantly feeling like a magical charm, despite never having heard it before.

The music, words and sound quality coming from the Stag's new speakers was fabulous. It brought Sally-Anne home to him. As it finished, Linus approached the *Long Estate*, then pulled up outside the Cohen's house. Steve Wright, said this song had just been released, but was already at number three in the singles chart. The band was called *Frankie Goes to Hollywood.* Linus switched off the engine and stepped out of the Stag. Tomorrow, when the record shop opened, he would buy that.

As Linus walked up, the door creaked open and Bernie's head came round and smiled, nodding at the Stag. "Bring that beauty into the driveway." He said. "You need to keep it safe."

Bernie came out and shook hands with Linus as they walked towards the Stag together.

"Everybody apart from you, tells me it's junk." Said Linus.

They reached the car and Bernie touched its roof gently with his fingers. "What do they know." He said rhetorically.

"Do you fancy driving it?" Asked Linus.

Bernie was genuinely delighted at the prospect of this. He smiled and said. "I'd love too."

Getting into the driving seat, he carefully closed the door, then looked up at the mirror and adjusted it. Linus passed over the ignition key and Bernie started the engine, touching the throttle gently, as its mellow bellow came from the exhaust.

He selected first gear and pulled gently out onto the backroad. Linus was both surprised and impressed, because Bernie was concentrating on driving with extreme care, clearly full of respect of both the car and him. They headed out onto Purley Way. Reaching the end of Croydon's old aerodrome on the left, then coming towards the hotel, Bernie looked down at the switch on the gear lever's knob and asked.

"So is that for the overdrive then?"

"Yes," said Linus. "It works in third and fourth gear, so now you're up in top, just flick it and we'll be in the equivalent of *fifth* would you believe. Some even call it *sixth* gear."

"I'm loving this thing." Said Bernie, smiling and glancing down the bonnet, then over to the airfield, the sun touching his glasses, and his smile subsided....

As they passed the hotel, the rays caught the old, abandoned runway and the control tower.

"I've just thought of something." Said Linus. "Jane is going to wonder where we are."

"Blimey," replied Bernie, looking serious. "I'll turn round at the lights and head back."

Pulling up in the driveway, Bernie switched off the engine, patted the steering wheel and said. "I absolutely loved that. What a great car you have."

"Thanks." Replied Linus, then looking over at Bernie's fabulous Silver-Shadow and said. "But it's hardly in the same league as yours, is it?"

"Well, that's an interesting point." Bernie said, looking over at Linus. "I use it simply because our agency is about image in everything. We have to connect with film producers, actors, advertisers and investors. The Rolls gives out an *impression*, when we turn up at a studio meeting, otherwise I wouldn't bother."

"I get that now." Said Linus. "Image is always a key in business. My old boss used to call this an *old Snag*, and I'm sure that was not just because of its reliability."

Bernie laughed and shook his head at the Rolls. "Don't even go there on that."

"Well," said Linus. "Whatever, I enjoyed the trip we had into town when Sally-Anne drove it last month."

"Good." Said Bernie, looking around the Stag's interior. "Maybe one day, we'll do a swap."

They both laughed at this, and then Bernie carried on. "That reminds me, have you got a date when I can get the cellular phone installed yet?"

"I'll sort it out and bring you the form." Linus replied.

Bernie nodded back and then went onto a different subject.

"Linus, I am not happy about this *Strip-O -Gram* business. I admire Sally-Anne's independence, but want her to be part of what I do with Esther. I hope that going Stateside is going to change her mind on this. Then, when she returns, she could join us here.

I know she is going to be stubborn on this, so I can set up an independent operation for her, but under our *umbrella*."

"So did she go out there to start the change?" Asked Linus.

"You mean did I send her out there for that reason." Bernie replied, smiling at him and then carried on. "That is partially true, but Esther needed some help and I genuinely believe that

Sally-Anne was the right person for that. I only want my girls to do this, because it's about confidence and trust, and I know if something does go wrong and they need help, they'd come back to be me and never try and cover it up, and that is the difference between *them* and *employees*. The girls are the most trusted people I have on this earth, and always will be."

"Thank you for telling me." Said Linus.

Bernie patted Linus on the shoulder, then tapped a finger on the Stag's steering wheel and said. "I *really* wanted to have a drive in this car you know. I didn't do it just so I could tell you about what I need from Sally-Anne. Come on, we better go in or Jane is going to shoot me."

Manfred von Sterne looked over at the security office by the port's exit barrier. On the post was the red circled sign marked with the words *Zoll Douane*, the port of Hamburg's, customs and export declarations point. The engine of the Volkswagen Type 2 van idled, as the security guard walked over to the window. Manfred wound it down, and stubbed out his cigarette in the ashtray, then he passed the document to the guard to examine.

Both von Sterne and the guard knew it was a fake, but they had to go through the process, because every exit from these docks was filmed by a camera on a tall pole.

Neither looked up at the camera, as the security guard examined the document and handed it back to Manfred, not saying a word.

Then he went back to the office, turned a knob and the barrier lifted. Von Sterne gently accelerated the engine in the rear of the van, and slowly drove away towards the road that ran around the port.

He smiled with relief as he started his journey back to West Berlin. Just because the guard was a *fourth Reich* member, didn't mean something might not have gone wrong. Heading towards the *Autobahn,* he glanced into the rear-view mirror at the clock tower of *St Pauli Landungsbrucken*, on the other side of the river Elbe. It was just coming up to 14.00hrs. He would be back in the *Spandau* district about four hours from now, then would meet Gerhard at the secure, storage site.

The plan was then to move it over to *Neuruppin* soon, and in a different vehicle, just to be sure this one had not been spotted or even, spoken of by that security guard.

The flat four, air-cooled engine was now working hard. He glanced over his right shoulder to the box, in the back of the van. It was not a surprise that the engine was struggling a little. Not when it was powering the wheels of a van with the weight of one million deutschmarks made out of gold bars, some forty-six years ago in it…

Monday in the *RADI-CAL* office was full of change. It was as if Mike Sentinel had become a different person, in a good way. There were only twenty-two days left before their cellular radio system was going live.

His PA, Julia had organised a new layout of the place and made sure it was tidy, as if a film crew were coming in. Everything now seemed more spacious and on the back wall, was a large white-board. It was laid out with felt-tip pen writing for the models of the cellular phones, and on the top were the names of the sales team. It was due to commence on the date marked just under the ceiling, 24th December 1984.

Linus looked up at the board, and then down at his Seiko. It was just on 17.30hrs.

Jeannie came up behind him. He felt the atmosphere of her presence and turned around. The dress was black, the hair was blonde and the heels were high. She was smiling. He felt the respect and confidence in connecting with her, was the finest he'd experienced in *this* life.

They stood looking at each other, but said nothing. Then Mike Sentinel came out of his office door and said. "Mmm, come on in you two."

He shut the door behind them and they sat down at his meeting table.

Mike went straight to the point. "Steve has just been on the line, and he's asked me to get you two involved with something in the City." He started reading the details off of his notepad. "Apparently, *City National Bank* have been in touch with Sir Dennis. They are looking into the possibility of supplying their stock traders with hand portables. It seems they have noticed the use of *Motorola 8000x* in America, and are considering a few for use here when we go live."

"Sounds interesting." Said Jeannie, and then went on. "But the *R3* isn't coming in until March is it?"

Mike looked out of the office window to see if anyone was listening and said. "That's true, but we have pre-stocked almost two hundred in the new Croydon warehouse."

Linus and Jeannie looked at each other with a little surprise, but both guessed why.

"Sir Dennis does not intend to mention this to other board members, who think the car phones and transportables are bad enough, but as for these things......" Said Mike.

"So what do you want us to do next?" Asked Linus.

"I want you to get a meeting with them." He tore part of his note off and passed it over to Linus. "Get onto this man and arrange it as soon as you can. Then keep it to yourselves and tell no one except me. Understand?"

They both nodded, then got up and left the room. As they walked down the main office, Jeannie said. "We need to go out and have a drink, so we can discuss this."

It was just coming up to 22.00hrs as he stared at the phone on his lounge table. With a bit of luck, she might be back in the apartment as it was 17.00hrs in New York. Last night, he could not reach her. But she only had to be running a little late after work, to make it past his week-day bed time. He knew she would be too thoughtful to call him then, and he also did not want to bother her, maybe appearing to be concerned or even being suspicious in some way. This was not easy. He just wanted to hear the sound of her voice.

Thinking back to the discussion with Jeannie in the *Anchor* pub earlier, it was clear Mike had given them a very interesting opportunity. Tomorrow, they planned to set up a meeting with the contact in the City. He sat back in the chair, still waiting for the phone to ring and thought about Jeannie's view on this. She believed it would be a potential deal, and felt the commitment to *RADI-CAL* of the Bank, could be a real transition for the *all* of the RITON board's attitude.

If the group's largest financial provider for customers went ahead with ordering the first batch of portable cellular phones from them in Britain, it could be a game changer for *RADI-CAL*. When they discussed this in the *Anchor*, she told him it was her genuine belief that *RADI-CAL* would eventually be the *largest success story ever* in the RITON group.

If she'd said that a month ago, he would have laughed. But not now....

He picked up the BT land-line phone on his coffee table and dialled Sally-Anne's number stateside. After a few moments the long *burr* sounded. But there was no answer.

Jeannie sat looking down at her coffee table. She was in her dressing gown. Upstairs, Paul was in bed asleep, he'd started snoring about an hour ago and she got up and came down to the lounge. Things were getting even worse; she could not abide snoring. She thought about men, and how they often turned out to be. When she first had the affair with Paul, he was attentive and exciting, but not now. It was as if he'd ticked the box of their relationship, and had gone into a boring zone.

She'd been there before with her first husband. He'd been the same. He didn't snore, but became tedious, it was as if all of the excitement when they came together had drained away.

She thought about Linus. What he told her on Friday was sad, and she'd felt that was so deep inside him. And however their friendship developed, even if they came together and eventually split, she'd never tell another soul on this earth about that. Never.

She reached over to her bag and took out the envelope of *speed,* then she laid it carefully out and breathed it into both nostrils with the straw. It took a short while to come in, for some reason longer than it used to, but very soon she began to feel uplifted. *This was a very good idea,* she thought looking at the almost empty wrapper, but tomorrow, she'd need to get some more…

The *Hairy Monk* bar in New York was starting to was grow on Sally-Anne. It was not far from their apartment and there was a good crowd in here. *'Like a Virgin'* by *Madonna* was playing as she went up to the bar with Esther. They both sat on the high-backed stools. They were rounded and comfortable, the yellow and white lights above the bar cast their rays down on them, and overhead in the centre of the room, flat against the ceiling, were lots of baseball team flags, and the Stars and Stripes.

The barmaid put down the two *Pina Coladas* and said to Sally-Anne smiling. "Now, are you sure you're over twenty-one?"

She laughed back at her and said. "A joke only lasts for so long, you know."

A few months ago, President Regan had raised the minimum drinking age in America to twenty-one. When Sally-Anne came in here for the first time, the barmaid needed to check her passport.

"What time did Ryan say he'd be here?" She asked Esther.

"He should be here any minute now." She replied, looking down at her watch and then over to the entrance door." Then, as if a magical co-incidence occurred, said. "Oh, there he is."

He came over to them smiling, the collar of his mac turned up, droplets of rain on his shoulders. Ryan's hair was dark and he was tall, and gave out a smile that Sally-Anne thought was really charming. As a contract manager at *NCD Global Studios Inc,* he was an important link for them. Ryan was tasked with number of new shows that were now required to be promoted across Europe, and Bernie had already established the agency rights to deliver them.

Esther got the barmaid to pour him a *Heileman's old style* beer. Sally-Anne watched the glass fill up and foam over. He took his first sip and then smiled at her. She thought about Linus and his lager-tops and how he'd always do the same, and then would light her up a Marlboro. She was missing him. Ryan was a nice guy and an important connection for them, so she'd need to keep social with him. But that was as far as it would go….

Chapter 19

New Street, London EC4
5th December 1984

They walked out of a building, which had over twenty floors, then Linus stopped on the pavement, looking up at the winter sun, glinting off the windows on the skyline.

Jeannie stood watching him curiously and asked. "What are you looking for up there?"

It was a good question, because he'd no idea why he was doing this. There were so many times he'd stopped and looked up at high buildings, when the light of the sun touched their windows. It was as if long ago, he'd dreamt about this and then, today, he saw it for real.

He came back to normality and said. "Just thinking about how big City National Bank is. I didn't know they were in every floor of the building."

Jeannie walked up beside him, thinking there was something else going on in his mind and said. "Shall we head back before the traffic builds up?"

Linus looked down at his Seiko. "Yes, let's get going."

They strolled to the end of New Street and stepped into his Cavalier. For a change, today he was driving. They headed back towards Tower Bridge, then Jeannie looked across at Linus and shook her head, as he accelerated a little too fast.

"So what do you think the outcome is going to be with City National?" He asked.

"Well," she said. "I think it's going to happen. They are already aware of how the *Motorola's* are working for the Wall Street lot, and given that piece of news in the newspapers on Julian's connection, who is also a stock market trader, then why not?"

Linus nodded back. "Yes, and of course, there is the long term profit that City National has made from the introduction of customers by RITON group over the years, and we have availability of enough units in stock for them, and only them."

Jeannie looked across at him, noticing he was accelerating more gently, and reducing her neck movements as a passenger to a minimum. This was always important for her, which was usually why she always insisted upon driving.

"And that is why if they do go ahead, it is going to be with *RADI-CAL,* and I reckon it could be sooner than we think, because we can supply all of the relevant stock traders and directors and they could use this as publicity too." She said in agreement.

The meeting up on the tenth floor, had involved not only the head of stock trading, but also finance and technical directors. They were all pretty laid back types. It often seemed that senior management were easier going than those, mid-management people, who were confrontational and disrespectful at times.

As they headed south over Tower Bridge, Linus looked out to the left along the River Thames and said. "Used to be up there sometimes with Mr Cannon, years ago."

Jeannie looked at him, and wanted to touch his dark hair in understanding, but just kept still and quiet.

He switched on the Phillips MW and LW radio, and to avoid the lack of FM, pushed in a cassette. Then he realised the only person who was always annoyed by that was not here.

The track was *"Nights over Egypt"* by the *Jones Girls*. It was a couple of years old now, but he was still obsessed by it. And for some reason today, it came into his head again, when looking up at that building....

Jeannie smiled at him, and he grinned back. They were in a cocoon of closeness and trust. It would not be physical, but was a connection of loyalty and understanding.

They pulled up outside the *RADI-CAL* office in Maidstone, just on 16.40hrs. Walking through the door on the first floor, they looked into Mike's office and saw Julia stood by his desk. Mike waved at them to come in, as if something very urgent needed addressing. Linus looked at Jeannie, expecting the worst as they entered.

Mike stood up and lifted the sheet of paper off of his desk, and Julia smiled at it.

"Mmm, you two better sit down." He said, pointing at the chairs by his now clear meeting table. He came over and sat with them, looking snootily down at the sheet and went on. "Seems you did alright." Then he passed it over and they both studied it in disbelief as he continued. "So that's one hundred and six *Motorola 8000x* HPU's ordered by City National."

Jeannie looked at the figure on the bottom of the order it was £370,894.00. Then she said to Mike. "But shouldn't that be over four hundred thousand?"

"It should be." Mike said in agreement and then carried on. "Just after you left there, the director you spoke to called Steve Rider, who offered a discount if they were prepared to place the order today. Then it came in via fax to him, and he just forwarded it to Julia. You did well, and thank goodness Sir Dennis ordered the stock."

"Well." Said Jeannie, looking around at them all. "This is a game changer."

Hello." Said Sally-Anne.

"Well don't ask *is it me your looking for*, because it is." Said Linus, trying to include the Lionel Ritchie song words as an effort of humour.

"I was wondering when you would eventually call me." She replied, understanding but ignoring the joke.

"Actually, I've been trying but probably got the timing wrong. How are things going there?" Asked Linus.

"No, it's my fault." She said. "Esther and I have been out working later than we expected. It's because this whole thing has been delayed as you know, and the lot at *NCD Studios,* who we have to sort this with, expect us to be in their offices every afternoon until late, because they film in the mornings."

"So what are they there like?" He asked, remembering her question in the *Sandrock* pub about *RADI-CAL* staff. "Are they all women, or is there form of male decency in there?"

"There is one bloke we are dealing with." She said thinking about Ryan. "But Esther is in charge of that."

Sally-Anne looked across the room at Esther, the phone's cable stretching out. She was sat at the table, writing out the revised contract details that she'd been asked to get approved today, preparing to get it faxed over to Bernie.

"Things are getting there, we'll have it finished by March, and then I'll be back. Anyway, how are things going there?"

"Oh, so-so." He said. "A few weeks and it'll be live, I hope that I am too."

She laughed and said. "You better be, because you still owe me."

"Like I said, I'm missing you, so please don't spoil it." He replied.

"And I thought I was talking to Linus MacColl and not John Waite. Seriously though, why don't you chuck it all in and come here?"

Esther heard this, put her pen on the table and looked over at Sally-Anne with a mixture of this not being a good idea, but also why it could be....

"Every day I want to." He said. "It's just that I *have* to see this *RADI-CAL* thing through, at least until it gets going. And do you know what? I *really* don't understand why that is, apart from the money of course."

Sally-Anne understood what it was like to have an unknown spirit in your mind, something that could drive you forwards, but make no logical sense.

"I get that." She said. "And don't worry, it'll all work out fine for both of us."

"I know." He said.

"Now don't call me next time, I'll call you as it's all going onto dad's account. Speak to you soon. Love you." She said.

"Love you too." He said, and then hung up.

Linus put the receiver back down gently and sat looking at it, his mind going back to the deal with City National. It was not just about the cost of the cellular hand portables being close to half a million quid. No. It was the profit margin on the calls at twenty-five pence per minute. He estimated this would be at least two hundred and fifty thousand pounds a year paid into *RADI-CAL*.

Something else had been worrying him, and that was the higher cost of making calls to cellular radios from BT phones rather than just to other land lines, but despite the *RADI-CAL* team always advising customers of this, it very rarely seemed an issue. For him, this had been a key concern, but now it had pretty much gone away.

The commission payment that he and Jeannie would receive when the City National deal went live next month, was going to be the highest bonus figure he'd been paid in all his years at RITON group. And then there was being one of the first people involved in something that could possibly change the way the world communicated. If nothing else, supplying these cellular phones would be a one-off in Britain.

Then he kicked himself about his thought stupidity, still looking at the normal phone on his coffee table. Without that, you could never call anyone overseas.

"Right." He said to the invisible Sally-Anne Cohen. *"Once I get paid and you come back, we'll go to Hatton Garden and I'll buy you a ring."*

The Cessna 152 light aircraft banked to the right and lined up with the field's markers. The sky over the virtually deserted area, some ten kilometres from the village of *Neuruppin,* west of Berlin, was darkening but the wind was light. It needed to be for a landing onto an exposed field.

Gerhard Baum and Manfred von Sterne had put the landing markers carefully in place and now, stood by the end of the abandoned looking fall-out shelter, both looking out attentively as the aircraft touched down.

Gerhard could tell from Manfred's dark concentration, that he hoped it would crash. That way, the annoying Lord Atkins would be dead and they could put this new venture on hold until *they* were ready. And pilots were always expendable.

But of course whilst that would be satisfying, not only would they miss out on the balance of the agreed gold deposit, but could lose the connection with his attacking force of *Fourth Reich* supporters in Britain. This was all about getting their own back. Atkins needed to stay alive, at least until they had commenced this...

The Cessna landed safely, then reaching the end of the field, the wings rocking a little as the pilot increased the *Lycoming* engine's revs, turning right towards the barn. Then, when it was close as possible, he switched off the engine.

Silence came into the vast area of open land, as it's propeller stopped spinning.

The pilot, wearing head phones and dark glasses, checked the controls and instruments. Then the door under the right wing opened and out climbed Lord Atkins. He walked towards them wearing a light grey overcoat, with a cigar in his mouth.

"Gentlemen." He said, shaking the hands of Gerhard and Manfred. "How lovely to see you again."

Both nodded their heads in the classic German way of an honourable meeting. Then Atkins raised his right arm and said *"Seig Heil."*

Gerhard and Manfred glanced at each other with a painted on smile, and Gerhard said.

"Please, come to our office Sir." Waving towards the stairs going down into the old nuclear fall-out shelter.

As they walked towards the entrance, Manfred looked over at the pilot, who was now spreading a green, canvas cover over the Cessna, both shaking their heads and smiling in mirth at the bizarreness of this annoying old man.

Entering the fall-out shelter, the fluorescent lights shone into a very tidy layout. There were desks, chairs, filing cabinets and maps of Britain and Northern Ireland, fixed to high standing art easels, because the walls were all concave, designed to help offset atomic bomb blasts. In the distance, there were four men sat around a table, looking intensely at a map of what Atkins perceived to be central London.

An armed guard watched them all, and then stood, looking Atkins up and down, a cigarette between his lips. He was good looking, blonde and clearly of Aryan race.

Atkins felt his small penis tingle, immediately attracted to this man. He looked down at the *Chesterfield* cigarette packet on the desk and said. "I see you are smoking fags made in one of our lovely towns. One-day comrade, that place could belong to you."

The man stared at him, as Atkins walked to catch up with Baum and von Sterne.

Manfred whispered into Gerhard's ear. "That idiot is from England, yet does not realise that *Chesterfield* is an *American* company!"

They both kept their humour under their breath as Lord Atkins followed them to the door in the far-end of the shelter. Von Sterne stood in front of the lock-code knob and clicked it until it released the door's shining steel handle.

He walked in and switched on the lights. The room had steel cages around it, each with padlocks. The closest cage had a pine box inside it, and Atkins knew what was in that. Manfred took out his bunch of keys and unlocked the cage's door, then stepped in and lifted the box's lid, looking up at Atkins as he came in beside him.

Every bar of the delivered bullion was there. Lord Atkins knew it would be, this was purely a standard generation of trust by the *Fourth Reich* people. He patted Manfred on the arm and smiled, as he shut the lid.

That first part of the meeting was completed. Next on the agenda was the discussion as to how they would light the fuse of their *New Order* for Britain, then go forwards to influence *all* of Europe.

Gerhard now believed this could actually be achieved. Subtlety creating political jeopardy for those still in power, and then restoring the *Protocols of the Elders of Zion* in a modern way, was just the beginning. With the establishment of power and trust for the *Fourth Reich* across Britain, a new world order could be created. He knew Hitler would have been proud.

And so too would the facilitator of the concentration camps, *Heinrich Himmler*....

Lord Atkins would open the door to Britain in a matter of months. Then Manfred would enter and light the fire.

All they had to do now was keep Atkins ticking over until it started, take what he owed and then he would be disposed of...

A trip to upstate New York in a *Jeep Wagoneer* was not on Sally-Anne's agenda, but she was doing it, and it was starting to feel alright.

As they left the city, Ryan was driving steadily on the Interstate highway 95, and she could not resist looking at the map of the route they were taking to a town called *Mystic*, in Connecticut.

The first thing that came into her mind, was the number of towns on it that seemed as if they were in England, including Greenwich, New Haven, Wallingford and *Manchester*. She thought about good times in the *proper* Manchester with Linus, not least, the chance meeting with the fabulous singer, Sade...

Then, she considered this place Connecticut. She always thought the area was called *Conneticut,* because that's how it sounded. And another thing was that made her think of cellular phones. She was amazed at how many she'd already seen in

New York. Maybe twenty or thirty perhaps, being used on the streets.

But the weirdest thing of all, was that Ryan had one in the glove box. Her mind went back to Linus. Just over a week to go and they would be going live in London. She wanted to be there right now, looking at him, messing around with him and feeling a *real* connection.

Ryan switched on the radio as Sally-Anne continued to look over the map. The *WNBC* radio station from New York City played the record *'I feel for you'* by Chaka Khan. This was right on top of the chart.

She started to feel guilt. True, she was only out with Ryan over the weekend, as he generously offered to give her some company, because Esther had to go off on a round trip to LA.

And based upon the work they were doing together, it was a positive thing to spend time out for *NCD Global Studios* and *Bernie Cohen Entertainment Ltd.*

Looking up through the *Wagoneer's* windscreen, she saw that the blue sky was darkening, the incoming clouds looked full of snow.

"Is it always so cold here in December?" She asked, looking across at Ryan.

"Sure is," said Ryan tapping the steering wheel and smiling over at her. "That's why I drive one of these things."

She laughed, enjoying seeing his charming smile, then said.

"Figures. At least you are prepared for snow. Back home, it comes in and everyone gets stuck. The papers call it a *whiteout*. The roads are blocked and people are either wandering around with shovels, or just staring out like zombies."

"But apart from that…." He replied, smiling.

"I know, I know," she said, lifting her hands. "Everything is fine."

They both laughed.

Another hour and the exit slip came up for Mystic. It was dark now, but fortunately there was no snow coming in. They'd chatted about their lives and backgrounds. Ryan had been a New Yorker all his life and was now twenty-nine. His parents had moved out of the City almost ten years ago, and were now living out here.

They went along the high road, and the headlamps flickered off the river that ran along into Fishers Island Sound. It was like the backdrop in an old movie scene.

Ryan slowed down and then pulled into the driveway of a large white house.

It was full of old-style windows on both the floors, all with black shutters, and had three, large chimneys of the roof. There were trees around it, the ground floor lights were on, shining out onto the garden.

He switched off the engine and said.

"What do you think of this old pile?"

"Nice," she replied. "There are plenty of lights on too."

"My folks are in waiting for us." He said. "And my mother has got your bedroom all sorted out."

"That's kind." She said, still looking around at the place.

"My pleasure. It's going to be your *private* castle."

She smiled back at Ryan. She realised that he wanted to re-inforce the point that although she might be out with someone she hardly knew, he'd arranged a safe place for her to be.

Then he opened the glove box and reached in to take out his cellular phone. Sally-Anne looked at it, as the box's little light came on. She noticed it was the same as the one in the brochure Linus had showed her at the Midland Hotel in Manchester.

"That's a *Motorola* isn't it?" she asked.

"Yes," replied Ryan. "It's called a *DynaTac,* it was given to me by my boss last year when the thing started up. He passed it over to her and she gently ran her fingers over it, as if her heart was on her sleeve.

He closed the glove box and it went dark in the *Jeep* again, save for the house's lights still coming through the windows a little. Then he looked over at Sally-Anne, she was still touching the *Motorola* and he said with genuine understanding.

"You're missing him, aren't you?"

She smiled back, handing over the cellular phone to Ryan and replied.

"I could say I'm *not missing him at all*. But I'm not *John Waite* am I."

Ryan laughed, opened the driver's door then said. "That's true, you are a hugely attractive lady, but you're not one of the finest British born singers to top the charts on this side of the pond. "But *that* guy is."

They both stepped out smiling, as she walked beside him towards the front door.

Driving to the Kent office, just approaching mid-day on Monday, the Panasonic's green light was on. There was just a week to go before the *RADI-CAL* network went officially live, but now, each of cell sites installed, were switched on. Linus decided to make a call to Colleen at the Croydon office, and see how things were going with her and Steve Rider. But there was something else he needed to ask her too.

He dialled the number, as he pulled up at the lights near Addiscombe, on the edge of town. He lifted the handset and pressed the SND button, waiting for if to make a connection with her desk top phone.

The traffic lights were still on red, and a yellow Ford Escort pulled up alongside. The *burring* sound came into the handset as he held it against his ear, then Colleen answered her phone.

"Hello, this is Mr Rider's office, can I help you?"

"Linus here Colleen, just wanted to see how things were going." The man in the Escort looked across at him, trying to work out what this bloke was holding up against his ear.

"Yeah, all fine today, so far anyway. How are you doing?" She asked him.

As the lights turned to green, Linus glanced at the Escort driver, now pretending to talk into an imagined microphone, mouthing the words *blah, blah, blah,* as he accelerated away.

Linus turned left, heading towards Upper Shirley, holding the handset between his ear and shoulder as he accelerated away and changed gear. "Yes, all good, off to the Maidstone office to see what's happening with a few things."

As he approached the roundabout, he put the handset in his lap for a moment, then accelerated up the hill, and could hear Colleen's voice coming through.

On the left, his eye spotted the gate of his old boy's school, he changed gear and brought the handset up to his ear again.

She realised what was going on, the same thing happened whenever Steve Rider called her from his Ford Granada.

"Look." She said. "Can I suggest you either pull over and carry on, or wait until you get to the office then ring me back?"

He knew she was getting annoyed. "Sorry," he said. "I'll give you a call later."

She hung up, shaking her head. Not with anger at Linus, but rather in concern of the potential danger of using these things when driving.

As Linus headed out towards the Surrey and Kent border, he took on board her comment. She was right about that. Anyway, he needed her advice on something personal. It would be better doing that from his desk phone later, so he could concentrate on what he needed to say, and not be disrupted by driving a car while speaking on a phone....

He switched on BBC Radio 1 and the super Gary Davies show came on, and that was so much better than the madness of attempting to make a cell phone call...

The office in Maidstone was full, with the exception of Jeannie. She had taken a few days off and would be back in on Friday. Julia said that she needed to sort something at home. At one point, Linus considered giving her a call on the off chance she was out in her car, but that wouldn't be appropriate.

Their relationship was based solely upon being friends, but being male and female could arouse suspicion and he certainly did not want to cause an issue for her with Paul.

Mike Sentinel waved at Linus, and then beckoned him into the office. Then he got up from his desk and closed the office door as Linus sat down.

"I wanted to discuss something with you about Jeannie." Said Mike.

Linus looked at him somewhat concerned as Mike sat back down in his chair and carried on.

"It's to do with this order from City National. Now, the EC4 post code has been allocated to you of course, but Jeannie was there too."

Linus now understood what was coming and already worked out his response as Mike continued.

"Now, technically the commission payment should all be allocated to you when it goes through next month, but Steve and I think it would be good if you could split it fifty-fifty with Jeannie."

"I should be delighted to do that." Said Linus. "She was very generous with the *Trans-ship* order and, without her, I probably would not have signed *City National*."

Mike smiled back, pleased at Linus's response. "Good," he said. "I'll let you know when the figures come in from the accounts department, but one thing is for sure, this shall *always* be the largest cellular phone deal in Britain, *before* the system went officially live anyway."

Linus looked at Mike. If he'd been told this less than three months ago, he would have laughed. But now, it was for real.

Chapter 20

*Hyde Park, London
24th December 1984*

It was coming up to mid-day, and the group walked through Lancaster Gate and turned left towards the cordoned off site near the Italian Gardens, in Hyde Park. Although the weather was still quite bright, the low and hastily assembled stage, was surrounded by huge, round lights on poles, shining down onto it as the crew began to position the cameras. The power cables ran over to a white Ford Transit van, its back doors open and a generator sat on the ground behind it, running quietly.

The Maidstone based team stopped and looked over the scene. It was more complex than any of them imagined. There were a lot of people here, running around, adjusting everything, and sound checking.

Linus asked Mike. "What time is Frankie Howerd expected to arrive?"

"Should be here by 14.00 hrs," said Mike, reaching inside his overcoat taking out a letter. "He's coming with his agent, a chap called Alex Judd, and it should all be finished by 15.30 hrs. Shortly before the *official* going live time of course."

Linus knew what he was referring to. The event would *indicate* the network going live at 17.00 hrs, and Frankie would *appear* to call Sir Dennis Ogilvy. The producer would sort that. It had to get on TV for news tonight.

The winter chill was starting to increase, and Mike noticed Robbie Robson was stood with his collar turned up and looked somewhat miserable. He thought this could be due to the cold giving him an ache in his body, from that old bike accident….

"Right," said Mike to the team. "No point in just waiting around, I suggest we go into the pub and get back here in an hour or so."

The pub was across Bayswater road, on the left of Lancaster Gate. Without making any comment, they all began to walk back towards it.

They entered the *Swan* pub and Mike with his usual generosity, walked up to the bar and asked what they wanted to drink. There was a total of eleven *RADI-CAL* staff, all stood by the bar. As this was Christmas Eve, they all knew that Mike wanted to look after them, and perhaps he even felt guilty that this was going on today, when they could all be lazing about at home.

The bar was decked out with holly, with wires connecting coloured lighting, and in the corner was a large Christmas tree, covered in sparkling silver and gold barbells. The speakers around the bar played out *'Do They Know It's Christmas?'* by *Band Aid.*

It was a traditional public bar. There was solid, dark oak around it, and the floor had no carpet, just Victorian planking, albeit somewhat worn as would be expected, but warmly traditional, and the seating was in a *Chesterfield* style.

The two barmaids placed the drinks on the bar. Everyone picked them up, then as the next words of the song came in, looked at their glasses in guilt.

"The greatest gift they get this year is life, where nothing ever grows, no rain nor rivers flow, do they know it's Christmas time at all? Here's to you raise a glass to everyone. Here's to them underneath the burning sun…"

Linus continued to look down and imagined the tragedy and desperation in Africa. He thought about the curse of humanity, such a terrible thing was happening there and yet, here they were in a bar, involved with launching a mobile phone device. What good would that *ever* do for the world?

Jeannie looked at him and touched his shoulder, she was thinking it too, and so were the rest of the *RADI-CAL* team.

Then Mike, realising their guilt said. "If you haven't already done so, make sure you all buy this record, that way you'll be putting something into a good cause."

Julian said. "Here, here." And everyone raised their glasses. Buying these might only be a small commitment, but at least they'd feel a little better. The group stood around the table chatting to each other, mainly about what would happen today.

Jeannie was on a vodka and tonic. She took a sip, put her glass on the bar and started to remove her blue coat. Linus helped her, taking it back from her shoulders. Underneath was a slightly off-white dress. It was tight fitting and the bar's lights touched on her shoulders, the blonde hair swept down her back. Everyone stood around in the group, could not resist looking at her.

"So how's it going with Sally-Anne in New York?" she asked Linus very quietly.

"I think it's alright." He said

"Do you mean that you're not *really* sure?" she asked, now taking this deeper.

"Well, put it this way. Getting in touch has been difficult over the last week or so. She has been moving around with her work." He said.

The music from the bar's speakers changed to '*The Power of Love*' by *Frankie Goes to Hollywood.*

She pointed up at the closest speaker, the light touching her red painted nails and gold wedding ring, and then said. "That's spooky, don't you think?"

Linus felt a bit taken aback. But deep down, he *was* getting concerned about the lack of contact with Sally-Anne. It had been almost two weeks since they had spoken.

He was on the edge of responding, when the bar's door opened and in walked an older man in a raincoat, someone he instantly recognised, so did Jeannie and everyone else. It was Frankie Howerd.

Mike walked over to him, extending his hand and said.

"Ah, Mr Howerd I presume, come and meet the *RADI-CAL* team.

"Oh My Gawd," he said looking around at them. "I didn't realise *you lot* would be in here."

The *inflection* that he used in his words made every one of them laugh. It was as if they were all settled in his show's audience.

"What can I get for you?" asked Mike, pointing over at the attractive barmaid.

"I'd *rather* just have a *Boddingtons*." Frankie said.

Linus, Jeannie and Robbie laughed at the innuendo, but no one else got it.

"Oh well, please yourselves." Said Howerd.

Jeannie was still laughing in her usual deep and sensual way, then asked him.

"So what do you think of our thing?"

"Oooh err, Missus." He replied, as she continued to laugh. Then smiled at her, genuinely liking her style.

Bizarrely, although he'd only been there for seconds, it was as if he was now one of the team. He was a famous celebrity, but somehow, instead of everyone being star struck, they felt a connection of friendship to him. Weird but wonderful.

Frankie reached inside his overcoat and took out something that surprised them all. It was a *Motorola 8000x* hand portable cell phone.

"Blimey," said Robbie. "How did you get hold of that?"

"Simple my dear fellow," replied Frankie snootily. "One of *your* lot sent it to *my* agent as a gift."

Mike laughed, he knew that Steve Rider had arranged this. Not only would that have given Frankie a chance to play around with it before the filming, but also, it might even make him an enthusiast, and that could reach out to a lot of other stars.

"Have you given it a try yet?" Robbie asked.

Frankie looked at him in surprise and said. "What, do you mean it's working?"

"Yes," said Robbie. "Officially, after *you* have made the first *ever* call in Britain today from the park, but actually it's live now."

Passing the Motorola over to Robbie, Frankie said with a mixture of interest and disbelief. "Go on then, show me."

Robbie Robson asked the barmaid, pointing over at the grey phone by the till, near the long row of *shorts* bottles. "Excuse me, could you let me have the number?"

"What for?" she asked. "You're already stood in here."

"I know said Robbie, holding up the *Motorola*, I just want to show Mr Howerd the way it works."

"Oh please yourself." She said looking at him as if he were crazy, then wrote the number on a piece of paper and passed it across the bar to him.

"That's my *line*." Frankie whispered into Robbie's ear, just loudly enough to make all the others laugh.

Robbie dialled in the number, pressed the SND button and passed the *Motorola* over to Frankie. The whole bar room went quiet as they watched, not just the *RADI-CAL* team, but everyone else who had come in. *The Power of Love* song had finished, and no other sound came from the speakers.

Frankie Howerd looked at Robbie suspiciously the moments ticking by, suspecting this was nonsense. But then, the phone by the till rang and the bar maid answered it, saying "Hello," as she looked across at him, the *Motorola* up against his left ear.

"Oooh, and hello to you Missus." He said. "Can you pour me a *Boddingtons* please?"

"Certainly," she said and put down the phone, annoyed by the stupidity of this.

Laughter and applause surrounded the room as she walked up to the beer pump on the bar. *This,* thought Linus looking around, *is one exceptional moment in a decent pub.*

Mike Sentinel raised his glass at everyone in the bar and said out loud. "And that ladies and gentlemen, is the first *pre-*official cellular call made by Mr Howerd in this wonderful country of Great Britain."

Everyone cheered and whistled. Frankie Howerd smiled and bowed.

They had all left the *Swan* pub and were waiting by the filming site in the park.

A lot of *RADI-CAL* staff were here. Steve Rider was stood with Colleen on the stage, talking to someone Linus thought must be a producer, with headphones placed round his neck and holding a notepad. Steve looked very focussed, as he explained something to the man, and Colleen was clearly comparing the discussion with some planning notes that she was perusing. She was wearing a black fur coat with the collar turned up, and high boots.

I must ask her something. Thought Linus as he looked over at her. Then Jeannie came up beside him and smiled. "Now this is getting very close." She said, then pointed over at Colleen. "She used to work for Mr Cannon before joining Steve, didn't she?"

"She did," Linus replied. "She was his PA for years."

"Good looking." Said Jeannie.

"You're not gay are you?" Linus asked.

Jeannie laughed and said. "Touché. I should have a glass of Moet to raise up to you. I deserved that!"

"*I'll never forget Paris,*" he said, in a terrible impersonation of Humphrey Bogart. "Or should I say *Rochester.*"

The producer went to the front of the stage, as Steve and Colleen walked off. Then he raised his hand and spoke out to the audience. The *RADI-CAL* team now mingling with some passers-by.

"Ladies and Gentlemen please welcome the fabulous Mr Frankie Howerd."

The audience all cheered and clapped as Frankie walked up to the producer, staring at his *Motorola* and appearing to be keying a number, as if his mind was elsewhere.

He looked around, stepping back in shock, as if he was not expecting an audience, the laughter and clapping continuing.

"Sorry," he said. "But I'm really hooked," then pointed at Jeannie and said. "But not on you *Missus*. You're out of my league, in more ways than one."

Colleen came over to Linus and Jeannie, as the audience laughed. Frankie continued, looking around at them all. "*Titter ye not,*" he said in feigned annoyance. He pointed over at Colleen who was clearly not impressed, and said. "Yes, I know your type dear, all fur coat and no knickers."

The crowd's guffaws continued as Frankie went on. "Right, Ladies and Gentlemen, I'm just off to see the nice catering chap for a sausage." He Looked at the *Motorola*, waiting for the laughter to die down and said. "Then, I'll come back and get this thing set off, so it can *change the world.*"

Everyone clapped and some whistled, as he finished the warm-up, and left the stage.

"Hi," said Jeannie, as she shook hands with Colleen. "I'm Jeannie Sands, I've heard good things about you from Linus."

"Thanks," she replied. "I've heard *lots* about you too."

Linus then said to Colleen. "I'm sorry I didn't get back to you the other day."

"Never mind," she said, still looking at Jeannie. "I realise you've been *very* busy."

Jeannie looked over at Mike Sentinel and said. "Excuse me folks, I need to have a chat with Mike about something."

Colleen watched her strut along seductively and said.

"Nice. I can see why she is so appreciated by you."

"But not as much as you are." He replied.

"So," she said. "What is it you want?"

"I was wondering if you had the direct number for Karen Solomon in the New York office?" He said. "I have looked everywhere, but can't find it."

"Sure, but can I ask why?" Colleen replied.

Linus came straight to the point. "I appreciate that she is busy, but I'm worried that I haven't heard from Sally-Anne for a while."

"Have you not called her then?"

"That's the problem." Replied Linus. "I agreed not to do that, firstly so I could fit around her time-line and secondly, Sally-Anne being as generous as she always is, insisted that I wouldn't be paying for the calls."

"I see." Said Colleen. "So you are thinking of getting Karen do a bit of snooping then?"

He could not argue with that. "Yes," he said. "If you put it like that."

Colleen opened up her bag and took out the notebook with RITON Group contact details. She flicked through it, found the 34th street phone number, and then passed it over to him. He took a small diary from his coat pocket, then noted Karen's number down.

"Thanks," he said, passing the notebook back. "I'll bear that in mind."

"If I can give you some advice," she said, her gloved hand reaching out and touching his bare one. "Whatever she does or does not do, for some reason which I cannot fathom, you two are meant for each other. It hit me like a ton of bricks when she came in and stripped for you."

He laughed, remembering that event and also thinking of the weird co-incidence that the person he was standing with now who arranged this, felt the same as he did.

She looked over at Jeannie, now chatting with Mike and Steve and said. "Don't ever believe that people are what *you* think they are. However, I believe that Sally-Anne Cohen is an exception to that rule."

The lights came on around the stage. The camera operators were clearly ready and the stage manager came to the front, touching his lips to ensure the crowd piped down. It reminded Linus a bit of the BBC event in their Manchester studio, but that was a lot warmer than this one…

Frankie Howerd came on to the stage again. He was wearing a black overcoat, done right up to the neck, and an ancient looking, *Bicorne* hat, as if he were Napoleon for some reason.

He went up to the microphone, then reached into his pocket and took out the *Motorola 8000x*. Then he looked at it as everyone cheered, and dialled in a number.

He attempted to put the cell phone up to his ear, the corner of the hat struck the antenna.

The laughter came in, as he removed the hat and pointed over at Jeannie, now stood at the front of the *RADI-CAL* group audience.

"Don't forget to tell them to look after the *knobs* when they start using these things *Missus*." He said, still looking at the antenna.

"Cut." Said the stage manager.

"Oh well, *please yourselves*." Said Frankie. "I'll alter the position of my hat then."

He turned the hat around so that its corners faced backwards and forwards.

The audience settled down and the stage manager re-started the filming.

The scene had already been practised by Frankie Howerd and the producer in the film studio. It involved a call to Sir Dennis Ogilvy, the recording of which had already been made. Frankie gave the impression of an actual conversation, but naturally, was able to *ham* it out, full of *double-entendres* as if it were on the BBC show, '*The Good Old Days.*'

The *RADI-CAL* staff were all pleased that the filming had been completed. The actual time was 15.25hrs. It was nobody's fault, but as the event disbanded, most of them felt somewhat deflated.

Frankie had been superb of course, but although everyone felt the way the show had been derived was a good idea in a practical sense, it might have been better if it had gone ahead at mid-night on new-year's eve perhaps. The bells would have rung and the fireworks gone off. But it was done, and *RADI-CAL* was the leader of a new way for people to communicate.

"What time do you plan to get the train back?" Linus asked Jeannie as they walked back towards the *Swan* pub.

"I'm in no hurry." She said and carried on. "I would guess around seven, I should be home before nine. How about you?"

"I've got nothing to go home for." He said, sounding sorry for himself.

Jeannie stopped by the gate, looking him in the eyes as the others passed by, and said. "Do you have any relatives?"

Linus looked down at the ground, absently twisting the sole of his shoe. "Well," he said, continuing to look down in what seemed like embarrassment. "I don't really have any. My mother went away when I was young and my father has a different life-style, with another woman, very far away…."

Jeannie nodded in understanding.

"Well," she said. "A positive thing is that there's going to be a few days for peace and quiet. "And if you get really bored, give me a call and then you can come over to ours."

"Thanks." He said. "I appreciate that. Anyway, I can always watch '*The two Ronnies*' on the TV."

"Talking of which," she said smiling. "Didn't you say your TV was black and white?"

"Yes," he said. "And I'd rather die than have a new-fangled, colour thing."

She put her arm through his, as he stood with his hand in the pocket of the overcoat.

"Come on, she said, nodding over at the *Swan,* it's time to celebrate."

The dusk was now turning to darkness and on the other side of the road, an old man stood wearing a trilby hat, the collar of his overcoat turned up, under the awning of a small shop front. He watched them walk into the *Swan* and Dick Kelson said under his breath. *Typical, that yid bitch has cleared off and now he's out with some other bird.*

Kelson shook his head, in disgust. Being a murderer was one thing, and that was generally just a required job for the good of the righteous.

But going off with another bird...Anyway, that was not his concern. The real issue was that letter written to MacColl by Rupert Cannon. Sure, the only copy he *previously* thought existed, was the one he'd made from the original, before Lord Atkins had set fire to it.

There was no indication at all as to why there was another copy out there with someone. But he could not get it out of his mind. He watched more of the crowd, who had been out by that bonkers event in the park, enter the *Swan's* bar.

What the fuck was this all about? Filming a lunatic, camp, comedian, dressed as Napoleon on a bad day, holding a plastic brick against his head. Then he laughed as he remembered seeing that stupid brochure, when he'd gone into the hotel room of that annoying pair in Manchester.

He thought about going into that pub to do a bit of spying. It was too risky. That MacColl bloke might recognise him from when he was in the Midland hotel bar.

Kelson walked down the Bayswater Road in the opposite direction from the *Swan*.

His Passat was parked on Leinster Terrace, out of site from the park. The hobble was getting worse every day now, and the walk was painful.

He was in no doubt that his work, and therefore as far as Lord Atkins was concerned, his life was fast reaching its end.

Since his wife 'passed away' he'd become a loner, so it didn't really matter. In fact, he'd killed her, and the bitch deserved it. Over the years, he'd taken out loads of others, one of the recent ones being Rupert Cannon. It always amused him when he thought about this, because that bloke was the son of the man his *own father* had killed in 1938. A funny old co-incidence. But *where* would he go after his own death? That was the thing that bothered him now…

He reached the Passat, parked in a dark corner of the road. He'd chosen this space because the street lamp above it was out. He looked around to make sure he was not being followed or watched. This was unlikely, but still a habit.

He opened the car door and then sat behind the wheel, and considered his own death again. Maybe, he would be taken into a *new world order*, one where he was accepted for the scum that he'd taken out, and for his respect of what Hitler had so nearly achieved.

He looked down the Passat's bonnet into the darkness, drumming on the steering wheel with his fingers, imagining a new age. A *new* Adolf would be his leader, providing so much more for the *decent* people of the world, including atomic destruction of the enemies.

Time was running out for him now, but his final effort would be in greatness.

Lord Atkins might be his current leader, but things would change. He started to look forward to their next meeting, once 1985 had arrived….

The bar in the Swan was full of *RADI-CAL* people.

Steve, Mike, Julia and Colleen were engaged in a deep conversation, and there were a number that Linus recognised from the *Heath-Field* House training course, in other regions. The two new starters in the Kent office were there too, stood at the other end of the bar with Kevin Aaron.

Jeannie ordered the drinks. The barmaid who had answered Frankie Howerd's call, brought them over. Linus raised his lager-top against her vodka and tonic. She nodded over at Mike and said.

"He mentioned that you agreed to split the commission with me on the City National deal. That is good of you."

"That's the least I can do." He said, lighting up a Marlboro. "You are the one who made it happen. I was behind the lines."

"Thanks." She said smiling at him.

"Also, I really appreciate you listening to that *school thing* I told you about." He said, feeling embarrassment.

She would never tell anyone. whatever happened between her and Linus, that would never change.

"I am sad about what happened to you, but honoured that you shared it with me. I'm always here if you need me, and I'll keep it locked inside, forever." She said in sincerity.

Linus looked over at Steve, his group still chatting, stood around a bar table, and on it, stood an *R2* transportable.

"I'm going to ask Steve if I can make a call to New York on that." He said to Jeannie, nodding over at the *R2*.

"I get it," she said smiling. "You're going to tell him it's to let the new RITON lot there know it's live."

"I am," he said, realising her knowledge of his plan. "Then I'll ask one of them to do me a small favour."

She continued her smiling and said. "So would it be an old *friend* of yours, that might go and take a look at what a *certain* person is doing when she's out at night by any chance then?"

Linus smiled at her. "It might be." He said.

Jeannie took a sip of her vodka and tonic, then said. "Well, take my advice. Women can be devious. What's your *friend's* name?"

"Karen Solomon." Said Linus. "She's an area manager in 34th street office. We had a great time in Manhattan one night."

"I'm sure you did," said Jeannie laughing. "I know I'm shooting myself in the foot here, but just remember the words of that *BB King* song. '*Never trust a woman*.'"

"And on that note," he said. "Would you mind coming outside, whilst I try and make the call?"

"No," she said, still smiling. "I need to have a chat with the new guys that are with Kevin." She strutted away, then looked back at him over her shoulder and said. "Let me know how it goes."

The bar's lights touched her blonde hair, the seams on the back of her stockings visible. People in the bar watched her move, including Colleen. *That was something of an irony*, he thought, given her attitude at their first meeting in the park. Linus walked over to Steve.

"Well Linus, what did you think of today?" He asked.

"Good," said Linus, pointing at the *R2* transportable. "Could I borrow it for a minute? I need to call the RITON office in New York, just to let them know we are now live."

"Yes," replied Steve. "But good luck with getting through. Still if you do, at least it'll be the first *official* overseas call made from the UK on a cellular phone."

Everyone laughed except Mike, who watched Linus lift up the heavy, grey boxed, transportable and walk towards the door. He wanted Linus to get through, sensing he was concerned about something.

The front garden was in darkness and empty, except for two men in conversation by the entrance, Frankie Howerd and his agent, Alex Judd. Linus put the *R2* on a table and sat down. The Bayswater Road had virtually no traffic, there were no passers-by on the pavement, and the moon shone down from a cloudless sky. It was now 18.00hrs local time, so middle of the day in New York.

Linus flicked through his notebook. Frankie and Alex noticed the transportable on the table, and it took their attention away from their conversation. They watched Linus starting to key a number into the handset, and clearly could not resist what he was doing, so they both walked over to him.

"Oooh," said Frankie, looking at the *R2* transportable. "I see *you've* got a *big one*, are you making a call then?"

Linus looked up at them both and said. "I'm going to try and call our group's office in New York." It felt surreal being asked this question by a huge star, but also slightly off putting, given the nature of the call he was going to make.

Frankie and Alex laughed. Then Frankie said, pointing at the bar. "Well I'm going in for a night cap."

Alex Judd looked at his watch and said to Frankie. "I need to get off, let's keep in touch."

"*Oooh yes*," Said Frankie in his sarcastic way. "*Let's*."

They both went off, and Linus pressed the SND button and waited for the signal to dial in. A clicking noise came into the handset and then it buzzed a little. He waited for a while, but it did not connect.

He pressed the red cancel button, and put the handset back onto the box. Looking up at the bright moon, he decided to try again.

As he dialled in and pressed SND once more, he thought about the complexities of this. The number to New York would be transferred from the press of a button, to a board of electronics inside the *R2* transportable, which would then send out a signal at 900 MHz through its antenna, across the sky to a cellular base station, close to Victoria. This would connect the signal onto a BT line, which the *RADI-CAL* base station technology would convert from digital to analogue, travel across the country and then, go into a cable under the Atlantic Ocean.

Around four thousand miles later, the signal would reach the New York land-line network and re-connect with their cables. The number would travel over to the RITON office's central phone hub, which would put the call through to the desk of Karen Solomon.

It's a long shot, he thought, now listening intently into the ear piece of the handset. He looked through the bar's front window, and saw Frankie Howerd stood talking with Mike and Robbie. *Three old soldiers chatting.* He thought.

A few more clicks came into his ear and then, a long burr sounded.

"Hello, Karen Solomon, can I help you?"

"This is Linus MacColl," he said. "How are you doing?"

The voices clashed somewhat, as the words travelled across the Atlantic, causing a delay.

"I'm doing fine," she said. "And how about you?"

"Good," said Linus, backing off speaking for a few seconds, and then carried on. "I wanted to ask if you could help me with something…"

The weather in New York was milder than usual at this time of year. Ryan and Sally-Anne sat in the corner of one of the *NCD Global Studio* rooms. On the table in front of them, was the final approved contract with *Bernie Cohen Entertainment Ltd.*

This had moved faster than most had thought, primarily because Sally-Anne had been focussed on this with Ryan, and it had proved an efficient connection.

It had given her confidence too. Esther had been so busy with the work associated with the L.A people, that trying to manage what was going on here at the same time, would have been impossible.

Her dad, as ever, had been right. Esther had needed Sally-Anne's help and the outcome had been excellent. She was pleased with what she had achieved and grateful for the kind support of Ryan, who as a senior contract developer for *NCD*, had been key for what was now going forward.

A lot of new, American produced TV shows would go into Europe through Bernie's company.

"So," Ryan asked. "What's your plan for tonight?"

"Nothing, Esther is still finishing off in L.A today, and staying out there with some friends. She asked me if I wanted to come over, but it's better that I don't." Replied Sally-Anne.

"Why?" asked Ryan, somewhat puzzled by this.

"Because I think she has a *very close* working relationship with a producer she met over there." She said smiling at him.

"Ah, yes." He said nodding, also with a smile. "I've heard something about that."

"So, I am staying here, watching the TV, resting up in the apartment, and then I can book my flight back home in a few weeks, way sooner than expected thanks to you." She said.

"I seem to have been over efficient then." He said looking down in a pretence of sadness.

"That's always the case with a genius," she said laughing. "Cleverness can get in the way."

"At least you should let me take you out for a few final drinks in the *Hairy Monk* bar tonight." He said, still feigning misery.

"Why not." She said, smiling.

Frankie Howerd was in a deep conversation with Mike and Robbie. In fact, the whole bar was now in a state of discussion. There was an atmosphere of drinking, smoking and laughter, typical of Christmas Eve. But also, there was an element of excitement, following today's launch of cellular phones.

Linus lugged the *R2* transportable up to the bar, and placed it in front of Steve Rider. It weighed eleven pounds, almost the same as six bags of sugar.

"Did you get through alright?" Steve asked Linus.

"Yes, only took two attempts and it was fine thanks." Said Linus.

The song playing through the speakers was *Like a Virgin* by *Madonna.* Steve then shouted over the music to Mike, who was still deep in conversation with Frankie Howerd, as he pointed at the *R2*.

"It got through to the States!"

Mike nodded his understanding, and gave him the thumbs up.

Steve waved at the barmaid pointing to the lager, knowing exactly want Linus wanted and being very efficient, so did she.

Looking around the bar, everyone it seemed, was still in here, except Jeannie Sands.

In the pub's ladies' lavatory cubicle, Jeannie sat looking down at the *speed* powder on a handkerchief, placed on her lap. Bending forward with the straw, she inhaled, first into one nostril, and then the other. The effect was now taking even longer to hit in, she needed more of the drug every day now.

She wiped the back of her hand across her nose and began to laugh in self-sarcasm, shaking her head at the song's words she could hear playing from the bar speakers. *'Like a virgin, hey, touched for the very first time.'*

She stood trying to get herself back on-track for returning to the bar, knowing without a doubt, that she was now an addict.

Frankie and Mike were in a deep discussion about their experiences as soldiers. But as was often typical with the those who had faced dangerous and tragic experiences whilst fighting for their country, they kept the post-traumatic stress in their minds, and not coming out of their mouths.

"Anyway," said Frankie. "If I think about all the mistakes I make when on stage, *none* of them are as embarrassing as my boat breaking down off Normandy on D-Day, and putting me behind all the others. What was your worst experience?"

Mike Sentinel looked Frankie Howerd in the eyes through his extraordinarily thick lenses and felt his inner self falling, as the guilt and horror of shooting a young boy in Aden so very long ago, struck him.

"Oh," he said, pointing over at Robbie Robson who was now stood talking to Julian. "I had to go and pick him up when he came off a *Norton* one winter up in Scotland, after he left the barracks to go and meet a woman in a pub."

"And I thought I had a bad day back in forty-four." Frankie said, shaking his head.

As he did this, Mike felt sure that he saw the hair on his head slide to the left, *but surely that could not be true,* he thought, staring at it through his thick glasses.

Frankie took his final swig of the *Boddingtons* bitter, then looked at the empty glass and said to Mike.

"Life is like an escalator. People get on it at the bottom, and then as it goes up and nears the top, we realise that it's all been wrong. Then we turn and try to run down it, but the motor speeds up, and we are running out of energy. Then, we are finished. Life and war Mike, it's the *same* thing."

Mike looked at Frankie, taking that in with a mixture of surprise and agreement.

"*Aw gaud*," said Frankie looking at his watch. "I better be going."

He placed his empty beer glass on the bar, then took a card from his pocket and gave it to Mike. "That's my address and phone number." He said, pointing at it. "That's a *real* phone, and not one of these new bonkers things you are trying to sell. Anytime you and your *Missus* want to come round for a chat, you'd be more than welcome."

Mike looked at the card, wanting to say thanks, but was overcome and just nodded as he thought. *This man is not just a star.*

Frankie walked up to the *Swan's* door, turned and looked at everyone. "*Titter ye not!*" He shouted, and stepped out into the night as they all waved and cheered.

It was cold now, and he turned up the collar of his overcoat, walking out into the darkness. Leaving the pub's garden gate, he turned right into the side road.

The street lights shone down and at the far end of the road, one was over the top of his car, a 1965 *Austin Westminster* saloon, two tone in colour, light blue and white. He always preferred to drive home to Kensington, rather than take a tube or a taxi.

He took the keys from his coat pocket, then opened the driver's door and stepped in.

As he put the key in the ignition, he noticed the street lamp touching the bonnet.

It was like looking at the sun glinting off the English Channel on the 6th of June 1944, as his invasion of France vessel drifted without power, after its engine failed.

As an army sergeant, this delayed his Normandy landing. But when he finally made it to the beach, there was carnage as far as the eye could see. He put his head into his hands as the memories of something so awful from over forty years ago came back. It was certainly not the first time. For some reason it always came at him when he was out, and spoke of his army life with someone in a pub, just as he'd done with Mike Sentinel tonight. He felt huge guilt that he survived due to a twist of fate, and so many did not.

He wanted to speak to an old friend, who was there with him on that day. The problem was, he was always out alone when this anguish of the past affected him, and desperate as he was, what could he do? The only option was to dive into a phone box and make a call to him. But that was dangerous, people might look in the box and recognise him.

But then he remembered that cellular phone thing in his coat pocket. It was now officially live, *thanks to him,* he thought sarcastically. As he took the grey brick out, he noticed it was still switched on, the green light shining out. He keyed in his old friend's number, he knew it off by heart. Then pressed the SND button and put it up against his ear, after a few seconds, he heard the long *burr* sound coming in.

The old friend in Stepney answered and Frankie said. "Good evening Corporal Harding, just wanted to wish you a merry Christmas."

"And the same to you Sergeant Howerd." Said the delighted man at the other side of town. "Or should I say, *Titter ye not,* old friend."

Frankie realised this thing he held up against his ear was of some use.

Jeannie glanced at her watch. The last train home for her from Victoria was leaving in under five minutes. They stood together by the gate, the last of the passengers walking past, some clearly a little tipsy. Both wanted to say something but it was still on hold. Then the whistle blew and the chance was over. Linus looked down, and Jeannie very gently, touched his hair with her fingers. Time stood still for an instant, then the whistle blew again. She turned and ran down the platform, stopped for a second, smiled at him, then stepped up through the train door as he waved back. The final whistle blew, and the train went off.

The *Hairy Monk* bar was not as busy as she thought it would be. She was just about to tell Ryan that, then a crowd came in.

There were fifteen of them, men and women, overcoats on, the bar lights glistening from the raindrops on their shoulders and hair, all laughing and she considered that it was a work crowd, out for a Christmas Eve celebration drink.

Ryan turned his back on them, wanting to focus on his conversation with Sally-Anne.

"So, tell me the date you're planning to leave our *New York state of mind.*" He said, using that *Billy Joel* song's title.

She took a sip of her *Margarita* and replied.

"I'm leaving on the 24th January now, as Esther is coming back from L.A a few days before. That way, I can sort everything with her, and head off home with all the details for my dad to get into place."

"So what do you want to do in between now and then? I'm going to L.A sometime in January, but am around for a while. Would you like a bit of company?"

"I'd like a bit of company," she replied laughing. "But aren't you going to be with your folks?"

She thought back to their weekend in New England. It was as if she'd been out with an old friend. They had walked around the town, gone down to the river, been in bars, had dinner, and then sat chatting with his folks by the log burning fire, in the lounge of their lovely home.

She'd been safe in her own room that night, but all she did was lie awake and think of Linus, feeling guilt, even though she'd done nothing *really* wrong. Maybe, this was why she had put her calls to him on hold? But the reality was, her job here was coming to an end, and it was going to be just great to be home with Linus.

Ryan had been looking at his beer glass and swilling it round a little as he considered her question about folks.

"No," he said. "They are heading over to my sister's in Wisconsin, and then they'll be back just before new year."

Sally-Anne could tell he was not too happy about this, so decided not to delve in any further, and said. "Well, you'll have to put up with me then."

Ryan put his glass on the bar and gave her a hug in delight. Sally-Anne was not uncomfortable about that, as it was more friendly than sensual, but it took her by surprise, and she automatically, for some reason put her arms around him, the *Margarita* still in her right hand.

At the other side of the bar, a woman was staring at them. She had only come in a few minutes ago with some members of her team at *RITON Electronics Inc*. From the East 34th Street office.

Karen Solomon had already heard the dark haired woman's voice as they came in. She was clearly from England and matched how Linus MacColl had described her on that cell phone call earlier today. She smiled, and thought, *this could make my walk in the rain worthwhile then.*

Looking along the train carriage, the revellers were still drinking from the bottles and cans they had probably taken from office parties or bought from an off-licence. Many stood in the train's corridor, wearing the paper-hats from crackers, and some blew on party horns.

As the train rattled through Battersea. Jeannie could see the smoke bellowing from the power station on the left. *The electrical supply into London must be huge tonight,* she thought, and then wondered how the poor seagulls in flight from the Thames would cope, when they undoubtedly inhaled that awful smog in the air.

Her mind was multi-tasking across a huge web of confusion, regret and guilt. The good effects of *speed* inhalation had gone. In fact, the come down had created serious negativity. She looked at the train's door handle. *Maybe this was why people jumped out? s*he thought.

There was no more powder in her bag, she had taken in three today and the rest was at home. She would need to wait until this slow train got back.

She thought about Linus. *It was life's fate wasn't it? Right person, right place, wrong time, etcetera.* Days of boredom with Paul lay ahead. She needed to get away, time was running thin. *BB King was right* she thought, *never trust a woman,* and whispered out *'especially one like me.'* She looked down at her red, patent leather high-heeled shoes, and put her head into her hands.

Linus walked down the platform to his own train. He wanted the next two miserable days to fly by as quickly as possible, so he could get back to the office on Wednesday. As he stepped into the carriage, he imagined that Anna, who dumped him years ago, was sat waiting in there, expecting him to walk over and beg her to come back. He'd dreamed of this for years, always hoping. But from the start of joining *RADI-CAL,* it had begun to drift away, and now even if she'd *really* been there, he would ignore her.

He thought of the extraordinary strands of sensuality and seductiveness from Jeannie. It was like a deep breath of excitement, but also safety. She had helped him start to overcome his self-hatred, and the *if only I'd done things better* thoughts that were derived from the past.

The friendship with Jeannie was the most unique he'd ever experienced. It was as if she had the natural compassion and skills of a psychiatrist, and the looks of a movie star. It felt as if there was a reason beyond his comprehension, for him coming into the *RADI-CAL* team.

But, the real aspect of change to his life had come from someone who he wanted by his side forever.

Someone who he felt enormous trust for, and a sense of being with in another world. But most of all, someone who he loved beyond any doubt. He believed meeting Sally-Anne under such a strange circumstance was not luck, but had been created and passed down to him by his G-d.

Chapter 21

Notting Hill, London
2nd January 1985

Dick Kelson sat back in his tatty old armchair. On the other side of the lounge coffee table, was his wife's empty chair. He still felt a little guilty about strangling her when she was sat in it. Normally, it didn't bother him, but she always had a thing for Christmas, all that *mistletoe* and *wine* stuff.

But he'd had no choice. The silly cow had prised open his desk draw at the other end of the room and read a document, it was private, and not for the consumption of anyone else. When he came in that night, she was sat in that chair seething.

Well, he just had to do her in, didn't he? Luckily, he'd come in with that piano wire still in his overcoat pocket. It was there for another job he hadn't done yet. He quite enjoyed her last seconds of anger, choking, shock and her realisation that she was going to die. It was always the most satisfying part of carrying out a murder, and he believed it was even more painful for the victim than shooting, because it was slower.

The document was out of here now. It was where he should have put it in the first place, in the safe of his villa in *Fabron*, just west of Nice, in the South of France. Still, so what? He was sat indoors in peace and quiet, and been enjoying that for months, since doing her in.

Kelson had removed a lot of money over the years from Lord Atkins. Initially, he did this to get his own back, because of how Atkins's father had stitched up his *own* father. Taking a lot of money from the undercover workers in their company scams, had paid for his villa in *Fabron*. No one knew about that villa, except his wife...What the undercover workers did know however, was that if they told anyone about the money they handed over to Dick Kelson, they too would be taken out.

But things had gone much further. His own relationship with the *Fourth Reich* went back a long way. It was after all, one of their people who had saved his life after being shot in East Berlin all those years ago. And that was because his *Lordship* had sent him to the wrong fucking place.

He enjoyed the clandestine method of taking money from Atkins, to help fund the new Reich, ironically passing back some of it that was stolen by his father.

He was still angry, but had been instrumental in helping build up the *New Order* for Gerhard and his loyal subjects. The huge change was coming.

The news story about that cellular radio thing going live, reminded him of what he'd seen up in Hyde Park. Frankie Howerd was just taking the mickey out of it. But maybe, what von Sterne had told Gerhard, could work?

There was now a huge number of undercover *Fourth Reich* members ready to go and start the riots in the cities of England. Communication between themselves and those in other areas could expand and control this. These new cellular phone things could be useful.

What if they could use them out on the streets? There would be no need to call each other from an office or phone box. They could contact each other and plan the attacks. Should they need to change direction, or be warned about people setting up gangs to fight back, calls on these things could help.

The police would have no idea where they were. *They could keep moving, keep killing and keep burning*, he thought, smiling.

Next to his BT phone on the table was a device preventing calls being tapped.

Good job, he thought. Five minutes ago, Gerhard's call had been with a passion for their potential to change this world for the better. Nazi power was returning, the first aim was to take over Britain, and Adolf would rise up from the past. Their work and future joy of success was coming.

But, there were things that Dick Kelson needed to do first. It was time to remove his Lordship now, but something else was worrying him too.

That bloke Bernie Cohen. He was in the film business and also associated with the people in television. What if that twit MacColl and his bird or even that other bitch he'd seen him out with, had a copy of the *real* letter?

What if it had got to Cohen, and he could put it on the TV or in newspapers? He thought.

Then he looked over at his murdered wife's chair and said out loud, smiling.

"There's only one way to be sure. That *fucking* lot needs to be *removed*."

The rain came in onto the office's windows and Croydon aerodrome's abandoned runway disappeared from his view.

Linus turned away and stared over at Colleen, sat behind her desk. She was thinking about Mr Cannon.

"So why are you in here today and not the Kent office?" she asked him, taking a bite of her apple.

That was a good question and there was no real answer he could give. Steve Rider was out and he wanted to ask her *real* feelings about something he'd already told her on the phone.

She had listened to this, but had sat on the fence. That was why he'd come in here, she realised that, despite her question.

"You know what," she said quietly and with sincerity. "We are all only human. Even if Karen Solomon was right about seeing Sally-Anne with that bloke in the bar, it probably came to nothing."

Linus nodded in understanding, but she could sense that he was still concerned. Karen had spoken to Linus on Monday from the New York office. He had called her, otherwise she would not have mentioned what she had seen in the *Hairy Monk* bar. Initially, she did think about calling him, but decided to let it go. After all, everybody made some mistakes.

"Look, thinks happen." Colleen carried on. "In a few weeks she'll be home you said, and if I were you, I'd keep in touch and put everything on the table when she is back."

"What do you mean, *put everything on the table?*" He asked.

"People miss each other and then have affairs when they are apart." She said. "Sometimes, they have an affair as they *really* love the person who is far away. Ironic, I know, but there you are."

Over the last two days, he'd stayed indoors. He considered going over to the pub yesterday, but decided against it. Two calls had come in from Sally-Anne.

She sounded a bit distant in the first one, as if her mind was far away. But on the second, she was back to her old self, telling him that she was really looking forward to coming back much sooner than was planned.

Given what Karen had told him, and the point Colleen made, it could be that she really did want to be with him again. But what if she came back and told him that she had moved on? What if she, being up front and strong minded as ever, wanted to do this face to face? Would Sally-Anne turn out to be another *Anna*? That did not bear thinking about.

The café on 34th street had emptied. It was just on 09.00hrs, and most New York office workers were already at their desks.

Esther Cohen sat looking over at Sally-Anne in a mixture of understanding and annoyance. Sally-Anne was staring down at her coffee cup, her mind in another place.

"Right," said Esther. "You need to snap out of this. We all make mistakes, but this is not just about you having an affair, it's about our dad's business."

Sally-Anne looked up at her, tears running down her cheeks. Esther opened her handbag, took out a handkerchief and gently wiped her sister's cheeks.

It was cold out on the street, and the café's windows were steamed up. A police car's siren wailed as it streaked past. Sally-Anne shook her head and said.

"And I thought I was the fucking *siren* around here."

Esther smiled and said.

"We are only human after all. Now, this needs to be sorted, and I have planned out what we can do."

"Like what?" said Sally-Anne, looking down at her cup again in misery.

Esther ignored her misery and said. "You are lucky, because Ryan is off to L.A tomorrow and is going to be there for a fortnight. I know this, because the guy I get on with out there at *NCD Global* told me. So, you can finish off here with his assistant and then, get the flight home before he's back."

Sally-Anne looked at Esther and said. "I know he was going to L.A this month, but didn't realise it was so soon."

Esther looked over at her dead-pan and said. "Sometimes people get asked to travel quicker than was anticipated don't they? Like you going back home sooner than Ryan expected, because a work thing in London came up." Then she turned on a smile.

Sally-Anne got this. She knew Esther had arranged it, and that was the reason why she was back in New York, long before her originally planned time. She had out-manoeuvred this problem situation in every element, just like her dad would always do. *That's why Esther was so much cleverer than she was.*

She'd be back home by the 15th January.

Linus and Jeannie had been in the Kent office all day again. There were two issues which they had now sorted out. One was with *Trans-ship* and that was because some of the Manchester units were not connecting to the local base station.

In Rochester, the coverage was even worse. But they had made it clear right from the start, that in Manchester, the cell site's antennas were still being adjusted, and when the trucks left Rochester, they would pick up coverage when they reached the A229 and M20. But they needed to keep *Trans-ship* patient, and be very supportive.

The other problem was with *City National*. It was to do with the delivery of their *Motorola 8000x* units. Eventually, they got this sorted out with the help of Steve Rider. They had been concerned that the stock might have been sent out to others. But Steve was highly efficient, and Colleen Walker was overseeing everything in her style of monitoring paperwork for delivery activity.

These were the first large businesses, to order cellular radio telephones in Britain, so it had been a stressful couple of days. But now, it was Friday and coming up to 18.00hrs. Jeannie looked over the desk at Linus, and pointed at the door smiling.

"Come on," she said. "Let's go to the *Anchor* for one."

Everyone had left the office, except for Julia. They asked if she wanted to come with them, but she had to finish something off, then wanted to get home.

The *Anchor* was virtually empty. Jeannie and Linus walked from the bar to a table at the far end. The jukebox was not playing, and the pub was more subdued than they had ever seen it.

Linus said, looking at her as they sat at the table. "I wanted to tell you something earlier but we were too busy. I think that Sally-Anne has been having an affair in New York."

"So how did you find that out?" Jeannie asked, curious but unsurprised.

"One of the *RITON* staff in New York, saw her out with a guy in a bar."

Jeannie waved her hand around the *Anchor's* bar, and said sarcastically. "Rather like us being seen out together."

"That was just the start." He said. "My contact saw them go to his apartment. The next morning, she happened to walk past it again, and saw Sally-Anne leave there."

"Ah, now I see." Jeannie said.

"I called her last night." Linus continued. "She is coming back into Heathrow on 15th, which is a week after next Tuesday I think. Anyway, she was sounding distant on the phone, so I didn't say anything."

Jeannie took a diary from her handbag and flicked through it, checking the date.

"It is." She said. Looking at him thoughtfully.

"What do you suggest?" Linus asked her.

Jeannie sat back considering this and said. "I think you should say nothing until she is back here. That way, you'll pick up on the truth when you look her in the eyes."

Linus nodded in understanding. Jeannie knew it would be difficult for him to wait until he could do this, and said.

"I tell you what, let's cheer each other up. I'm having some problems with Paul too. I won't bore you with that, as you've got enough on your plate, but a night out would do us both good. What do you think?"

She reached over and touched his hand, the ceiling's light glinting off her gold wedding ring.

Linus looked at it and said. "Let's do it then. Would you come over and stay at mine?" Then he added. "I have a spare room."

Jeannie smiled. "Yes, that would be great. Let's go for next Tuesday."

Bernie Cohen looked through the hotel bar's window at the old, abandoned Croydon airport runway. Every time he saw it, he felt the memory flood back. For so many years, he'd tried to take it out of his mind, but was never able to. The odd thing was though, that it wasn't about *his own* experience. It was something he'd seen through the *DC-3* aircraft's window, as it stopped near the control tower.

Bernie watched a man and two ladies being marched by men in black uniforms. They appeared well dressed and walked staunchly, the women looking down at the ground. The black uniformed man on their right wore an official flat-hat, and looked morose, but the one behind had a cone-shaped helmet, appearing to be jolly.

As they went past the aeroplane, Bernie noticed the men in uniforms were not armed, so were probably not soldiers, but might be police, remembering the *Kristallnacht* destruction in Vienna. He watched as the people were taken towards another aeroplane, across the runway, and then disappeared from view.

That was forty-six years ago, almost to the day, and Bernie was eight years old.

Now he believed, these people had been abducted and sent to Poland, then ended up in a death camp. But he, like others, had no proof.

Linus walked over to Bernie and he stood up, grinning.

"Good to see you. Now, have you got the Stag today? I hope so."

"Sorry," said Linus. "But I have got the *RADI-CAL* form."

"Oh well," replied Bernie, nodding out at the airfield. "I'd rather be in here with you, than out there in the rain again...."

They drank tea, enjoying each other's company. They had both felt a real connection, since they first met, when Bernie's front door had creaked open. He signed the document, and Linus gave him the envelope with the other details inside.

"This is for you." Bernie said, passing him over a large, brown paper bag. Linus opened it and took out an album. It was by Sade, called *Promise*.

"It's not officially out yet, but we have been given it by the Power House studio in Battersea, thought you might like it."

"Thanks." Said Linus, looking on the back at the track list, remembering some from the BBC event in Manchester. "That is great."

Bernie, smiled. "My pleasure." He said. "It's the least I can do. I appreciate you arranging the guys to come over and install my phone at the end of next week, rather than me having to go over to them."

"I'm sorry it's taken longer than it should, but things have been busier than expected." Linus replied.

As they walked out into the car park, the rain had eased off and Bernie said.

"Sal is coming back in ten days." Linus nodded, he knew that and wanted to tell him something, but couldn't. Bernie carried on.

"The least I can do is organise for us all to celebrate, she has done a great job out there for my business, you know."

Linus realised that, and said from the heart. "I have missed her so much."

Bernie smiled, giving him the thumbs up as he went towards his Silver Shadow.

Linus walked back to his Cavalier at the other end of the car park. Then he noticed something strange happen. A red, Fiat 127 started up and tore past him. It was a typical, rusty little old thing, and he noticed it streak out and turn right, in the same direction as Bernie.

Weirdos are here on a Saturday, he thought, remembering a trilby hatted bloke sat in a Passat, when he was with Colleen, after Mr Cannon had passed away.

Anyway, he needed to get things organised before Jeannie came on Tuesday, there was no time to waste....

Chapter 22

*Queen Anne's Gate, London
7th January 1985*

Lord Atkins looked through his window on to the street. It was 3.30pm and the darkness was coming.

Dick Kelson was due in at 4pm, and for the first time, he did not care if the man was running a little late. *Not that he could run with that gammy leg*, he thought, smiling.

His mind was bathed in an element of sadness, because he knew that today would be the last time he would see the man. It was strange. Part of him felt disgust of this *commoner*, another part felt a little guilt because of the *connection* with the son of the man his *own* father had used and then, *removed*. But it was time for Kelson to go.

Atkins sat down at his desk. It was strange but, he'd always felt some sexual excitement when he forced Kelson to stand up with his coat on and perspire. Arranging for him to be shot in the leg in Berlin of course, had been very useful. He smiled remembering sending him there, just to get that done.

There was no chance that Kelson would be assigned to another employer after that, so there was the benefit of him being locked in, but also the excitement of excruciating pain that he put him under. Lord Atkins felt a tingle in his penis as he smiled.

But, there was something far more important to consider. He was now making a comeback for Hitler, even though he was dead. The man who could have changed Britain, Europe, and much of the world for the better. His thoughts moved to things that most did not appreciate about what happened to Germany following the humiliating Treaty of Versailles, when they lost the first world war in 1918.

The loss of much, including large territories and the demand of 269 billion Goldmarks by the French, brought Germany to its knees. The worst of it though, was France allowing the huge acquisition of German land by Poland. Over two million Germans living there, were taken under Polish control.

Lord Atkins considered what his father had said about where this would ultimately lead. He told him that there would be a new war in the East of Europe, when Germany restored the power to strike back. David Lloyd George, Britain's Prime Minister had felt the same, and warned the French of this, but they did not listen.

But Germany had no choice. They had to comply with the armistice agreement. The Reich had already surrendered its fleet, air force and large weapons. They had no possibility of a negotiation with France, for the Treaty of Versailles.

Atkins sat back considering something else. The Prussian, Jewish ministers had pushed to accept this Treaty, because Germany had *no* choice in the matter.

This was why Adolf Hitler had decided to go into politics. In his book *Mein Kampf,* Hitler stated that: *"hatred had grown into him for those responsible."* It was, Hitler considered, the betrayal of the nation by the Jews.

Atkins wrestled with something that now came into his mind increasingly. *But other German ministers also knew they had to acquiesce, and accept the Treaty of Versailles and they were not Jews. They had no choice. The Jews were not the only ones responsible. Germany did not have the resources.*

He shook his head, confused. But that was of no relevance. Hitler was *still* his hero and, his *ghost* leader.

Dick Kelson stepped out of the Passat and hobbled along Queen Anne's Gate. It was five minutes past four. As he came to the building's steps, he smiled up at the first floor lights shining out from Lord Atkins' office window. *Fuck you*, he thought. Opposite, a black Ford Transit van was parked. The driver gave him a nod, and Kelson then returned it with a touch to his Trilby hat's brim, and entered the building.

"Come in." Shouted Atkins. His trip up the stairs had been painful, but today, Kelson did not care. He hobbled up to his *Lordship's* desk and stood bolt upright.

Atkins got up slowly, considering something very odd was going on here. Kelson would always try and move as if he was not limping or in pain, although that was clearly not the case today. The hobble over to his desk had been extremely bad, almost as if it had been overacted.

He walked around Kelson, hands behind his back, sniffing his neck but smelt nothing, and the sweat was minimal. Atkins felt no excitement, his penis as small as a worn down pencil.

"Right Kelson," he said, sounding a bit disheartened, with no sneering or anger.

"Sit down, we'll go through a few things that need sorting out."

"So," said Dick Kelson, sarcastically." What do you want to sort out then?"

Atkins did not like the tone of his voice.

"Before I go any further *Dick*, you better be polite, and remember how important I am."

Kelson nodded in respect and said. "Yes, your Lordship. In fact, I do know how very important you are, so I have brought you in a present today, to show you how much I like you."

Lord Atkins smiled and said excitedly. "Quite right, *Dickie boy*. Now, show me what you've got."

"With pleasure," said Kelson, as he reached into the inside pocket of his over coat.

He pulled out his *Walther PPK*, the silencer was on, and the safety catch off. Atkins looked stunned and went pale, his lips parting but could say nothing. Kelson aimed the gun at his forehead and smiled.

"I'd like to call you a cunt." Said Kelson, still smiling. "But you are not that nice."

Dick Kelson put the first shot through Atkins' forehead and then stood up, hobbled over to him, the head now on the table, oozing blood and brain matter, then placed the silencer against the left side, and squeezed the trigger. Just to be sure.

He needed to check if there was anything of interest in the desk, so opened the draws, carefully removing the files with his gloved hands. There was some blood dripping from the edge of the desk, so he made sure no globules touched them.

I'll go through these later, after our SICS van driver has taken out the body. He thought, limping over to the safe in the corner.

Kelson had the code, even though his *former* Lordship wouldn't have known that. He turned the knob to each number and released the handle.

Inside was a lot of money, not that Kelson needed it, he'd already made his million. It was more about the documents of history. But he would take the money ….

Chapter 23

Godstone Village
8th January 1985

They walked into the *White Hart* and up to the bar. Linus noticed a change in her today. She was distant, and her clothes seemed, well, *plain* in comparison to her normal style. The green dress was long and her shoes were low. She asked for a tonic water and made her way silently over to a table in the dark corner of the room.

Outside, the winter sun was bright in a cloudless sky. Both their cars were parked next to each other, the black *RADI-CAL* roof antennas pointing up, as if they were rockets on a count-down.

He took over a *Schweppes* and his lager-top. They clinked glasses, smiled at each other and said, "cheers."

"Are you alright? Only you seem, well, not yourself." He said, feeling concerned for her.

Jeannie looked him in the eyes.

"I'm worried about this Linus. Maybe we are going too far, we work together, I'm married and I know you've had a bad let down in the past. But you have a woman in your life, despite her being far away just now. We're on the edge of being more than good friends, and I don't want us to blow it."

Linus took a sip of his lager-top, then sat back and stared at her. He expected this, and having something on your mind is one thing, but the reality of how to react is quite another. The moments ticked by slowly, as he tried to work out a response that would be right for both of them, and then it came to him.

"Jeannie, you are so right. I have been thinking about this as well, and suggest that we do things based on our friendship, so I'm going to take you out to the finest restaurant I know, then go home for as much *Moet* as you want, and my bedroom is going to be your *private* castle."

He bowed his head, pretending to take off an imaginary Elizabethan style hat, waving it down with a flurry. He had no idea where the term *private* castle came from, but he would be in the spare bedroom alone, when they finished their night out together.

She sat back for a moment, deep in thought then laughed and nodded back, continuing to smile. She raised her glass up to his, clinking them together again.

Jeannie followed Linus back to Upper Norwood and they parked both cars in front of his place. In the driveway sat the white Stag, looking pristine. Like everyone, she smiled at it and shook her head, but she *understood* why he kept it.

She went to the rear of her Cavalier, raised the hatch-back, taking out her overnight bag and a long-dress inside a black cover. It was clear that at least part of her wanted to stay, or maybe she could get changed, go out with him and then drive home. Linus was not sure, and neither was Jeannie.

After their conversation in the pub, she was still uncertain. Although she knew Linus was not the type to be pushy, a few drinks and dinner, plus their extraordinarily close connection, could take her over the edge. A similar encounter had led to the end of her first marriage.

She took her things upstairs to the bedroom. There was lots of space in here, and he'd wanted her to be comfortable and in private. Closing the door behind her, she hung the dress up on the wardrobe's front, then placed her bag on the bed and opened it. She slowly took out the contents, carefully laying them out. Taking a pace backwards, she studied every item, her mind deep in thought….

In the lounge, Linus switched on the stereo amplifier and flicked through the albums. But now he wondered if they were appropriate, and even so, would it make any difference to the situation? Then, something occurred to him, and he reached out to the turntable.

Jeannie took the folded tissue and a paper straw from her handbag, then put them gently on the bedroom's dressing-table. Carefully unfolding the tissue, she stared at the pink powder. Resting the straw against it, she placed a finger against her left nostril and inhaled the powder into the right. She took a step back, closing her eyes as the *'Speed'* began to enter her head.

The music came on downstairs, its sound serenely entering the bedroom. She recognized Randy Crawford's *"Time for love."* She liked this song, and took another, deep inhale.

Gently, she touched her underwear laid out on the bed. The Basque looked exquisite, as did the crotch-less, lace panties and *'Aristoc'* stockings. Everything was new, bought for this occasion, she had tried it all on at home yesterday when Paul was out, ensuring the fit and look, was perfect.

The *'Speed's'* effect began to increase, bringing a feeling of excitement, emotion and sensuality. This addiction had closed in on her, and she was sure there was no going back. She looked up at the ceiling, as the song's words came at her, she mouthed them out and started to cry.

"Good friends, night whims,
Won't you listen to the snowflakes fall
We're slow but we're fast
Got a good question to ask
Love is the answer
Now is the time for love."

She stared in the dressing table mirror, shook herself, dried her eyes and walked down into the lounge.

Linus was still looking at his albums as the music continued. Guessing where his mind was, she said. "They all look good to me."

"Thanks," he said. "Anything in particular you'd like me to play?"

"No, I just want you to be in charge of the situation." She replied.

Linus opened a bottle of *Moet & Chandon*, the cork hitting the ceiling with a bang, then the champagne's bubbles flowed over the table. They both laughed and he said. "Are you *sure* that you want me to be in charge then?" He filled up her glass and passed it over.

"I want to stay," she said, sipping from it. "But I need to make a call home first, to see if I can."

Linus realized that she was on the edge, staying could be a danger to her personal life, or perhaps a way forward. But he was sure that asking permission to stay was not the reason for the call, having undoubtedly already told her husband Paul, she was away on business tonight.

Jeannie wanted to find out if there was still a feeling of *any* affection for Paul. They were becoming more distant every day, but now the moment had become critical. Her feelings for Linus MacColl had grown to a point where she wanted things to become physical, but could not predict the outcome.

"I understand," said Linus. "I'll go out while you make the call." Nodding at his phone on the table.

"No," she said. "I'll do it from the car. Whatever happens, and even if I can't stay, I'll get changed and we can go out tonight."

She stood up and walked to the door, taking the glass of *Moet* with her. Linus realized the call would be in total privacy from her Cavalier's *R1*, and that it could go either way.

He watched her go out of the door, feeling as if he was on the precipice of life.

The minutes seemed like hours.

Jeannie Sands returned to the door, smiling at him and said. "I'm staying."

MacColl stood by the door, wearing his black dinner suit and blue-velvet bow tie, waiting.

Sade's *"The Sweetest Taboo"* played on the Hitachi stereo, as the lounge door opened and his life changed forever, instinct told him so.

She stood looking across at him, and he felt both knees go weak, not an expression, but a reality. The brilliance of the full-moon and stars came through the lounge windows, and on to her, like the goddess in a dream.

She was always attractive, but the way she looked tonight, was beyond anything he imagined. This was Cybill Shepherd in a magical scene. Fabulous, three-quarter length, slightly off-white dress, gold necklace, red high-heels, bright lip gloss and glorious perfume, giving out a heart stopping aroma. On both hips was a very slight contour of the dress, from the edge of the Basque that was under it. She strutted over, hips swaying, whispering the song's lines.

'There's a quiet storm and it never felt like this before, there's a quiet storm that is you. There's a quiet storm and it never felt this hot before....'

Linus passed her another glass and she clinked it with his, took a sip then looking into his eyes, she continued.

'You give me the sweetest taboo, that's why I'm, in love with you....'

In unison, they rested their glasses on the table, the moon glinting off the chilled rims, she put her arms around him, touching her lips against his. This was not a full kiss, merely a glance, but ecstasy, guilt, love, desire and fear all came at him like a thundering tidal wave. She knew that, and smiled...

If I live to be a hundred, he thought, *nothing could ever compare with this moment....*

Linus opened the passenger door of the Stag and she stepped in, the left-side of her dress rising slightly, the stocking-top flashed at him provocatively. He got behind the wheel, they both smiled and then laughed somehow uncontrollably, as if all the pressure of their lives had rescinded and they were now on a fabulous roller-coaster.

The brilliance of the stars touched the bonnet as he turned the key and the V8 fired up, making that mellow, low-burble dedicated to the Stag.

Their laughter continuing, as they pulled out onto the main road, and he pushed the tape into the *Blaupunkt*.

Out came *'Ain't Nobody,'* by Chaka Khan. He said that he believed this song *was* about her. She just continued laughing.

This was a moment of infectious, two-way happiness, and a humanity connection that he wanted to hold-on to forever. But *how* could he do that?

Heading towards Shirley Heights, they passed the old boys school on the left. The abuse he'd experienced there and never dared speak to anyone except Jeannie about, was still hanging over him, but for the first time ever looking at this place, he *was* in control of his emotions. He *really* didn't care now, because next to him was a beautiful woman, who had given him a level of self-confidence, that he had never experienced before.

Storming up the, dual carriageway over the roundabout and into Upper Shirley Road, the song continued, sounding great in treble and bass out of the Stag's speakers.

'And now we're flyin' through the stars, I hope this night lasts forever. Oh oh oh oh.

Aint nobody loves me better. Makes me happy, makes me feel this way....'

She continued to smile at him, and said. "I love the way this sounds." She genuinely thought that, because Linus and Julian Rayne were popular music buffs, both obsessed with the latest stereo turntables and radio cassette players, and she loved hearing them enthuse about all their gadgets when on the Kent site together.

First stop of the night lay ahead on the left, *The Sandrock.* She had been there with him before, but this was their first *real* night out, and she was *not* going home...

He took the Stag into the car park and switched off the engine. The moon and stars shining through the windscreen, glinting off her blonde hair. They looked into each other's eyes in silence, so close to connecting their lips. Both felt a strong fight of *"yes or no"* inside them. The moment trickling to a *"no"* as they stepped out in an atmosphere of personal, white-heat.

Standing at the bar, they gently touched their glasses of Pink Champagne together and in their hearts, felt the reason for *The Connection* had finally come. They instantaneously kissed, lips entwined with passion. There was no going back.

Heading down the back road, they turned right into Coombe Lane and then left, into the courtyard of the *Chateau Napoleon*, the finest restaurant in South London.

Rolling up outside the entrance, the parking valet opened the passenger door of the Stag and then came round to the driver's side. Jeannie and Linus walked on the laid out red-carpet and up the steps under the canopy, to the entrance. On either side, glowed a Victorian street lamp, adding to the magical image of this place.

The *Maître d* opened the door and shook hands with them both. She smiled at him, basking in the enjoyment of coming here. He guided them across the glittering room to their reserved table, with Linus in front, and eased the chair back for Jeannie, suavely slipping it under her. Linus ordered a bottle of *Moet* as they scanned through the menus. To him, this was a blur.

He didn't care about what he ate tonight. Jeannie's tongue ran over her lips as she looked into his eyes, running her sharp heel gently down his leg. "I want something that I'm going to enjoy the taste of, but it doesn't need to be *too big*," she said dryly to him. "What would you like?"

They both had soup and filet steaks. Linus ordered the same as Jeannie, because he lacked the ability to make his own choice tonight. During the main-course, she had asked him if he wanted her. There was no time to waste, it was a full-on. This was *the Jeannie way*....

The valet brought the Stag up to the red-carpet, side-lights glowing. He opened the passenger door and she stepped in, closing it carefully as she reached for her seat-belt.

Linus fired up the engine, then ejected and turned over the cassette, pushing it back into the *Blaupunkt*.

"Moonlighting" by Al Jarreau, played out across the car, recorded specifically for this moment tonight, from the pre-released album he'd been given as a present, when he left New York.

She reclined the seat, and smiled at him with a depth of approval. There were many times when she'd been stopped in the street and asked if she *was* Cybill Shepherd. Sometimes, surprised by this, but mostly she liked it, occasionally, *fake* signing an autograph....

'Charming and bright, laughing and gay, I'm just a stranger, love the blues and the braves.'

Turning right into Oaks Road, Linus opened the Stag's throttle, it's glorious burble increasing, the four headlights on full-beam, their glare catching the trees ahead of them on the side of the woods. Jeannie caressed his leg, then his left hand on the wheel, easing it over to her lips, she began to suck on the fingers.

'Some walk by night, some fly by day, something is sweeter when you meet 'long the way.'

Linus wanted to pinch himself to see if this was for real, but feeling her lips on his hand and glancing over at her closed eyes and flickering blonde hair, he knew it was.

Reaching the junction with Upper Shirley Road, he looked to the right and across at *The Sandrock*. "Do you want to go in?" he asked her.

She looked at him and said. "I'll do whatever you want." Her voice had gone into the glorious, deep mode that reflected her unique personality, and exuded sensuality to the core.

"Let's go home," he said, turning left and gunning the Stag into Upper Shirley Road like a screaming banshee.

Pulling up outside his place, the music had changed to the last track on the cassette "*Leaving me now*" by *Level 42*. They kissed as if they were in a Hollywood movie scene.

"Come on," said Jeannie, nodding at the door. "We've got unfinished business."

Chapter 24

Notting Hill, London
9th January 1985

"So," said Dick Kelson to the *scrawny*, unshaven young man with glasses, and a tatty black pullover. "Are you sure you saw MacColl pass over the envelope to this Bernie Cohen bloke?"

The café was empty now, and the two of them sat at the far end in privacy.

"Yes," replied the scruff, now perspiring, despite it being cold outside and not a lot warmer in here. "He took one sheet out, and seemed to write something on it and gave it to MacColl, but Cohen took the envelope away when he left, and I'm sure there was other stuff in it."

Kelson sat back thinking as he looked around the Café, then smiled at the bloke and said. "You better be right." Then he drew a finger slowly across his throat, depicting a knife's blade and said. "Or…"

The scruff was now perspiring more, nodded over and said. "I am sure, Mr Kelson." And then he wanted to impress him by adding something he'd found out yesterday.

"I did some checking with our *SICS* man in Heathrow, and that bloke Cohen's daughter is flying back in early on the 15th from New York."

Dick Kelson smiled, feeling a little more like Lord Atkins today. "Is she now? That's very useful." He said. "I wouldn't be surprised if they weren't all waiting at Cohen's place for her to turn up, including that MacColl."

"Right," he said. "Now give me the exact address of that *yid* bloke you followed."

Linus stood looking over at her empty desk It was 15.30hrs and Jeannie had not come today. He glanced around the *RADI-CAL* office and everyone else was there.

He sat back and thought about last night. Although it was something that he could only describe as surreal, he knew deep inside that whatever happened to him for the rest of his life, he would never experience anything so wonderful. And, he would never have the ability to find the words to explain it, not just the excitement and passion, but the *connection.*

Robbie Robson came over, noticing his mind was elsewhere and said.

"You look far away, are you alright?"

"Yes," said Linus, now coming back to the present. "Just thinking about how fortunate we are to have got these HPU's delivered to us."

On his desk sat the *Motorola 8000x* that had arrived this morning, along with one for each of the team. This was due to *City National's* contract, and Steve Rider wanted all *General Activity Managers* allocated with any the City postcodes in the *square mile* to have them.

Robbie could see that something was not right with Linus. He did not want to push it, and said. "If you want a quick one tonight, I'm up for it."

"Thanks," said Linus. "I need to get home to do something."

As he headed back to Upper Norwood, the Panasonic R1 rang. It was Jeannie Sands.

The sound of her voice was magical as it entered his system, not knowing what he could do or say.

"Sorry I didn't call you earlier." She said. "I was in a bit of a state, but one thing's for sure, I am missing you."

He pulled over to the side of the road. There was no way he could drive, and have this conversation with her.

"I'm missing you too." Linus said, hearing the noise of her car's engine in the background and asked. "Where are you?"

"I'm going home." She said. "I have to. But I want to see you somewhere tomorrow."

Linus thought about this and replied. "Why don't we meet at the office, then we can go our separate ways, and meet up somewhere behind the scenes?"

"That would be great," she said. "Whisper where it is to me tomorrow, when I see you."

"How are you?" He asked, tongue tied.

"I'm so horny," she said, in her deeply sensual way, "That I can hardly drive."

Dick Kelson looked at his watch, as he dialed the number of Manfred von Sterne, it was just on just on 5pm, the time in Germany was an hour later.

As von Sterne answered, Kelson pressed the button on the box of tricks, that made the call impossible to be listened into by anyone trying to monitor it.

"Hello Manfred," said Dick. "I wanted to let you know that Lord Atkins has now departed from our future work together."

Von Sterne looked across the table at Gerhard Baum, both sat in the closed room at the far end of the fall-out shelter.

He smiled and ran his finger across the throat, and Gerhard nodded, understanding that, and giving out a sigh of relief.

"Thank you for advising us Mr Kelson, the timing is good to take things forwards. One moment, I'll put you on the speaker phone with our *Fourth Reich* leader."

Kelson smiled, things were getting better.

Gerhard went straight in. "So Dick, we need to go to the next stage. Firstly, are you able to secure the rest of the funding to us from Lord Atkins soon?"

"In a matter of a few weeks." Said Kelson.

"Excellent," said Baum. "To help matters, Manfred is going to come and help you soon."

Kelson was expecting this. He planned to remove personal treasures from Atkins' place in Hertfordshire, then hand what was left over to the *Fourth Reich*. That way, everyone would be happy, rather the like the way Goring had planned things but didn't make it.

Kelson would not lose out. He would take these magnificent things, and be the leader for all of the *swine* removal in Britain when the *new order* was achieved.

"That would be very helpful Gerhard. In two weeks, I'll be ready for Manfred." He said.

"Good," said Baum as von Sterne smiled back. "Let's keep in touch."

Baum was about to hang-up, as he remembered something.

"One more thing," he said. "We believe all of our leaders on the streets of the target cities in Britain need to communicate. Manfred has suggested we order these new *Motorola* cellular portable telephones for them all. Can you look into this?"

As if I haven't got fucking enough to do, thought Kelson, and replied. "Yes, I'll do that, and then sort it out with Manfred when he arrives."

Gerhard Baum put the phone down and said. "He is an annoying old of a man, but we need him now, Manfred."

Von Sterne smiled back and said. "I know, but it shall be rather like the order I am sure the *Fuhrer* gave for the father of Atkins in 1940. Once we have taken Britain, we shall kill this *schwein*."

They laughed and raised up their glasses of *schnapps*.

Linus answered the phone. It was just on 22.00hrs and he was sure it was coming in from Sally-Anne in New York.

"Hello," she said. "Did I get you out of bed?"

He waited a few seconds before replying into the phone line running under the Atlantic.

"No," he replied. "I was just about to go. How are you?"

"I'm fine." She said, and then. "I just want to see you and tell you how much I've missed you. Dad's going to pick me up from the airport on Tuesday, and maybe you could come over to the house later?"

"Yes," he said. "I'll look forward to it."

There was silence for a moment and then Linus said from his heart. "You know what, I *really* have missed you so much."

"Me too." She replied and then said. "Got to go, I'll see you soon."

She hung up the phone, looking down at the floor of the apartment. The darkness had fallen, the rain came down, and a siren wailed out on the street. Esther was back in LA and she was on her own, and that was fine because she didn't want anyone to see her tonight. The feeling of guilt was tumultuous, and tears ran down her cheeks. She looked at the phone and said out loud.

"I'm sorry Linus. I'm the real *schmuck*. But what more can I do? Whichever way it goes when I come home, *I'll never stop loving you.*"

He stared down at the table, now swathed in feelings of guilt and irony. Then he shook his head at the ceiling. *I spent years missing a woman who constantly made me feel as if I was a fool. She was vicious yet scornful and expected me to pay for everything, then dumped me. And now look what's happened. I have met two of the kindest, generous and beautiful women on this earth, but both at the same time….*

Jeannie stood looking into the tall mirror in her bedroom. She was alone, as Paul had gone for an early meeting at work. When he left, she had looked out and watched him drive away, and she felt guilt. But there was also her inner belief that she had done the right thing. Something was telling her that time was running out. Surely, it was her right, and everyone else's, to do what they wanted, whilst they still had a last chance?

She smoothed her hands down the blue, *coat dress*. She could not make her mind up what to wear today. This was always her fall back, but looked pretty good.

The weather was milder than expected, and she decided not to wear stockings. There was still a good tan on her legs, following the decent summer and autumn of last year. On her right leg was a significant, red birth mark, it was just above the knee and for first time in her life, she wanted it exposed.

Linus saw this two days ago. He ran his fingers gently over it, and then touched his lips upon it. No one had ever done that before and it had been heart-lifting for her. She wanted him to see it again today, to give out her confidence and gratitude. She felt born again.

She looked into the mirror as her tears began to well up, and whispered.

> *'Come bring me your softness*
> *Comfort me through all this madness*
> *Linus, don't you know, with you I'm born again*
>
> *Come give me your sweetness*
> *Now there's you, there's no weakness*
> *Lying safe within your arms, I'm born again.'*

Dick Kelson checked over Lord Atkins' office. It was tidy, emptied of all valuable and secretive items, and any DNA had been cleaned away by the *SICS* man.

Atkins never had any permanent staff in here. That was too risky. It was either *SICS* temporary staff, or just him. All required paperwork was completed personally or through the management of Kelson, who would take it to the *SICS* people to do. That had increased Kelson's power, and now put him at the top of the tree. Everyone in *SICS* was under his leadership. Now, Lord Atkins had gone and Dick Kelson was in control.

He looked at the photo of Atkins' father on the wall. The tables had turned, now Kelson had got his own back for what this man had done to his *own* father. He took the picture down and placed it in his brief case, then he hobbled to the door, looked around for the last time and switched off the lights.

The Passat was parked in dark place. Lord Atkins' Bentley had been removed by one of the *SICS* men and taken to an isolated storage place. He wanted no one to question why that car was parked here, as the office were now deserted. This was the Kelson method of planning to reduce any risk.

He stepped in to his car, and felt an increase in pain. Things were getting more difficult for him, when moving around.

He stared over at its glove box. The copy of that document Rupert Cannon had intended to give to Linus MacColl about what his father had been forced to produce in 1938, was still in there. It's criminally contrived content on Jewish refugee actions, was a potential powder keg for this nation's history, even though it had been an undercover plot, unknown by virtually everyone associated with the government.

The chance of developing the *Fourth Reich* in Britain was now becoming imminent. His concern for a possible copy of that document having somehow made it to MacColl or that Bernie Cohen was now a critical worry.

Cohen was involved with news and television and MacColl with the global electronics company that could somehow use his findings to its advantage. If it did come to light, this opportunity would be destroyed, because the nation would learn about the past and there would be no decent chance for the *Fourth Reich* to go forwards.

He thought back to the day he took Rupert Cannon out. It was a very simple action. Kelson sat next to Cannon in his lounge, having entered as a *fake* doctor, arranged by that RITON medical support bloke, Brian Callaghan. Strangely, it was as if Cannon had worked out what was really happening.

Cannon sat back in his armchair, as Kelson gave him the two cyanide pills. He smiled at the tablets, squeezed Kelson's hand as if he was actually *thanking* him, and slipped away.

Kelson had initially felt a liking for Cannon. It was the only murder he could remember carrying out where the victim held his hand and smiled. It had actually been very pleasant. He doubted if *his* father felt the murder of Cannon's father was that good, back in 1938 when he took him out in a taxi…

But now looking back, Kelson felt that Cannon might have stitched him up. Could it have been that Cannon knew his letter to MacColl would be taken away by him, but a copy had been put somewhere else? And, because he now wanted to die, this would be carried out by a professional killer very quickly, and as it happened, rather nicely. A *win win* perhaps?

Kelson looked down the street and thought. *Mr. Cannon was a smooth operator.*

The finger was now pointing at MacColl, Bernie Cohen and that *yid* bitch he was hanging around with. Although he could not guarantee there was no one else involved, he needed to take this lot out. He was *sure* they had a copy. If he didn't act now, then it could spiral out of control. He then shivered on how

Gerhard and Manfred would react, were they to find out about this.

That bitch was back from New York on Tuesday, and the rest of them would certainly be there to welcome her back at Cohen's house in Purley.

He would go there too and join the fun....

Linus drove slowly to the *RADI-CAL* site. It was just after 09.00hrs and most of the staff were in.

As he looked at Jeannie's Cavalier, his heart missed a beat. But stepping out into the unusually mild winter's morning air, it started to pound with excitement. The guilt was there in his head, but he could not help it.

She was standing at the far end of the office, watching him and smiling, as he walked towards her.

He felt completely inappropriate for her. His looks, the way he walked, his clothes and intellect, were not in her league.

Julia, Mike, Julian, Robbie, Kevin and the two new guys watched him, and although Linus could see them all, they were in a kind of blur, as if they were animated and not humans. The only *real* human he could see was Jeannie.

They came up close, smiling at each other. Neither caring if anyone in there had actually worked this out. Everyone and everything was shut out of them. Inside this mystical and magical bubble, it was only about each other.

"You look nice." He said, despite having seen her in this *coat-dress* before, something was so different now. Her legs were bare.

"Well," she said, looking down at her red, high heels and her birthmark, as his knees went weak. "You are the one who made it possible for me to do this."

He wanted to get closer, gently touch her leg and then hold her, and never let go.

She increased her voice level and said. "You just caught me, I'm off out soon."

"Me too," he said. "I just came in to pick up some stuff." He felt the entire staff look over in suspicion, as if they were watching two forbidden lovers in a movie.

"Where are you going?" she asked.

Chapter 25

Croydon
15th January 1985

Steve Rider looked at Mike Sentinel across the office meeting table. It was dry outside, a few faint rays of sun came in from over the old, Croydon Aerodrome.

"My point is Mike, "he said. "The great news is that things are taking off in *RADI-CAL,* beyond our expectations. But we have to now manage the demand that is coming in, or there is a chance we could lose our efficiency image."

Mike nodded back in agreement and said. "Mmm, yes I understand that Steve, but we have to keep the regional teams chasing new business, particularly in the bigger corporates who are showing interest, or we could lose out."

"I fully appreciate that Mike." Steve replied. "That is why our recruitment drive is essential, but we must align this with our established team. An example of this is the guys you have in your region. Some need to be allocated purely on to the corporate opportunities. We must get our foot into the door of the big boys."

Mike was in full understanding of this. It was the way things had been developed in *Rate-Syrex* when they worked there together. He smiled inwardly, remembering that both he and Steve were often called the *blonde bombshells*, and so was Jeannie Sands.

"So," said Mike. "Is there any of the team you want to take this on? Given the fifty or so around the country, the choice needs to be discussed with all the regions."

"Yes, I know that." Steve replied and then carried on. "I appreciate that you are in charge of the South East region but should like to suggest a couple if that's alright?"

Mike nodded, guessing who these might be, but got it wrong as Steve continued.

"I think Jeannie Sands is essential for this, but I'd also like to have Linus MacColl in the role."

Mike thought about this. Jeannie was undoubtedly the right person, although suggesting Linus was not what he expected. But then realised why. He was a long-term RITON man, who had a respected sense of loyalty from the group directors, but also had helped the *RADI-CAL* image look good to the board. But he was not completely sure, Linus was not the most gifted sales person in the team.

"Mmm, I see that Steve. Linus is a decent bloke, but not as experienced in the new business roles as some others."

"I appreciate that," said Steve. "That is why I suggest that Jeannie and Linus work together for new corporate business, because she can help with her skills, and he'll keep delivering good reports to the main board. Call it a *win-win* if you like."

Mike smiled back at Steve. He certainly did agree with that.

Colleen knocked on the door and brought in a tea tray, then put it down on the table.

"Thanks Colleen." Said Steve. "Have you spoken to Linus recently?"

"Yes," she said looking over at Mike. "But he is off today, as his lady friend is flying back from New York."

Mike looked out at the old abandoned, aerodrome runway. "At least she is flying into Heathrow and not Croydon."

All three of them laughed.

Linus MacColl drove slowly towards the *Long Estate.* He'd already agreed with Bernie to be there by 14.00hrs. The flight in from New York was on time. He knew that because Bernie had arrived at Heathrow early to avoid the traffic, and phoned him from a call-box in the terminal. They had a laugh about this, as after Bernie had told him about Sally-Anne's flight time. He said that next time, he would call from his car when the *RADI-CAL* phone was *eventually fitted.*

There had been a slight delay, as the demand for these cellular radio phones had exceeded expectation. Bernie had been among the first in Britain to order one, but had kindly told Linus he was in no rush, because he understood the pressure was on the *RADI-CAL* team.

Heading along the Purley Way, he passed the RITON building on his right and thought about going into the new *RADI-CAL* division head office, for a chat with Steve Rider and Colleen Walker. He'd also heard that Mike Sentinel was in there today. But he decided not to. He needed to focus on a problem in his mind and think it through alone, besides he'd booked today off.

On the right, the *Aerodrome* hotel appeared out of the January mist, he indicated then took the Cavalier into the car park. He pulled up and switched off. The dashboard clock came up to 12.00hrs.

He looked around the site. The car park was virtually empty, except for a rusty, old red Fiat 127, that he seemed to remember left behind Bernie, when they met here last week to fill out his *RADI-CAL* contract.

The control tower was just visible, but the runway beyond was almost impossible to see, as if it never existed, but it had. Like so many things in life, or death for that matter, realities of the past get hidden away. Some *prefer* to hide them, whilst others spend their lives seeking the truth, but when that is found, the outcome can be crippling.

The bar area was almost empty. There were a few sat around a table in a discussion, with note books in front of them. At the far end was a scruffy looking bloke with glasses, sat reading a newspaper.

The waitress brought Linus over some tea. He did not want anything to eat.

His mind was running over the time he'd spent with Jeannie on Thursday.

Following her to the pub in Godstone village, he felt every element of Jeannie. She was driving in her steady, careful way as ever, and he could see her blonde hair through the car's rear screen. Reaching the M25, he noticed she was on a call. The grey handset of the Panasonic R1 up against her left ear, it's lights glinting in white and green. He felt the atmosphere of her with him, even though she was in another place.

They stood in the pub's car park holding each other, neither wanting to let the other go.

At the bar, they stared at each other in silence. They looked for every element of thought and human impulse within each other.

"I've been thinking," she said. "Something has connected us, and I can't describe it."

He looked down taking in her words. "I know." He said.

She continued.

"We are both in relationships, and to be honest, I no longer want to be with Paul. It's not just because of what happened with you and me, I feel there is no future with him. But your situation is different, I think."

"Yes." He said looking in her eyes and gently touching her face, not wanting this magic to ever end.

"The thing is, you have to decide what you want." She said, looking at his dark hair, as she ran her fingers through it. "I feel that time is running thin in life and you need to tell me. I am not a great woman Linus, I have been selfish, I have lied and cheated but have learned how wrong it is to steal someone from a *good* person."

Jeannie continued to hold his gaze, she knew he was trying to find the words, but he was struggling.

"I understand," she said, now touching his face. "You have to make the decision, and its only right that you should be meeting with Sally-Anne first."

Linus nodded. He was sure that Sally-Anne had an affair in Manhattan. If she had not, then would he have been involved with Jeannie Sands? Was this just a travesty? Did Jeannie really want him, or was it because she had lost the passion for her husband?

"I'm going to see her next Tuesday afternoon at her parent's place, when she is back from New York, and are you prepared to wait until then?" He asked.

Jeannie looked down at her birthmark, the bar's lights touching her blonde hair, her head nodding deep in thought. Then she looked up at him, tears starting to come from her eyes.

"Yes, she said. But please, don't leave it any longer."

Linus left the *Aerodrome* Hotel and walked towards the Cavalier. The fog had lifted and although it was dull, he could see the runway. His mind went back to what Rupert Cannon had told him on that fateful day last year. The words he remembered were of sadness, but he'd also felt a connection with guilt and sorrow. And there had been an undercurrent of something that he could not get out of his mind…

He leant on the car's roof, looking up at the *RADI-CAL* antenna, and over at the airfield again. *Regrets*, he thought. *Minds losing control of bodies, connecting with confusion, guilt, passion, It's all there….*

He got into the car and looked into the mirror. *How fucking much can one manage? There is no excuse, you shall always pay for what you do wrong.*

It was now 13.30hrs. He turned the key, and the Panasonic R1 went live as he waited for the green light to show the signal was connected with the cell base station.

What was he going to say to Sally-Anne? He felt the self-hatred yet again, for letting her down. But was Jeannie the one chance in a million? And, did he deserve it if she was? One thing was for sure, with or without her, he'd never forget their night.

He was tempted to call Jeannie and was about to dial her number, then decided he would wait a while.

Driving out of the car park, he noticed the scruffy bloke he'd seen in the bar was stood outside the hotel's doorway, and looking at him for some reason....

He switched the Cavalier's radio on to the Gary Davis show on BBC Radio 1.

On came the song, '*A New England,*' the singer was *Kirsty MacColl.*

Chapter 26

The Long Estate
15th January 1985

Linus drove slowly onto the *Long Estate*, in the Jeannie way, he thought.

As he approached the back road, he was still in remorse, and probably would be forever.

Up ahead on the left, was the Cohen's house. His mind raced back to this good man, his wife and daughters, fighters and full of humour and generosity.

His thought process switched to his work responsibilities in the RITON Group, before he was transferred to *RADI-CAL*. It was about taking things forward. Staff made errors and there could be misunderstandings with their supply chains, and sub-contractors in the world.

Things went wrong, usually people were not to blame. They tried hard and made mistakes. It was not through lack of effort. The RITON approach was to sort these things out, and encourage those who had got things wrong to go forward in an understanding and supportive way. This was why it was, in his opinion anyway, the finest and *kindest* electronics business in the world.

Sally-Anne had an affair, and so had he, but they were only human too. And for them both he believed, there was *something* in the past, in another age, that connected them. He needed to tell her, and she needed to tell him…

As he neared the house, a ray of sun came from between the clouds and shone over the drive's gates. Then it glinted from the raven hair. She stood watching him arrive, wearing a black dress and high heels. Her arms were folded and she drew on a Marlboro. On her wrist was the Star of David, and he saw the sun touch it. He felt she looked like Carly Simon, about to start a fabulous concert.

The Passat was parked about seventy yards past the Cohen's house. Kelson saw MacColl's Cavalier in the driveway, next to that *yid bitch's* Metro and her dad's *Roller*.

There was a rise in the road, and as it then dropped down the hill, Kelson pulled over to the left, that way he would not be seen from the house.

He looked around to make sure there were no pedestrians around, or anyone looking over at him as, he opened the glove compartment.

He took out his Walther PPK pistol, then he screwed on the silencer and slipped it into his large, overcoat pocket, made to enclose this by a *special* tailor.

Stepping out of the car, he straightened up his trilby, looking at his reflection in the door's window. It always felt good to be smart, when you were about to blow your enemies away….

Jeannie drove very slowly onto the *Long Estate*, and as ever when she was behind the wheel, with care and concentration, just like everything else she did in life.

As Kelson hobbled up the hill towards the Cohen's house, he realised something. A stupid error.

He felt the PPK against him and then remembered there were only six rounds in the magazine. Given that there were four people in there, he might need another magazine as back-up. Just in case. After all, as a professional killer, he always prided himself in being prepared for anything.

Kelson went back to the Passat and opened its tailgate. He kept a number of *things* in there, under the spare-wheel cover. He lifted it up and took out a magazine clip. He held it up in front of him, looking at it, as the sun touched the brass shell on it's top.

In that exact instant, a blue Vauxhall Cavalier went silently and slowly past him

"Fuck" he whispered, watching it head down the road. *"I couldn't even hear that coming."*

Through the hatch-back's rear window, he noticed the sun briefly catch the blonde hair of what must be, a woman driver. On its roof, he noticed the black antenna, for one of those new cellular phone things no doubt.

He watched the car head slowly down the hill and into the distance. He closed the Passat's hatch-back and slipped the magazine into his coat pocket.

Some daft bird lost. He thought, still looking down the road, as the car was now gone. Then he shook his head in anger at himself. *I've never made a fucking error like that before.*

But he was now comfortable she had not seen the magazine. *No bird could be that bright, especially a blonde.*

He started to hobble up the hill again, the pain increasing. This was getting worse.

Still, at least fucking Atkins was gone. Noticing the aerial on that bird's car, it reminded him that Gerhard and Manfred expected him to get hold of these cellular radio phone things to co-ordinate the *Fourth Reich* attacks in the cities.

He smiled at the thought of that, as he hobbled on, sweat now running down his brow. *Well,* he said to himself, touching his pocket with the spare magazine in it, *I certainly won't be placing an order with that Linus fucking MacColl.*

Jeannie looked in the mirror, not moving her head as she headed down the hill. Seconds earlier, passing the man stood by the car's open, hatch-back, she had seen the sun glint off something in his hand. Her eyesight was excellent, and so was her total focus on everything, no matter how small, when she was driving. She was sure it was a pistol's magazine, like something in a movie.

Fear came at her. Inside, a thought told her that this man was going to the house where Linus's car was parked outside. The house of the woman he loved. The one she had felt a sickening jealousy for, but never showed this to Linus. Maybe she was going to be shot for some reason by a jealous old git? But perhaps Linus was too?

She dropped down the hill slowly, went round the bend and was out of site, then pulled in.

She looked at the Panasonic R1. The green light was on. She could call 999, but had no proof of what she had seen. Anyway the police could take ages to come and maybe they would think the call from a cellular phone was a hoax.

But that was not the real issue was it? She thought. In the boot of her car, under the hatch-back, was a huge amount of the *Speed* powder. In a combination of addiction and now, distributing it to certain connections, she was working with the dealer she trusted, as a supplier. It was a side-line, but gave her an unrestricted amount for her own use. If the police came, and they looked in her car, then what? End up in jail? It was far too risky.

There was only one thing she could do. She had to reach out to Mike Sentinel.

Some thirty minutes before Jeannie had passed Kelson's car, Sally-Anne and Linus were stood at the bottom of the back garden. It wasn't that she wanted to avoid her parents, but needed to be with him alone for a while, to look into his eyes. To show remorse and beg forgiveness, wanting to feel love between them, if it were still possible.

The wind started to increase and the tree branches moved around, the last of the leaves falling. They sat down together on the bench in silence.

"I need to tell you something." She said, squeezing his hand as if she never wanted to let it go. "I did something wrong there. I could give you a list of excuses and try and make it sound as if it was not my fault. But it was."

Linus guessed what was coming. She continued.

"I was working with a guy there and we had a get together. It was brief and it should not have happened. It's my fault, I have no excuse. Yes, I *really* missed you every moment of every day, but that can never justify it. I am so sorry."

The tears welled up, as she fought them back. Then they won, and came down her cheeks.

But he felt as if he was the really guilty one. What he truly feared about seeing Sally-Anne today had gone. She had been brave enough to tell him the truth, but he *really* knew that she still wanted him. He was so scared that she would not.

He knew the most difficult to find words and guilt, needed to come from him now.

"I made a *connection*. She's in the *RADI-CAL* team. One night we got together."

What he *could* have said was that she took him forward in a new business for something that could, he now believed, very much change the world. He *could* have said that a connection deep inside, gave him the chance to tell someone for the very first time, about what happened to him when he was a boy.

But most of all, how they went on a night out, which had every element of magic that would stay embroiled in his mind, for the rest of his life. But he knew Jeannie was a like a burning candle, he could never hold her forever.

And there was something so extraordinary linked in his head to Sally-Anne, it flashed in the memory of another world and another life. She was the only one for him.

She continued to hold his hand tightly. In her mind, the fact that they had both behaved in a similar way, would balance things out between them. There was nothing else to say on the matter. Things would recover. She would make it happen.

Two crows walking by the fence took off, and they both watched them climb into the sky.

"Come on," she said looking at the back door of the house. "It's getting cold, let's go inside, we can talk later."

The gatekeeper swung up the barrier and Mike gave him a cheery wave as he drove through it. As he reached the junction with Purley Way, his Panasonic R1 bleeped.

The road was clear and he accelerated the Vauxhall Carlton over to the right, planning to go through Purley Cross, then out to Caterham, the M25, then on to the M26 towards Sevenoaks. He wanted to head for home.

The Panasonic R1 continued to ring out. Mike looked down at it, considering not bothering, but then decided to answer it.

"Hi Mike, its Jeannie." She said, knowing that he'd not see her number, although should recognise her voice. "Where are you?"

"Heading for Purley Cross, then to the motorway through Caterham. Why?" He replied.

"I'm on the *Long Estate* in Purley." She said. Mike noticed there was an element of concern in her voice, as she continued. "I knew Linus was over here and have just seen something weird. Then I called the office, and Colleen said you had just left."

"Why did you go there?" he asked.

"Because Mike, part of me wanted to be in his company and another is jealous. It's hard to explain but there is something else going on here at his girlfriend's house. I can't be sure, but I think a man is going in there with a gun."

"Have you called the police?" He asked.

"I was going to, but wanted to call you first." She said. "In case they won't take it seriously from the cell phone signal."

"Mmm. I'll be there within a few minutes. It's by Purley Cross isn't it?"

"Yes," she replied. "Turn left onto the entrance road, follow it down and you'll see Linus's car on the edge of the house's drive way. Keep going over the hill, and I'm parked down on the left."

Mike pressed the end button and clipped the Panasonic back on its holder. As he floored the accelerator, the Carlton touched seventy, as it streaked past the abandoned airport. He knew there was something bad going on here, and it wasn't just about a man who might have a gun. There was something that Jeannie was being dishonest about.

Mike drove slowly onto the *Long Estate* and looked over to the left so he could spot Linus's car in a driveway.

His glasses were starting to steam up because he'd put the heater on full blast, and so he wiped the inside in desperation, using his thumb. Then he spotted Linus MacColl's red Cavalier in the driveway of a large house, beside a Rolls-Royce and a Mini Metro.

He continued slowly past the house, and over the brow of the hill, passing a Volkswagen Passat and then, on the left, Jeannie stood beside her Cavalier, looking out for him. Mike flashed the headlights of the Carlton and pulled up very slowly behind her car.

He stepped out, wiping his glasses with a handkerchief, as he walked towards her. Jeannie leaned against the side of her car, and they looked each other in the eyes as he kept wiping them. He put them back on and said.

"So Jeannie, tell me why you *really* did not call the police?"

She looked at him with an expression of guilt and sadness, then moving off the car she said.

"I need to show you Mike."

Mike followed her to the hatch-back, and as she opened it, guessed what was in there. And he was right. A plastic storage tray was across the boot, from one side to the other. Inside it were a mass of plastic bags, all with *speed* powder in them.

He stepped back, shaking his head in anger, but also in sadness. In the typical Mike Sentinel style, he blamed himself. Five years ago, he'd worked hard to get her off an addiction. Now, she was not only back on it, but probably in the trade.

"Mmm," he said. "Clearly, you have now failed to follow my instructions. If you weren't so important for *RADI-CAL*, I'd bloody well report you."

She looked down at the ground in dismay at her stupidity.

Then Mike reached up and closed the hatch-back.

"Right," he said. "At least I now know why you did not call the police."

"Sorry." She said, still looking down.

Mike touched her arm and then said. "We'll talk about it later Jeannie." He understood humanity's mistakes.

"It's never too late to sort out something bad. I'll always be here to help you. That's what I'm on this planet for anyway." He said, looking up at the cold, blue sky. He shook his head, the blonde hair flicking about. "I've got to make up for what I did wrong."

She looked at him in confusion, then realised where he was coming from. Robbie had told her about the Aden tragedy. But, Mike had saved *his* life up in Scotland *before* being sent out to Aden....

She knew that it wasn't just feeling guilt for what happened. It was because the man was massively kind through and through. He was an exceptional human. She pointed back to the Passat. She'd already written down the registration number in case Mike could not see it, and passed it over to him. "That's the car he came in." She said.

"Right," he said. "I'm going to put a call into Julia. She can phone the police so they go straight to their house. That way, they'll know the call is genuine as it is from the office line, and so won't need to come to *your* car."

They got into the Carlton, then Mike put in the call from the Panasonic R1 to Julia. Her phone rang, but then switched to the desk's answering machine.

Mike explained the situation after the bleep, in a very calm and practical way, so that Julia would follow his instructions and note the Passat's registration number, when she picked up the message. His final point being that she must call Jeannie on her *Motorola 8000x,* immediately after she had rung the police for assistance.

Mike clipped the handset back and looked at Jeannie. She knew he'd left the answer phone message and said. "If she's gone out, then how is that going to help? Why not call another member of staff?"

"No," said Mike. "She is in today and is one of the few who can cope in an emergency. I won't risk it with any others. I am in charge Jeannie, and you need to trust me."

"But if the man has gone in there with that gun, how do we know the police are going to be there in time to stop him?" She asked, highly concerned. "Even if Julia gets straight onto it?"

"We don't," Mike replied, reaching over with the car's key to the glove compartment. "That's why we are going there with this."

He took out a large pistol, a *Browning Hi-Power automatic.*
Jeannie stared at it in amazement.

"*Fuck*." She said.

Mike looked at her, *his* amazement was in *that* swear word. It was something she never used. But, now he could appreciate why.

"Where did you get that from?" She asked

"I stole it when I left the Army," he said, looking down at it disdainfully. "I shouldn't have done, but managed to get away with it. I kept it because it reminded me of guilt first of all." He continued to stare at it in remorse, and carried on.

"But then, I realised that if I did something wrong again, I should use it on myself. So I kept it with me, to remind me that life is about helping others, if not I would take my own life. It shall always be with me."

"Do you have a licence for that thing?" she asked, bringing him back to reality.

"No," he replied. "But so what? We have to save people's lives."

She continued to look at it in shock and said, "Better than using the *F* word then. You take that, and I'll get the *Motorola 8000x* out of my car for Julia's call. We both always knew *RADI-CAL* was going to be of value, but this has gone beyond..."

They smiled at each other. Their joint skill at recovering from a bad situation and going forward with confidence kicked in. And this new cell phone could be a life saver.

"Right," he said. "This is what we are going to do...."

He had everything planned up to the last detail. Kelson was always a perfectionist when it came to organising the removal of his victims. A *SICS* operative would arrive in a black Transit van in a couple of hours, to do the collection.

The darkness would be in by then, and the van would be reversed up to the front door. The houses up on the *Long Estate* were all far apart, so nothing was likely to be seen.

The house cleaner had given the layout details to another one of the *SICS* people. The *connection* of both innocent and associated people to members of their team was common place. A good example of that was with Rupert Canon.

His cleaner was part of *SICS*, unknown to him of course, but in the Cohen's house it was different. Their cleaner had just talked about it in innocence to someone she considered to be a trusted friend, Rupert Cannon's cleaner.

And now Kelson knew everything about this place....

As he approached the house's driveway, he looked around the road and saw no one. He knew the lounge area was down on the left, and his journey was to go through the front entrance gates, past the hedge on the right. This was the most exposed part of his plan, and as he hobbled along as fast as he could, for some twenty-five yards to the garden gate, it reminded him of the walk to the lift in that *Midland* hotel in Manchester, last October. Only this was worse.

As he reached the gate, he lifted the handle very quietly, then turned and checked if there was anyone watching him. The coast was clear, and he went carefully into the patio area.

The back door leading into the kitchen storage area was not locked either. His gloved hand pushed the handle down gently and he crept in. He walked up to far end door, standing by the wall, out of sight.

He reached inside his coat, taking out the *Walther PPK*. Creeping through the kitchen, then onto the hall's parquet flooring, the layout reminded him very slightly of his place in the South of France. He walked slowly up to the lounge door, for some reason it was half open, and that was useful. He stared through the gap and took everything in.

Linus MacColl, Bernie Cohen, his *Missus* and that annoying bitch of a daughter, were all stood around the centre table. Each held a glass of champagne, and there was a plate of cakes on the table. In front of the window by the side of the room, was a piano. The walls were covered with pictures, and some frames had records in them. And there were some comfortable looking chairs in there.

That's good, he thought. *At least I can sit down once this is sorted out, my fucking leg is killing me.*

The door opened and everyone stood in shock. An old man pointing a gun at them stood smiling.

"Hello," he said. "Sorry to disturb you all, and before you ask, no I don't want a drink thanks, but would ask you all to sit down."

Kelson hobbled into the room and then waved the pistol at the two sofas by the table.

They continued to stand motionless and he shouted.

"Do it now!"

They put their glasses onto the table and followed his order. All of them were in shock. As they sat down, Bernie asked, "What do you want from us? I guess you are in here to take something?"

Kelson laughed, then stepped slowly over to the Steinway piano, keeping his eyes on the four of them, the pistol raised in his left hand. Then with his right, he grabbed a China doll from the top of the piano, and slung it at the door's frame, its head shattering and the rest dropping into the entrance.

He looked at Sally-Anne and said. "I remember seeing you buy that from a *chinky* bloke in Manchester *luv*. Now let me think," his finger touching his lips, feigning the use of memory. "That's right, I seem to remember it was five or maybe *four* quid."

Sally-Anne was overcome with anger and attempted to stand up and then run to Kelson. But Linus held her back, knowing the danger, and realising the man was winding her up.

"To answer your question," Kelson said to Bernie, looking over at the broken china doll in the doorway, its base upright in the centre. "As you can see, it's not about stealing *valuables* is it? No, it's to collect some written information from a man called Rupert Cannon that you have got."

Bernie stared at Kelson. "*What* information?" he said.

Kelson was suddenly taken aback. The look on his face and the genuine sounding question from Bernie, was not what he expected. On the table, he saw an envelope with the *RADI-CAL* logo on it. It was open, and a sheet was partially extended out of it.

"In there," he said looking over at it, and then pointed to Linus. "Something one of my staff members saw you take from this Mr MacColl at that *Aerodrome* hotel last week."

Bernie and Linus looked at each other, both unsure of why a man should threaten them with a gun because of a *RADI-CAL* agreement.

"Give that to me," he said, now pointing the *Walther PPK* at Jane.

She stood, picked it up from the table and carried it slowly over the Kelson, then went back to the sofa. He pulled out the paperwork and flicked through the sheets. The only thing in there was the *RADI-CAL* cellular phone contract document for *Bernie Cohen Entertainment Ltd.*

He threw the envelope on the floor in anger, pulled back the hammer on the pistol and pointed it at Bernie's head. *"Where is that fucking letter from Cannon then?"*

Bernie raised his hands and shook his head.

Then Kelson slowly nodded and smiled in understanding. It seemed that he'd been right about this the first time, and had recently worried for nothing. No one, except him and Lord Atkins had ever seen this letter from Cannon.

Kelson pushed the hammer forwards, he noticed everyone in the room take in a deep breath, as if they felt that they might survive. He enjoyed doing this, because they wouldn't.

He reached inside his coat and took out a folded sheet, the last remaining copy of the Cannon letter. Then he waved it towards Jane and said. "Here, you read this out."

She walked slowly over again and took the letter, staring at the pistol he pointed at her, and then she went back to her seat.

Linus looked at the bloke, trying to piece this together, recognising him from the *Aerodrome* Hotel, and now, sure he'd seen him up in Manchester.

"I must tell you what happened," said Kelson in amusement, as if he were chatting to some friends in a pub. "I was given the job of taking out the man who wrote this. He was very sick and a nice bloke, so I helped *him on his way*." He laughed again, pointing the gun at Linus.

"I was told to exchange the *actual* letter he wrote to you for a fake one. Problem was my *guvnor* was not happy with my version, so I had to exchange it for that shit article about your old banger."

He looked at Sally-Anne, then said. "To give you your due, or should I say *Jew,* miss *perfect,* I noticed you'd kept your hotel room tidy when I swapped it over."

She scowled at him, wanting to run over, to take a chance, grab the gun and blow his old head off. He *was* that fucking aftershave stinker. Linus gripped her arm.

Jane unfolded the letter and looked at the hand writing. She could tell it was photo-copy, as some of the words were blurry. Kelson pointed the pistol over at her, and she started to read it.

"Dear Linus

I am writing to you for two main reasons. Firstly, to try and explain why I said something at Croydon Aerodrome, when I leaned on your old Snag, and secondly about my father and what he did. Or rather, what I believe he was forced to do before the war started.

My father died in an accident. He was knocked over and flattened on Beak Street in London. At least we were told that it was an accident. The driver was never found apparently."

Dick Kelson laughed, then interrupted. "Actually, it was my dad that did him in. It's a small world isn't it?"

Jane looked at him in ever increasing hatred, and continued the reading.

"Walter Cannon was my father's name and he was a clerk in the Home Office. He was the document producer for the Assistant Permanent Secretary of State for the Home Office, a man called Atkins. The day before dad died, he told my mother about what he was told to write by Atkins for the Nazi government, then gave her a smuggled out carbon copy to hold on to.

She showed it to me just before she passed away. Most of it was impossible to read because it had faded so much over the years, but I can still remember the words she spoke, and I am sure she was right about what had been behind the scenes of this document written in 1938.

Atkins had set up a personal, secret pact with the heads of the Nazis. It was a method of taking extra money from refugees across Europe, many from Poland, Czechoslovakia, Austria and Germany. The Nazis took property, businesses and possessions via the Gestapo, and then when refugees arrived in Britain, Atkins used the police to collect their money, telling them it was an official secrets act operation from the government, and that it must never be spoken about, or they would be charged. The police communicated it solely to Atkins.

Atkins acquired undercover thieves, faked as members of the home office, and they collected the money the police had taken from the refugees. These people gave everything they had, but if Atkins was not satisfied, they were deported and ended up in death camps. It was part of the deal he had with the Nazis.

I have never been able to tell anyone this, because my father was forced to produce the documents and so I felt acute shame. But I needed to get it out before I died and the only person I felt I could trust was you.

Linus, I believe this was the start of something even more sinister. The criminals must have acquired so much in terms of property, creating businesses from the money they took, and other possessions. But also, perhaps Atkins was able to acquire items such as gold bullion, flown in from Nazi criminals like Goring, before the invasion of Britain took place. Maybe, even Hitler was not aware of this? The invasion never happened and they lost the war of course, so perhaps it is still here. Who knows?

My biggest concern was that Atkins acquired so much and must have built a relationship with those Nazi's who survived, or perhaps with some sort of new order, who want to make a comeback. Perhaps there is an unknown and huge bunch of scoundrels who could endanger so many people again?

Anyway, I digress.

You are a good man and I wish you had been my son. I'm heading out across the ocean soon and one day, I might see you on the other side.

Yours sincerely, Rupert Cannon"

Jane finished and looked up in silence. "Right," said Kelson, pointing at Sally-Anne. "Take this letter off your mother, rip it up and set fire to it."

She carefully took it from her mother and tore it up, feeling as if she was destroying something which was the final link to the masses who were robbed, humiliated and then murdered by a huge covered up crime syndicate in Britain. It showed who was responsible, and was a chance to put this out to the world.

Part of her wanted to be shot instead of burning this, but she knew it would be destroyed anyway.

The Nazi's were good at forcing burning.

Sally-Anne screwed it into a ball, put it into the table's ash tray picking up the lighter. She lit it and watched it disintegrate into ashes, the tears running down her cheeks. She felt lost and guilty, her mind connecting with how millions of men, women and children in Nazi death camps, were murdered.

The burning glow then died away. Kelson pointed towards the side window, looked at Sally-Anne and said to her.

"Get up and pull the curtains across, then turn on the lights."

The darkness was coming in now, and he knew there was no possibility of anyone seeing them through the back garden's windows, but the side one might be a problem, if anyone was walking past on the pavement.

Time was running out. It had been a bit of fun listening to this woman read the copy of his Cannon letter, but now he needed to take them all out. Nobody on this planet would ever know about it. That was the only remaining copy, and now it was gone.

Sally-Anne walked slowly over to the curtains. The daylight was fading fast, as she glanced out. She thought this was going to be her last view of the sky.

Then, on the pavement, she saw two people. A tall man with glasses and a blonde mop of hair, wearing a raincoat. Next to him, was a woman. She was wearing a black coat, was also blonde, and looked like an actress from an American TV show. *Cybil Shepherd* she thought. Against her ear, she was holding one of those very expensive *brick* looking mobile phones. For a split second, their eyes *connected*.

Then Kelson shouted at her. "For fuck sake you *bitch*, just pull it across!"

As she took out the last light of day, she guessed that was someone called Jeannie. Returning slowly back to her seat, she stared at Linus. He could see that there was a *message in the wire* she was trying to get across to him. Taking him back to the John Waite song, '*Missing You.*'

They all sat in a mixture of sadness and contempt. Bernie decided to buy some time, he thought Sally-Anne might have seen something out there, maybe there was a chance….

"I'd like to say that's come as a surprise." Bernie said to Kelson. "But it hasn't, because I picked up on something when I was at Croydon Aerodrome at the start of 1939."

Kelson looked at Bernie Cohen, now considering that he might take this bloke out first and then finish the others, but also felt an interest to learn a bit more about this.

"Go on." He said.

Mike and Jeannie had carefully examined the front of the Cohen's house, although merely walking along the pavement, as if they were in a conversation with each other, and heading towards another place. They could see no lights on in the front, but worked out that whoever was in there, was in a room on the left, towards the far end. Jeannie had seen a raven haired girl behind the window, as she closed the curtains. She guessed who it was, as their eyes met for a second….

"Shall we knock on the door?" Jeannie said quietly to Mike, walking past the gate. She had spoken to Julia on the *Motorola* and told her exactly what she had to tell the Police, but knew time was running thin.

"No," said Mike. "That is too risky. The police should be on the way now and the horns are going to be on. A knock on the door at the same moment could bring on the shooting. We need to creep around the back."

Jeannie nodded, then thought about his words, *the horns are going to be on.* Most normal people would call them *sirens.*

"Right," she said. "We should make our first move by going towards the front door as if we are just visitors. If we see no one, we turn right towards the side gate."

The gun was inside Mike's raincoat pocket. He turned up its collar as they walked towards the door, and then headed for the side gate.

"I'll tell you what," said Bernie, looking over at the barrel of Kelson's gun. "The treaty of Versailles made in 1918 ruined everything. If France had been *fairer* at Germany's surrender after the first world war, then the chances are that Hitler would never have been in power."

He looked around at the others and continued, he was trying to buy time, but actually really meant this.

"There might not have been a second world war. Germany would not have lost its land, especially to Poland who took loads in 1919, being a prime example of why another war happened. The huge funds demanded from Germany by France could have been reduced. And Britain would not have become a burning pile of debt, that has *still* not been fully paid back to America since their borrowings in the *last* war, because there would have been *no last* war."

"Yeah, maybe," said Kelson, as he pointed the gun's barrel towards Bernie's heart. "And when Germany lost the first war, it was Hitler's angle to say it was the *fucking* Prussian Jews in parliament who gave into the *Frogs*."

Bernie, nodded back at Kelson, and said. "But the reality was that virtually every German in politics gave into the French, because they had no weapons or anything else left, whatever their parties or religions, the ministers had no choice."

Mike and Jeannie went through the gate then moved slowly down the path and onto the patio, then up to the door of the kitchen's storage room. Mike pushed the handle and stepped in slowly, Jeannie right behind him, into the darkness, closing the door behind them quietly.

Dick Kelson smiled at Bernie. "I've heard this before. The thing is Mr Cohen, you are not wrong."

They all stared at Kelson in surprise.

Then he carried on. "You see, Hitler's rage against the Jews was certainly sparked by what he saw as an opportunity. That was down to the blame he put on those who said the Versailles Treaty had to be agreed with, because there was no choice after they lost world war one.

Just like you said, they were right. There was no choice. Hitler knew that of course. But by getting his Anti-Semitism rage of blaming *them* out to the German people, it was his way of taking power."

Kelson began to walk slowly backwards, now level with the piano. Things were coming to an end. He wanted to shoot them all from a greater distance kill anyone who tried to run towards him. He stopped, close to the end of the Steinway and carried on.

"Hitler might have wanted to take out the Jews, and he *did over* six million. But you see, it was also a massive earner for so many others, you know, like Herman Goring. They set up companies building death factories, and *arrangements* for sending immigrants over to other countries. They called it the *conveyor belt*, to take away loads including dosh, send them abroad, then demand even more on arrival by undercover operatives. They either stayed or most likely, were deported, and *done in* at the camps in Poland and other places."

Kelson nodded in the direction of Croydon Airport, then carried on.

"Atkins was behind it all here. He conned the *Old Bill* into believing they were following *official* government instructions, but in secret. He built up a big squad of money collectors, and despite Hitler losing the war, made a fortune through some clever activities. We are now going forwards again. The *Fourth Reich* is coming."

Kelson raised up the *Walther PPK,* towards his first target, Linus MacColl. But as he did so, the sound of footsteps in the hallway came in, and all of them looked at the room's open door. Mike Sentinel tore into the doorway, holding up his *Browning,* he could see four people sitting down, then looked to his right at a man wearing a trilby hat and holding a pistol. This time, he knew it was *real.* He took a final step, aiming his *Browning* at the man's head, tripped on the China doll, falling forwards onto the floor.

Jeannie was right behind him, and now she had become the target. She crouched down, but it was too late.

Kelson fired and hit Jeannie in the chest. She fell.

Sally-Anne was the first up, immediately running towards Jeannie. Kelson pulled the trigger again and the shot touched her left arm. She fell too. He aimed the gun at her raven hair. *Time to finish this yid bitch*. He thought.

Mike Sentinel's glasses came off as he fell down. But he didn't care, still lying on the floor, he pointed the *Browning* at the man's head and squeezed the trigger. The bullet entered Kelson's forehead. He was dead before he even hit the floor.

Linus ran over to Sally-Anne. She was getting back up on her feet, like a wounded lioness. Mike had saved her by a split-second. She looked quickly at the outside of her left arm. It hurt, and the blood patch was coming through her dress's sleeve, but she could tell it was only a flesh wound. She ignored it, this was not her priority.

She moved towards Jeannie with Linus, and they knelt down on either side of her.

Mike was on his feet and looked down at Kelson. The trilby was still on, but now soaked in blood from the shot that had instantly killed him.

Mike turned towards Jeannie and realised she was dying. *It's my fault.* He thought.

He looked at the *Browning*, then cocked it and put the gun against his head.

Bernie came across the room towards him, shouting. "No, don't even think about that, I need your help now!"

Mike put the gun down by his side. His instinct told him that he should always be there to help someone.

Then he stared at Bernie in confusion as he came over, the mop of blonde hair flicking.

Bernie gently took the pistol from Mike's hand, pushed back the hammer, placing it on top of the Steinway.

Jane was on the phone in the room's corner, she dialled 999 wanting at least two ambulances....

The sirens were wailing now, as the police cars entered the *Long Estate*. Within seconds, the first car pulled up into the driveway. Jane went over to the side window and pulled back the curtains, so they could see the room's lights coming out.

She ran down to the far end, opening the back door, then headed around to the front of the house. She needed to keep the police away from Jeannie in the room's hallway entrance. They had to get the ambulance medics there first.

Mike took his coat off and went over to Jeannie. He could see the blood stain growing on her chest. He gently pressed the inside of his coat against the wound. Her face was white, all colour gone from her cheeks and she was shaking with shock. Mike knew she was not going to make it. He had seen this before in Aden, the bullet had cut through the renal artery.

Sally-Anne touched Jeannie's hand.

"Sorry I let you down Mike." Jeannie said. He could find no words to respond. He was devastated.

Linus touched her blonde hair and she smiled at him, blood now coming from her lips. "I knew that I'd ran out of road. I'll always......"

She closed her eyes and her life ended.

Linus was sat with Sally-Anne in the rear of the ambulance on the road of the *Long Estate.* The front entrance to the house was cordoned off now, and three police cars were there with blue lights flashing. Opposite, a number of local people stood looking over.

"Morons." She said, looking over at them. The medic had put a blanket around her after bandaging her arm, but she was still shivering.

"That's it. I'm going back in." She said, getting out of the ambulance. Linus followed her to the gate and put his hand on her shoulder.

"You need to go to *Mayday* Hospital." He said.

"Why?" she asked, looking down at her left arm. "It's only a scratch, unlike what's happened to someone."

In front of them were the police cars, and on the right was Bernie's Rolls. They walked over to it and leaned back on its far side. He reached into his coat and took out the Marlboros, lighting up two and passing one over.

"Thanks," she said, taking her first drag and looking at it. "I fucking needed that."

The police officer standing by the front door, moved over as Mike Sentinel came out, a grey blanket also over his shoulders. There was another officer next to him, as they walked towards one of the cars together. Mike stopped, said something to the officer, and walked over to Linus.

Mike's glasses were off, they were smashed. But strangely, he looked as if he didn't need them. As if he was told he did, but could manage without them.

"The police are taking me home. I'll get my car collected later. I am not being questioned anymore today, but I've been told they are going to again at some point." Mike said.

Linus looked over to make sure no officers were coming over, or even listening from a distance.

"What about *your* pistol?" Linus asked him.

"Oh, it wasn't mine," replied Mike. "I found it in the back room as I came in."

Linus moved up to Mike's ear and said even more quietly. "I wonder if they'll ever find out who it belonged to?"

Mike shrugged and replied. "Mmm, I don't know. However, I did notice that the serial number seemed to have been filed off it for some reason." He pointed at a black police van on the far side. Kelson's body was in there. "Maybe that bloke left it in the kitchen as a back-up?"

Mike then spoke very quietly into Linus's ear.

"No one shall ever know."

Then he reached into his jacket pocket under the cover of his blanket, taking out a car's key and handed it undercover to Linus and said.

"Take this into Julia and tell her to get one of our guys to collect Jeannie's car and then bring it back to the office." He glanced around at the police again and carried on. "I told them Jeannie came here with me. I don't want them looking into her car. It's parked down the hill on the left."

Sally-Anne took another drag of her Marlboro, staring at the flashing blue lights. She realised there was something a bit odd about what Mike was saying.

The officer stood by the car waiting for Mike, looked over.

Mike said to them both very quietly.

"Whatever you do, don't mention anything about what Mr Cannon wrote in his letter, especially regarding the police. They are going to have all of us in to make a statement over the next few days, so we've got time to come up with something between us that is different from what he *really* said. We could have uncovered a catastrophic situation which is ongoing."

Sally-Anne looked at Mike and said.

"I'd better warn my parents as well then."

"Yes," said Mike. "But I'm sure they both already realise why they can't risk saying anything."

Then he turned and made his way to the police car.

They all knew why. Cannon's letter was gone, and the four of them who heard its content must not tell anyone.

There was *every* possibility that the Atkins crime syndicate was still running…

Linus and Sally-Anne held each other gently and in silence, watching Mike as he disappeared in the police Ford Granada. He was right. They needed to keep *schtum*, and both believed there was a huge criminal *connection* here. Maybe, they could work together and undercover, to find a way of exposing this hateful history and perhaps stop another path to destruction.

Sally-Anne looked over at the house. *If for no other reason, I'm going to fight this for that Jeannie woman,* she thought.

She had only met her as she was dying, but somehow felt an inexplicable *connection* with her, something that she had never experienced before and probably never would again.

Epilogue

Brighton Palace Pier, Sussex
19.05hrs 20th April 1985

She took her hand off his shoulder and pulled her hood down, the raven hair was flicking in the light wind. Linus continued to look out to sea. Jeannie's *Motorola 800x* hand portable cellular telephone had now sunk. Lost forever.

Sally-Anne stood alongside him, waiting in silence. After a while, she touched his dark hair very gently, the Star of David on her wrist taking a last flicker of light.

She guessed what he had done, looking down at the now calm sea. But she would say nothing. He turned and they stood looking deeply into each other's eyes. Two gulls cried out, as they swooped over.

"How is it in the bar?" he asked as they turned and walked arm in arm, away from the end of the pier and back towards the town.

"It's Good." She said. "Your pint of lager-top is already in there."

"I suppose it's on my account then?" he asked.

She laughed.

They came off the pier and onto the pavement, heading left towards the *Queens Hotel*. Coming to East Street, along Grand Junction Road, they could see the outline of the *Grand Hotel*, still covered in sheeting, undergoing a re-build after last year's IRA bombing.

"We are going to fight this," she said as they strolled slowly. "Problem is we can't disclose the Cannon thing. If we exposed it to our press or anyone for that matter, they could take us out. The chances are, this *Fourth Reich* is huge."

They stopped and looked at each other as she carried on.

"It's been over there months now since…"

They both looked down at the ground, remembering what happened as if it were a moment ago, both knew it would never go away.

Sally-Anne carried on. "We have all kept *schtum* about what happened and what we discovered. But now is the chance for us to get more information. Once we have it, we could get it into America's news via a third party, keeping us in the clear perhaps?"

They started to walk along again, then crossed the road to the *Queens Hotel*. Looking into the bar's window, they could see Bernie and Jane Cohen, sat down at a table with Mike Sentinel, raising their glasses up together. All three looked extremely sad. Linus and Sally-Anne guessed that they were toasting Jeannie Sands.

Sally-Anne took out her pack of Marlboros and lit two up, passing one over to Linus.

"I've been thinking," she said. "Neville Chamberlain was a good Prime Minister because he bought time to get Britain in shape for the coming war by trying to pacify Hitler, so this nation could build up its defences."

Linus took a drag of his Marlboro and said. "I know, so what are you getting at?"

She looked around. No one was near, the only person she could see was a man stood on the corner of the street opposite, collar up and looking in the other direction.

"Maybe because this was Chamberlain's priority, criminals in government could use this to their advantage in setting things up undercover. You know, the focus being on the danger of a war, not on what the staff were doing."

"True," said Linus, flicking cigarette ash into the gutter. "Humans are like monkeys really, because they focus on the banana they are holding rather than the storm that's coming. As if one day Britain walks out of the E.E.C, and everyone is more concerned about watching TV shows than the effect that would really have on Europe."

She laughed. "That won't *ever* happen," she said. "But if it did, you'd be right and there could be *another* Atkins."

He shook his head, looking through the bar window again at Bernie, Jane and Mike, then smiled and carried on.

"I would never have believed we'd get into an undercover fight-back on this, with my boss and your dad at the helm."

"Well," she said, still laughing. "Given their backgrounds, maybe there is a chance. But we must be extremely careful, we can trust no one, including the police of course."

"Five of us taking on the world then." He said. "One being beautiful and looking like Carly Simon."

"Yep," she said. "And by the way, *one* of the five still owes *me*."

Linus pointed at himself and she put her arms around him, kissed his cheek very gently and whispered in his ear.

"Yes, Mr Linus Simon MacColl. You belong to me, and of course, loving you is the right thing to do."

Manfred von Sterne watched the two of them head into the hotel, still stood on the street corner, his collar turned up.

The information gained from an informant back in January had shown nothing obvious about why the incident with these people that probably took Dick Kelson out, had occurred.

Gerhard had been slightly concerned, but the main reason for Manfred being in Britain was to recover as much as possible from the safe of Lord Atkins. That had been easier than expected, not least due to the assistance of his butler...

Manfred had followed the individuals of this group around occasionally, and this was the first time he'd seen them all together. But he guessed it was just in memory of what Kelson did to that woman. He kept asking himself *why* Kelson had done that?

There was no evidence. He walked back up the hill. At the far end was a red Bentley, false number plates on it. He stepped in and put his hands on the steering wheel, looking down the bonnet.

He smiled. Now Lord Atkins and Kelson were gone, the benefit was not just about gaining back all the old Third Reich possessions smuggled in by Goring ready for the invasion that never happened. Then he looked around the Bentley, smiling, *and it certainly wasn't for taking of this thing.*

No, it was about him and Gerhard going forwards with the new *Fourth Reich* to take over Britain. His mind went back to seeing that man in Berlin on his cellular phone, coming out of the bar. He was convinced they would help them when going forwards here now. They could make the *connection* across this *new order*.

He started the Bentley up. It made a screeching noise and smoke bellowed from the exhaust as if its engine was almost ruined. *Typical British crap*, he thought. *This car is new!*

As he drove up the hill into the darkness, he decided to call Gerhard when he arrived back in London tonight. The people he'd been watching seemed innocent, although he could not be sure. But keeping them alive could be useful for further information. At least for now....

EXODUS

Egypt
1265 BCE

He was the last one in the column. The sun was rising fast, its rays glinted from the sand dunes and onto the tribe ahead of him.

The column went as far as he could see across the desert. He was a slave, thrown away when he was a child, and had never experienced teaching, so could not translate into numbers how many were in the *caravan line*. He could see their leader at the end of the column, taking the men, women and children forwards. Their leader was Moses. With his commitment to god, determination and pride, he would guide them all to the promised land, but first, they must reach Mount Sinai.

Moses reached the horizon, the sun touched him, and cast a powerful reflection onto the desert. He looked down towards his long chain of souls, now free from the slavery of Egypt.

He did not stop, but walked backwards as he came to the top of the dune, making sure all were still following. And they were. Although tired after walking through the night, they were determined not to stop, and many felt the help from the hand of god upon them. They had to keep moving. Some fearing the Pharaoh might send his army.

The last man in the column was falling further behind. He stumbled but kept going, looking at his hands. The blood from building work on the pyramid he had toiled on had congealed, but the pain remained. His body was still covered in dust from the temple site. A rough, linen kilt, was his only clothing. The cuts on his back from whips of the slave beaters, for the work demanded by the Pharaoh, were still throbbing.

His feet were bare and sore, but he knew he had to continue, not for himself but for his god. But the gap between him and the last human in the *caravan line* was now much further. No one turned back to help him. He was on his own. It was not their fault, if he knew anyone at all it would be some other building slaves, but they were all closer up the line to Moses.

Then he stumbled, and fell onto the desert sand. He knew that without a shawl to protect his head from the blazing sun, water for his parched throat, and bread to eat, he would not survive. He closed his eyes as a fly landed on his forehead, followed by another and then, another.

His mind drifted and began to bring in strange images of a dream he had, when sleeping amongst the slaves outside the pyramid they were building.

He was somewhere in the cold, there was no desert, just buildings, so high it seemed they were reaching up to the stars. The sunlight was somehow coming from *them* and not the sky. But how could this be? Because the sun was covered by dark clouds.

But as the clouds moved over, the sun flickered from the gaps in the tall, straight and grey towers, as if it was shining off the Euphrates river. The streets were full of people, moving like lemmings. The ground was flat and grey. The coloured chariots had no horses, but somehow still moved with a strange noise and the smoke from what must have been hidden fires, came out from behind them. On their sides, he could see the images of men, their bodies under coverings of mystery.

On the side of the street, he saw humans holding grey, black and thin boxes against their heads as they walked along. Some stopped, looking down the street, and he was sure he could see their lips moving, but they were stood alone....

His memory of the dream faded, and insects buzzed around his dark hair, starting to land on his face. He knew the *caravan* had moved on, and began to close his eyes. It seemed the moment had come to stop living....

Then, a soft noise in the sand gently vibrated by the side of his head, as he rested it down for the last time. A foot came close to his eye, inside a palm fibre sandal. The front piece covering the toes had tiny rocks of many colours, the sun glinting from them, touching his eye with their rays, making him blink against the brilliance.

He felt he'd been caught up by one of the Pharaoh's men. He was the last in the line following Moses to Sinai, so would be the first to die. He tightly closed his eyes and held his breath, waiting for the pain of a spear to destroy him.

But nothing came. There was silence, excepting for a light breeze and it brought a fine dusting of sand onto his face. From the foot of this Pharaoh's man, he looked up slowly, squinting against the blazing sun's rays, taking a last look at the world and his killer before death came.

He continued to move his eyes upwards, and saw something unexpected. The s*henti* flax clothing was white and reached down to the ankles. Over the head was a long shawl, these were the clothes of a woman. His tongue ran over his lips, like an automated begging for water.

Suddenly, their eyes touched. The slave was startled. He was sure that he'd seen this woman's face before, but he could not think where. *In another life, in another world perhaps?*

She took the shawl from her head and the sun touched the long, raven hair and a smile came from her lips as she bent down beside him. Then, she touched his dark hair and reached into her flaxen bag, taking out a brown terracotta jug, she removed the top and put it down in front of him, pointing at her lips, indicating he should drink.

The slave put out his hands onto the desert and pushed up his body with the last of the strength in his arms. He looked at her and she waved at the jug, smiling. He swigged at the water. Whoever this was, she had saved his life and there had to be a reason for this. It was a gift from their god.

He felt a sense of pride and determination come into him. She had given him the determination, but the reason for pride he did not know.

Then he wobbled, she placed her hands on his shoulders. As he looked into her eyes, a crow flew past them, and headed for the horizon. They both turned and watched it, no words were spoken.

She reached into her flax bag again, then took out a piece of unleavened bread and passed it to the slave. He ate it quickly and desperately. Then as he finished, she sensed his guilt, smiled in understanding and touched his face.

He looked down at the desert, not knowing what to do next. Then, she took another white shawl from her bag, it was her miraculous spare. She draped it over his head and then spread it gently across the shoulders. The *flax* would become his name. *Linus.*

They turned and looked at the end of the line, it had now reached the top of the dune.

They walked into the sun's rays, following the *caravan*. He looked at her with gratitude and passion. They did not speak. *How can I ever give back to you?* he thought, still staring at her raven hair.

Mount Sinai was ahead and there would be a river to cross, but they *would* reach the promised land together.